Call Me Kismet

PJ Mayhem

Book Reality

Helping Writers Become Independent Authors

1

'What do you mean there's someone around you for a relationship?' Catherine barks down the phone, all hard edges and elder-sibling superiority. 'I thought you were off men?'

'So did I, but Amethyst told me fate has other ideas.'

'You can't be serious?'

'Of course I'm serious. My Anahata was quite badly out of sync. Amethyst picked up on it when she was rebalancing my chakras.'

'Oh, for God's sake. Your Ana-what?'

'My Anahata—heart chakra.' I realise Catherine isn't the best person to share my news with. She hates this sort of stuff, even though I've explained a thousand times that Amethyst is a qualified energetic and spiritual healer. 'He's hovering in my auric field, waiting for me to notice him.' Now I've started I'm like a train gathering speed.

'Of *course* he is.' Catherine's sarcasm curls her words like they're old paper. 'So who is it?'

'Not absolutely sure yet, I still need to figure that out. But according to Amethyst, there will be signs. I just need to stay tuned in enough to notice them.'

Amethyst had also said to me, 'Oh, and my guides are telling me that it will help if you keep your head up. You need to look him in the eye, that's how you'll connect with him.' I think better of sharing that last bit with Catherine—definitely one spiritual step too far for her.

'Holy mother of God.'

Maybe I should have stopped a step before.

'Naturally, my Sahasrara—that's my crown chakra, Catherine—had gone berserk …'

'That wouldn't be the only thing.'

Higher ground, I remind myself. 'With my Sahasrara whirring at a million miles an hour, my mind scrolled through the obvious potentials.'

I don't give Catherine the details: Desmond at work—absolutely no trouble looking him in the eye, although a 49-year-old finance officer who still lives with his mother is hardly relationship material. Jack, my morning barista—definitely not—he's delightful and we've certainly got a connection, but under no circumstances should coffee ever get complicated. Bruce the courier who always asks for me when he comes in to work—sweet but unfortunately not with that halitosis … perhaps if I got him some Listerine—no, not a good way to start a relationship and I'd only find his lisp annoying after a while anyway.

'Did you come up with anyone?' Catherine's voice is tight with exasperation. I'd suggest meditation but know that now isn't the time.

'Initially, no. But then waiting for the bus I had a spiritual epiphany.'

'You mean you thought of who it might be.'

'No, I mean a *spiritual epiphany*! Clear as day, a vision of the guy from Putney Gourmet Green Grocer appeared on my psychic relationship radar.'

'What makes you think it could be him?'

Oh Catherine, it is so not to do with *thinking*. That's the whole point of it being a spiritual epiphany. I opt for the path of least resistance. 'I don't mean to be presumptuous, but I've seen him watching me as I go by his shop some mornings. His eyes follow me.'

'So, what's he like? What's his name?'

'Well, he's, um, he's … OK, here's the thing. I haven't actually ever spoken to him, and as for his name, I'm not too sure of that either. I just know him as the Singing Fruitologist—for obvious reasons.'

'I can't believe you're wasting your money paying some crackpot psychic to tell you that crap.'

'Amethyst is not a crackpot psychic. She's a qualified professional, remember! Besides, destiny doesn't concern itself with details.'

'Whatever. I just think you'd be better off putting your money towards something practical rather than trying to catch smoke. You need to think about your future …'

Spare me! One of Catherine's boringly sensible lectures is the last thing I need. Not that I blame her; astrologically she's a Capricorn—they're obsessed with stability in all its forms, particularly financial.

'Thirty-five is hardly ready to be living for my retirement plan.' I don't bother retaliating to the jibe about my four uncompleted degrees that she throws in every time. Some people take a while to find their groove. None of those degrees were really *me*. What is me are my Mandarin studies that I've 'fluffed around with at evening college for years' (as Catherine put it). I would formalise them but it's not that easy on top of full-time work.

'And if you *do* want a relationship maybe you could do something where you're likely to meet someone you share an interest with. Getting to know them first might be a good idea, Fiona.'

'It's Kismet! *Six months*. It's six months since I took my spiritual name and you still can't get it right. Honestly, I don't know why you and Mum have such a problem with it. And Dad, it's like he hasn't got a clue.'

'Excuse us if we haven't managed to break the habit of a lifetime in six short months. Look, I haven't got time to argue about that now, Brian will be home from work soon and I still haven't started dinner.'

It's 6.05pm. Catherine will be striding from her Ikea kitchen breakfast bar to the Duck Egg Cream wall (I lived through the colour charts) where their family organiser hangs to check how far behind schedule she is. In approximately ten steps she'll reach the 'bible' that holds all the manoeuvres of the military-style operation that is their life. She's probably a good three-and-a-half minutes behind by now.

Before either Catherine or I have the chance to say anything more, Brian's words rise over the echo of their front door thudding closed. 'Catherine, where are you? I have a surprise for my darling wife.'

'Gotta go. Bye!' Catherine rushes off, leaving my love for the kids still forming into words on my tongue.

What was I thinking? Catherine really doesn't have a clue. She probably thinks the spiritual path is a new style of pavers available at Bunnings.

Maybe Catherine's right. My self-doubt is there before I've even opened my eyes to the bright January Saturday morning. She usually is—Catherine was busy being right before I was even born.

Once I've intention set, done my *You Can Heal Your Life* affirmations, a heart-opening chant and a quick 'powering up for positivity' meditation, I flick on my radio. With Triple J to keep me upbeat, I open the back door and settle down at the kitchen table to create my Action Plan to Improve my Life list. I start with the heading, as good a place as any.

Fifteen minutes later I'm still coming up blank when a gust of wind bursts in and whips the list off the table. Until now the morning has been deathly still. That has to be one of the signs Amethyst was talking about.

Back in my bedroom, I fossick around the bottom of my wardrobe until I find the heart-shaped box of Lovers' Oracle cards that my dear friend Stephanie gave me three years ago. Hope restored, I rip the plastic off the box, close my eyes and focus my energy on manifesting the perfect card as I shuffle. When the moment feels right, I pick a card, open my eyes, and shazam: *Romance—Cupid's arrow strikes.*

'No time to waste. Destiny awaits!' as Amethyst would say.

I'm about to rush out the door—in as much of a rush as changing three times, doing my make-up twice, curling my eyelashes four times and brushing my hair in every direction to add body allows—when I hear the *whoop, whoop, whoop* of my phone. A call from my mother. No one else warrants the emergency alarm ringtone. Although Catherine is getting there.

There's no way I'm answering it. One of Mum's special Bev-style interventions—a Mumtervention—trying to save me from myself and my 'whimsical acts and witchy-woman moon-worshipping pursuits' (her words) is the last thing I need right now. I'll be bashing my head against the wall before I can say, 'I'll have some raspberries, tomatoes and you, thanks,' to the Singing Fruitologist.

Mum wouldn't understand that, as a Taurean, I don't do whimsical anyway.

Two hundred and five steps later, I'm looking at a sign that reads PUTNEY GOURMET GREEN GROCER—PURVEYOR OF PUTNEY'S FINEST FRESH PRODUCE SINCE 1963. My heart is beating so hard it could burst out of my chest and land on the other side of the street. I take a moment—something as monumental as meeting my destiny cannot be rushed—then step inside. Manfred Mann's 'Blinded by the Light' is on the radio. Positive—it's tuned to the fruitologist's preferred Retro FM. Negative—I can't hear anyone singing along.

I walk between the produce—a panther could only dream of my stealth. In my 'focussed on the Singing Fruitologist' state I can't think of anything I actually need. I really should have made a list to give this mission a more natural feel. I throw some mixed greens into a bag, put a punnet of strawberries in my basket—a nice romantic choice of fruit—but then take them out. What if he sees them and thinks I'm buying them for a passionate evening with a special someone?

I'm heading towards the deli section at the rear of the shop when I hear the storeroom door open. I duck behind a towering display of pumpkins. I'm not at all prepared for this. I could be mistaken for a human pin cushion, the way every single hair on my body is standing on end. I have no idea what I'm going to do or say if I do see him. 'Hello, you don't know me but I think you're destined to be my next relationship,' could be a bit too full on for our first conversation—and where would we go from there?

Up on my tippy-toes, I peer through the display to the storeroom door. Half of me is willing the Singing Fruitologist to come out, while the other half is tied up in the critical task of willing a badly balanced pumpkin to stay in place.

'Frankie's just texted me, he's not coming in,' a guy who isn't the Singing Fruitologist announces as he emerges from the storeroom.

Frankie? That must be the Singing Fruitologist's name—he's the only regular missing. Or perhaps they've just nicknamed him that after Frank Sinatra.

But maybe this means the Singing Fruitologist isn't the one. Surely if it's meant to be, he would have been here, waiting for fate to deliver me?

2

Tucked away at a corner table, I watch Jane approach through the crowd in the glow of the red silk lampshades. Brandishing two drinks as though they're trophies, she blows at her fringe, which tonight is the same colour as the lampshades, to keep it from flopping over her eyes. Jane's tights match the cerise velour of the couch against the wall that the early birds have secured. In between her hair and her tights there is an explosion of colour, like a bomb has gone off in her art studio and she hasn't had time to change. Even though I'm wearing black, I feel positively beige—everyone here looks a bit like Jane. No wonder this is her favourite bar.

Opposites attract. People have been saying that about Jane and me since we met in kindergarten. It makes us sound like we're a couple. We're not, but in lots of ways we might as well be betrothed, sans the sex.

'Shit, Kiz, sorry I'm late,' Jane says once she's close enough to see my best attempt at faux anger—brows knitted above a smile. That's as angry as I can manage with her. She plonks the drinks down, pulls her chair close to mine, sits. We wrap each other in a tight hug, and she doesn't quite release me. Hands on my shoulders, she studies my face, as if I'm a subject she's about to paint.

'Holy Govinda. This is not a mocktail!' I splutter, sipping my drink to break the intensity.

'Oh God, shit, I'm hopeless tonight. Sorry, Kiz. I don't know why I always forget you don't drink anymore. I guess you can put it down to Mercury being in retrograde or whatever. I'll go get you something else.'

It dawns on me that Jane, in her slightly sceptical if supportive Aries way, is right. Mercury *is* in retrograde, which would explain why the Singing Fruitologist wasn't there—our communication would have been stifled.

'No, don't be silly. One drink won't hurt. We know I love a vodka cocktail as much as the next girl. Not like I'm on the wagon or anything. It just interferes with one's alignment to the cosmic forces.'

Jane raises an eyebrow. 'Amethyst?'

'Yep.'

'Speaking of being aligned, *spill*.'

'What?'

'Don't you "What?" me, Kismet Johnson! You've got *the look*. Something is going on, I know it. You look fantastic.'

'Don't be ridiculous.'

'What ridiculous? Lucky for me I got here when I did and no one came along and whisked you away, I'm telling you.'

'You can't be serious! I feel like such a wreck. Work's a nightmare—I've been there all hours. It's playing havoc with my biorhythms and my sleep patterns are completely haywire.' I'm sure it's probably Situation Singing Fruitologist that's having the most effect on my biorhythms and sleep but I'll fill Jane in on that later. I just need to hang onto it for a little bit longer. As soon as I mention it, Jane will do a full dis-section, coming up with a plan of what I should do. But it'll be a Jane plan not a Kismet plan. Jane plans are something only Jane can carry off. Withholding information temporar-ily technically isn't lying, so karma won't mind. This week I've been leaving home before Putney Gourmet Green Grocer (PGGG) opens and getting home after they close, so nothing has happened in the six days since I last ventured in anyway.

'Work schmerk. I know you and this, my dear, is *nothing* to do with work. I think someone might be about to get back on the bike—and about time.'

'Thanks for changing nights.' I'm aiming for distraction.

Jane waves a hand dismissively. 'So? Have you got a date tomorrow night? You have to tell me—you know I'll only drive you insane trying to guess.'

True, Jane's like a hound on a hunt once she's onto a scent. 'A date? Shiva, no! You know I don't do dates. My per-fect sister's perfect husband has surprised her with a perfect gift so she'll have the perfect birthday in perfect Phuket. So my perfectly adorable niece and nephew are staying with my perfectly—well, my parents, but Mum and Dad have to go out tomorrow night so their imperfect daughter is on child-minding duty.'

'Oh, that all sounds *perfectly* lovely! And steering the con-versation in that direction is the perfect deflection. But I'm still waiting for you to tell me what the hell is going on with you.'

'Why don't you tell me about you—how are you? What's happening?'

'Nice try. For the record, it's deadly boring at the moment, I'm spending my days and half my nights locked in my studio to finish those dull office art commissions. A girl's gotta pay the rent. Now out with it.'

'I know this sounds a little out there.' After my initial out-pouring to Catherine, I've realised Amethyst's prediction does sound a bit insane when I say it out loud. 'Well, Amethyst sort of mentioned that there's someone around me for a relationship.'

'I knew it! I *knew* there was something going on.' Jane leans in, so close now that her knees touch mine. 'I could sense a little *mo*, or it might have been *jo*—whichever—part of your mojo is back. I felt it across the room! This is so exciting. Now tell me, who is it?'

'The Singing Fruitologist.' I hold my breath and brace myself.

Jane frowns. 'What?'

'I'm a bit light on details but he works at the Putney Gourmet Green Grocer—Purveyor of Putney's Finest Fresh Produce since 1963. And he sings.' We spend a minute laughing at their purveyor tagline, then she's off again.

'So no name?'

'Not definitively.'

'But?'

'It might be Frankie.'

'What's he sing?'

'Whatever's on the radio.'

'What station does he listen to?'

'Just your average, middle-of-the-road commercial stuff.' Jane will have a conniption if I tell her it's Retro FM.

'Oh well, I guess we all have to make compromises. Good singer?'

'Buddha above and beyond, no—appalling! The fact that he does it anyway and doesn't seem to care, even when he isn't completely sure of the words, is quite ... I don't know ... endearing.' I feel like a tennis pro facing balls fired at a million miles a minute from one of those machines. I've broken out in a sweat.

'Age?' Jane fires again.

'Hmm, I'd say he has a good few years on us … maybe forty.'

'Marital status?'

'Unknown. I haven't seen a ring.'

'Oh, OK. That's not necessarily a deal breaker anyway. Owns the business or works there?'

'Works there, I think, not one hundred per cent on that one either.'

Jane laughs. 'Jesus, Kismet. What exactly *do* you know about him?'

'It's not so much about what I know, it's what I've seen.'

'Good, that myth about it's not what you've got it's how you use it can only get a guy so far.'

'Yes but no, not that. I've had a sign.'

'Hold it right there. I need another drink for this.'

Jane is off before I can stop her, a kaleidoscope swirling to the bar. I can guarantee it won't be a mocktail she brings back for me.

'So, a sign?' She settles in even closer than she was before.

I take her through my session with Amethyst and trip to PGGG. 'After getting myself all het up then not seeing him when I went in, I took a walk through the park to clear my head and get rid of some of the nervous energy fizzing around in me. The fruitologist's absence raised a bit of a question mark, so I put Situation Singing Fruitologist in my spiritual pop-up toaster …'

'Your what?'

'My spiritual pop-up toaster. When you don't know what to do about something, you put it in a metaphorical toaster so an idea or answer can spring up from your subconscious when it's ready.'

'You distract yourself and wait for an answer to come,' Jane says, somewhere between a question and a statement.

'Exactly. When my toast was done it popped up with the solution. All I had to do was ask Spirit for a definite sign he's the one. Why I hadn't thought of that before I don't know, put it down to the anxiety short-circuiting my brain. I mean, Amethyst even told me there'd be signs!'

'I hope you didn't say, "If I see a kid on a bike or people throwing a Frisbee it's him", given you were in a park.'

'Thank you very much, oh, she of little faith. No, actually I was very prescriptive—miniature red short-haired dachshund.'

'What else!' Jane's laugh inches towards a snort. She doesn't need an explanation. She knows that miniature red short-haired dachshunds go beyond being my favourite dog; 'besotted' would be the appropriate term.

'I was totally preoccupied with practising keeping my head up so as not to do my whole staring at the ground and avoiding eye contact thing, when for some reason, Spirit guided me to look down and there it was. A divinely delivered dachshund literally under my nose. Karma was almost kissing my feet.'

'You're insane.' Jane gives a full snort this time.

'Quite possibly certifiable,' I manage through a countering snort.

Pretty soon we're snorting like we're part of some carefully choreographed synchronised snorting team. But then, we've had a lifetime of practice.

'Fuck, I can't believe I forgot to ask. Celebrity lookalike?' Jane wheezes.

'Hmm ... maybe a younger Kevin Costner but with a bit more, well, character.'

'And by "character" you mean?'

'A slight bald spot and eyes that have a bit of a seagull quality about them, but it works on him.'

Jane doubles over, snorting into her knees. To most people it wouldn't be that funny but a few years ago we'd watched *The Bodyguard* at a 'Cheese & Sleaze' evening and spent the six months or so afterwards singing 'I Will Always Love You' to each other very badly, very often.

'Oh well, we can't fight fate.' Jane sits up, wiping tears from her cheeks.

'Yep, that's what Amethyst says. What is fated must be lived.'

Shiva, Shiva, Shiva. Why aren't alarms more intuitive? It should have known I needed to get up! I jump out of bed in a panic the next morning. Last night's vodka makes my head spin. It takes a moment to catch up with the rest of me. I really should have stopped a few drinks earlier or at some point when I was sober enough to remember to set my alarm.

I should text my mother and tell her I might be late, seeing as I definitely will be. She's not going to take it well. She's organised a Mother–Daughter–Niece–Nephew day for us before I mind Sammy and Sonja tonight. I'll text on the way.

It's grooming essentials only before I fly out the door to hail a cab.

Fuck, fuck, fuck, of all the times! Forgive my swearing, Spirit, but extreme circumstances—the fruitologist is out on the street chatting. I haven't got time to breathe let alone try to negotiate an appropriate greeting and I *so* don't want to be seen with my hair still wet and only a quick slather of foundation and mascara—eyelashes totally uncurled.

Oh no … please, Spirit, no—but, oh yes, dharma it. He looks in my direction and something in my brain snaps. I put my head down and run across the road. I try to ignore the sound of the horns.

'Fiona, what is wrong with you today? You're all over the place.' My mother looks at me as I sip my coffee at the zoo café. She refused my offer to get her anything with a pointed reminder that she'd had two cups of tea while she was waiting.

'Nothing. Why?' I say, thinking, *Oh my Buddha, I don't know—I've been wondering that exact same thing since the traffic incident myself.* Now the fruitologist probably thinks I hate him and threw myself into traffic to avoid him.

'Gran, can we go out there and play?' Sammy points to the play area that, at ten (Sammy) and eight (Sonja), they're a little too old for, but they're kicking the legs of the table and rocking back on their chairs, prisoners of boredom.

'Of course you can, my little daaarlings,' Mum says before I can offer to buy them treats to save myself being alone with her.

'So,' she begins as my niece and nephew race to the door.

'How's Dad?' I ask with enthusiasm.

'To be honest he's a little … well, he's lost a little of his old spark. I've got him some vi—'

Oh Great Ganesha, if she says Viagra I am going to die.

'Are you sure you're alright, dear? You're looking a little pale.'

'Yeah, I'm fine, thanks. Dad?'

'I've got him some vitamins. I blame the golf! He's obsessed with it.'

'Nothing wrong him enjoying a game of golf, Mum. He could be up to a lot worse.'

'He certainly could be up to a lot better too. I mean, look at Brian, whisking Catherine away like that. Your father wouldn't do anything like that in a million years. Now, speaking of Catherine and speaking of men, she mentioned that you might have met someone.'

Mum and Catherine, they're two Capricornian peas in a pod. I stir the dregs of my coffee.

'I'm so happy for you, Fiona. All a mother ever wants is for her children to be happy.'

Oh Spirit, save me.

'Sometimes I blame myself, maybe I should have been a better mother somehow. Catherine did OK but then again ...'

'Then again what?' Snapping is a mistake, and pain ricochets through my head. I rub my temples.

'No need to get huffy, dear. All I was going to say was that she was always a little more sure of herself. But now that you mention it, you always were a little—'

'Different,' I jump in, stealing her chance to declare me *odd* or *weird*—though it wouldn't be the first time.

'That's one way to put it, but that aside, I don't think you're doing yourself any favours, particularly not today. Look at you, you've hardly made an effort.' Mum is wearing one of her favourite pant suits, her dyed chestnut hair sprayed into a helmet and her face heavily powdered. 'And with all that *stuff* you're into these days, I mean there are certain things men like in a woman, Fiona ...'

'It's Kismet now!' I hiss—I'd scream if it weren't for the fear my head may actually split in two. 'And I'm fine. I am perfectly happy as I am and, yes, there might be a potential someone but you don't need to go shopping for a mother-of-the-bride outfit yet.'

As if.

'*Gran!*' Sonja wails from just inside the doorway. It's as though Mum's wearing a jetpack, the way she launches across to her. She coos and fusses over Sonja for a moment before giving me a 'come on, let's get going' look. The wailing was obviously the result of a minor sibling altercation.

'I'll carry mine, Aunty Fee.' Sammy skids to a halt beside me as I gather our bags.

'What, don't you trust me with it?' I wink and pass him his precious South Sydney Rabbitohs backpack. He stops just long to put it on, then speeds off—a blur of red, green and white.

3

They say you shouldn't define someone by their job, which I'm pretty happy about. I'd hate for people to think I'm nothing more than the Academic, Operational and Compliance Coordinator at The Centre for Strategic and Financial Excellence. I didn't *choose* that role. When I started three years ago I was employed to do straight admin, which is bad enough. But then private colleges were hit hard with regulatory and funding changes—one additional task after another made an emergency landing on my position description until my role became something else entirely. Now I do—it's quite hard to define—everything I used to do plus *really* boring stuff like coordinating government compliance requirements and trying to make sure we maintain accreditation and a whole lot more all equally as dull. And all things that don't align with my aura in the slightest.

'Fiona, where's Broomstick?' It's Monday morning and Desmond is leaning on the low petition at the front of my desk, a cascade of grey from hair to Hush Puppies. This isn't the sort of place that could cope with a Kismet, so at work I'm still Fiona.

I'm not really in the mood to talk at this hour, least of all about our boss, Broomstick—Dr Cybil Raynard. It's not even 9.30am. I don't do mornings, apart from with my caffeine dealers, then I'm no better than a crack ho with her pimp. After Jack on Putney Bridge Road, there's Bing downstairs. I see him at lunchtime too. Bing calls me 'Mei Mei'—'little sister' in Mandarin. In return I call him 'Da Ge'—'big brother'. My visits to Bing are right up there on my list of favourite routines—a chat in Mandarin *and* a caffeine fix. Who could want for more?

Back to Desmond. I don't want to discourage his conversation. It's so rare that he manages to scramble out from the piles of folders and financial documents that tickle at the ceiling and cover half the floor of his office. But he's so caught up entertaining himself he fails to notice the collective sucking in of air from around the office.

'Fiona, I need you to find a compliance consultant and organise a meeting for next Tuesday. Oh, and Desmond, it's Dr Broomstick to you.' Dr Raynard says, all tense under her beige trench coat. She really does look like a broomstick with a bun.

Desmond's face goes from grey to red. He scuffs across the carpet back to his office with such speed, I'm sure I see sparks. The archetypal Cancerian mummy's boy, he's bound to phone Mummy (he still calls her that) as soon as his door is closed. I'm pleased he at least has someone to debrief with. I don't do emotional crises verbally before 11am—via email I'm good for 10am.

'Sure, Cybil. How was your weekend? Monday certainly came around quickly, didn't it?' I chirp, despite the time. I've been trying to get a smile out of Broomstick ever since she started six months ago and I don't like my chances today. I'm convinced she'll die of some horrible disease, with all those toxic emotions stewing and festering inside of her. I can literally feel them bubbling away in there. I get quite queasy whenever she's near me.

'Oh, you'll need to do up an interim internal audit report to send to the consultant before they come,' she shoots as an afterthought. She's another Aries, so bossiness is built in. I do try to make allowances but, seriously, there's no need for her to go spreading her toxic misery around so liberally.

I get to work on finding a compliance consultant. By the time I've narrowed it down to a list of ten to make initial enquiries and emailed them all, then dealt with some of Broomstick's other random demands, my usual work and a last-minute crisis for a lecturer who couldn't fix the paper jam in the photocopier and needed the notes for his class immediately, the day is over.

Unfortunately so are my plans of going into PGGG tonight. It's already 6.50pm so I'll never get back in time. And to think I've wasted my favourite workday outfit—a super short black sheath dress with subtle grommet trim, which also serves to cinch the waist a little. But my favourite feature is the great asymmetrical mesh panel at the hem that runs three-quarters of the way around. It gives movement, so I feel feminine without being girly. Today I'd combined it with my black cigarette pants—I avoid bare legs at all costs.

Even at 6.45am, Jack's café oozes warmth. I know it's summer, but still. The rusticness of the furniture and the open hessian sack of coffee beans beside the door is immediately comforting.

'You're early, Fiona, this must be a record.' Jack checks his watch as I stumble up to the counter somewhere between asleep and awake.

'Don't remind me and definitely don't expect it to become a habit.' I thrust my KeepCup at him.

'If you were that desperate for coffee all you had to do was call, I would have brought it round for you ... well, call *and* give me your address.'

'Coffee delivered to my door? Then I'd never leave home.'

While Jack chuckles and gets on with making my coffee, I lean on the counter to flick through the paper. People probably assume I'm the sort of person who goes straight to my stars but I don't. With Amethyst and my own intuition, who needs a newspaper column for guidance? Astrology's more a tool to help me understand people and where they're coming from. I don't know what sign Jack is yet. To ask would ruin the fun and challenge of figuring it out. Last time I really thought about it I had him down as either a sexy Scorpio or playful Sagittarius. He does have that eternally youthful Sagittarian way about him.

'Thanks, Jack, have a good day. See you tomorrow.' I'm running on autopilot but my reflexes are still quick enough to whip my fingers away before he has time to grab them during our coffee and change exchange.

Of course PGGG isn't open yet, I hadn't expected it to be. I'd just hoped that maybe destiny would see fit to throw a little miracle into the mix. *Everything is as it is meant to be, flowing in perfect harmony,* I remind myself, repeating my mantra.

I don't really have time for a miracle right now anyway. I need to focus on how I'm going to get Broomstick her report by Friday. So for the next four days, this is my life. My Lovers'

Oracle cards go back to gathering dust, my I-Ching itches for attention, even my intention setting is lacklustre—nothing more than a token effort as I dry my hair. There's certainly no time for any 'powering up for positivity' meditations and I can't fit in a chant to save myself. When I do arrive home from work somewhere between nine and 10pm, I fall into bed in a crumpled heap. My phone lives at the bottom of my bag until I get to it on the train on the way home in the evenings. I listen to messages that I'm really too tired to take in, let alone return calls.

Jane calls on Monday: 'Just calling for an update on Situation Singing Fruitologist. Did you carry out the action plan?'

Tuesday, it's Mum: 'Oh good lord, Fiona, your father is driving me insane. Jealous of his own grandchildren, can you imagine! Just needed to get that off my chest while he was out at golf and with Catherine away … Hope you're well, would be nice if you called sometime.'

It's 8.45pm on Friday before I hit send on the email to Broomstick with her so 'super urgent that she went home hours ago' report attached. At least she can't say I didn't meet my deadline. Now that's out of the way I can focus on getting on with Situation Singing Fruitologist. Maybe finding a new job should be up there too.

On the train home I check my voicemail. Catherine has called.

'OMG, Fiona, you have to go to Phuket! It is *amazing*. Did you see the photos I posted on Facebook? Oh, that's right, you don't do social media. I'll show you at Mum and Dad's at lunch on the weekend. Mum said you'd been ignoring her, or maybe it just wasn't in your stars to call her this week.'

'Oh, go screw yourself, Catherine,' I say to my phone, throwing it back in my bag. Why I bothered listening to her message when I was in anything but the mood for Catherine, I've no idea.

'Oh Buddha, have mercy!' Saturday morning, I jump back from my bathroom mirror in fright. My solid eight hours' sleep has done nothing to repair the ravages of the week. I look like a corpse that's been dug up and dragged through a hedge backwards.

Still, there's no getting out of heading down and sorting out Situation Singing Fruitologist. I committed to it in a text to Jane—unfortunately before I saw myself in the mirror. All I have to do if I see him is muster the courage to keep my head up, look at him, attempt a smile and hope he doesn't scream and recoil in horror.

Positive Lovers' Oracle card endorsement: *Cast away your concerns, come rest in my embrace.* I feel more likely to pass out in it but anyway.

I can do this. I'm going to go and buy my produce like I would in any other shop. Simple. It's just my fate riding on it, no big deal. But first, I slip off my jeans, take off my knickers and put my jeans back on. Like I can afford the distraction of worrying about VPL in such critical circumstances.

Before I head out I check that the $50 note is still in my pocket. After the last time I can't rely on my hands to stop shaking long enough to get a note out of my wallet. Pay-Pass feels too impersonal. I throw in some coins for coffee as well.

Of course coffee must come first. 'Nice to see you slept in a bit today, Fiona,' Jack says brightly.

'I'm exhausted. I feel like I could sleep forever.'

'Like Sleeping Beauty but then you'd have to wait for your ...'

'No.' I know where this is headed. 'I don't need a Prince Charming—just a new job.'

'I'll give you a job. One catch—no pay.'

'Why would I work for no pay?'

'For love.'

I give an Oscar-worthy sigh. 'I can't afford to work for love. What about coffee and love?'

'For sure, as much of both as you want.'

'I'll think about it.' I wink as Jack passes me my coffee. Today my reflexes are too slow to get my fingers away before he grabs them.

'Hi,' I say and smile as I walk into PGGG, head up. Unfortunately it's not the Singing Fruitologist I'm saying it to but one of the other regular guys who works there—slightly younger than the Singing Fruitologist. I have totally no attraction to him, so feel perfectly safe.

I grab a basket and commence my access-all-areas tour of PGGG—Retro FM is on so I'm feeling optimistic. I'm bent over getting some chai from a bottom shelf when, from the adjacent storeroom, I hear what can only be the Singing Fruitologist. Thinking no one can hear him, he's belting out Rod Stewart's 'Da Ya Think I'm Sexy?' with such abandon it runs the risk of turning the smile that's galloped across my face into a fully-fledged snort.

Still bent over—for all the world looking like I'm very focussed on my choice of chai—I wonder how I can fill in time until the Singing Fruitologist comes into the store, without making it too obvious. I'm certain the answer is about to rush forth from my neurons when I sense someone behind me. I look over my shoulder and see the 'hi' guy from when I came in. He's staring at my arse. I snap up and give him an indignant look. Does he have any idea what he's done? Not only has he ruined my moment listening to the Signing Fruitologist, there's no way I can hang around and wait for him to appear now.

I storm to the counter and make a point of staring out at the street to avoid looking at the 'guy with the roving eyes' as he cashes up my items. Infuriatingly, he's still smiling at me.

'Raymond.'

The guy and I both turn. The Singing Fruitologist is just inside at the storeroom door. He's dressed in a bright green, branded sports T-shirt and reasonably stylish jeans.

'Can you do a count of the organic pastas when you're done there?' The Singing Fruitologist calls.

Hmm. I'm not sure I like his speaking voice—it's got a strong nasal twang. This could be an issue if we're going to have a relationship. I can always use a gag in some sort of sex-play scenario so I don't have to listen to it—not sure about the rest of the time, but an answer will come. The Universe always provides.

'Did you look at him in the eye? Smile?' Jane launches in immediately on answering when I call her to report.

'Well, sort of.'

'There is no "sort of", Kismet, either you did or you didn't.'

'I sort of had a practice run.'

'Practice run? How can you "sort of" have a practice run?'

I explain the rationale of my smiling at the other guy.

'No harm and you usually are open and friendly with everyone. Well, everyone other than guys that you fancy or that you think fancy you.'

'You won't believe it, but it sort of backfired.'

'I know I'm going to regret this … but how exactly can you smiling at someone in a shop backfire? Although I realise if we're frolicking in the fertile fields of your imagination the possibilities are endless.'

Of course Jane won't regret it for a second, she's dying to know. So I run her through the events at PGGG. She finds Raymond's antics much more entertaining than my Singing Fruitologist sighting.

'Go Kizzo! I told you your mojo was back. Ha, let's see if the Singing Fruitologist sings Beyoncé songs next time you go in.'

I have been known to do some of 'How to Get a Body like Beyoncé' workouts on YouTube—not that I'm not *ever* going to breathe a word of that to anyone, least of all Jane. She'd die laughing.

'Very funny. It's just made everything worse. What if my mojo is conjuring the wrong sort of man or the wrong sort of attention? I'm not up for those sort of shenanigans with just any frisky fruiterer. I most definitely don't want to be turned into a sex object and discussed by them like a skank as though they are boys down at the pub, if anything happens with the Singing Fruitologist.'

'Do you think you might be overreacting just a tad, Kizzo? There really weren't any shenanigans—it's pretty standard male behaviour. I wouldn't be worrying about getting a rape whistle for when you go in and get your fruit and veggies just yet.'

4

One very uneventful week on from my last failed attempt, I'm back at base camp heading out my door on another 'conquer Situation Singing Fruitologist' expedition. The sun's radiant smile makes me certain it has come out specially to welcome me. I can practically hear it whispering, 'Kismet, today is a day where anything is possible.' I float down to PGGG on a cloud of possibility—OK, so maybe it's more a rapid dog paddle in a sea of anxiety. The weather's a good sign at least.

The terse woman who never seems pleased to be at work is at the till. This is disappointing but not critical—I've observed that she and the Singing Fruitologist are rarely on shift together. I confess that I've wondered if they don't often work together because they're married; I wouldn't want to work with my partner either. Still, the fact that I can't hear him singing along to the Bee Gees' 'Tragedy' is far from ideal. I mean, who can resist the Bee Gees? Even I want to sing along.

I have a feeling that something or someone is interfering with the fruitologist's and my cosmic connection and I think I know exactly who it might be. The woman's eyes burn into the back of me as I dawdle down the aisle. I know I look dodgy—dodgy *and* uneasy. She probably thinks I'm a shoplifter. Mind you, a quick frisk by the fruitologist may just get this karmic-relationship-in-waiting underway.

Given there's only four aisles and the deli, it doesn't take me long to discover a silent fruitologist in the deli section. He's up a ladder, back to me. My eyes are exactly at the level of his butt and I let them wander upwards. I'm not perving, I'm just taking a moment, maybe two, to appreciate the physical aspects of what fate has in store for me—obviously the Universe put me in this position for a reason. I watch him move jars of organic baby food from the box resting on the top of the ladder to the shelf. Sweat prickles against the red fabric of his T-shirt. The flush I experience as I watch him, the way his back and shoulder muscles stretch against his T-shirt, is from nothing more than the heat of the day, I swear.

I so hope the baby food isn't a sign though. I love children—provided they're other people's. I don't really do babies, and definitely not nappies. Babies aren't on my karmic blueprint for this lifetime, Amethyst tells me, so it's a good thing I've never wanted them anyway.

I could say hi. I *would* say hi, but then I imagine him jumping with fright and falling from the ladder to his death—slicing his jugular on the glass of a broken jar of baby food or slamming his temple on the corner of the shelf. That would be lifetimes of super bad karma and his death is really not ideal for my destiny, not to mention his. I step away extra quietly.

John Farnham's 'You're the Voice' comes on as I gather my items. If the fruitologist starts singing to that, it's over. I know it hasn't really begun but that would be the end right there. Surely fate could not be so cruel?

At the checkout the woman is a little less super rude to me than usual, dealing with my items in her speedy way.

'Sorry,' I say, not even trying to keep up. I'm stringing things out today, just to make sure I stay to the end of 'You're the Voice' so I'll know for sure if the fruitologist sings along.

'That's OK, take your time,' she says over the beeps of the scanner.

What does she mean by that? Does she mean, 'Take your time stealing my man'?

If the fruitologist and I are destined to be together as the Lovers' Oracle predicted pre-trip—*Your soul mate is already with you in spirit*—Ms Terse-at-the-Till and I are obviously going to have to embark on some sort of turf warfare.

I step out into the street with the final bars of 'You're the Voice' drifting into silence, mercifully unaccompanied by the fruitologist. I immediately feel as though I've forgotten something but I've no idea what; every item on my list is ticked. However, my intuition sends me back in to search for whatever it is, and I almost run smack bang into the fruitologist coming out.

'Hi,' he says as we weave our way around each other.

'Hi,' I mumble to the ground, unable to look at him, sure he'll be able to see the guilty blush of my earlier appreciating-his-physicality session. The tingle I feel being so close to him only makes it worse.

It's perfect though—now the fruitologist has opened the lines of communication by saying 'hi', I can say 'hi' if I see him without worrying about seeming like a stalker. I know it may not seem like much, but to quote Lao Tzu: 'The journey of a thousand miles begins with a single step.'

A single step may be all well and good for Lao Tzu, however I'm about to self-combust. I consult the Lovers' Oracle. *Mystery—all will be revealed in good time.* But Great Guru, Govinda and Ganesha give me strength—I'm not sure what the oracle considers 'good time': it really should be more specific. It is now five full days since the 'hi' incident. There hasn't been a single fruitologist sighting, let alone an opportunity to facilitate advancement on the 'hi'. Not even the sound of his nasal twang chatting to a colleague or the lyrics of an out-of-tune song have come wafting out as I pass each day, making sure I look like I don't care.

I need to take control of this situation before another day passes. But it's 9.30pm on Thursday and PGGG is closed, so my options are limited. Meditation feels too passive, chakra dancing too wafty and my I-Ching hasn't been so reliable on the relationship front in the past. I consider a spell, briefly—probably a bit too extreme this early on. At least an entire interaction-less month would be required before I go googling white Wicca tricks.

Only a Manifesting Miracles affirmation is right for these circumstances. I write out the miracle I want to manifest—that's the obvious part. But it's equally important to make a couple of key declarations, such as 'I am a magnet to miracles' and 'I am open to miracles and welcome them into my life', before launching into asking the Universe for the miracle. It's also vital to visualise the outcome you want to manifest—burning a candle is good too. The final steps—which most people miss—are repeating it every day and sleeping with the 'miracle' under your pillow until it manifests.

It worked. By the next morning the miracle of the Singing Fruitologist has been manifested—in my dreams at least. In the dream the fruitologist and I were sitting next to each other at a local meeting when he leant towards me to ask me a question of no great consequence and, disappointingly, not at all romantic in nature (typical of the men I seem to attract—I must work on clearing this negative pattern with Amethyst). I leant even closer to him and put my cheek against his to whisper my response into his ear.

That's when I saw the list of items he was going to raise at the meeting. Item one was for people to put the egg boxes back in a neat stack when they disturb them grabbing their dozens and half-dozens. This very much appealed to my medium- to high-scale need-for-order tendencies.

He then wrote me a note: *Are you free 24th, 25th or 26th?*
And that's where the dream ended.

Unfortunately, a few days on there's still no sight or sound of the Singing Fruitologist in person. Note to self: Remember to say 'in person' in manifestation affirmations in future. Destiny may not concern itself with detail but sometimes the Universe can be dharmaed pernickety about these things.

But tomorrow is the twenty-sixth.

Sure enough, now the fruitologist has started infiltrating my dreams there is no stopping him and I wake on Saturday having had a dream that PGGG were out of yoghurt. When I began seeing Amethyst eight months ago she told me I'd get a lot of messages through my dreams as my intuition developed, but I've never had them with such clarity before.

Dressed, make-up on and eyelashes curled (only twice but worked perfectly) I add extra glisten to my face with a quick spritz of my refreshing rosewater mist, try to keep breathing, do my hair, apply lipstick then do my hair again. It's just not happening, my eyelashes seem to have used up my positive hair energy quota for the day. I can't afford any more time fussing with it. I've spent so much time getting ready and mantraing myself up (*I will look the Singing Fruitologist in the eye today, it will be easy and I will do it seamlessly and with grace*) that I have less than thirty minutes before Stephanie comes to collect me for our swim at Pebbly Beach.

As I approach PGGG, I begin hatching a plan. If they've run out of yoghurt I can ask the fruitologist to call me when it comes in, the perfect cover to provision him with my number. Yes, I can well imagine that I'll be able to carry that off! Ms Cool, Calm and Collected Seductress will be *so* suave and sexy. Not!

Keep it simple, Kismet.

Best I settle for: 1) Trying to look him in the eye, and 2) saying hi.

A point to fate—the fruitologist is at the checkout when I walk in. He's too busy with customers to see me or be singing. And it sounds like a younger staff member has taken control of the radio so I doubt he'd know the words to The Killers 'My List' at any rate. They're my all-time favourite band so I notch the song up as another point to fate.

The next revelation has to be worth at least a thousand points and I grip the refrigerator door, unable to breathe at the magnitude of it. They're out of yoghurt! With my second dream coming true, the chance that the first one might too, or the note bit at least, is overwhelming. These are the spiritual rewards Amethyst promised will come, if I maintain faith and stick to my path.

In the queue my ability to eavesdrop on the fruitologist's exchanges is inhibited by the couple behind me speaking unnecessarily loudly. Totally inconsiderate. My evil-eye glare silences them immediately.

'Had a great day at Pebbly Beach yesterday,' the fruitologist says to the woman in front of me.

Pebbly Beach! Like that isn't another sign. Still my Scorpio moon sends tiny pulses of astrologically borne jealousy through me at the friendliness and familiarity of their interaction. Lucky for her she is no competition—middle-aged and, dare I say it, downright dowdy. Otherwise she may have received an 'accidental' scuff to her heel and a wide-eyed innocent 'sorry' when she turned to see what was happening. Not ideal for enlightenment but all's fair in love, war and fruitologist flirtations.

As the woman leaves I hand over my items and miraculously find the voice and courage to say, 'Do you know when you'll be getting more organic sheep's milk yoghurt in?'

'Wednesday,' he says with a smile and starts bagging my items.

'Oh, that's OK thanks, I don't need a bag thanks.' I wave my enviro bag at him partly as evidence but mostly in the hope it will distract him from my ridiculous use of 'thanks' twice within ten words.

Seemingly undeterred by my bagging rejection the fruitologist tells me the yoghurt delivery will be 'between one and 2pm'.

I do love someone with such attention to detail. So very helpful.

I feel the pressure build as we wrap up our little exchange. Brave me as opposed to the other me, whose armpits are sweating and feels like she's going to faint, comes out with 'Fantastic! Guess I'll see you Wednesday,' in an attempt at flirtation. I do have to look down slightly to carry this off. He's smiling at me when I look up.

It's a funny lopsided smile. The kind of smile that looks like he's holding something back, which only makes me more determined to find out what that could be.

The fact that I have just enough yoghurt to last me until Wednesday can't be overlooked. My intuition is telling me that this is the start of something big.

5

'Good morning, sunshine.' Jack beams from the coffee machine. Normally this level of enthusiasm would be too much for me on a Wednesday morning, but today's a different story.

'Hi, Jack. How are you?'

'I'm awesome but not as awesome as you.'

'Why?'

'You just are.'

'Thanks. I'll be even *more* awesome when I get my coffee.'

Jack laughs. 'Sheesh, don't rush me. It's a fine art.'

'I know, and it's worth waiting for—you're a master.'

'True. Nice dress by the way.'

'Thanks, it's a top actually.' I take step back from the counter, showing Jack my wrap top. 'It's one of my favourites—I wear it all the time, hadn't you noticed?'

'Yes, I just hadn't mentioned it and today it looks different. It's making your eyes look even more beautiful, like emeralds.'

I know I've got a glint in my eye—and a glow—but it's good to see that my grooming efforts have paid off. I'd pulled out all stops in case I don't have time to go home before I go into PGGG for my yoghurt tonight.

'Ha, you can't cover it up that easily. Now you've upset me I'm going to take my coffee and leave.'

'You're killing me, Fiona!' Jack calls after me as I walk out backwards, both of us smiling.

The door of Jane's studio is slightly ajar when I get there that evening.

'Yoo hoo!' I step inside.

No sign of Jane. I sit my shopping bag among the creative chaos of charcoal, oils, brushes and paint canisters that covers the large table she uses as a desk. She's probably out the back. I'm about to head out to see when I hear noises coming from the bathroom: low muttering, grunting. I should have called ahead.

'Who's there?' Jane calls as I'm tiptoeing out.

'It's only me. I'll go and we can catch up later.'

'No, wait, I'm done in here, well, nearly.' Jane gives a husky giggle—it isn't meant for me. I step outside to give them some space.

A few minutes later a flash of youthful handsomeness gives me a parting wave.

'Aren't you meant to be somewhere picking something up yourself?' Jane emerges from the bathroom red-faced. It isn't a blush; Jane would feel no need. I envy her this. She stops in her tracks as she peeks at the contents of my shopping bag. 'Oh dear, triple chocolate mud cake. This can't be good.'

'Who was that?'

'No one special—spectacular but not special. What's going on, Kismet?'

'You know my "See you Wednesday" comment?' I say once we're both plated up with cake—Jane a sliver, me a slab. Naturally I've told Jane every minute detail of my visit on the twenty-sixth.

'How could I forget? It was brilliant.'

'Thank you. I was feeling totally Mae West about it myself.'

Jane nods. 'Very.'

'I can't believe it! This morning, I'd done all my preparations to go in tonight—I was mantraed up, meditated, positively affirmed and had intention set like a mad thing to manifest the interaction with the fruitologist that was best for my highest good.'

'What about your I-Ching and had you zhoozhed your zing?'

I shoot Jane a 'don't mock me in my distress' look, but smile anyway. 'I'm off the I-Ching, it's not doing it for me at the moment. And if my interaction with Jack was anything to go by, my zing was adequately zhoozhed, thank you very much. Anyway I was on my way down to the bus this morning and saw the fruitologist in the street. He deliberately—*deliberately*—turned away from me! Fuckwit! Sorry, Buddha.'

I grab my fork to continue conducting my one member orchestra of outrage. 'And we're not talking some innocuous half-turn of the head but a "practically throw his neck out" type of manoeuvre. I was left in the street—my best smile falling from my face with a huge, humiliating thud.'

'Prick,' Jane spits.

'How dare he, how *very dare he* think he can turn away from me? And even more how very dare he think he can reject me? Who does he think he is? And what was with the "hi" the other week? Why even bother "hi"-ing me and being so nice and smiley when I asked about the yoghurt if he was just going to carry on like that? I have enough "pleasant exchange and hi" people in my life! I'm the Queen of Hi! I say "hi" to people I'm not sure I even know if they look familiar, just in case I do know them and they think I'm ignoring them!'

'Exactly. I second your fuckwit and raise you a effen C!'

'Totally. And effen C is being nice!'

'What did you do?'

'What was there to do? I breathed in all the pride I could summon, stood tall, flicked my hair and walked on by.'

'You didn't say anything?'

'Like I'm going to beg him to notice me! The worst part is I'm now completely out of yoghurt—no way was I going to swallow my pride even for that.'

'Fuckwit. He isn't worth a sniff of you, Kiz—you should forget him immediately.'

'Well, perhaps ... but even you said we can't fight fate.'

Thank the Goddess for Amethyst. From the moment I step into her waiting room on Saturday morning I feel as though I've been wrapped in a cloak of comfort. Amethyst floats out like a butterfly and scoops me up in a hug, draping me in the silk wings of her kaftan sleeves. She places a feather-light kiss on my third eye then takes my hand and leads me to the treatment room.

With all that charm and grace I'd say she's a Libran but I don't know for sure. Whenever I've asked her birthday, she flutters her hands like little versions of her butterfly self and says, 'So many lifetimes, so many birthdays.'

I fill her in on Situation Singing Fruitologist, right up to the point of catching the quick shuffle of his sneakers back into the store as I passed this morning. I may have had my head down and only darted my eyes in using my peripheral glance technique but I know they were the Singing Fruitologist's sneakers—I've spent so much time looking down when I go by I could write a paper on *How to tell a Fruiterer by His Footwear*. Not that I can tell Amethyst that.

'Do you think the sausage dog could have been a coincidence, not really a sign at all? I mean, given everything, do you really think there's any point?' I squirm in the talking chair, feeling like a spiritual traitor.

'Hmm' is all Amethyst says. Then she closes her eyes and presses the tips of her fingers to her temples—a dead giveaway she's receiving a message from her guides. I lean forward and wait for the revelation.

'It is not my role to play matchmaker—I am a spiritual healer, an artist of energy not a walking, talking version of RSVP!'

Yikes.

'Kismet,' she continues, 'in a world full of possible timings and sequences, do you really think that we can sweep Spirit and the Universe aside and put things down to mere coincidence? You have to learn to *trust*.'

'I just don't understand how it can be this hard if it's meant to be.'

'The greater plan of how things will work is not always obvious in the immediate. It's not for us to judge. How often have you heard people say something makes sense in hindsight? You're overanalysing it—have faith. Now, let's get you up onto the table, your aura is a complete mess!'

Amethyst magically weaves my chakras back into balance to rewire my energetic short circuit—I'd fused out my Sahasrara with my overactive mind and my Anahata with my fear.

When she's finished, she says, 'I have something I need to share with you. I don't get permission from the Universe to share this with just anyone, as it goes slightly against the manifestation theory.' She lowers her voice to a whisper before continuing, 'By focussing on something too much you can actually drive it away from you and, conversely, obsessively focussing on one thing can get in the road of other things that are meant for you—block them from coming to you.'

Who would have thought destiny could be so complicated? Doris Day made it sound so much easier in 'Que Sera, Sera' but then again I don't believe Doris Day was actually a qualified energetic and spiritual healer.

'Blessed be.' Amethyst farewells me with another kiss to my third eye once we're done.

I check my obsessive-overthinking-self in at the door on the way out and step into the rest of my life as Ms Totally Well-Balanced, Non-Obsessive, Middle-of-the-Road, who lives with grace, acceptance, balance and harmony.

I feel so entirely Om Shanti that enlightenment must be imminent.

6

'I know, I know, sorry I'm late.' I rush into my parents' kitchen the next day and plonk the plate of brownies I've baked for dessert on the orange laminate bench. It's that time of the month again—the Johnson family lunch.

I go first to my mother, who proffers her cheek for me to peck, barely slowing her hands as they swish away at the iceberg lettuce she's washing. Catherine stops spooning olives into a serving dish and turns stiff as I rest my fingers on her shoulders and barely kiss her cheek. None of the adults in my family are very good with physical affection. I'm OK with women I feel comfortable with, like Jane and Amethyst, but it took work. Kids, on the other hand, are a different story.

Sonja is sitting at the pine kitchen table chopping carrots with the same blunt knife her mother and I learnt our kitchen skills with. As I kneel beside her she puts the intergenerational knife down and wraps her arms around my neck.

'Just as well you're here, big girl,' I say, layering kisses over her golden, baby-soft hair. 'I'm so tired I couldn't be trusted with that job today. I hardly slept a gazillionth of a wink last night.'

'You should have tried medicating, Aunty Fee, you told me it helps you sleep,' Sonja offers in her sweet, caring, Piscean way.

'Oh honey, it's meditating, and yes, usually it does help, you're one hundred per cent right.'

Catherine swivels around, hands on hips. 'Don't go putting any of your new age, hippitty-doo-daa ideas in her head, Fiona, she's only eight.'

I take a breath. I won't correct Catherine's 'Fiona' in front of Sonja, I don't want to make her feel bad for calling me Aunty Fee. To her and her brother that's who I will always be and I'm more than happy for it to stay that way.

'Seriously, Catherine, meditation is scientifically proven. Psychologists use it to treat depression and PTSD these days.'

Dad enters from the backyard, extinguishing the embers that are sparking between Catherine and me. Sammy is hot on his tail.

'Hi guys. What have you been up to out there?' I give Dad the Johnson greeting.

'I've been teaching the young one here a bit about putting,' Dad says proudly of Sammy, who squirms and wriggles under my hug. He's a Gemini but the squirming has nothing to do with his star sign, it's because he's a ten-year-old boy. Only his grandmother can get away with hugs without resistance these days.

'Don't encourage your father to start up about the G subject, Fiona.' Mum pats the tea towel she's using to dry the lettuce with renewed vigour.

'Where's Brian?' I ask, but I know what Catherine's answer will be before she gives it. Even for a Virgo, he's spending an exceptional amount of time at work lately.

'Catherine, speaking of Brian's work, didn't you have something you wanted to mention to Fiona?' Mum gives Dad a nudge, handing him a plate of marinated steak and sausages. 'Sammy, you go out and help your grandfather with the barbecue. Sonja, you supervise the boys.'

A nervous quiver starts in my gut and rises until the skin on my head feels stretched. There's something brewing here and I don't like the smell of it one little bit. The intergenerational knife isn't the only thing that hasn't changed in this place. Sure, Sammy's and Sonja's paintings now decorate the fridge where Catherine's and mine used to hang but everything else is fundamentally the same, especially Mum and Catherine.

'Is anything happening with that guy your psychic told you about, Fiona?' Catherine asks with a smile or a sneer—sometimes it's hard to tell.

'It's Kismet! K-I-S-M-E-T! Kismet!' I snap now the children are out of earshot. 'And she's an energetic and spiritual healer. We've had some exchanges, nothing concrete quite yet.' I try to sound confident.

'Do you remember Grant from Brian's work? You met him and his wife at that lunch Brian and I had last year. The senior statistician.' Catherine always identifies people by their jobs.

'Maybe vaguely.' I attempt to cross reference the bevvy of bland couples that were at the lunch. I've virtually succeeded in wiping the whole torturously *pleasant* event from my memory.

'He and his wife separated a few months ago and he remembered you—well, you and your brownies—from the lunch. He asked Brian if you were still single and if he could get your number.'

'Oh no, what did Brian say?' Having to withhold my spiritual exclamations around my family is really an added pressure I don't need, although being remembered for my brownies does take the edge off a bit. I'm quite chuffed at being renowned for them.

'Of course he said he'd ask me first. So can I?'

'What?'

'Tell Brian to give him your number?'

'Let me think about it.' A statistician is so not me but I should get back on the straight and narrow in terms of entertaining other opportunities and not over-focussing on the fruitologist. Grant could be a good distraction and I think I might need one.

Being Ms Middle-of-the-Road had all seemed well and good when I was high on the wave of my chakra cleansing, bathed in sunshine, taking in the beauty of Crystal Beach as I stood on Amethyst's porch. To be honest, it was a bit of a relief initially; the whole obsession with Situation Singing Fruitologist was becoming exhausting, however the middle of the night sent Ms Middle-of-the-Road veering a little off course. 'Just one last Fruitologist Fixation fix and I'll kick off my Fruitologist Focus Rehab tomorrow,' I'd promised myself after I'd had a light-bulb moment recollecting Amethyst's RSVP comment.

I'd searched page after page of online dating sites and apps for slightly less attractive than the real thing Kevin Costner doppelgangers to see if I could find the fruitologist. At 2am I was still trawling through the endless pages of the profiles of men between thirty-five (he could just be wearing badly for his age) and fifty (or particularly well) that live within twenty kilometres of Putney. One page after the next brought a fresh wave of relief. At least he wasn't putting himself out there for the entire world to see. I wasn't sure how I'd cope if I'd discovered the fruitologist was on a dating site yet had turned away from me in the street.

'So, can we give Grant your number?' Catherine does little to hide the exasperation in her voice, or any part of her, as she bangs cutlery down on the bench, bringing me back to her question.

'Sure, why not.' The words are out before I realise what I'm saying and, Buddha help me, my mother is witness to them.

7

Day four of Ms Middle-of-the-Road and the rewards are already materialising. First, on my way to work, I transitioned from walking with extreme dignity to a hair-flicking flounce when the fruitologist looked at me as I passed. Love, light and perfect harmony deserted me. I'm sure I projected a 'Screw you, you don't get to ignore me again, sweetheart!' vibe, which wouldn't be surprising as that's exactly what I was feeling.

It's as though by reclaiming my power I've created the energetic shift I need for my life to move forward, because when I arrive home Wednesday evening and check my email, I find a message from the Office of the Australian Consulate in Shanghai. I have a phone interview for a job as the Executive Assistant to the Consulate General next Wednesday. With all this Situation Singing Fruitologist business going on I'd forgotten I even applied for it.

Amethyst must have had a spiritual connection malfunction, a simple case of spirit guide crossed wires. China has always been my destiny, she's even said I have a future life there. And the timing of the interview so soon after the fruitologist's rejection can't be overlooked. If I'm going to have a destined relationship surely it has to be with someone there.

Six years ago when I began studying Mandarin it was like coming home. I'd decided I wanted to learn a language and Mandarin made perfect sense as I was seeing a Chinese guy at the time. I was fascinated by the stories he'd tell, the myths and customs, and hearing about that world. We all have a 'soul place' and as inexplicable as it is, China is mine.

The next morning, sitting at my desk, I'm the portrait of composure and quiet positivity, surprisingly contained. I haven't even phoned Jane to squeal excitedly about the interview. It feels too big. Besides Jane hasn't called me. I suspect that has to do with the guy from the other night. This happens sometimes: 'spectacular' can have Jane MIA for up to a fortnight. But two weeks with a man is her limit.

'Fiona, we've changed our minds.' Broomstick's arrival crushes my composure and positivity. She seems quite excited about whatever it is that 'we've' changed our minds about. Her lips aren't quite as pursed, like she's been sucking on a tube of superglue, as they usually are. 'We're not going to use the Education Compliance Consultant after all. You and I are more than capable of taking care of it. I've found a work-shop next Thursday to bring us up to speed on the latest requirements. Book that, cancel the compliance consultant, then come into my office and we'll start making a plan.'

Deep breath—I just need to focus on Shanghai.

In Broomstick's office, I start making my own plan of what I'll have on my New Life in Shanghai vision board, then abruptly wonder why Grant hasn't called. Anything to escape being fully present with Broomstick. Maybe Grant doesn't want to appear too keen. Not that I even care. A statistician—he's bound to be a Virgo. That sort of nit-picking is *so* not something I need. Still, a girl doesn't like to be shelved by a lonely separatee.

Out of the torture chamber, Broomstick's plans outlined on my notepad, my mobile beeps with a message. It'll be Grant—I've manifested him into action with the power of my mind. I'll look at it in two minutes, I don't want to appear desperate.

Then I remember what the whole boredom of the Broom-stick meeting has made me forget: I don't need to care about Grant or any of it. I'm about to embark on my new life as a successful globe-trotting woman of international high-calibre executive support. I pick up my mobile.

OK, not Grant but Amethyst. I had just been thinking of her too, sort of.

Darling Kismet. Apologies if my RSVP comment seemed a little harsh the other day. My energies were grating against the cosmic forces. It came to me in a meditation that your gentle soul needed an apology for that.

Much love until next time. A xxx

I guess even energetic healers are human.

Wednesday morning there's still no word from Grant. It's not like I'm waiting, I've got much more exciting things to think about. Still, I can't help but wonder. Maybe he's not such a lonely separatee after all, perhaps his separation has pro-pelled him into a mid-life crisis and he's busy swiping twenty-somethings on Tinder. They probably can't even bake.

'You're looking lovely again this fine morning, Fiona. Do you have a date tonight?' Jack's words bounce out, little bubbles of joy as always. I can imagine him at seventy, still sounding as young as a boy. His brows arch over dreamy Mediterranean eyes that match his coffee. Who needs Grant?

'Oh no, don't tell me, I don't want to know. It'd break my heart.' He throws his forearm dramatically across his forehead.

'Then best you never know.' I half-laugh. Until now, I'd never noticed how hairy he is. Pity, I really don't like hairy men.

Our fingers brush in a playful but zing-free way as I grab my coffee. I flutter mine into a wave, rallying myself from the disappointing hairy revelation. At least I can always rely on Jack for a fun distraction. It's nice to have something consistent.

As for the fruitologist, there's been four sneaker sightings, another catching of him glancing at me as I went by one night and a slightly disappointing Singing Fruitologist–free visit. Not that I'm counting, just observing. I've been so Ms Middle-of-the-Road this week that if maintaining my focus on the centre white lines of the bitumen was an Olympic event, I'd have scored a 9.5 out of 10.

Coffee in hand, I call Broomstick. It's still early, so I'll get her voicemail. I can't possibly go in to work today, there's no way I'd be in a fit state to face the interview for my new life as a successful globe-trotting woman of international high-calibre executive support after a day in that place.

Forty-five minutes later my bedroom looks like the change rooms during a Myer Boxing Day sale but nothing in the mountain of clothes is right. Not that it matters what I wear—it's a phone interview—but still, it's important to embrace the energy I want to project. I finally settle on my plain black linen skirt and matching shirt.

When my phone beeps with a text from Bing asking if I'm OK and why I haven't been in for my coffee, I practically jump through the roof. I may be a positive 9.5 out of 10 on my Ms Middle-of-the-Road scale but my nervous energy reading is off the Richter. If I don't do a quick session at the gym and get rid of some of this nervous energy, I may implode.

At the gym I run faster and faster on the treadmill until I have to grip the rail to stop myself flying off the back of it. But I can't move my legs fast enough to stop my brain getting itself caught up in knots of anxiety over the interview, and then about the fruitologist. When I'm not much more than a sweat spot, I look up at the TV screen and there it is, a sausage dog. I've been seeing quite a few of them lately, but seeing one right here, on the screen at the gym ... I couldn't even take a stab at the odds.

At precisely 5pm Shanghai time (8pm AEDT), my phone rings. I stop dead in the middle of one of the caged tiger circles I've been pacing around my living room in for the last hour.

'Good afternoon, Fiona Johnson speaking.' I feel as though a bandage is being wrapped tightly around my chest and my voice sounds all wrong.

'Fiona, this is Elizabeth Mercury from the Office of the Consulate General, sorry, is this a bad time? I'm sure this is the time we had allocated for you.'

'No. Thanks for calling, Elizabeth. I really appreciate the opportunity for the interview,' I say, thinking, *God, why didn't I just answer the phone like it was a normal call?* Already I can feel my words becoming loose on my tongue, slipping out beyond my control.

'I'm just going to patch in the Assistant Consul. He and I will be conducting the interview.'

'Great.' Oh Govinda, why did I say great? That is so unprofessional.

'Yes, I have excellent Microsoft Office skills.' Introductions out of the way, I answer the first question confidently but my mouth has started to go dry and the bandage around my chest is getting tighter. I have to sit on my left hand to stop it shaking.

Each question wrings me out a little more. My voice moves from quavering to breaking when I try to answer scenario-based question four. I can barely breathe and can think even less. The bandage is working its way up and down, round and round, to mummify me. Without knowing the environment or processes they have in place I have no idea how to respond. I chase words around like peas on a plate.

Out of kindness, the Assistant Consul offers a prompt but from their reactions when I do stammer an answer, I know I've lost them completely. The rest of the interview I'm like a salmon swimming upstream. The current gets stronger with each question until I'm caught in rapids—tossing and tumbling, the pull dragging me under. Words are coming out but I haven't got any idea what they are anymore.

8

The next morning I force my stuck-in-a-vice-feeling head off the pillow. I should be in my well-deserved place under the doona for the day—if not the rest of my life. I would be, except for the stupid Education Compliance workshop.

I dress in a shapeless grey dress—not to please Broomstick, who'd asked me to wear something 'normal', by which she meant to leave my signature monochrome, angular-cut, urbane chic clothes on their hangers—but so I can be invisible. My dress looks a bit like one of the hessian sacks filled with coffee beans at Jack's, not that I'll go in there today. I don't want him to see me in this state—my eyelids all puffy and froglike despite my make-up, blotchy skin showing through my foundation. Unwashed and slicked back in a plain band, my hair looks more dirty blonde than the 'golden wheat' and 'caramelised blonde' that Diego, my hairdresser, so artfully highlights it with. I couldn't manage a flirty front even for coffee. And going to Jack's would mean I'd then have to go past PGGG, like I'd do that looking like *this*.

All is as it is meant to be, everything in perfect harmony.

It's not easy but I get my mantra out from under the black cloud that hovers above me. I churn it over step by step down the backstreets, grateful at least that I don't have to face public transport or pretend I'm OK in front of everyone at the office.

I reach the old hospital with its buildings plonked around like Monopoly pieces and check the map. The conference room where the workshop is being held is in a shiny new research centre opposite the hospital proper. Doctors run importantly across the street, patient files tucked under their arms, stethoscopes thumping against their chests. 'Quickly, quickly, out of our way, we've got lives to save here!' their auras seem to say.

'Sorry.' I turn to apologise to one of the medics who runs into me. Doing so, I nearly run into someone else. I do a double take. It's Raymond from PGGG. I give him a forced smile of acknowledgement (my new life being over is no excuse to be rude). He doesn't seem to see me at all or maybe he just doesn't recognise me with my butt so well concealed.

It's a bit of a relief when I reach the workshop venue, but then ...

'These are my people, Fiona,' Broomstick says with something approaching a grin, as she runs her eyes down the list of participants.

I take my place next to her, pick up my folder and glance at the list. I see what she means. Besides mine, there's only one other name out of the thirty-five participants that doesn't have PhD after it.

'Dr Cybil Raynard—Centre for Strategic and Financial Excellence.' Broomstick lurches across the table to shake the hand of Professor Emeritus Bartholomew, as identified by his nametag. He hasn't even had the chance to sit down.

Halfway through the well-worn workshop protocol of in-troductions, I begin to wonder what Raymond is doing at the hospital. The seed of concern that maybe the fruitologist is here plants itself.

As the day moves on it becomes obvious that the P in all the participants' PhDs is not for 'practicality'. By morning tea I'm so bored and frustrated that Ms Middle-of-the-Road has vacated the premises and my earlier concerns have taken root. I'm convinced that the fruitologist has had an accident or maybe a heart attack and is lying dying in the hospital somewhere. During the Reliability of Automated Compliance Software presentation, I imagine myself rushing to his bed-side, mopping his brow—kind, concerned and caring. I stop my imaginings short of me in a nurse's outfit—best not risk it, especially in case it was a heart attack that put him here. It would be too tragic if I stepped up to his bed in a sexy white miniskirted uniform and divulged my desires as I leant over to pop my thermometer under his tongue, causing him to die of coronary arrest. What a way to thwart our future and leave me in the limbo of being a near-grieving widow forever. (Not that I want a husband but it works for the dramatic tension of my fantasy.)

At lunchtime the workshop facilitator gives us the directive to 'mingle with attendees from other organisations, swap compliance ideas and share how you implement compliance strategies in your organisation'. Kill me now. I can't believe my life has come to this. I hide in the bathroom. Starvation is preferable to making compliance small talk, even if it does mean having to sit cross-legged to hide my feet in case Broom-stick comes in and catches me.

I fill in time texting Jane, thankful I hadn't told her about the interview. I couldn't stand having to relive the experience.

Back in the workshop, I glance at the agenda. The cruel truth of how I'm going to spend the rest of the day and low blood sugar make my mind run amok. Before long I'm back beside the fruitologist's hospital bed, where, in a moment of lucidity (he'd deteriorated to being in a coma by this stage), he'd asked for someone to bring me to him. Of course I'd rushed to him immediately, sung bad Retro FM–style songs and chatted to him to try to bring him out of the coma he'd slipped back into immediately after making his request. I did not move, eat or drink (OK, I did drink but only to sustain my life with water and a reasonable mood with the occasional off-the-trolley, totally flirtation-free coffee) until the miracle of my voice, presence and affections brought him back to consciousness.

By the end of the workshop, the fruitologist had recovered and we'd moved from our honeymoon period to a three-bedder and mortgage in suburbia with him complaining that I spent too much money on clothes, make-up, hair, gym membership and going out with friends.

The Lovers' Oracle doesn't have anything like: *You are about to enter a suburban nightmare.*

Saturday morning I remain none the wiser as to the fruitologist's welfare. Not that I should even concern myself, but it does provide a welcome distraction from the vultures of the memory of the interview when they come pecking at my brain.

On my way out to meet Stephanie, I glance in at the PGGG in a very non-attached Ms Middle-of-the-Road way, careful to make sure I don't appear like I'm looking, let alone care. Thursday night's prayer of 'Goddess, I don't mind if the fruitologist wants to have a mortgage and whipper snips and mows the lawn every Sunday and I have to give up Diego (he is quite pricey) ... so long as I can keep at least my coffee habit and gym membership—I just want him to live!' (I'd gone full circle again by the time I got home from the workshop) is answered. The fruitologist is there, alive and seemingly well.

I appreciate that asking for two miracles in one morning might be a bit much, especially since I threw the first one away on the fruitologist and his welfare. Now I'd confirmed he was fine, I was back to being upset about him ignoring me. But a girl shouldn't limit herself. 'The Universe has an infinite capacity to deliver,' Amethyst is constantly reminding me. Maybe I have miracle magnet energy today and should take advantage of it and focus on manifesting another one. Because a miracle is what it will take for me to formulate a Stephanie-digestible version of Situation Singing Fruitologist.

You can choose your friends, but you can't choose your family and I'm still surprised that I chose Stephanie. She's Catherine if someone had taken an angle grinder to her and smoothed off all the really hard edges.

When I arrive Stephanie waves wildly at me from the middle of the crowd of people waiting for their tables at yum cha. She's already got a ticket, I see. Of course she's already got a ticket—that's *so* Stephanie. I often wonder if she has a secret Advent calendar for her life: everything perfectly planned out so she just lifts the flap when the time comes, and—*wham*—there it is. She's always been like that, ever since I met her when we worked together in a bank. What some people miss, though, is that Stephanie is also intensely kind—even if she's not overtly demonstrative.

'Hello, Kismet.' The air kiss she gives me is so air that she's barely closer than arm's length. Still, she adjusts my hair where it sits on my shoulders in case the 'hug' disturbed it—that's her way of showing she cares. Stephanie's black pixie cut never has a strand out of place.

Our greetings are barely over when our number gets called.

'What's happening with you? How are James and the kids?' I say, once we're seated. I've got one eye on the trolleys that trundle by—inspecting the contents of the steaming bamboo baskets and pointing at plates and dishes.

'James' work ... This week, little Lily had a dance rehearsal ... We've found an under-five's martial art class for Aiden. I think it ...' Stephanie lists in her efficient, factual way. I offer her a dumpling but she looks at her chopsticks as though she's about to receive an anal probe.

'I'll get some forks and spoons for us.' I have no problem using chopsticks but I don't want to make Stephanie feel awkward.

'I ... work's been really busy so I haven't been up to much,' I say when Stephanie asks what's been happening. I'm so focussed on the trolleys and the food that I've got no hope of coming up with a version of Situation Singing Fruitologist that Stephanie could digest.

Our conversation moves into the easy flow you have when you've been friends with someone for over ten years.

'I think that's probably enough, Kismet,' Stephanie says as I peer into another steamer. She's a bird-style eater so I'm a bit disappointed. I like to leave yum cha groaning and promising I'm never going to eat that much again but knowing I will.

Before we leave, Stephanie phones James to collect her but first she wants to take advantage of not having the kids and do some shopping in the city. I'm happy to leave her to it. Given events over the last few weeks, I need some downtime to contemplate my next move.

9

Who can explain why I decided it was a good idea to go into PGGG again but fate is a powerful motivator and here I am, 7.15pm Monday, striding in. Naturally my eyelashes have been recurled, my hair brushed and re-brushed, my make-up touched up and my face spritzed. If nothing else I could show the fruitologist I'm completely unaffected by him.

Ms Middle-of-the-Road can't help but hear that he and some guy who resembles a sporty version of Harry Potter's Gregorovitch are talking about ... sport. The fruitologist is wearing one of his trademark T-shirts with a brand emblazoned across the front. He seems to have quite a thing for them.

Apples are the final item on my list, actually they're the second last before pears, but don't ever let it be said I won't be flexible when desperate measures are called for: the apples are closer to him. I go about choosing them at the pace of a semi-comatose tortoise, inspecting each one, turning it up, down, round and round, trying to project a wrap-it-up-boys vibe.

Halfway through selecting my apples two things happen. The fruitologist finally bids his friend farewell and Prince's

'I Would Die 4 U' comes on the radio. If he hadn't started singing along to it I might have been OK but, as though he has a window directly into my fantasies, he does.

An apple slips from my shaking fingers and hits the stack. Before I know it, I've created an apple avalanche. Half-a-dozen Pink Ladies tumble to the floor.

A large Adidas sneaker rolls one of the runaways towards where I'm crouching. 'Are you OK there?' the fruitologist says, his voice getting closer as he crouches beside me.

'Yes, sorry, thanks,' I squeak. Apart from the fact that I'm going to die of humiliation right here, right now!

I keep my head down and reach for the apple resting against his all-too-familiar sneaker. He's so close that if I could breathe I'd probably be able to smell him. His big hand makes it to the apple before mine. As he passes it to me our fingers touch. A small village could be powered by the current that runs through me.

'Thanks,' I squeak again. I can feel his eyes on my face. I continue looking at his feet. The moment is so intense that I can't stand it. Before he can say anything I jump up like a jack-in-the-box and dash to the counter, where one of the casuals—a bored-looking girl—is waiting for someone to serve. Seriously, where is Ms Middle-of-the-Road when I need her?

The next morning it's as though Broomstick has picked up on my excitement from the spark at PGGG (I'm trying to focus on the positive rather than my questionable reaction), and is set on ruining my mood.

'Fiona, my office.'

Angela from Marketing, who's walking past, gives me a sympathetic look.

I bustle into Broomstick's office projecting efficiency, hoping that will make it brief.

'I was talking to one of my old colleagues about their compliance strategies,' Broomstick begins.

Oh, karmic kindness—as if the workshop the other day wasn't more than enough compliance talk for one lifetime. All I hear through her excited monologue is, 'Blah, blah, blah …' and now she's extinguished the excitement from the spark, my mind drifts to thoughts of why I'm such a complete mess around the fruitologist.

'On Friday,' she says and brings me back. If there are deadlines to be met or something I have to organise, I'd better focus.

'I've called Professor Emeritus Bartholomew, he thinks that getting the submission in early is the best strategic move as well.' Broomstick's lips unglue themselves from her teeth into a proper smile. The creases at the corners of her mouth leave little lines in her face powder.

I must look like a stunned mullet, because she says, 'You remember Professor Emeritus Bartholomew from the workshop, Fiona?'

How could I forget! But why are you smiling about him? And what is with the make-up these days, Broomstick?

'You mean this Friday?' I splutter.

'Yes, this Friday, Fiona,' she says in her 'Why are you asking such a stupid question?' voice.

This Friday, I think, blood draining from my face then my body, until the only colour I have left is on my Got the Blues for Red OPI–pedicured toenails. I can't find the strength to speak.

'I have stuff on this week,' I finally manage. Like my life. I'd so been enjoying having it back after the last report, doing all the normal things: full sessions at the gym, dinners, coffees, phone conversations, having a moment to laugh with people at work again (not Broomstick obviously), not to mention yum cha. I'd even contacted the evening college about going back to Mandarin classes again.

As much as I want to scream, 'Go screw yourself!' at Broomstick, I bite my tongue. The interview experience for the Consulate job is still too much of a gaping wound in my confidence to hunt down a new job immediately. Besides, I survived deadline hell last time. I'll survive this too.

'What would have been so hard about staying there and matching his gaze, Kismet?' Amethyst asks in my next appointment, then says, 'What happened the next time you went in?' She's probably got a perfectly clear answer to the first question just by tuning into my thought field.

'He wasn't there. That "manifesting your mojo" mantra you gave me was completely wasted!' I sigh dramatically, hurling my arms around for impact, and laugh.

'I mean, the next time you *saw* him Kismet? Did you look him in the eye?' Amethyst holds her temples and squeezes her eyes tight. I can safely strike humour off the list of enlightenment's essential attributes. 'They are virtually screaming at me that this is what you have to do: *look him in the eye*. My guides aren't ever wrong.'

'I try, but it's as though ...' I fiddle with the tassels of the cushion I'm nursing and attempt to come up with exactly what it is that I feel. 'Like there's a power beyond me—I've got no control over it. I've made myself go in twice since the apple incident. I did say "hi" to him the day he was there and I tried to raise my head but as soon as I got to his eyes I looked down again.'

'Why?'

'There's a force, an intensity when I look at him that I can't explain. I've never been great at this sort of thing but this, it's insane.'

'What's your gut instinct telling you if you let go of fear and just feel? Go in there.' Amethyst leans across, laying one hand on my heart and the other on my stomach. 'What is it saying?' Her voice is as soothing as a warm bath.

'That it's bigger than me, that if I fall for him I may never stop falling. Which I know is ridiculous—I don't even know him. I mean, I know nothing about him.'

'It's not so ridiculous from where I'm sitting.' Amethyst smiles. 'And of course you can stop falling. You are always in complete control.'

'That's just the thing. With him, I don't feel like I would be. I'm not already. Just look at me!'

'You are far stronger than you realise, Kismet.'

'Maybe that's part of the problem. I'm tired of being strong, always coping, always being responsible.' I wish my sigh was for dramatic effect but it's real.

'Spirit doesn't ever send us anything we can't handle, although I do think it would be a good idea for you to see someone who might be able to help with your anxiety, especially considering the interview. Being strong doesn't mean being without support. Give Lionel a call. He's an amazing hypnotherapist. Hypnotherapy can be a great help.' She scribbles a number on a piece of paper and sits it on top of my handbag.

'And in terms of your fruitologist,' she continues, 'he's just another person, Kismet, another soul, in another physical body. He's probably as fearful as you are. We're all in this together. What you see in yourself is not what others see in you. You can be quite intimidating in your self-contained way.'

I hold in a scoff as Amethyst tunes into the cosmic forces.

'I'm going to give you an exercise to do for homework,' she advises a minute or two later. 'It will help you get clarity on whether the fruitologist really is who you want in your life or if you've simply got yourself so tangled up in this obsessing that you can't see Buddha for his robes.'

A little plume of nervousness tickles at my chest as I imagine Amethyst giving me some highly evolved spiritual practice to connect to the universal energy source and my own guides for answers. I always find those things a bit challenging. I don't know how to tell if I'm right or wrong—is it imagination or intuition, hope or holism, a psychic message or projection? Which is why I like to go with definite, tangible signs.

'It's a list of what you want and need in your next male love relationship.'

'A man wish list?'

'No, no, no, Kismet—it's much more energetically sophisticated than that. It's a highly attuned clarifying tool. It literally sweeps away the dust of misguided wants to define who and what you truly value. All of my Goddesses- and Gods-in-training who have created a list with focus have had success within twelve months.'

Twelve months seems like a very long time to wait but I guess Spirit does have quite a few people to cater to.

'It's practically homoeopathic in its principle of like curing like. The whole "opposites attract" idea is passé. With the energy of the world shifting and the cycle we're in today, it's all about fitting together in completeness but not expecting anything of someone that you aren't already doing or aren't prepared to do, be or become yourself. So, List A: *What I need and want to have in my next male love relationship list.* Here you list things you want, but in a specific way. Are you with me so far?'

I nod patiently at Amethyst's remedial explanation. She hasn't picked up that in terms of list making, at least, she is talking to a fully-fledged Goddess.

'List A has to be in the positive form. Let me give you an example. You cannot put "not married"—you must put "available". Got it?'

I nod again.

'Now, for List B. That is your *What I am and love list.*'

I'm to list the items from List A that I also have. So if I put 'available' on List A I could add that for myself on List B.

'You ready for List C?' It's becoming more and more obvious she's used to dealing with list-making novices.

I give silent nod number three.

'List C—that is your *Work to do list*! You have to list anything that you aren't or don't have but are prepared to do or work on.'

I think of the item that will top my C List: 'Loves job.'

'So, in the end everything from List A must appear on List B or List C unless they are physical traits of the male. Clear?'

'Perfectly,' I say with a final, emphatic nod.

I get cracking on my list as soon as I get home. By 2am Sunday I have everything down in draft form. Just over two hundred items—yet to be categorised into Physical, Emotional,

Spiritual and Mental attributes by means of a nicely designed spreadsheet. Tomorrow I'll sort it to ensure it carries the right energetics of effort, functionality and aesthetic appeal.

Spirit won't let my efforts go unrewarded.

10

First thing Monday morning I phone for an appointment with Lionel, the hypnotherapist. After that, work takes over and the week speeds by as though I'm watching it from a bullet train.

When I arrive at Lionel's office at 4.30pm Thursday, his receptionist, a middle-aged barrel of a woman, points me down a hallway. 'He's running a tiny bit behind, I'm afraid, just take a seat down there. He should only be a minute or so.'

The hallway opens up into what looks like someone's lounge room. I sit on the couch and grab an early nineties *Home Beautiful* from the selection on the coffee table. I move to a less relaxed-looking waiting chair; it better suits my mood. I flip through the magazine, quickly discard it and reach for a replacement, hoping to find one that has a publication date inching towards this decade, however the 2011 *Angler's Annual* does little to distract me.

I attempt to slow my breath to the tick of the dark mahogany clock that sits on the mantle. I wrap my left leg over my right, unwrap it and wrap my right over my left. I can't settle. Hidden from the receptionist's view, I feel no qualms about changing seats again. The expansive lounge room set-up adds to the anxiety—my presence is so pronounced. I feel as though I'm meeting a boyfriend's parents for the first time and everyone but me is in the kitchen gathering the accoutrements of afternoon tea.

When a door opens I almost expect someone carrying a tray laid out with a Royal Doulton tea set and cake stand with a perfect Victoria sponge.

'Kismet, come in.' A bear of a man with grey hair and matching beard steps through the door, not a Victoria sponge in sight.

'Please, take a seat,' he says after I enter his office, pointing to the chair set at right angles to the desk, where he sits. 'As you will have guessed, I'm Lionel. I like to start with a thorough case history, so please indulge me for a moment.'

We run through my family, my childhood, my life to date— I paint my past with broad brush strokes in response to his questions. He raises his eyebrows and studies my body language. I feel like a bug under a microscope.

'So how do you think I can I help you?' Lionel asks when I've finished the somewhat abstract self-portrait of my life.

'I sort of have a bit of an issue with anxiety.'

'I see.' He watches me fidget for a moment before continuing. 'Hypnotherapy is very effective for anxiety. Are there any specific situations that create these moments?'

'No, not really.' It feels too revealing to mention the fruitologist, too soon in my relationship with Lionel to reveal that side of me. And the job interview seems too humiliating to share with someone I don't know. 'I mean, I do get a bit fixated on things too. Maybe we could work on that as well. They seem to go hand in hand.'

'The first step is to get you to a point of being able to experience what it is you are actually feeling,' he says. 'I'm going to run you through a breathing exercise that will take you to a point of relaxation to establish whether you are able to wind down enough to go under hypnosis. Take a seat in whichever one of those chairs looks most inviting to you.'

Oh no, this must be a test. The chair I choose will hold some deep significance. He's going to make an assumption about me based on which reclining-chair I pick. I rule out the chocolate velour one with the matching teddy bear—obviously the kiddie chair. My other two choices are an apricot-coloured leather armchair—potential for mother issues particularly given that the other choice is a navy velour Jason recliner (definitely father issues in that one).

I've begun to sweat from the added anxiety of the choice, so I can rule out the apricot leather one; I don't want my black linen pants sticking to it. I move to the navy Jason recliner, even though it goes against the grain of my style—I can't abide navy and black together.

'I'm going to count back from ten and I want you to slow your breathing in time with my count.' Lionel begins counting, then, 'Four … three … two … now go inside to that place no one else can know, get in touch with it … and one. Let it all go, feel yourself melting into the chair, release yourself from everything that has gone before and tell me what comes into your mind.'

The realisation that I've forgotten to tell the receptionist that my health insurance is in the name of Fiona keeps circling but I'm sure that isn't what he wants to hear.

'I can see tension in your body, Kismet. Just relax, let go.'

It's very exposing—reclining there, eyes closed. I force myself to be still, to look as though the tension is melting away. I visualise myself playing with Sammy and Sonja, and a smile warms my face.

'That's better,' Lionel says just before the buzzer goes. 'Next time we'll get further. I just needed you to experience a sense of trust and relaxation with me before we progress to the next phase.'

The bullet-train blur hasn't bypassed Jane, and I've been looking forward to seeing her all week. But something seems a little different when I hug her on Saturday night, nothing major, just a slight edge to her aura. Once we're settled at our table, she's all smirks and near snorts and I'm sure I must have imagined it.

'Ladies, have you decided what you will have this evening?' It's Erice, the ever-attentive owner of Marrakesh on Moore.

'We might need a little longer,' Jane says to him. 'Do you want to tell me about the Lionel session first or update Situation Singing Fruitologist?' she asks me.

'Not much to tell about the Lionel session really.' I try and skim the surface but eventually have to confess.

Jane practically explodes when I say I wasn't quite ready to tell Lionel about the fruitologist. 'What the fuck are you going for if you're not going to tell him about it? Give me eighty dollars and I'll draw a white line on the pavement and make you follow it—they say it works for chickens.'

'You know me, I'm not the sort of girl who can divulge that much before I get to know someone a little.'

Erice sweeps back over to us.

'I'll do mains, you do starters,' Jane says and immediately looks at Erice. 'Chicken tagine.'

'Any drinks, ladies?' Erice asks as he scribbles down my addition of a mezze plate.

'Sparkling mineral water, please.' It's my usual.

'I'll have the same.' Jane hands Erice the menus and wine lists.

'What's wrong with you? Don't tell me you're detoxing,' I ask once I can lift my jaw to speak again. I've never known Jane not to drink with dinner.

'Not exactly. It's no big deal, I've just had a few too many big nights.'

'Oh, I see,' I say, not really seeing at all. Multiple big nights haven't ever stopped her before, although it helps explain the edge to her aura I felt earlier.

'What's happening with the fruitologist anyway?' Jane narrows her eyes at me, as though she's daring me to tell her something negative so she can lay claim to being right about him being a fuckwit.

It's going to be awkward if anything does happen with him. I'll have one of those 'Help! My BFF hates my BF' situations that Tiffany and Angela from Marketing were sharing from one of their social-media feeds in the lunchroom the other day.

'This morning I took a little pre-shopping walk to put a bit of colour in my cheeks—I'd woken with a migraine—but once again, no freaking fruitologist! What's he doing energetically interfering with my affections if he's not going to commit to me even for a shopping trip?'

'God, why are you even wasting your time? I can't believe you bothered to half-glance in his direction once, let alone twice after everything you've told me.'

'I don't know myself. It's like there's some magnetic force drawing me to him, or maybe it's more a moth to a flame. And I cannot tell you how freakishly often sausage dogs are appearing.'

'Even if he or that woman are trying to kill you? At last report you assumed he was so not into you that he was going to have you stowed away under a mountain of salad greens, slowly asphyxiating in the PGGG cool room.'

'It was being poisoned, actually, and I'm still not sure they're not. I have been feeling a bit queasy and nothing tastes quite right.' I chuckle as I recall my chat with Jane where my creatively paranoid self had conjured up a 'death by poisoned yoghurt and feta' scenario for entertainment.

Jane sighs. 'I know it sounds like a cliché, Kizzo …'

'Oh, Great Govinda, you're not going to tell me you've turned and realised you've always been in love with me, are you?'

'I know your imagination is one of your gifts, but don't be so ridiculous. I just think you deserve someone who, well, is really into you, and the fruitologist—if we disregard spiritual pop-up toasters and sausage dogs and call a spade a spade—isn't! Why don't you give Erice a go? At worst it'd get you back in practice if anything should, miracle of miracles, ever happen with the fruitologist.'

Across the room Erice is seating a table of women who, by the look of them, are out for a big night of cougaring. Glimmers of light from the perforated pressed-metal Moroccan lampshades make patterns on the tight curls of his heavily oiled hair. One of the cougars must have caught her prey, as the head cougar pulls out a tiara and veil for the hen and pink-feathered fascinators for herself and the others. From the way the youngest looking of the brittle-haired pack is cooing at Erice as she strokes his generous pelt of chest hair and the gold chains that nestle in it, she definitely has hers in her sights.

'No, I think not!' I say to Jane. 'Besides I have to go home tonight.'

'Why?'

'I promised Jack.'

'Well if not Erice, then Jack? And why is it any of Jack's business whether you're going home or not?'

'Running past his café on my way here, he asked where I was going and whether I'd be coming in for coffee tomorrow morning. I've given him my word.'

'You take it all too literally—like you owe any of them anything. You think he'll even remember?'

'Jack always notices if I don't go in. But it's irrelevant anyway. I'm not sure I want to get involved with anyone.'

'Why not?'

'I took advantage of the empty change room at the gym the other day to do a complete body inspection in the full-length mirror—there's no concealing anything with those neon lights. My butt looks like an elephant's hide stuffed with golf balls! I nearly died. I *so* couldn't get naked with anyone.'

'Let me tell you something, Kismet, if you seriously think that any red-blooded man is thinking about a dimple or two—or even ten—on a thigh when he's about to launch the rocket, you're in bigger trouble than we thought.'

I snort. Not in humour, more in doubt.

'He's in his caveman state and when he's into you and you're both into it, any teensy bit of flubba-dubba—not that I'm saying you have any—that you've spent time angsting over in the mirror is completely invisible to him.'

'Like I said, it's irrelevant anyway. I think I need to reinstate Operation Escape to China.'

Even though Jane doesn't know about the Consulate interview, she knows better than anyone that China is where I've always wanted to be. She looks at me, then down at her phone that's just buzzed with a message. She's got that about-to-explode look again.

'Why don't you make up your fucking mind!'

It takes a moment for me to realise the comment isn't directed at whoever sent the message, it's meant for me. My heart lurches as though it's been dropped from a thousand feet.

'Sorry …' I can't keep the tears from welling in my eyes. I put my fork down and focus on the table. I have no idea where this has come from. We've had these conversations thousands of times. I could count on one finger the number of cross words Jane and I have had over the years.

'Sorry—just had a bad day. I didn't mean it.' Jane brushes spilt cous cous off the tablecloth.

'They probably think we're a couple having a tiff.' I try to laugh as I point my chin in the direction of the cougar collective. Their platinum heads have turned towards us. They look like a row of sideshow alley clowns waiting for ping-pong balls to be dropped into their mouths.

Jane takes a gulp of water then looks at the glass accusingly, as if it's to blame for its contents. 'It's not just you, Kismet, we all have problems. Sometimes, between you and Mum, your bloody indecision and faffing around gets a bit much. I love you both, but seriously it's like being stuck in a tug-of-war.'

I would try to explain or at least apologise but she snatches up her bag and stands. 'I've got an early start, I better go.' She drops a handful of notes on the table and strides out before I can get it together to try to stop her. Jane doesn't even do early starts.

11

If it weren't for Jane's outburst I'd ignore my phone's chirps the next morning. I'd left her a voicemail then sent a follow-up text—both went unanswered. In the hazy cocoon between being awake and asleep I can almost convince myself that it was just a bad dream. Almost, but not quite.

When I finally find my phone among the folds of my doona, 'Catherine' flashes disappointingly on the screen. I groan, put my head under my pillow and let it ring out. Catherine has been acting so Buddha-begotten Mother Teresa lately. She'd be likely to use one of her new favourite sayings, like 'First world problem!', if I mentioned anything to her about Jane, or work, or the fruitologist. And she'd undoubtedly call me Fiona while she was at it. I blame Phuket. It's as though she thinks taking a trip to a five-star resort in a non-Western nation makes her some sort of humanitarian aid worker like Angelina Jolie, holding the hands of people as they died of starvation or a flesh-eating bug.

I was having flesh issues of my own and not just the elephant's arse kind. When I got home last night, still shaken,

I poured water from the recently boiled kettle onto my hand and threw painkillers in the cup with the camomile tea bag. My hand is now wrapped in a bandage, underneath which is a thick coating of paw paw ointment and lavender oil.

Not that I blame Jane for being frustrated with me—I'm frustrated with me! And I hate to admit it, but Catherine may have a point about the first world problem thing. It's time I took control. Jane was right about the fruitologist and if he's going to come between Jane and me, there'll be a price to pay. What was he doing trespassing on my karmic path if he wasn't going to act with some intent? OK, so he may not *know* he's trespassing but still. My best friend had snapped at me like never before and wasn't returning my calls and my hand hurt, plus he *had* ignored me.

Two hours later, coiffed, curled and carefully made-up (indignant outrage cannot be carried off with anything less), I'm ready to take on the world, or the fruitologist at least.

I hurtle down the street, dodging crowds enjoying their Sunday brunches. I bypass Jack and caffeine for now. I don't want anything to soften the spikes of my filthy mood. I storm past the fruitologist spritzing salad greens; highly suspicious given the asphyxiation by salad greens Jane mentioned last night. She probably intuited it. She's good with that sort of thing, not that we're allowed to mention it. 'Just a feeling,' she always says.

I realise I've gone too far—quite possibly in more ways than one. I have to back track to get to what I need but I'm not going to let my bad mood give way to humiliation. I stride back past him. *Stomp, stomp, stomp.* I pass him a third time, as though I'm trying to cause an earthquake. One last chance for him to react. The fruitologist continues his spritzing but pauses in his singalong—I'm so huffy that I refuse to notice what the song is.

I stop beside him, hold my breath and wait for him to speak to me. Nothing. I snatch the tongs from the salad greens and snap them together—I have to put my other items down to achieve this, but with only one good hand, I then have to put the tongs down to get the bag. Not great for indignant outrage but now I've committed, I'm not going to stop. I need to successfully bag some greens so it appears that shopping was my only intention and the fruitologist has nothing to do with why I'm here.

It's not going to be easy, because my hands are super shaky. I can't do anything to stop them, not even put one under my arm for a moment to bring it into stillness and calm it down like I usually would.

He turns to me. 'Can I help you with something?'

I look up and catch a flash of his lopsided smile. 'No, thank you,' I say, clipping my words so much that I trim the end of the entire sentence right off: *I am perfectly fine without you and without your help, in fact everything was much more fine until you decided to step onto my karmic path.*

I don't imagine he would get subtlety anyway.

Mental note: *Add* 'Gets subtlety' *to the relationship list when I get home. While I'm at it,* 'Doesn't wear sneakers with jeans' *would also be a worthy addition.* That's what my eyes are focussed on, now I've lost my looking-up nerve.

'OK, then,' the fruitologist says as I snatch the tongs up again. We stand there with our weapons of greengrocer destruction—him with the spritzer, me with the tongs held like a fencer—until he turns and commences fussing with the broccoli. He starts singing again and this time the song does catch my attention—John Cougar Mellencamp's 'I Need a Lover'. If that wasn't a spiritual intervention by Retro FM, nothing was ever going to be.

Oh for Govinda's sake, man, are you blind? I want to scream and snap my tongs. *Can't you see when a girl is having an internal tantrum? Do something! Put up a bit of a battle! Don't back down so bloody easily!*

Even when I thrust my thigh against the roll of bags and snap one off with aggressive efficiency (impressive with only one good hand), he does nothing. He just stands there singing, rooted to the spot like a turnip.

I wait for him to move off so I can at least throw a few leaves in the bag for effect but we remain side by side. Despite the nervousness and frustration, a strange feeling of familiarity and ease like I've been here before begins to overtake me. That I've known him as part of me from somewhere, before this time, before this life. I've never felt anything like it. Just feeling that is enough—speaking doesn't matter. I hate to give into it but there's something comforting about him being so close to me.

It's ridiculous—I don't even know him, I remind myself.

I put the tongs down and mutter, 'I think I've changed my mind.'

Outwardly I turn, flick my hair and flounce off—inside I have to drag myself away. Although my departure is helped by the call of coffee. I stride down to good old—well, young (I'd say thirty, if that)—reliable Jack's. Jack wouldn't be oblivious, Jack would say, 'Fiona, what's wrong, are you OK?' Or something flattering or sweet. He probably still will and I won't have to hurl myself around the café for him to do so.

What? No, Jack? The gall of him after I overlooked Erice to keep my promise to him! Not that I would have seriously considered Erice but it's a matter of principle. And coffee quality—Jack's is so much better than this young guy will make but it will have to do.

As I walk home, my head is a whirlpool of Amethyst's, Jane's, Catherine's and Mum's words.

You need to look him in the eye, Kismet.

Just make a decision.

Do something sensible.

Your problem is you never think of the consequences, Fiona.

That moment in PGGG has sent me way off course and I need to get Ms Middle-of-the-Road somewhere close to the bitumen. I focus on what I know. From all observations and interactions, the fruitologist is entirely *not* What I Want and Need in my Next Male Love Relationship. He wouldn't even score a five out of the two hundred–odd items on the list, including the one specifically mentioning his sneaker size, just to give fate a head start.

My favoured drug floods my veins with each sip. I relax into enjoying my caffeine fix, the whirlpool of voices slows, and I'm even calm enough to think that everything wasn't really *that* bad with Jane. I probably just overreacted—there'll be a call from her when I get home.

A long, low rumble from close to the ground catches my attention. I'd literally bet the life of my mother's first-born child (Catherine, so really I've not got that much to lose if I'm wrong) that when I look, it will be a dachshund. It's a rare talent, to be able to recognise them by sound alone. Some people may even call it a little crazy but they're people who wouldn't understand that dachshunds are my spirit animal.

What does surprise me is that it's a red, short-haired, mini dachshund puppy.

The fact it's a puppy can only represent growth and beginnings. It's so perfectly timed with my questioning—the fruitologist's behaviour must be a lesson for me to trust the Universe and have patience.

There's still no call from Jane when I get home. I'm back to feeling sick about it again. I'd call her but Jane can't stand needy. A text will be OK, so long as I don't say anything heavy.

Are you still alive??? Send word ASAP. Kxxx

I've just finished measuring the distance between the freshly dusted picture frames, knick-knacks and candelabras on my mantelpiece—the final touch in my afternoon's productive distraction of cleaning—when my phone finally dings with a text.

Hey Kizzo ... and kicking. I do want to talk but not over the phone. Let's catch up again this week. J xxx

OK so I'm a *little* disappointed. I'd hoped Jane would call and I still feel a bit sick. 'Talk'? Why didn't she use 'chat' like we normally would? 'Talk' sounds like a break up.

In a way it's a good thing that there's so much on at work. I throw myself into the week, probably more than I really need to but it's preferable to thinking about all the different reasons Jane wants to 'talk'. When I do calm myself about that, the buzzing mosquito of Situation Singing Fruitologist is there to take its place but that's hardly a priority the way things are with Jane.

Around lunchtime on Friday in what has felt like one of the longest weeks in history, a text from Jane arrives asking if I can meet her at her studio at 6.30pm for a takeaway. Of course I'm free—I'd put everyone else who wanted to make plans on standby.

Hi GJ (for 'Gorgeous Jane') *Just so happens your luck's in* ☺. *See you then. Love n hugs Kxxx*

I feel clammy and faint as I walk up to Jane's studio. It's madness that I feel this nervous about seeing her but the combination of 'talk' and her suggestion to meet at the studio (i.e. not in a public place) is like being called to the principal's office times ten.

I knock extra loud—I learnt my lesson about walking in unannounced.

'Kiz, come in!' Jane opens the door.

I step in hesitantly, not sure whether we're going to hug as usual or not. But Jane gives me a one-arm hug as she closes the door.

'Do you want a drink?'

I see Jane is over her alcohol-free period as she gestures to the glass of wine on her desk. Normally I'd make a jokey comment about it but not tonight.

'No, I'm good thanks. I'll just grab some water.' I head to the fridge. A drink might help. Mind you, the Recue Remedy I took earlier hasn't. 'How umm … how's your week been?'

'Look, Kizzo, I know the other night was extreme but, well, things were extreme.'

'Oh,' is all I can say.

'I thought I was pregnant.'

'Fuck—how? I mean I know how. But *how*? You're always so safe. And who?' I ask, sitting down. It's like a slap in the face that she didn't tell me. I so would have told her, I wouldn't have been able to *not* tell her.

'Broken condom with that guy who was here the night you came around. As if worrying about the whole STD side of things wasn't enough. Turns out I'm not—just a coincidence my period was a couple of days late.'

'That's good—well, the not-pregnant bit obviously. Why didn't you just tell me the other night?'

Jane takes a slug of her wine and looks at me for a moment before she speaks. 'It's not like anyone else gets a chance to have anything going on in their life with all your drama, Kismet. There's no *space*. You're so caught up in analysing everything to within an inch of its life. Can you even remember the last time you called just to ask me how I was?'

Thoughts swarm in my brain: *I thought you loved workshopping my life and indulging me in my crises and fantasies — they amuse you. And I do ask how you are!* (OK, maybe not quite so often since the fruitologist.)

'The thing is, it got me thinking. Maybe I want something more,' Jane says over my silence.

'What, like a relationship?' It comes out in a way that sounds so wrong it verges on sarcastic.

'No, not a relationship. Fuck, that was part of what was upsetting me about being pregnant: the thought of being tied to a man. But maybe having a child wouldn't be a bad thing.'

Of all the scenarios I'd thought of during the week, this definitely wasn't one of them. What about our pact to not ever have children? Neither of us had ever wanted them. I don't recall Jane ever even *holding* a baby.

But if anyone can do the single-parenting thing, Jane can. She's the most capable person I know. Besides, she's had first-hand experience, as the product of one. It was always just her and her mum. 'Darling, it was the eighties—days on cocaine—I can't remember what I did, let alone *who* I did,' is all her mum has ever said of her father.

'So a sperm donor?' I ask, trying to come to terms with what's going on. I may need a drink *and* Rescue Remedy for this.

'No, there are too many people in the world already. International adoption.'

Oh Buddha, as if Catherine going all Angelina Jolie wasn't bad enough, now Jane's at it too.

'Wow, you've given it serious consideration already then.'

Deep down I'd hoped it was just one of Jane's thought bubbles, like an initial concept for an art piece she never takes any further. I know she's capable of it but I still can't imagine her with a child.

'You know me, I've already done some research. It takes a couple of years so I can't afford to mess around if I'm going to do it.'

'No, of course.' Like Jane would mess around. If you want something done quickly, ask an Aries. I should say something like, *How wonderful* or *That's great* or *Good for you—you're going to make a wonderful mother*, but I know it'll come out sounding false. It's not that I'm not happy for her, if a child is what she really wants. But this is beyond major, it will change the landscape of how life has been with us for thirty years.

I'd taken it as a given that no matter what happened, Jane and I were always going to be closer to each other than we were to anyone or anything else. It'd always been the case, even through my previous relationships. And I thought it would always be that way but Jane has just cut my mooring ropes and I'm all at sea.

'Oh my fucking God.' (Sorry, Buddha.) I stand up and hug her. It's the most real thing I can do.

'I know. Who would've ever thought it?'

We look at each other in disbelief for a moment before convulsing into laughter.

'Let's order some dinner,' she says once we wind down, as though everything is fine and back to normal. And Jane would be fine. If you looked up 'water off a duck's back' in a dictionary you'd probably find an artsy black and white photo of her.

Me on the other hand—I'm still stinging and spinning.

12

This is going to be torture for them in a few years, I think, as my mother lunges at Sammy and Sonja, drops to her knees, wraps her aproned body around them and squeals, 'Oh, my little daaarlings!' They're not even fully in the door.

For now Sammy and Sonja are delighted. And who wouldn't be? They've just escaped a lesson on the finer points of edge trimming from their grandfather, who remains in the front yard with his tape measure and trimmer. Surprisingly given this, Dad's not a Virgo, he's a fellow Taurean, but we can be a little pedantic and houseproud. And not all of it is Dad—Mum's always on at him about making sure the front yard is neat. And it is, clinically so. As a teenager I used to tell people I lived at the pink flamingo because I thought the ornate concrete bird out the front was the only thing that gave our white brick bungalow some character. Plus it sounded so much more exotic than 27 Smith Street. The flamingo's so faded now it practically blends in with the bricks.

'Jesus, I'd prefer the golf.' Catherine storms in a minute or two after the kids. A figure hidden by a tower of Tupperware follows: Brian.

'I think it's great, very efficient and no second guessing,' Brian, the true Virgo, says of the edging.

Mum straightens one of her pride-of-place family portrait studio shots that's taken a hit from the Tupperware, then starts fussing over Brian, wrestling containers from him.

All the talk of edging sends my mind wandering down the path of the fruitologist and his imagined whipper-snippering ways. In the week since the salad greens incident I haven't seen him. He's probably off whipper-snippering for some woman who doesn't have a problem looking him in the eye or talking edges and hedge trimming and pretends she can't get her own salad greens just so he'll do it for her.

'Now, you three go out and play,' Mum says to Sammy, Sonja and me once we've all made our way into the kitchen.

I'm not fazed about being sent out with the kids, I prefer it; they're much more fun than the adults. But Catherine will be furious. It's obvious Mum is going to do one of her Mumterventions, giving their marriage a health check after Brian's absence last time.

'Aunty Fee.' Sonja wraps her arms around my hips.

'Yes, honey?'

'I'm not meant to tell you. It's supposed to be a surprise, but guess what?'

'What?'

'Guess.'

'Can't possibly.'

'Try ...'

'Give me a clue.'

'It's red and green.'

'Christmas?' I ask, having no idea.

'No.' Sonja's curls dance around her head, she shakes it so wildly.

'Warm?'

'Not even close. Ice cold, nearly freezing.'

'Oh, can't you just tell me?' I plead playfully.

'Aunty Fee, can you give me a push please?' Sammy interjects, twirling and untwirling on the swing that his mother and I played on.

I usher Sonja over to her brother. 'I'll need your help,' I tell her, holding up my bandaged hand. There's no time for talk of surprises—we've barely got five pushes in when Catherine flings the door open. I can almost see the smoke coming out of her ears.

'You three come in here and do something useful.'

The way Sammy, Sonja and I snap to attention and march inside, you'd think we're in the army.

Back home, I head straight to my bookcase and pull *Feng Shui for a Fuller Life* from between *Living with Light* and *Awaken to your Spiritual Destiny*.

I need to find the best place to put the surprise from Sammy and Sonja. It turned out to be a couple of bunny candles—one red and white and one green and white. I guess there isn't a whole lot of choice in aunty-appropriate presents at a school fete and anyway, I adored them for having bought me a present just because they were thinking of me. The candles are cute at least, which would have been Sonja's focus. Sammy would have gone for them because they're red and green rabbits—the colours and mascot of his beloved South Sydney Rabbitohs team.

Oh, great Guan Yin, Goddess of Mercy, no wonder! One look at the practical square bagua (those octagonal ones are so hard to work with—how are you meant to tell where your wealth or whatever corner is when your room has four corners but your bagua has eight?) reveals why everything has been going so wrong with the fruitologist. My Feng Shui is totally up the karmic creek!

Feng Shui for a Fuller Life is nothing if not clear: 'Don't ever have a single item in your relationship corner and nothing long, sharp or pointy.'

How can I have been so oblivious? I have a single golf umbrella leaning against the wall, smack bang where it shouldn't be!

I sit the bunnies paw to paw on the power box in my relationship corner. As a tenant, I can't do anything about the power box positioning, even though it's obviously less than ideal. But intention creates the energy behind everything, so I transform my thinking, turning the power box from toxic, electromagnetic energy–field polluter to a symbol of zing and sparking electricity. I give the bunnies a spritz with some rosewater (energy balancing, an aphrodisiac and said to open one's heart to love—a girl can't go wrong), and whisk the umbrella away.

I get an immediate text. Jane. Not quite the relationship I was aiming for but a positive start—the energies are shifting. I'm so relieved things are back to an even keel with her. I'm just going to need some time to come to terms with what she said the other night.

13

It's noon on Wednesday when Broomstick sidles up to my desk.

'I'll be back around 3pm. If Professor Emeritus Bartholomew should happen to call, tell him I'm on my way. He has my mobile, but just in case.'

The week's been so dull that I'm quite curious about what she's up to with Professor Emeritus Bartholomew. Her pinned-up hair has wispy tendrils tickling at her ears, which have earrings (!), she isn't wearing her trench and the top two buttons of her business shirt are unbuttoned. You don't need to be a psychic to know what she *wants* to be up to with him.

I have to get the thought out of my head—or into someone else's at least. I can't possibly 'go deep inside myself and explore my inner workings', as Lionel has promised we'll be doing in today's session, with that image in my mind.

I get up to make my way to Desmond's office to poke some fun at Broomstick but run straight into Marianne from Customer Service as I leave my desk.

'Sorry, Marianne.'

'Don't be—I was just coming to give you this.' She hands me the book she's carrying. 'I just finished it last night. I think you'll like it.'

We book swap sometimes, not that often, but I always enjoy the books she recommends. I'm about to tell her so when Desmond appears beside us.

'Sorry to interrupt, Marianne, I just need to see Fiona about something important.'

'Sure. Happy reading,' Marianne says to me. She's so customer service chirpy.

'Thanks,' I call after her as Desmond gestures to my desk. He pulls out the chair from the spare desk next to mine and we both sit down.

'Broomstick's out, isn't she?' His eyes dart around the office.

'Yes. You won't believe where …'

'Sorry Fiona. I need to talk to you.' He leans in a little closer to me. 'There's something I've been meaning to tell you for ages.'

Oh my Great Ganesha this has all the tell-tale signs of a car-crash moment. It's going to make work so awkward if Desmond confesses he's in love with me. I fan myself with the novel.

But what if Desmond is 'the one'? Perhaps the Universe only threw the fruitologist in as distraction so I'd focus on someone else and not block the love energy from Desmond by going all haywire around him. Oh no—'love energy' and 'Desmond' should not be combined in the one thought. I'm getting Broomstick and Professor Emeritus Bartholomew–type images about Desmond and they're not pretty. Sure, I can think of at least ten traits from my What I Want and Need in my Next Male Love Relationship list that Desmond has—which is more than I can say for the fruitologist. But my destiny cannot be with a man whose mother still cuts his hair. Besides, Cancerians are so clingy that he'd drive me insane. I put a quick prayer out to the Universe.

'I'm engaged.'

'*What?* I mean—congratulations!' I hadn't expected the prayer to be quite *that* effective. Oh my Buddha—his mother must be mortified.

'I was just skyping with Valeria, my fiancée. She's still in her home country at the moment but she's coming to live in Australia on the twenty-fifth of next month. I wanted to tell you first.'

'Congratulations, Desmond,' I say as I toss the novel on the pile of papers in my in-tray, where it lands face up. I catch a glimpse of the title, *The Thirteenth Tale*, as I lean over to give him a peck on the cheek. But he looks a bit panic stricken at impending physical contact, so I reach for my bag instead. It's time I was going anyway.

'There's this guy ...' I say to Lionel from the apricot leather recliner a while into my session. Even though not sitting in the same chair as last time goes against who I am, I've mixed things up to keep him on his toes and undo any assumptions he might have made from my previous choice.

I hadn't consciously decided I was ready to tell Lionel about the fruitologist. I *was* planning on talking to him about Jane. But I tell him everything—right down to the apple avalanche and rejection of the fruitologist's salad green–bagging help, to him appearing as I went by this morning and giving me a smile. And the fact that, as I hadn't braced myself to see him, I had no idea what to say or where to look and that I'd managed nothing but a 'hi' that was at a pitch and volume only a dog could hear. Plus I'd directed it at the ground, part automatic re-action and part embarrassment about my salad green antics.

'The issue,' I tell Lionel, 'is that my brain vacates and there's nothing but static in my head when I see him.'

'Hmm.' He looks at me, all bear-like grey-bearded comfort. 'I know what we're going to do with you today, Kismet. Close your eyes. We'll start counting back from ten and we'll go into the scene. You can have a chance to relive it—change the out-come to what you want it to be.'

Of course, under hypnosis my responses are warm but witty, the sort of lines that you only ever think of once you've walked away.

After the session, Lionel attempts to reassure me by saying, 'Just say the first thing that comes into your head when you see him. It'll always be the perfect thing to say.'

If only it were that easy.

When I get home after a few more hours at work, my mind starts to roam from the centre of the road again. I fall back on my 'what I know about the fruitologist' routine to bring it back into line, doing an inventory against my What I Want and Need in my Next Male Love Relationship list. Given that I don't know much beyond the physical, I focus on that.

- Fit—tick.
- Brown eyes—cross (even though I can barely look at them, I think they're blue and there's that slightly seag-ullish issue).
- Under 45—? But potentially on the wrong side of the line.
- Dark brown or black hair—cross, sort of mousy and not quite enough of it.
- Taller than me—tick, but that's not hard, I'm only 163.5cm.

- Olive complexion—not overly.
- Nice smile—lopsided, not sure I'd categorise as nice; does smile readily (usually for people other than me).
- Stylish—not unless you're into active wear.
- Reasonably hairless—unfortunately only the crown of his head, arms not too bad, legs have surplus and I can guarantee that there is quite a pelt on those well-formed pecs of his (best I don't think about his pecs—nice pecs aren't on the list anyway).

'How's work, Fiona?' Jack says the next morning as I flick through the papers.

'Please don't make me think about it when I'm here in my happy place.'

'Have you thought any more about my offer?'

'What offer was that?' I look up from the paper to focus on Jack and as I do I have a very disturbing realisation. The physical items on my list are undeniably, one hundred per cent Jack—apart from the hairlessness, but there's waxing.

'The one to work here.' He tries to act as though he's exasperated with me.

'Oh yeah, sorry. Can't afford it, unfortunately—love and coffee won't pay the bills.'

'You'd get food too.'

It isn't fair. Not only does Jack have all the physical attributes on my list, he's sweet, playful, into me and can make coffee, and I'm certainly not repelled by his touch as his fingers wrap around mine when he takes my money. But there's just no real zing and he's so ... so ... What is it exactly?

Eager and available!

Swamped by confusion over Jack I'm practically on top of the fruitologist before I notice him. He's on the phone, leaning against the PGGG doorway. *Arrgghh*. He's so sexy—I think I may melt. This makes no sense. He's nothing on my list and still, here I am, almost dropping with desire for him.

I could easily put my head down and ignore him, but he's thrown a complication into the mix: his lean is one of those madly seductive, casual ones that I can't resist. Without any time to get anxious or analyse it, I fall head-on into the moment and just go with what happens next.

He smiles and looks into my eyes—right into me. My natural, non-pained smile radiates from my eyes right back into his. We don't break eye contact as I pass but I'm not checking his eye colour against my list. I have no recollection of what I see, there are no thoughts, no noise and no one else. I'm suspended in time—suspended in everything. I feel like I'm floating.

14

Saturday leads me to a session with Amethyst.

'Could this dysfunction with men be some sort of genetic flaw I've inherited?' I ask her from the spotlight of the Talking Chair.

After last night my auric field is in desperate need of a cleanse. I'd gone around to Mum and Dad's to go through old family albums—as part of my Lionel homework, I was to sift through my past and try to identify contributing factors for my anxiety. I'd expected my parents to be out at the golf club enjoying the smorgasbord with their friends the Smithsons, like they've done nearly every Friday night for the last ten years. But Johnny and Vonnie are away; a cruise apparently. 'One of those Rhine things, not like an ordinary old *Love Boat Pacific Princess* one,' Mum had explained.

'I'm trying to find a shot of Jane and me from second class, we were talking about it the other day.' I'd been quite blatant in my deceit—I could never tell them about Lionel or having something like anxiety.

The evening was one long, happy stroll down memory lane until something flicked Mum's switch. Obviously to do with one of the photos but I had no idea what. She'd shot up from the kitchen table and gone to the laundry where she hurled Dad's golf clubs around like a sack of potatoes, quoting Dr Phil: 'If you wouldn't do it in front of your spouse, it's infidelity.'

Dad looked even more clueless than me, like he did every time she went off like that, but he stuck by her in his solid Taurean way, not making any waves. He'd done it our entire lives.

'What's for dessert tonight, Bev?' Dad asked, rather than take Mum to task over her abuse of his golf clubs. He knew exactly what he was doing; over the years Dad's got this down to a fine art. Halfway through telling him the details of her 'delectable' dessert offering, she'll slip into nagging him about his weight problem—completely distracted from whatever it was she was so upset about. It works every time.

I didn't hang around for the dessert drama, I had more than enough fodder to see me through a few sessions with both Lionel and Amethyst without that.

'I think I know what you mean.' Amethyst gives me her 'I'm about to reveal a great insight' smile. 'One day you go to sleep full of youthful superiority over your mother and the next you wake up and she's taken possession of your voice box. Things are coming out of your mouth that you'd promised the Universe you'd never say.'

If my expression is true to my feelings, my face is a traumatised mix of disappointment and panic.

'We all start to turn into our mothers at thirty, Kismet. It only gets worse the more years that pass. But, blessings for you, we can clear what you've picked up of your mother's karma that isn't yours. I'll work on that when I get you on the table. Tell me what else has been happening.'

I tell her about Jane and the night at Marrakesh on Moore, the conversation at the studio and her thinking about adopting and how it feels as though there's been an earth tremor and the tectonic plates of our relationship aren't sitting quite right anymore. Ever since those events our conversations have a little crack that we try to glue and polish away with some of our old banter, but it's not the same. Well, not for me. I doubt Jane even notices. I know it's my fault—I monitor my words and wait for her reaction, no longer sure where it's safe to tread.

I don't tell Amethyst that Jane's words also made me question my direction or lack thereof and highlighted just how lost and adrift I feel, trying to work it all out.

'Sometimes we have to let something go to let something new into our lives, Kismet,' Amethyst offers without a moment's contemplation. 'I'm not saying that you can't be friends but the question is whether there's the energetic space for another relationship the way you and Jane are. Even when people don't intend it, their responses are skewed to their needs. They have a vested interest in you staying the same—it's all they've ever known, it's comfortable for them if you don't change. It's a bit like how you feel at the thought of her adopting, but less extreme. Start by not telling her absolutely every single thing.'

I nod but stay silent.

'The amount you tell her, seeking her approval and answers, is a lot of pressure to put on Jane too. You need to trust your own intuition, call on your higher self for guidance. It will know what's best for you, not Jane. And she's got some big decisions of her own to make by the sound of things.'

I can't imagine not workshopping everything with Jane.

As usual, Amethyst seems to see straight through me. 'Just see it as the autumn of your friendship, a time for letting go of how it has always been so you can both have new growth in a way that is healthier for each of you. You'll be OK, your love has strong ties, you just need to unknot the tangle a little. Like I said, it'll also free you up to let other relationships into your life. On that note, what progress have you made with the fruitologist?'

'I really can't explain what it was and exactly how I felt because I don't understand it myself,' I say, as I tell Amethyst about seeing the fruitologist on the street the other day. 'The other times I've been around him have been intense but this was something else—like I'd disappeared into another world. There was no way I could speak or react like I normally would. It's kind of scary.'

'Remember what I told you last time—have faith that you can handle anything the Universe sends your way. Have you seen Lionel yet?'

'Yes, a couple of times. It feels like more.'

'That's great, if it feels like more you must have a bond. Has he helped?'

'Early days, but I'm feeling very positive about it. I'm seeing him again Thursday.'

'Good. I can really sense you're moving forward. Have you been doing all the things we've talked about? The list, how's that coming along?'

'Great. I've made it very ... comprehensive.'

'Good, good. And the signs, having you been keeping an eye out?'

'Yes, and they've been popping up all over the place. Even the songs that are on the radio when I go into the shop seem to have meaning, they're so in tune with the situation.'

'Of course.' Amethyst smiles knowingly. 'I don't know why you sound surprised. Now all you have to do is keep looking him in the eye. I get that every time. I'm getting it again now,' she says, pressing her temples, eyes closed. 'You can't escape it. One way or another it's going to happen, my guides are certain about it.'

Four days on from my session with Amethyst the meaning of Situation Singing Fruitologist still eludes me, let alone the meaning of life.

'Welcome, Kismet.' Lionel sweeps up from the maestro-like bow he gives me as I walk into his consulting room for my session. He sits at his desk and smiles at me. I follow his lead and sit in the office chair next to it.

'What's been happening this week?'

'I've seen the fruitologist a few times lately,' I say. To bemoan my work situation feels so dull; besides, it's a practical, tangible thing—I should be able to figure it out on my own.

'Have you connected with him in a non-regular-customer way yet?'

'No, not yet, but things are warming up.'

'How so?'

'I managed four or maybe five words in a row to him and looked him in the eye. There's been a smile too.' Having worked on it with Amethyst so thoroughly it feels unnecessary to go into too much detail with Lionel today.

'That's great progress, Kismet, well done.'

He's probably thinking that the smile, the looking in the eyes and the extended speaking (no more than a polite 'hi, how are you?') were all simultaneous events on the one visit. I don't bother to correct him.

And in terms of warming up, I don't confess that parts of me warm up every time I catch a glimpse of the fruitologist in action—the lean; seeing him reaching up to get something from overhead, the way his T-shirt—best I don't go on, I've started to blush. I don't want Lionel interrogating me about why.

'I want you to try that chair today please, Kismet.' Lionel points to the chocolate brown velour one with the bear. 'We're going to do some work with Positively. I have introduced you to Positively, haven't I?'

I stare questioningly at the bear. 'No, I don't think we've met.'

Lionel moves across to take the teddy from the chair. 'Hello Kismet, I'm Positively,' a voice suspiciously like Lionel's says from behind the bear's body, as it waves a badly mended paw at me. There's nothing to do but wave my now completely healed hand back.

'You did do your homework, didn't you?' Lionel moves Positively from in front of him and looks at me. He's not as cute as Positively but his face is kind and safe.

'Yes.'

'Good, because Positively can't help you if you haven't. It's forbidden. And there's something else you have to do if you're going to work with Positively.'

'Yes?' I say, an octave or two too high to carry off being entirely comfortable with the situation.

'You have to cuddle him.'

'Sure ...' The word comes out thin and reedy, uncertain. And who can blame me?

'You'll need one of these.' Lionel hands me a card. I look at it, hoping for the secret message that will open the door to

Positively's affections. All I see are two bears entwined, hearts dotted around them like lovers' thought bubbles. At the bottom of the card, printed in a very unattractive font (Comic Sans, I suspect) is: This Cuddle Card entitles the recipient to one cuddle.

'Give him that, I'm sure he'll appreciate it.'

Oh great Goddess above. I slip the card between Positively's paws, which Lionel is holding together. I wonder if Positively's surname is Ridiculous because that is how I feel.

Positively remains stagnant, stuffed and completely silent.

When enough time has passed for Positively's silence to be taken as a green light, Lionel passes him to me.

I sit back and pop Positively on my lap, gently holding him around his middle.

'No, no, no, Kismet. Not like that. That isn't even a hug! You can't just have him sitting there for protection like you try and get away with when you hold the cushions.'

Dharma it, he was onto me.

'You need to really cuddle him. You do know the difference, don't you?'

'Sure.' I hold Positively a little closer.

'Still just a hug, Kismet! Here, let me show you.' Lionel reaches across to take Positively. 'Cuddling is about the fondness factor—nestling, snuggling and tenderness. Hugging is just, well, like what you'd do with your great aunt or whoever—it's just an embrace of general affection. There is no real nurturing or intimacy there.'

I bite my lip to stop myself laughing at Lionel's demonstration.

He passes Positively back to me as though he's cradling a baby. I hold the bear to my chest and put his head under my chin. Many things cross my mind, none of them likely to induce a state of deep relaxation: I hope no one has dribbled on him; I wonder who has had intimacy with Positively prior to me; etc.

'Lie back, relax and let go,' Lionel begins as usual. 'I can still sense some tension, just give into it, nurture him, Kismet, go into the cuddle, feel it, explore the affection, embrace it—pardon the pun.'

I struggle to navigate my way through this whole cuddling business and how I can possibly carry this off without snorting. Maybe that's the point, maybe this is really humour therapy in disguise and I'm meant to start laughing? I get a shot of panic, unsure what to do. But Lionel seems to be taking it very seriously, so I get back to thinking of how I can manage the correct cuddling moves with Positively. A puppy, or a fully grown dog, even a kitten (though I'm not really a cat person); if I imagine Positively as one of those things I'll be able to pull it off.

'Before we start, I want you to just relax like that and tell me the most emotionally charged discovery you made doing your homework.'

I don't tell Lionel the full details of the family album search—I'll be so tense I might snap Positively's head off. 'There wasn't anything really—I was just sort of there, in my family, while life went on around me.'

'Hmm. OK, now just breathe the way I showed you. I'm going to count down from fifty. When you're ready, we'll travel back through your childhood to strip the layers of anxiety.'

Once Lionel has counted down he says, 'Kismet, I want you to think of yourself as a badly treated chair, coat upon coat of paint whacked one over the other, where no one ever concerned themselves enough to care what was underneath.'

Bullseye. I give a little cough to distract myself from what he's just said. My eyes are already closed but I squeeze them a little harder to stop tears slipping out.

'Now just relax, focus on Positively. He is here anytime you need him. On any day you come, now that you have his permission, you can cuddle him.'

By the time Lionel has stopped speaking again, my poorly cared for piece of furniture moment has passed completely. The image I'm getting is not of me cascading back through my childhood but a bird's eye view of this scene, looking down at myself, a 35-year-old woman sitting in a dark room, sprawled in a brown velour recliner, hugging a teddy bear that has seen better days. Now I'm wondering if Positively's middle name is Insanely: Positively Insanely Ridiculous.

But if this is what it takes to overcome my anxiety, then so be it. I'm prepared to do whatever it takes.

'Do you feel safe, Kismet? Comfortable?' Lionel asks.

I nod.

'Visualise yourself, take yourself to a place where your anxiety is at its premium. Don't rush. Just nod when you're ready.'

When my mind's eye has me at the counter in front of the fruitologist, handing over my items, struggling to even get a note from my wallet, I nod again.

'Give it a name.'

'What?'

'The anxiety—give it a name.'

Oh, Lionel, how could you? Does he not realise he's just added a whole new level of anxiety to this experience by making me come up with something on the spot? How am I meant to name my anxiety just like that and how am I meant to know what an appropriate or acceptable name for anxiety is? What if I call my anxiety something wrong and he thinks it's stupid? But I know exactly what he'll say if I ask what most people call theirs or what sort of name I should give it.

101

'Alex. I will call my anxiety Alex.' I am partial to alliteration and this way I don't have to decide whether it's male or female.

'Now ask Alex where it came from.'

'It's always been with me.' I breathe into my feelings, my words slow, considered, my voice softer than when I'm not 'under'.

'What's it telling you?'

'That whatever I do, it'll be wrong.'

'Ask it why.'

'Because I was different and being different wasn't just being different. It was wrong.' And so it goes. Alex and I have words, thirty minutes of them, then Lionel brings me back out.

'Here take one of these,' Lionel hands me a Cuddle Card as I'm leaving. 'You might like to give it to the fruitologist.'

What are you on about, Lionel? Do you think I would be here paying $80 to cuddle a bear in a dark room if I could just barrel right up and thrust a Cuddle Card at the fruitologist? It's looking very much like Positively might well be the most sane one among us.

'That may be a little premature. I don't even know his name,' I say diplomatically.

'Well, there you have it. That is your homework for the week. Challenge yourself, challenge Alex and introduce yourself or at least find out some personal information about the fruitologist or divulge some about yourself.' Lionel smiles, knowing he's caught me at my own game.

15

Lionel's homework is like a magic wand. Left to my own devices I'd faff about forever but now I have someone to answer to, I'll spring into action. I'm not sure if I'm innately obedient or just have a pathological fear of displeasing people or letting them down. Either way, the spots on the leopard appear the same.

I'm in a tricky situation. Obviously I'm not going to be able to find out anything about the fruitologist without managing to form a coherent sentence in front of him. But from where I stand (which happens to be wrapped in a towel, staring at my wardrobe, wondering what to wear for Mission Elicit Personal Information), that feels like a higher mountain to climb than Everest.

Then there's the summit—the fruitologist. How is it possible for him not to have a single one of the two hundred and twenty-nine items on my What I Want and Need in my Next Male Love Relationship list, for Buddha's sake? What sort of man is he? If such a thing as a spiritual intervention ombudsman existed, I'd be lodging a complaint before you could say, 'Aren't two hundred and twenty-nine items a bit excessive?'

Stuck with the issues of the earthly realm, as I stand here at ten on Saturday morning, dark jeans in one hand, light ones in the other, all I can do is wonder how I'm ever going to carry out my homework. Divulging some personal information might be easier.

'Kismet, my name's Kismet.'

'Hi, I'm Kismet, I see you all the time but I don't know your name.'

'Hi, um, I see you all the time but I don't know your name.'

'Hi, I'm Kismet—you are?'

'Hi, I'm Kismet, I was christened Fiona, but I really prefer to be called Kismet, so in fact just forget I said that first bit and call me Kismet. Your name is?'

Hmm. That last one isn't going to do; as if I'd be able to get that many words out in front of him anyway. And the second two are so similar no one else would bother to think twice about them, but in my mind the tiny difference could be make or break. I know no matter how much I rehearse them the lines will come out however they like. That doesn't stop me giving it a shot. I need to feel prepared.

The coy smile I road-test to accompany my introduction is far from ideal when I see it in the mirror. The seductive smirk I try just makes me look smarmy and, if past experience is anything to go by, my attempts at a red hot sexy seductress act around the fruitologist don't bode well for the friendliness of said greengrocer.

I think about choosing a Lovers' Oracle card for a clue. So I do—ten in fact. None of them offer anything I'm really in the mood for, so I listen to the little voice in my head that says, *Just ask his name.*

I get dressed, give my eyelashes one more curl (total: four) and, armed with my big plan, I'm ready to make the potentially life-altering trip to the PGGG. But first, a little affirmation and visualisation focussed on the Feng Shui bunnies in my relationship corner and an incantation for the Universe's support.

Arrgghh! My mobile buzzes over my mantra. My scream subsides when I see it's Jane, texting in reply to my call from yesterday.

Yes, I can meet you for lunch.

As much as I'd primed myself for Mission Elicit Personal Information and as much as I don't want to travel across town because I'm really very tired, and as much as meeting her today will mean I won't be able to get to the ho-hum domestics I planned to do and my routine will be all out for the week, and as much as Amethyst had mentioned about making room for other relationships, I can't not meet Jane. It'd only make things worse.

The fruitologist will still be there next week. Besides my hair hadn't worked that well anyway.

'Bless the Goddess!' I clink my glass of soda water against Jane's glass of shiraz. We're here to celebrate her STI-free results coming through—sure, there's a while to wait for HIV but she's pretty confident; Mr Spectacular but Nothing Special had been tested recently.

Jane seems light, happy, totally back to normal as she tells me about her week. I'm still having difficulty getting my head around the concept of Jane wanting a child and, yes, in spite of my best efforts to pretend I'm not stinging from the things she said, there's a little something inside me that just won't go away.

She looks at me in the new eye-narrowing way of hers that entered our lives with my fruitologist fixation. 'What's happening with you? Dare I ask, any progress with Situation Singing Fruitologist?'

I'm not going to tell her about Mission Elicit Personal Information and risk a lecture but I have to give her something. To not tell Jane anything would create a chasm bigger than the Black Cavern, which, as both Jane and I know from Year 7 Geography, is one of the largest in the world.

'I haven't seen him but I've come up with an inroad to conversation,' I tell her. 'Last night when I got home I was doing a bit of googling and came across an article on the impact of large supermarkets undercutting traditional specialised greengrocers. According to the article, the industry is in urgent need of reform.'

'You *are* kidding aren't you, Kismet? You're thinking of using that as an opening, with someone you—fuck knows why—fancy?'

'It's fate more than flat-out fancy, but I thought it was perfect, arming myself with something that's relevant to engage him in conversation. You obviously don't agree.' I'm probably skating on dangerously thin ice as far as keeping it within the boundaries of Amethyst's recommended approach to the change in my relationship with Jane, but now I've started it's not easy to stop.

'Well, what I really think, if you are going to persist and not face the fact he's a fuckwit, is that you should just stride in there and—'

'Yes, I know *that*. But given that's unlikely, what do you think of my 'hot topics in the world of fresh produce' as a conversation starter?'

'Seriously, you can't go in there and start making moves talking about bloody imported fruit and vegetable issues. You'll seem like the least good-time girl ever and as sexy as a dead otter floating on an oil spill.'

'I thought it might show I was caring, but I see your point. Anyway, whatever, I think PGGG may have back-up income anyway.'

'Here we go.' Jane semi-snorts, so I feel safe to go on. I know she can tell from my tone and little smirk that I'm about to skip down one of my midnight flights of fantasy paths—the type where something innocent going bump in the night becomes a machete-wielding homicidal maniac about to enter my bedroom. Jane will appreciate my theory in a way no one else would or could. As far as the autumn of our relationship is concerned, I'm just playfully throwing leaves in the air.

'I think they're Polish mafia.'

'Of *course* you do. Why, exactly?'

'Getting my coffee this morning, I'd just read the headlines of a story on the Russian mafia in the paper and next thing, a guy who used to work at PGGG and has recently returned came in.'

'Connection?' Jane doesn't subscribe to the 'no coincidences' belief but sounds curious, if not yet totally on board.

'He has a strong Eastern European accent, is quite short, stocky and thuggish. Not that being short is necessarily relevant, I just don't get a good vibe from him. I can well imagine him carrying out a hit on someone. He's quite disturbing to be around, actually.'

'You haven't ever mentioned the fruitologist being Polish?'

'Well, no, I think this guy—who I've christened "Thuga"—could be a relative from the old country who comes and goes on special missions.'

'Who's the godfather, do you think? This guy or your guy?'

'Thuga is definitely the godfather of the operation. The fruitologist seems more in charge in the shop. He's not old country at all—definitely born here. I think he's the local head. Everyone but Thuga seems to have been born here, so it makes sense that he would be the organiser.' I pause, partly for dramatic effect and partly to take a breath so I can continue. 'But now I have a problem. I was so caught up trying to figure it all out when Thuga came into the café that I have no idea what Jack said to me. I hope it wasn't anything too flirtatious that'll get back to the fruitologist. I might get whacked and packed off to Poland in cold storage.'

'The plot thickens.' Jane's smile quickly becomes a laugh. I'm grateful she's right beside me on my midnight fantasy express.

'Whichever way it goes, I'm done for. No matter what, now I have to get to know the fruitologist just so I can figure out who's who and what they're up to. You know I hate an unsolved mystery.'

'What happened to Ms Middle-of-the-Road?'

'She forgot to take a driver reviver, fell asleep at the wheel and drifted off course, momentarily at least. Was bound to happen eventually, all that straight and narrow is exhausting, constantly reining myself in. Actually exhausting and boring.'

'There's no harm in the adventure and entertainment of a little off-roading or whatever. But I don't get why don't you put your fantasies to good use—less dead otter and Miss Marple, more Mae West again.'

'Yes, well we both know how that went down. That aside, it's not like I haven't thought about it, but the logistics are all wrong. If they had space for a chest freezer then I *might* be able to just have a normal mojo-manifesting fantasy about the fruitologist taking me from behind as I bent in to get some frozen berries or something but alas the only way he can take me from behind with their setup is if I'm up against the fridge getting my yoghurt—I'd be far too unsteady when

I'm on my tippy-toes getting fresh nuts. And if any man thinks he can come between me and my sheep's milk yoghurt, he has another thing coming!'

'So between suffocating you under salad greens, possibly poisoning your yoghurt and feta and now packing you off to Poland in an icebox—not to mention commercial radio—do you really think he's a good choice for you?' The mirth has suddenly slipped from Jane's voice. Why did she ask if she was going to get upset about it again?

'So what's happening with Operation Baby Jane? Any more thought?' I attempt to scramble back to safe territory, a smile plastered to my face.

'Monday's the big day.'

'What?' I feel my smile slip. I'm all for it if a child is what Jane really wants but there's no need to rush into it. 'Shouldn't you perhaps give it some more thought?'

'Calm down, Kismet, I just mean I'm planning on telling Mum that I'm considering it.'

'How do you think she'll take it?'

'Hard to say. You know she can be pretty unpredictable.'

Maybe I'm not the only one at risk of turning into my mother here.

16

'No, James, just tell them. They're three and five—they don't need a choice. No … no! You are not putting me on to them to tell them to do it. They're your children too!'

I hear Stephanie's voice before I see her on Sunday morning, those brilliant Capricornian boundaries directing her husband over the phone. I run to catch up to her.

'Let me be sure I understand,' Stephanie says between our dessert plates being whisked away and our coffees arriving. 'He looks mostly like a younger Kevin Costner but also Tom Hardy, David Beckham but only the way David Beckham looks sometimes, David Hardy and the lead guy from NCIS but younger again?'

'Yes, sort of—well, not really—there's just something that reminds me of the fruitologist in all of them.'

'How is that possible, Kismet? They look nothing alike. And now when you see them you take them as signs?'

I shift in my seat. 'Yes.'

'Those and every sports brand logo you see, as well as the sausage dogs?'

Stephanie laying the cold, hard facts out on the table like that does make it all sound a little questionable. If I didn't have a bit of a headache from my sleepless night, I would have been more on point and not revealed all those signs to her. Although there's no need for the 'I can't believe you just said that' look she's giving me; a look she normally reserves for James.

The sausage dogs are no secret to anyone who knows me but the others I don't even try to justify. I bring out Ms Middle-of-the-Road and give her control of the wheel, which keeps the conversation on the straight and narrow for the rest of the afternoon.

'I'm coming back to your place, you don't mind, do you?' Stephanie says as we leave the restaurant. 'James has to learn to get a handle on parenting. He's hopeless. The kids know he's a pushover and they play him. There's only one way he'll learn. If someone has to drown at bath time, then so be it.'

'Sure. No problem.' A life is a small price to pay to teach your husband a lesson. I know she's joking but I do have a minor flash of concern that I will be implicated as an accessory if one of them really does drown. Doing time for aiding and abetting Stephanie teaching her husband a lesson won't look good on my resume, let alone the negative karma of it.

'I'll be gone by six thirty. He's got *very* clear instructions that their dinner is at seven. I need to arrive just after that to make sure they're fed.'

'Of course,' I say as I flag a bus. To be honest I'm a bit edgy; I hadn't planned for this. Unplanned things grate against the flow of my energy.

'Oh, a bus, how fun!' Stephanie is bursting with the enthusiasm of someone who doesn't endure public transport, day in, day out. When Stephanie isn't behind the wheel of her supermummy SUV, James runs her around, like today chauffeuring her into the city.

'I won't be training or bussing it home, I wouldn't know how. I'll take a cab, but this makes me feel like a tourist,' she continues, bouncing slightly on the seat. A very un-Stephanie move.

As we're getting off she starts thanking the driver, 'Thank you—'

Oh no, don't you dare.

'Please don't call him "Driver"—he knows what his job is,' I hiss at her. It's one of my bugbears and her overenthusiasm for the novelty of my nightmare reality has worn my tolerance thin.

At first when I see the figure step out of Jack's café as Stephanie and I are walking back to my place, I'm not absolutely certain it's the fruitologist. Side on, it's hard to tell. I slow my pace slightly, and he turns and walks in the same direction we're heading. From behind, I'm sure it's him. Having mastered How to Tell a Fruiterer by his Footwear, I've moved on to How to Tell a Fruiterer by his Bald Spot. It comes in handy for differentiating between him and Raymond when I do manage to look up. I'm also becoming quite familiar with the way his T-shirts pull slightly against his shoulders and back muscles.

I wonder what he's been doing in Jack's café? He's not carrying a coffee. I very much doubt he's been in there saying, 'Keep your hands off my Kismet.' For a start, he doesn't even know my name and Jack knows me as Fiona anyway—we were on a first-name basis well before I converted to my spiritual name.

I surreptitiously observe the fruitologist. Careful not to give any reaction that will alert Stephanie to something being afoot, I 'yes', 'no' and 'totally' at appropriate intervals.

You'd think I'd be excited to share him, but I feel slightly protective of him. I have no idea why. I mean, I know why I don't want to tell Stephanie it's him. She'd be likely to march right up and lasso him with some sort of project plan about how she thinks our relationship should play out. That would be after she's assessed him from all angles to see if she deems him worthy relationship material and interrogated him about his intentions. I wouldn't even put it past her to ask for a full medical history back to his grandparents, what his salary is, whether he has a super fund, its balance, and if he owns any property. She might even check his teeth while she's at it.

I'd die of mortification a hundred times over.

As Stephanie continues to list James's parenting shortfalls, I watch the fruitologist. He walks into the pub and alarm bells start clanging in my head. Is he an alcoholic? Is he a pokie addict? Is he off to watch sport on Foxtel there? Or worse, is he off to pick up virtually in front of my very eyes?

Maybe the fruitologist really is dying and was off to the pub to drown his sorrows. As I walk by PGGG the next morning, I don't catch a glimpse of him or his generously proportioned sneakers, nor do I hear a single off-key lyric. I realise that he could disappear and I wouldn't ever know who, when, what, how or why he'd gone or what this Singing Fruitologist debacle has been about.

The whole dying thing makes perfect sense. Perhaps, on the few times I've managed to ask him how he is and he has been civil enough to manage a mumbled reply, he's been telling me that he's dying. And I seem like a heartless bitch who doesn't even flinch at the news because I haven't understood him.

There are so many possibilities that he could have twanged out: 'terminal', 'contagious', 'mad for you' (unlikely, but a girl can live in hope), 'fine', 'good', 'well', 'OK'. Those last four are a bit dull. If he's coming up with responses like that then he's far too boring for me. I know for sure that I have 'interesting and amusing' right at the top of my What I Want and Need in My Next Male Love Relationship list.

A lack of response on my part to 'mad for you' certainly wouldn't encourage his heart to creep any further down his sports-branded sleeve. And of course if he *is* dying it'd explain why he isn't acting on his affections for me. I mean, it's not as though the Universe is going to send me someone who doesn't have affections for me as my destiny.

I'll have to conceal some secret device and record his response next time I go in, which I am planning on doing tonight, for Mission Elicit Personal Information. Then I can upload the recording and press a button like 'reduce nasal tones' (I'm sure there's a technical word for it) to clarify his response so I know what I'm working with. I've always fancied myself as a blonde version of Olivia Benson from *Law Order: Special Victims Unit*.

By 9.15am, I'm already bored. Which is not surprising given I'm at work tackling the compliance report again. My mind runs back to the fruitologist. After my last false alarm, I know it's unlikely that he really is dying but I've been ambling along, operating on the premise that I have the rest of my natural life to get it together with him. All the time in the world, as they say.

Well, not *all* the time in the world. I consider how long I might like the rest of my natural life to be. A reasonable period, I conclude, but that still takes some defining. Not too short and not too long. I decide a minimum of thirty-seven and a maximum of forty-five years will probably fit the bill. I don't fancy hanging around after eighty. It's not so much the years themselves; part of the problem is the aesthetic. It's not like I'm ageist and have something against old people or that I find them unattractive, I just don't really fancy the whole age-ing thing for myself. And naturally I cry at those old couples in nursing homes celebrating their trillionth wedding anniver-sary who appear on *Today Tonight* and *A Current Affair*.

I know it's putting the temple in front of the incense sticks but I can't stop myself running away with a fantasy of the fruitologist and me in old age. I imagine sitting with him on the porch of a nursing home, holding his gnarled, overworked hand, staring into his seagull eyes (that will be watering quite a bit by that age, I imagine), tufts of grey hair sprouting from his ears, his lopsided smile probably missing a tooth or two by then as well.

'You didn't ever have children?' the interviewer asks in my fantasy.

'No, we were all we ever needed,' I respond. The fruitolo-gist nods, or maybe that's Parkinson's—I haven't worked out that part of the fantasy one hundred per cent yet. We each share a little about the tangled web of misunderstandings and tortuous beginnings of us getting together.

'But it all worked out in the end,' the fruitologist says as he clutches my hand and gives me a camera-shy peck on the cheek.

'Fiona—the report. How's it coming along?'

Broomstick's bark jolts me from the world I'm lost in, saving me from a vision of a tragic end at the fruitologist's graveside when he's ninety-two or thereabouts. To be honest I'm a little relieved, all that thought of commitment and spending thirty-five years with someone had begun to make me feel a bit claustrophobic.

Speaking of claustrophobic relationships—I've just got my focus back on the report back when Catherine calls. 'Fiona, I have favour to ask.'

'More likely to get one if you play nicely and call me Kismet.' I have to whisper the last bit because I'm at work.

I hear Catherine's 'Hmph.' But she concedes: 'Oh OK, so, *Kismet*, it's like this: I've organised a date night for Brian and I.'

'A date night?' I know she can tell from the way my words hiccup that I'm laughing at her on the inside.

'Yes, a date night—sort of. I've got us tickets to a soccer game—I'm trying to get him interested in something masculine. All the other mothers at school's husbands are into that or AFL or something and Brian doesn't do any normal manly things to connect with them. I've organised a restaurant I *really* want to go to beforehand though, so there's something in there for me.'

It sounded like it was all about Catherine to me. She really didn't know when she was on to a good thing.

'So where do I fit into this?' I ask.

'I need you to mind the kids. You know normally I'd ask Mum but it's a generational thing. Everyone does date nights these days but she'd go getting those ideas of hers, thinking we're on the cusp of divorce or something. I can't endure another one of her Mumterventions over nothing again so soon.'

'Indeed, and where would she be able to pin all her hopes without her perfect son-in-law being "the son she never had"? It'd be like pulling at a loose thread and her world would unravel before the two of you had even got to the entrée!' I agree, enjoying a rare sense of comradery with Catherine.

'But there's one problem. It's Saturday fortnight, which is …'

'I know what Saturday fortnight is. It's something we're not mentioning because it's not happening.' It's vital that

Catherine does not utter the B word—I've banned any mention of it this year. Thirty-five is fine but once you topple into thirty-six you're a snowball hurtling towards forty and I'm not ready to be anywhere near forty. 'And there's nothing I'd rather do than spend the night with Sammy and Sonja, so of course I'll do it.'

'Great, thanks, Fiona. I've got to go but I'll see you at lunch on Sunday.'

I don't even take a gym break at lunchtime. I'm under the pump. I need to get the report done by 6.45pm—though that would be pushing it—so I can make it to PGGG and carry out Mission Elicit Personal Information.

Jane phones at 5.30pm.

'Kismet, do you want to meet up for a drink?'

'Sorry, I don't think I can. I have to get this dharmaed report finished today. Broomstick needs to send it off to the board tomorrow.' I try to keep the tightness out of my voice. It's not Jane—I'm going to be down to the wire so I need every second.

'Just tell Broomstick to fuck off!'

'I know. It should be easy right? N. O. Two letters, all I have to do is put them together and say them.'

'Exactly! So pack up your desk immediately, tell her to fuck off, walk out and come meet me at Bar Monk.'

'She's not here to tell. I'm sorry, I really can't tonight.' There's no way I can tell Jane that I'm giving priority to Mission Elicit Personal Information. She'd skin me alive and use me as some sort of installation, hung against a backdrop of a wall graffitied with 'The fruitologist is a effen C!' before I've got a chance to defend myself with 'Sorry but the Universe works in mysterious ways'. It's not like I'm choosing the fruitologist *over* Jane. She'd got Saturday.

'How did it go with your mum?' I ask, updating some figures in the Statistical Comparisons of Long-Term Savings against Initial Outlays in Compliance Implementation table of the report.

'That's what I was going to tell you about. Seriously, if Broomstick needs it done tonight, she should fucking well be there doing it herself.'

'I know, but once this is done I'll get my life back. Give me a quick snapshot of what happened with your mum now and we'll do full disclosure when we catch up.'

'Not great. She thinks she's too young to be a grandmother.'

'She's sixty already.'

'Sixty-two this year but you know how she is.'

I do—the opposite of my mum in nearly every way. 'Maybe we can catch up Friday?' I offer, already feeling guilty about choosing to carry out my mission.

'I'll see. I might be catching up with that young barman I did the feature wall for. But it's really not that hard, Kismet. Just say NO! If you don't say it, things are only going to get worse.' And she's gone.

I shoot her a quick text: *Love you! Let me know about Friday. Kxxx*

I hate un-ended endings and if I don't send something to smooth the water I won't be able to concentrate on getting this bloody report finished.

'Fiona, don't you have a home to go to?' Desmond says as he struts by my desk like a peacock.

I check the time.

Shiva—6.15pm.

'I won't be far behind you. I should be done with this in ten or fifteen.' I smile despite my urge to strangle him. Ever since his fiancée arrived he's been all man about town. I have my suspicions that 'my beautiful bride-to-be', as Desmond refers to her, strong-armed him directly to David Jones' men's department when he collected her off the plane. It certainly looks as though she's put an end to his mother cutting his hair.

'Take it from me, it'll never end. The more you do, the more they'll throw your way.' Desmond's voice echoes down the stairway.

I think I liked the burn-the-midnight-oil Desmond who barely left his office, let alone left before me, better. It's his smugness, not his happiness, that I resent. Mind you I could have done without his unsolicited advice so close behind Jane's.

When I check the time again it's 6.25pm and things look promising for a hasty exit by 6.35. Then my email dings with a new message. It's Broomstick. She has a couple of last-minute inclusions she's just finished discussing with PEB, as she now refers to Professor Emeritus Bartholomew.

Karma had obviously jumped up to bite me on the arse for being less than one hundred per cent truthful with Jane.

I've got two choices here.

17

It takes some effort to squeeze myself between the train doors as they close but I make it. Having put Jane off for Mission Elicit Personal Information, I could hardly let Broomstick take pride of place. I'll go in early tomorrow and make her changes. I do the best I can with my make-up, but the swaying of the carriage doesn't make it easy and the lighting is hideous.

Make-up done and Rescue Remedy taken, the next thing is hypno-breathing. I close my eyes and focus on my breath—in through the nose, entire torso expanding, out through the nose with a slightly constricted throat. Each breath gets deeper as I count down from fifty and tell myself, 'I am relaxing.' I sound a bit like Darth Vader when I hypno-breathe but the other passengers will have to live with it—I'm determined to turn my nervousness into anticipation rather than paralysation.

It's 7.20pm when I get off the train at Central. Critically short of time, I jump in a cab.

'Just here is good, thanks,' I tell the driver. We're a block before PGGG but there's no way on this sacred earth I'm going to get out of a cab in front of the shop like I've rushed to get there. I jump out, not waiting for my change, and run until I am close enough to PGGG to be seen. I pat my hair down.

The fruitologist and the Big Italian Guy (BIG) from the bakery next door are standing in the doorway of PGGG like two Chinese stone lions, nothing moving but their jaws.

'Hi,' the fruitologist says and takes a small step backwards to let me past. The squeak of his sneaker drowns out my response, which was only 'Hi', so it's hardly critical. I'm still trying to catch my breath from my sprint.

The doorway isn't big enough for the three of us, and I have to turn side-on to get by BIG's girth. Facing the fruitologist provides the perfect opportunity for me to conduct a little olfactory research on what he might have been up to at the pub last night. I take a short, sharp sniff. His breath is clear of alcohol but not minty, like he's trying to cover it up. I cross 'Alcoholic?' off my mental list of pub activity concerns. Which is a good thing considering what an effort I'd made for my mission—I'd have hated for it to be wasted, although 'Pokie Addict?' and 'Pick-Up Artist?' are still up for grabs.

Under the cover of my hair, I catch the fruitologist and BIG giving each other a look as I take a basket.

I motor through the store. Time does not allow me to do my full tour. These days, I rotate what I stock up on to make sure I get into every nook and cranny of the shop. Jane called it obsessive, I just call it maximising opportunities. Clearly the Universe placing the fruitologist out the front tonight was to compensate for my time restrictions.

Ms Middle-of-the-Road stays completely focussed, all the time telling me, 'You can do this. You can act like he is just any other shopkeeper, you can act like he is any other person, you can act like he is any other man, any other "soul in a physical body"—to paraphrase Amethyst—and you can certainly act like someone who isn't an obsessive semi-stalker.'

BIG is waddling back to his bakery, I see, when I sneak a glance at the doorway.

I steel myself, which unfortunately results in me giving the fruitologist a steely glare as he comes up the aisle towards me. Still, I keep my head up and hoping for a repeat of our moment in the street, I look him in the eye and say, 'Hi, how are you?'

He looks briefly at my left eye, then down, directing his mumble of an answer to the floor. As I tell myself that it was only because by the time I spoke I was almost beside him so to look at me fully would have been super awkward, he disappears out the side door.

Calm yourself, Kismet. He's probably doing something entirely legitimate, not preparing for your death by salad greens asphyxiation and readying the polystyrene chiller box to pack you off to Poland.

What he's been up to is worse than I thought.

'Eighteen to six—Souths are losing,' the fruitologist calls to the guy on the till as he bursts out of the cool room. He slumps like he's taken a hit but recovers quickly and starts singing along to Blondie's 'Dreaming', which is playing as he takes over at the till.

I can't believe I hadn't thought to add 'Sports Bettor?' to my list of pub activity concerns. I'm not sure if it's possible for someone to come up with a negative score on my What I Want and Need in my Next Male Love Relationship list but the fruitologist is definitely headed in that direction. How could destiny be so cruel?

I stride up to the till. The stride, like the edge to my voice and the glare, is there to cover my nervousness. The old lady in front of me is going to take forever—you can always tell, they've virtually got a 'slow moving vehicle' sign plastered to their back. She starts putting her items on the counter one by one.

The fruitologist eyes her basket and pats the counter. 'Just sit it down there,' he says, sounding sweet, not twangy at all. Just that takes her an eternity and a half. But he seems to have all the time in the world for her, whereas my toes are squirming in my shoes and I'm scuffing at the floor, thinking I'll be ready for a hip replacement myself before I even get out of here if she doesn't hurry up.

'Here, I'll get that for you.' He takes the green shopping bag she's been fussing with, snips the tag off and packs her items.

'Oh, thank you,' she says.

The lovely, delightful, sweet, gentle, kind fruitologist helps her lift her bag off the counter. It's so adorable that football scores, sports betting addictions, homicidal tendencies and organised crime rings disappear from my thoughts. Actually, my mind disappears completely—even more than the moment in the street. I take my first full trip to Planet Swoon, swept away to another world, thinking how beautiful he is, in that 'beautiful from the inside out' sort of way.

It's only when he looks at me and smiles that I come back to earth. In my panic at being caught out thinking sweet, soppy the-fruitologist-is-gorgeous thoughts, I look at him sternly then down at the counter.

Arrgghh! What is wrong with me? Why can't I ever have a normal facial expression when I'm in here?

'Hi,' he says to me again as the old dear shuffles off.

My breath catches on the anxiety that now sits heavily on my diaphragm. It's hard to say if I'm looking at him, because I'm hovering above my body, but I have to do this.

'What's your name? I see you all the time,' I say, regrettably ungracefully.

'Frankie.'

'I'm Fiona,' my out-of-body self responds but very little sound must come out, because, 'What's yours?' Frankie the fruitologist says as though he'd heard nothing at all.

'Fiona.' Oh Buddha, why didn't I tell him Kismet? But Fiona just sort of came out.

'Another F.'

In my freaked-out state, I say, 'Oh, yes, two Fs.' *What a ridiculous thing to say! He probably thinks I've already made us into a couple.*

Maybe we say bye, maybe we don't—I'm still not back in my body as I step away.

Ouch. I smash my hip into a trolley on my way out, caught up with trying to regain my cool, calm and collected Ms Middle-of-the-Road composure. A reminder to be careful with my thoughts.

18

'So what time did you leave the other night?' Jane asks.

Even on a Wednesday, Bar Monk is buzzing and I struggle to hear her. A situation not helped by the damp cotton wool that fills my head from my blocked sinuses. I caught a cold last week and it's now fully blown consumption. Not being able to breathe isn't doing anything to help nor are the miracle cure Chinese herbal drinks that Bing's been forcing me to drink before he'll give me my coffee. I think they make me feel worse.

'So what plans did you have on Friday night?' Not feeling well always makes me more feisty and I'm still not sleeping, so I don't have the reserves to cushion everything to the degree I usually would.

'I asked first.' Jane licks a drop of wine from her lips.

We look at each other and simultaneously realise how ridiculous us trying to have a stand-off is and begin to laugh.

'Later than I'd hoped.' I'm still sort of laughing, but my hacking cough is taking over. Technically it's not a lie; I *was* later than I'd wanted to be. 'Now you,' I wheeze. 'So who or what did you do Friday?'

'Drinks at a bar that wants a mural done and then the bar owner. On that note, I guess I have to ask: the fruitologist?'

'I made some conversation, not a dead otter in sight. Actually asked his name—it's Frankie—and he asked mine. That's pretty much it but there was a spark, I'm sure. Then this morning when I went past he was singing along to the Stones, "You Can't Always Get What You Want". What do you think that means?'

'That he's got crap taste in music and is therefore completely incompatible.' Jane pulls a face and laughs.

I should have known better. Jane *hates* the Rolling Stones, she especially hates Mick Jagger's lips.

Suddenly Jane stops laughing and my stomach drops. I hate it that I'm on such tenterhooks around her these days but I just can't make it go away.

'Kismet, what's wrong with your eye?' She leans forward squinting at a scaly patch on my eyelid, through the dim light.

'Oh no, not you too. Catherine was going on about it at lunch on Sunday.' I'm pleased Jane hasn't noticed that I'm also losing eyelashes from my right eye (potential over-curling). Now I haven't got a good eye between them, I won't be able to get away with wearing a designer eye patch to cover my bad eye and dramatically fluttering my eyelashes of the other one at Frankie to compensate if I happen to see him on the street. It's been a major concern all week so I've been trying to come up with contingencies.

Jane leans in a little closer. 'And, sorry, but what's wrong with the rest of you?'

Almost a week of fever, flu and night sweats hasn't done me any favours. My eyes are the least of my worries if I do see Frankie.

'Oh, it's my consumption, a bit of stress at work and lack of sleep.'

'You should have told me you weren't well, we could have met on the weekend.' There's that Aries for you again—fire signs, they flare up then they're over it again just as quickly.

'No, it's been too long. I wanted to see how things are with your mum after the other week and what's happening with Project Baby Jane.' I squeeze her arm.

'She didn't take it well but I wasn't going to pander to her. I knew she'd come round eventually and she has. It's vanity, really.'

'A curse.'

Jane and I nod, smiling, knowing how much we relish being mistaken for much younger than we are.

'And it was probably quite a shock for her too,' I venture. The ground feels more solid but I don't want to sound barbed.

'I think I shocked myself.' Jane hugs me as she stands to get another drink.

When she's back we go through the details of her mum's reaction, her work, the mural and Mr Mural the bar owner, and yes, the more she's thinking about the adoption, the more she's warming to the idea.

As we're leaving, Jane says, 'I know we're not meant to mention anything about the anniversary of someone's birth rolling around but what are you up to Saturday, Kiz?'

'That's right and that's the last word I want to hear on it. But seeing as you asked, I'm babysitting Sammy and Sonja on Saturday night. Want to join me?' I don't think Jane needs a reality check but some time with kids may not go astray.

'Yep. That vanity's a curse,' she winks, 'But no to babysitting, I'm catching up with Mr Mural—baby-making practice.'

'Ha ha.'

'Why miss out on the fun bits? And you? Any plans to go in and make progress on the name before you die a born-again virgin?'

'Shiva, no, not looking like this.'

'You should take tomorrow off. You do look ghastly,' Jane says, once we're in the full light of the foyer.

She's right, I should, but the mountain of work still isn't going down and now the board want more urgent changes to the report.

The late night and the cold damp air do nothing for my consumption. I wake (I use the term loosely) after another night of fever and night sweats feeling like death, but still I force myself up and soldier on.

'Fiona, where's your KeepCup?' Jack holds out his hand.

'I was too tired to wash it, sorry. I'll just have to do a take-away.' It's me over Mother Earth this morning.

'Poor Fiona. You should have brought it anyway, I would have washed it up for you.'

Oh, Jack, so sweet and kind. But even through my brain fog I'm thinking, *Oh my Buddha, there's Frankie*, as I pass PGGG and see him. Or, more accurately, his torso, as his head is lost behind the spices he's reaching up to get. He really has to stop doing things like that. He could bring on a flutter of longing and desire even if I was no longer in possession of a pulse. Jack ... well, Jack feels like a little brother to me.

I struggle through the next two days at work.

Adding some final touches and reformatting my What I Want and Need in My Next Male Love Relationship list isn't the most thrilling Friday night I've ever had, but I need to rest to be well enough to look after Sammy and Sonja tomorrow night. Plus there was an essential area of the list that I'd overlooked, which I was alerted to this morning.

I was waiting for my coffee, Jack thankfully preoccupied with orders, when Thuga stomped in. He held up three fingers to Jack and left but not before looking at me in that disturbing way he has.

Naturally, I'd done my hair-veil thing. I didn't want him to go back and report my flaking-off face to Frankie, especially with the breakthrough of the name exchange. I'm hoping to have de-flaked by Monday so I can go in after work.

Seeing Thuga reminded me of the flight of fantasy my imagination took me on when I'd stopped into PGGG on Sunday for some biscuits to serve as dessert after lunch at Mum's. Frankie hadn't been there but Ms Terse-at-the-Till had caressed (it felt like a caress) the back of my hand as she'd passed me my change and I'd had a sudden thought that she and Frankie might be swingers. I had visions of being tied up in the PGGG storeroom, taunted by the reward of a taste of my preferred yoghurt if I performed certain sexual favours. Standing in Jack's, waiting for my coffee, I worked my way through nearly as many different contortions as the kama sutra to try and figure out how to add 'not a swinger' to my list. Given I'm not allowed to use a negative, it's not that easy.

Sexually normal ... No, not definable, and I certainly don't want to end up with some lights-off, 'everything but missionary position makes a girl a slut' sort of guy.

Good in bed. For a moment I think I am onto a winner but then when I poke and prod it from a few angles I notice a flaw: what is 'good'?

I'm right up flummoxed creek without a paddle, stuck on this new item, but there is always a solution and I know the way to find it: the pop-up toaster.

I'm rinsing dishes that don't even need washing (I find dishwashing a very therapeutic task) that night when *Sexually compatible* bursts through the cobwebs of my brain. I shunt a few things around on my list and add 'Sexually compatible with me'

(I realised I should refine it—clarity is key) at number five on my A List, after: 'Kind', 'Amusing', 'Caring' and 'Generous'.

Come Saturday night, thoughts of swingers and European mafia sex-slave scenarios couldn't be further from my mind.

'Don't throw popcorn at your sister, Sammy,' I say during our second viewing of *The Secret Life of Pets*. My attempt to sound authoritative is undone by me throwing popcorn at him. Pretty soon popcorn is flying in every direction, the kids are jumping on the couch, squealing and screaming, and I'm wheezing with laughter.

'I want you to promise me you won't tell anyone about this, especially your mother.' I try not to sound panicked once we've all calmed down and I look at the popcorn shrapnel scattered around the living room.

'Yes, Aunty Fee.'

'Cross your hearts,' I demand over the sound of the handy vac, lifting couch cushions, making sure I get the nozzle into every crevice. If I leave even the tiniest trace of evidence, Catherine's bound to find it. Then she'll get all Catheriney and be telling me I won't ever be allowed to mind the kids again if I can't be responsible and set a good example.

As Sonja helps me clean, Sammy drifts away into his room.

'This is Greg Inglis, he's the captain.' Sammy emerges with his football cards to squeeze between Sonja and me, now back on the couch.

'I see.' I study the card that Sammy passes to me with great concentration. It's for Sammy after all.

'I think I know someone who might be a South Sydney fan like you.' I was pretty sure from the way Frankie deflated at the score the other night that they had to be his team. Despite myself (rugby league, for Buddha's sake!), I hear a little a smile creep into my voice.

'Really? That's a coincidence.' Sammy sounds quite serious for ten.

Environmental factors, I think, looking around the house. It's so oppressively staged and sterile.

'Maybe, but do you think there's really such a thing as co-incidences?'

'Of course—it's in the dictionary, Aunty Fee. Here, I'll google it for you.'

'No, don't worry. I believe you. I meant something sort of different.' I take another card from him.

At around the fifth card, Sonja, who'd disappeared into the kitchen, returns. She's got a look of such concentration on her face, making sure she doesn't drop the tray holding three plates, all of which have a brightly iced cupcake. 'Mummy helped me make these for you, Aunty Fee, but she said we can't call them a—'

'We'll call them beautiful cakes because that's what they look like to me.' And they do, despite Sonja's luminous, un-even icing and blobby piping.

'Sonja and I gave you the candles early because we knew we weren't allowed to give them to you today.'

'You sneaks! Thank you. I love the candles but I love you two more.' I bite into my cupcake and my teeth tingle from the pure sugar of the icing. The rest of me tingles from pure happiness.

19

'What? What's wrong? Why are you looking at me like that?' I demand of Lionel.

Lionel smiles. 'Like what?'

'It's my carrot legs, isn't it? I hate them, that's why I hardly ever wear skirts.' If I weren't flipped back in the apricot recliner, legs in the air, I'd tuck them under me. 'Sorry,' I splutter immediately. I've no idea what came over me, talking to Lionel that way, especially after the high five he'd given me when I'd told him I'd learnt Frankie's name, but Thuga and his mates have made me a little oversensitive about being looked at lately and soldiering on through my consumption seems to have eroded my filters. I take a breath and compose myself. 'I just don't like it when people look at me like that.'

'Like what?'

'Like *that*—all focussed and concentrating on me, like they're thinking thoughts about me I don't know.'

'Why?'

'I don't know, it's just the way I am.'

'I was just thinking it's the first time I've seen you in a skirt, actually. And while it would be entirely inappropriate for me as a practitioner to make a comment on your legs, I can assure you, no one would ever think your legs were anything close to resembling carrots.'

'Still, I don't like them. Can't we talk about something else?'

'Like what?'

'Frankie.'

'But you just said you hadn't seen him since the name exchange. When are you planning on going in again?'

'Probably on the weekend. I was thinking maybe we could do some work to prepare me for that, taking it to the next stage.'

'Can I ask you a question first?' Lionel says after considering my suggestion for a moment.

'Sure.'

'I'm pretty certain I know the answer but I want to be clear. Do you ever think that someone might be thinking something positive about you when they're looking at you?'

'Well ... no, especially not when they're really focussed.'

'I thought as much. I've noticed you're much more relaxed when you're not aware anyone is looking at you. At ease with yourself.'

My skin prickles and I can feel myself blushing. I blink my eyes to bat away unexpected tears.

'I'd like to work with that,' Lionel continues. 'I have a feeling this might be where part of your anxiety stems from. Are you OK if we work through to see where that fear of being focussed on came from?'

'I guess so.' It'll probably help with Situation Frankie in the long run too.

I don't ask for Positively but Lionel hands him to me then leads me back through time. I raise my right index finger to let him know I'm there.

'Where are you, Kismet?'

'Sitting on my bed, in the room I shared with Catherine.'

'How old are you?'

'Around four.'

'Be precise, go there.'

'Four and a half.'

'Tell me, who is there with you?'

'Catherine.' My voice is quiet, meek, scared—my little girl self.

'Just Catherine?'

I nod for yes again and clutch Positively a little closer to me.

We traverse my childhood with Catherine, travel through teenage years, enter early adulthood and end up at today. Lionel hears about how, under Catherine's gaze, my ears were deformed, or their lobes at least, my top lip too thin, my nose too fat and flat, nostrils far too wide, my hands far too big for a girl—more like a man's, my feet the ugliest to ever set foot on the earth (her pun, not mine), my hair mousy, too straight, too lank, my thighs had saddle bags, my freckles that are too freckly, how make-up makes me look like a whore; on and on it goes until we're at today. I'm a mosaic of all my flaws plus the ones adult Catherine has added to the list: not acting my age and not dressing appropriately for it. I could go on. I don't tell Lionel about my breasts—the ridicule of them coming, then the ridicule of them not coming enough. I really don't want to draw his attention to my chest.

'Catherine is a bitch,' Lionel says. 'Tell her that, Kismet.'

Even under hypnosis I hesitate. She really can't help who she is.

'Tell her.'

You know what? I think he's right.

'Fuck you, Catherine, you're a fucking bitch. Who are you to say who I should be? Like you're so fucking perfect.' I don't need to apologise to Spirit for expletives under hypnosis, I'm sure.

'Good on you, Kismet. I told you you were making progress. I'm proud of you. It's challenging work,' Lionel says gently, once he's led me out.

I can't say I feel entirely back when the buzzer goes but I hurriedly drag the half of me that's still in another world out and get myself together.

'Thanks, Lionel, I'll see you next week.' I sit Positively on the chair as I stand.

'Take care and be kind to yourself, Kismet. If you'll permit me, I'd like to give you a human hug. I think you could do with one.'

'Sure.' I stiffen slightly as Lionel wraps his arms around me. Not that there's anything wrong with the way he does it. As I've mentioned, I'm not great with random acts of physical affection from most adults, especially men.

On Saturday morning I wake from a nightmare. The PGGG had closed and been turned into a swanky bar, Frankie had disappeared and I hadn't ever got any further than asking his name. It was another reminder that I don't have all the time in the world, a message from my subconscious that I better get a move on with Frankie and look him in the eye when I do it. My eye isn't fully recovered but it'll have to do. Who knows when the chance won't be there anymore?

The next morning, the stars are aligning, everything really is working in absolute perfect harmony, and I'm certain I'll see Frankie. The eyelashes I do have curl perfectly, my make-up glides on, even my hair is behaving itself. The affirming message of *Transformation—your relationship with another is about to deepen* from the Lovers' Oracle only boosts my confidence.

Frankie is spreadeagled at the refrigerator doors right in front of my yoghurt. On a sheet of newspaper on the floor next to his big Adidas-adorned feet are gaffer tape, a screwdriver, a Stanley knife and a handtowel. I'm not sure whether I should take a second to observe and appreciate his physicality before I run for my life. Is it OK to even think of letting my eyes linger when I'd been committing yoghurt adultery for a fortnight while I waited for my eye to clear up?

Before I get the chance to do anything, Frankie turns and runs out to the store room.

Three things cross my mind. Maybe he's noticed me—or 'felt' my presence—and is rushing out to prepare my hostage quarters. He was probably multitasking, checking his implements of torture out on the shop floor while keeping an eye on things. Given our cosmic connection he was bound to know I'd be coming in. The efficiency is appealing, the plans to hold me hostage and torture me not so much. Obviously the whole nice and sweet to old ladies thing was just a ruse. How can I have been so naïve?

Secondly, I wonder if it's true what they say about big feet on a man.

And thirdly, given the way he bounds around, could I even keep up with him if anything did happen?

In truth more things cross my mind. Like wondering if he'd seen me and was so overcome with desire he'd rushed out for a wank in the bathroom, or maybe he'd gone to make sure the security cameras were recording so he could pleasure himself watching it later, replaying it over and over, screaming out my name. I know it's not a terribly spiritual thought—blame Frankie for interfering with my energies. Ever since the lean, I just haven't been the same.

Perhaps he'd gone out to check on the shrine of yoghurt he has set up in the hostage quarters—maybe with some stills of me from the surveillance camera and strands of my hair that he scours the floor for after my exit stuck above the yoghurt, next to the cash I've used to pay for my items. I'm probably flattering myself, but I'd seen something like that on TV once, although there was no yoghurt involved.

I know the thoughts are just Ms Middle-of-the-Road blowing a tyre or two. So I call the equivalent of spiritual roadside assistance and imagine what Amethyst would tell me about the way I'm letting mind carry on. I quickly take control of the wheel again.

However, if I *wasn't* reining myself in, I'd have to say that I hope the surveillance camera shots have caught my left side. It's my best side.

I take the opportunity to safely grab my yoghurt. Tina Arena's 'Chains' comes on the radio, as though the Universe is trying to give me a warning, but before I can get away, Frankie returns to his implements of torture.

'Hi, Frankie.'

He gives a bit of a start at my super enthusiastic delivery. I may have overcompensated for my alert and alarmed state. He looks at me. It's the look of someone who's just been asked an incredibly loaded question and is contemplating their response or formulating a plan. I take a small step back. I'm not going to let my guard down and risk having him pull a chloroform-soaked hanky out of his jeans and end up gaffer-taped in the store room, corn husks around my eyes as a blindfold. The Stanley knife and screwdriver, I don't even want to think about.

'I don't know your name,' he says. 'You told me but I forgot.'

How dare he—how very fucking *dare* he! (This is no time to be apologising to Spirit!) And to just blurt it out like that!

But for him to try to get away with a nameless 'Hi' in response to my overly zealous one would have been totally inappropriate and we both seem to know it.

I force a smile to keep the devastation from showing on my face. Aftershocks of silent questions follow the major earthquake in my brain as I stand there and fully register that he's forgotten my fucking name!

If I were able to think, I'd be giving the screwdriver and Stanley knife some serious consideration as tools of torture myself right now, but I'm far too busy dealing with the disappointment that is crumbling the stumps of my foundations. Not even a deep hypno-breath and positive-thoughts mantra is going to get rid of this.

How can I be fated to be with someone who can't even be bothered to remember my name? Why do I feel like I disappear into a sea of karmic connection when I look into his eyes? What's the magnetic pull about? And what of all the signs?

I wasn't planning on needing a list for my aftershock questions but there you go, you just don't ever know what the Universe is going to throw at you.

'Sorry.' I take a step away.

What am I doing? Why am I saying sorry?

To come back from this situation I have to flip it on its head and find a positive.

And there it is immediately—it gives me the opportunity to correct my original name exchange misnomer.

I look back at him. 'Officially it's Fiona, but you can call me Kismet. I won't be telling you again though.' As bad as it is, I can't stop flirtation flooding my voice. Then I turn with a flounce to walk away.

'I won't forget again,' he says.

I turn back and catch him making a little 'locking it into my brain' gesture at his temple.

I'm mad at myself that I find it sweet, but I'm even madder at myself that I look into his eyes. I shouldn't, he's like Kaa in *The Jungle Book*, I'll be hypnotised by his python ways and either floating off to Planet Swoon or in a storage locker by midnight.

Either seems preferable to the current reality.

20

I chop, dice and stir-fry my way through the afternoon, flinging myself around the kitchen. My music is so loud it's as though I'm trying to blast every thought and feeling about Frankie not only out of my head but out of my energy field.

I usually try to envision myself as a multicultural domestic goddess—think Nigella Lawson with an Asian bent—when I do my weekly cook-up but today I'm not up to it. Who could blame me? However, I'm not going to let a little Frankie-forgetting-my-name depression interrupt my routine. As a Taurean, routine is my best medicine.

Each time I stop long enough to think, I have to try to convince myself that Frankie only *pretended* to forget my name to show me that two can play the 'I'm so cool, calm and collected, acting like I don't care' game. Although even Ms Obsessively-Overthinking-Eternally-Hopeful-Against-Hope can't convince herself he'd be so complicated or into game playing, so Ms Middle-of-the-Road doesn't stand a chance.

By the time I'm heading out to meet Stephanie for dinner I've managed to bundle the whole incident into a tidy little package that I can live with. I had to try quite a few different boxes for size but the only one I can put it in is excusing him on the basis that he was so shocked at me actually speaking so many words in a row when I asked his name that he couldn't take it in. And reflecting, I did sort of mumble, so he probably didn't hear much more than that it started with an F. I pack the thoughts away and shove them into the mental equivalent of the space under the bed.

All of my thoughts and feelings are knocked aside when I walk into the restaurant and see Stephanie. Unguarded, alone, it's obvious she's beside herself. Her face is St Bernard sad and slack and I can see the frown line between her brows from the door. She's aged ten years since I last saw her.

'Mum's got cancer,' Stephanie says, without any of her usual crisp efficiency.

'Oh, Stephanie.' I reach across the table to take her hands but she pulls them away. I know she's trying to keep it together. 'I'm so sorry.'

Even as I say it, it sounds feeble, words are always so inadequate at times like this. I want to say, 'Cancer's not a death sentence anymore, treatment has really progressed, heaps of people go into remission,' but she looks so shattered, trying to turn it into something less significant than what she's going through would come off as patronising.

'Where is it?'

'Liver.'

We look at each other, our eyes speaking the words our mouths won't say. We saw what a woman we worked with years ago went through—it was evil. The success with treatment is low because by the time liver cancer is discovered, it's generally quite advanced.

Stephanie rallies herself. 'It's only stage two. She starts chemo next week.'

From entrée to dessert, I let Stephanie talk, telling me things she probably can't say to anyone else—I let her be sad, angry, outraged, frustrated, scared—although neither of us really have an appetite. But Goddess above, when it comes to dessert I'm only human, and what sort of girl is going to leave any baked ricotta cheesecake on her plate (or Stephanie's), particularly in an Italian restaurant in the aftermath of her own, now comparatively insignificant, life crisis?

Before we leave I need the bathroom.

'Ciao, bella,' the cute young Italian delivery driver says to me, dismounting his Vespa, which I've just had to side step as he zipped into the back of the restaurant. We're still laughing at my surprise as I disappear behind the bathroom door. Alone, my laughter is extinguished by the memory that Frankie forgot my freaking name.

During my thirty-five minute wait for the bus, I'm harassed, harangued and perved at by way too many drunk guys. The curse of being single and travelling solo on a Saturday night. *Seriously, must you?* I think time and time again as I wrap my coat tighter and tighter around me until it's practically a tourniquet. I decline every offer with a smile, including one not unpleasant and reasonably sober guy who tries to pick me up. I'm not feeling it, but then again I'm so cold I'm not feeling anything.

Still, he and the Italian—hell, even the drunks—are a welcome gift from the Universe, obviously sent to remind me that I am not insignificant, let alone repellent to men, despite the behaviour of some I could mention.

The string of the box I'd so neatly packed the name-forgetting incident in unravels on Sunday morning and Frankie jumps around in my mind like a hyperactive child on a trampoline. There is no way I can justify his oversight. Even Amethyst's 'what is fated must be lived' and her denouncement of the Baader-Meinhof phenomenon have worn beyond wafer thin.

I've got Bing's daughter Lulu's sixth birthday party this afternoon but I need to get out immediately. If I stay here stewing in my own thoughts it'll only get worse. Armed with my laptop and a hard copy of my What I Want and Need in my Next Male Love Relationship list, I take myself on a spiritual date to work on it in the anonymity and peace of a café in the next suburb. I hypno-breathe to ease my despair (not easy when it really should be done with your eyes closed). My shortcut through the park offers the bonus of not having to pass PGGG.

A dog barks from the deck of a house as I run across the road. With my highly attuned ears I'd bet my own life that when I look up I'll see a sausage dog. I admit my life isn't feeling worth a whole lot of prayer beads right now so I don't have much to lose, but still, I'm pretty sure I'll see a sausage dog.

There's a miniature red short-haired dachshund up on the balcony, and the fabric of Amethyst's wisdom strengthens again.

Two triple-shot lattes later, the thirteen pages of my list sit on the café table, untouched and unread. My mind has been darting around like a ball bearing on a washing machine with thoughts of Frankie, from him forgetting my name to the inexplicable feelings I have around him, including the trip to Planet Swoon while watching him with the old lady and those moments when I'd really felt I'd connected to him, not to mention the things that happened to me when I was appreciating his physicality. I'd even started a mental list of Endearing Things About Frankie after the old lady incident.

Before I realise it we've crossed the threshold of midday and I still haven't picked up my list. It's time for me to head to Lulu's party. As un-party as I feel, I have to go. I'm the only adult she's invited, plus she made Bing text me to check the date before she set it so she could be certain I'd be there. I refuse to disappoint her. It'll be fun, playing with them all, chatting in Mandarin and being able to switch off the geyser of Frankie thoughts.

When I get to the station and discover there's trackwork I want to cry. It's quite a trip to *World of Bounce* where Lulu's having her birthday party. Of all the people I could end up standing beside in the crowd waiting for the rail replacement bus I end up next to a couple who look like unattractive rabbits—which I could live with but then they start to kiss.

Gross. Get a room. Or a hutch.

I want to hit them with the energetic equivalent of a dose of myxomatosis, throwing the full strength of my current life crisis behind it. It's only karma that stops me. Being irresponsible with the force of universal energy isn't going to get me anywhere. Still, I doubt I'll be able to contain it. Those two slurping away at each other is more than I can take—I have to move away. I appreciate that it's not their fault they're unattractive, they can't help it. I do *try* to think, *Oh, isn't it lovely, there's someone for everyone. When you're ready for love you draw it to you.* I'm just not in the best space to carry it off at the moment.

An hour and a half later, Lulu has my hand and is taking me to meet her friends. This place is amazing—there's a jumping castle, big blow-up slides, some spongy rock-climbing contraption, huge blow-up gorillas (I'm not sure what they're about) and loads of squealing. The kids are having a ball. I take off my shoes and prepare to bounce.

I'm breathless and wishing I'd worn ear plugs by the time I flop down in a chair next to where Bing, his wife Bibby and a couple of other parents sit, chatting. 'Da Ge, why didn't you come bounce? You're no fun.' Bibby is excused from bouncing—she's about to pop with their third child. But Bibby wouldn't be a bouncer even if she wasn't pregnant. She's so quiet and shy—totally the opposite to Bing.

Later, when everyone but Bing, Bibby, Lulu, Jie—her elder sister—and I have gone, Lulu runs up to me. 'Ayi, will you come back to our place?' I love that Lulu calls me 'aunty'.

'Come on, Mei Mei,' Bing says, when I hesitate. 'We can have an early dinner—I'll make your favourite pork and beans then drive you home. Don't be boring. What are you going to do home alone?'

Some cleaning, washing, drive myself insane thinking about Frankie forgetting my name—thoughts that my mind had been clear of for the afternoon.

'We'd love you to come. Don't worry for me—Bing will do everything.' Bibby seems to intuit that part of my hesitancy is because I imagine she's exhausted.

'That'd be great,' I say.

'Yay—I can show you my best-ever birthday present.'

Back at their place we pile out of the car. I can barely keep up with Lulu and Jie as they run into the backyard where a grey, floppy-eared fluff-ball of a bunny that Lulu tells me is named Minky is hopping around in a cage.

'I can't believe you didn't tell me you were getting Lulu a bunny,' I say to Bing once we're inside.

'I didn't know. No one ask me—I just make money, pay bills ...' The words 'reactive' and 'excitable' are an understatement when it comes to Bing. Even in English it's hard to understand him when he's off on one of his rants.

'Maybe it was pregnancy brain.' Bibby winks at me. 'But Lao Tou, I think maybe you should start dinner now.'

'How do you live with him?' I shake my head as Bing carries on and heads into the kitchen.

'No one's perfect but he's perfect for me.' Bibby's so sweet. 'Besides I didn't ask him—I knew he'd say no and he still would have reacted like that.'

Ha. Bibby had Bing worked out, which was no mean feat, but neither was working out what all this rabbit and bunny energy around me was about. After the candles and Ugly Rabbit People, Minky's presence didn't feel like a coincidence.

21

'He forgot my freaking name!' The words I've been holding in rush out before Lionel's even closed the door. I only just managed to keep it in for our initial pleasantries.

'How did you react?'

'I said sorry,' I wince. I'm perched on the edge of my seat, thumbnail in my mouth.

Lionel thumps his palm against his forehead. 'You what?'

'Isaidsorry.' I suck my words in on a breath so they join together, barely audible.

Lionel looks as though I've sworn at him—very badly.

'It's that English background thing.' I try to explain: '"Oh, you've just axe murdered my entire family—I'm sorry." I told you I'm of English stock, right?'

'No, but that's not really that relevant right now. It's about acceptable behaviour and the patterns you set up,' Lionel says in a manner that suggests he's about to launch into some *Super Nanny* tactics and I'll spend the session in the naughty corner having a good hard think about what I've done.

147

I admit a sorry from Frankie would have softened the blow a little. It certainly wouldn't have gone astray.

'Look at the positives.' I try to lighten Lionel's mood, because his face is all crumpled and disappointed. 'It's a good thing that he just came right out and said it. It shows he's honest and it also gave me a chance to clear up the whole Fiona/Kismet thing.' I'd been calling on these lifebuoys quite regularly to get me through the week.

'That is one way to look at it.' Lionel raises an eyebrow. 'But how do you *feel?*'

'Obviously I wasn't happy. Upset, humiliated, mortified—to be honest devastation may have been fluttering in the mix too. But now ... well, it's sort of funny, don't you think?' I screw up my face up in a strange little smile that I worry makes me look like a cross between a hyena and a pig but it's what I need to do to keep the smile firmly in place. It's part bravado, part trying not to snort. I don't want to topple too far either way.

'You quite like a challenge, don't you? I think you'd be bored without it,' Lionel observes, kind enough not to ask why I'm pulling a hyena-pig face if he does notice it.

'Maybe.' I shrug, but he's right. Honestly, without some playfulness, flirtation, teasing, fun and a challenge with a guy, I'm bored in five minutes. Nothing worse than someone fawning all over me—turns me off them immediately.

'And you're quite competitive in your own subtle way. You certainly don't like not getting what you set out to achieve, but is the prize worth the effort?'

'You don't know till you get it,' I say, finding my stride. 'Besides, it's like Frankie has some spell, or maybe curse, over me. I just can't quite manage my normal reactions around him. I know it makes no sense when there's Jack. Jack is far sweeter and in theory he's more attractive than

Frankie and probably more suited to me. I haven't ever heard him mention sport.'

'One thing at a time. Let's just pop Jack aside for now. Tell me about this *spell*.'

'Normally I'd be able to at least have a rational level of up-settedness over something. I know that's probably not a word, but you know what I mean.'

'Yes, I like your made-up words. But the question is, do you ever act on being upset? Tell people how you feel, say what you want, rather than just make allowances and accommodate them? Not just with Frankie, but anyone? At work, for example.'

'That makes me sound like a doormat, Lionel.' I'm quite affronted. Sure, Catherine might have got all the stand-up-for-yourself genes in our family but I'm hardly a martyr.

'I wouldn't say that, Kismet, however, you didn't answer the question.'

'I just think "appropriate behaviour", "don't let people treat you as though you're less than you're worth" is a bit … not so much clichéd, as concealing.'

'How do you mean?'

'Everyone's so focussed on boundaries and "people will treat you how you let them" that they don't realise that if you don't focus on that, you get to see who someone really is, get an insight into their own moral compass, whether they do unto others as they'd have them do unto them.'

'Interesting, I'd never thought of it that way.'

'Most people don't.'

'While that idea may have some merit, I'm not sure it's the best approach.' He pauses. 'You look tired, as though trying to keep things so together and riding everyone else's waves is taking its toll.'

'It's the rats.'

'You haven't mentioned the rats to me before. Do they come to you in your dreams? They could be very significant.'

'No, they're in my ceiling, not my dreams. Don't be offended, I haven't mentioned them to anyone.'

'So, it's not being upset over Frankie, work and trying to figure out what to do that's keeping you awake?'

He's right of course, but I really don't want to go down that path today—it's too heavy. And the rats aren't helping.

'No, it's just the rats. Riverdancing rodents that have taken up residence in the ceiling space right above my bedroom, I fear a decent sleep and I may not ever meet again!'

'Riverdancing rodents! Kismet, you crack me up. Tell me more.'

'This family—or maybe it's a colony—of rats are making so much noise at terribly unenlightened hours. I'm sure they're morbidly obese too.' I create quite the scenario, imagining rats on tour through ceilings across the city but then realise I'm paying Lionel eighty dollars an hour to tell him a story about rats. 'Perhaps I should move across to the recliner for some hypnosis now.'

'I want you to do something for me, Kismet,' Lionel says once the buzzer has ended our session.

'Sure,' I say, still a little hazy.

'Perhaps it's time to be kinder to yourself, try an easier path.'

An easier path—that homework's going to be painless.

'I want you to ask Jack out. Just see what happens.'

What Lionel doesn't understand is that I have never asked a man out in my life. Not that I don't think women should,

I'm just not an ask-a-man-out sort of girl. I've never had the need.

And is asking him out worth the risk of making coffee complicated and ruining one of the highlights of my day? And what if 'it may be fated but I can't be bothered to remember your name Frankie' finds out? What of the lack of zing factor with Jack? I guess sometimes sizzle just has to build up from a low, slow simmer—so low, maybe you can't even feel it's there at first. So many questions.

I'm not at all happy that Amethyst has cancelled my session today. Having my Spiritual Support Pit Crew appointments is very comforting, reassuring. Although with the timing of her call, just when I'd got out from Lionel yesterday, I can't help wonder if maybe this isn't something I'm meant to figure out for myself.

Time for Ms Middle-of-the-Road to embrace being a mature, in-control woman, driving her own destiny. However, I'm not planning on getting caught speeding; I need to work up to it.

And then Jack's busy when I go in anyway. Saturday mornings are always like that. I do make a point of not letting Frankie reaching up to get some spices divert me too far from the centre lines as I pass PGGG. Dharma him, it's as though he senses when I'm ebbing towards Jack and does something to tempt me.

Maybe I'll come back down to Jack's later and ask him out—mornings not being my forté and all.

That afternoon I take a walk around the park and phone Stephanie.

'Mum's pretty much the same, maybe a bit worse,' she tells me.

'Would you like me to mind the kids so you can do something special, spend some time just the two of you?'

'No, that's—I want to keep it all as normal as possible. Thanks.' Her voice is tight, strained, her words stilted rather than just efficient. She immediately changes the subject and for the remainder of the conversation we talk about the most insignificant of things. The sorts of things you talk about when you're facing an abyss of pain so deep you don't know how you'll ever get over it, so you just have to pretend it's not there.

It's not intentional that I don't go back to Jack's, somehow the afternoon disappears. Besides after Stephanie, my mood wasn't upbeat enough to contemplate asking a guy out. I wanted to wrap her up, make her tea, feed her brownies, hug her and tell her everything would be OK—even when it so obviously wouldn't.

'How was your night? Did you get up to anything exciting?' I ask Jack, testing the waters. I'm not getting anywhere with Frankie so why not give Lionel's crazy idea a try? I'm a little later than usual, even for a Sunday morning. Not that I've been fussing around with my hair and make-up any more than normal, I just had to imbibe a plunger coffee from my emergency stash at home. Asking a man out was definitely not a feat one should approach entirely uncaffeinated.

'Quiet, I had to be up early. But I'll be having Sundays off from next week.'

'That's good, you'll be able to go out on Saturday nights.' It's the perfect cue to ask him out. I could so easily slip straight into it.

'Next time I go to a party we can go together,' Jack says, saving me the trouble.

'Perfect!'

We look at each other, our eyes as wide as shocked owls'.

Jack keeps talking but I'm too busy assimilating what I've just done to focus on our interaction now. It seems to have happened too quickly, too easily. Do I even really want to go out with Jack?

I talk myself down: *It's attending a party, Kismet, not necessarily a date*. Amethyst's always told me if something comes to you seamlessly, it's meant to be happening.

22

Monday morning it's business as usual in at Jack's—no mention of parties. I'm not going to push it.

I wait so long for a bus I almost forget where I'm going—wishful thinking. I make good use of the time to clean out my wallet. I'm throwing a handful of receipts into the bin when I see Frankie environmentally inappropriately ripping cardboard into the matching rubbish receptacle fifteen steps away outside the store. Surely simultaneous bin usage must signify a deep, karmic, soul connection. If we were recycling I'd put the connection down to a past life.

Frankie notices me noticing him. We hold our look for a nanosecond, so short it's even shorter than those stubby little eyebrows that aren't long enough for the tweezers to grab yet that drive a girl crazy. Frankie is just as frustrating.

I look away first.

At the station I have to jostle for space. The platform is a seething mass of grey auras, drowning in 'How can the weekend be over already?' energy. Mine is the same.

I'm quite late so when the train does finally arrive, I visualise myself holding my space to make sure I get on board. Twenty minutes later I'm trudging into work.

I've not even sat down before Broomstick begins boring me half to death. 'The directors have commended my new approach. Multiple strategic projects that are all offshoots of the bigger picture of a robust and comprehensive realigned compliance framework.' Her lips pull away from her teeth in a quarter-smile. 'We're about to enter a very, very exciting time, Fiona.'

Exciting, my aura—which I can feel is now greyer than it's ever been.

If I had been planning on going into PGGG, which I wasn't, I would have missed them. Dharmaed Broomstick and her never-ending amendments. What's worse, she'd headed off to yet another 'meeting' with Professor Emeritus Bartholomew, so again my mind was filled with images of them that I really didn't want to be having.

They're nothing compared to the dream I have that night. Between midnight and 4.30am, my delta brainwaves dance around in a direction that I won't ever be able to admit to anyone.

'Have you been a good girl?' Frankie asks.

'No.'

'Do you need to be spanked?' In the dream his voice is deeper, husky.

'Have you got the shallots?' I say in a way I wouldn't ever be able to carry off in reality.

He looks at me, his seagull eyes narrowing with curiosity.

'To spank me with, Frankie.'

In the convenient world of dreams, it just so happened that there are some snake beans next to us, so right there, on the dream-space of the shop floor, Frankie picks a bunch up and starts whipping my behind with them, saying, 'These are better, they'll sting more,' as he sings along to Billy Idol's 'Rebel Yell'.

I was happy with my subconscious for having come up with something still in the Retro FM bracket, but beyond the obvious—The Divinyls' 'Pleasure and Pain'.

We didn't get any further than that. My work anxiety cut through our potential and woke me.

'Are you going out, Fiona?' Jack says as I run by Tuesday evening, clutching my shopping bag so hard my nails are biting into my palms. I'd rushed out of work to get home, touch up my make-up, spritz, recurl my eyelashes, remove my underwear— don't want my destiny thwarted by VPL—and change. My hair isn't behaving itself but every day is a bad hair day lately.

'No, just going to pick up a few things.' I swing my bag and smile at him even though I feel like I'm about to vomit and pass out. It's true what they say about a butterfly flapping its wings on the other side of the world and creating a tidal wave: when there's an entire aviary of them flapping away inside your stomach it's a tsunami of anxiety.

He goes to ask me something else, but I don't have time to chat and I need to stay focussed. I've only got twenty steps left to give Alex, my anxiety, a good talking to. Of course I feel bad, brushing Jack off like that, but I'm a woman on a mission. The dream had changed my stance on things.

But only somewhat—I'm definitely not fine with Frankie forgetting my name, I realise when I step across the threshold of PGGG. I spot him and briefly wonder why his hair seems to be so much darker today. Perhaps he's using Just for Men or something in an effort to appear younger for me in compensation for his hideously unforgivable oversight?

I pass Frankie in not just a hoity but a super hoity, you-are-beneath-me way, not looking in his direction.

'Hi, Fiona,' he calls even though he's in the middle of serving someone else. It's like he's been waiting for me to come in, bursting to say it. He seems so eager to please that I don't think of turning around and snapping, 'It's Kismet, for Buddha's sake. Can't you get it right, man?'

'Hi, Frankie,' I say instead, in my best sing-song, swoony voice and turn my head vaguely in his direction. 'You remembered.' I toss my hair as I strut into the fruit and vegetables.

When I get to the till he isn't there, thank Buddha. A strutting arrival is one thing but I can't possibly interact with him. What was I thinking? But now there's no one to serve me.

'Frankie, there are people to be served!' the young casual evening shift girl yells from her position leaning against the avocados, swiping the screen of her phone. The broom next to her indicates that she should be sweeping the floor.

Not just people, sweetheart, one of them is me. The other one—in front of me—is a woman with two little boys. I sort of hide behind her as Frankie returns to the till. I look at my nails, out to the street, at the floor, at the back of the woman's head, anything to seem like I don't care. Only when I'm sure he won't notice do I steal glances at him.

'How was school today?' he asks the boys, giving them a smile that goes all the way to his eyes. I do have a weakness for men who smile right up to their eyes, making them crinkle in the way Frankie's just have. Dharma him.

'What's your favourite thing to do? Do you like your teacher?' he continues, then he makes a comment to the mother about an item she's bought for their lunchboxes being something he loved to eat as a child.

Dharma him again. His voice doesn't have any of its nasal twang to it, it's soft, warm. I feel as though I'm being wrapped in a cloud.

He says something else and makes himself laugh. I miss it, having begun my transit to Planet Swoon. Overtaken by the force that's pulling my heart out of my chest. The most adorable person I have ever seen is in front of me (actually, a little to the left given the counter). It's as though a whiteboard eraser has been applied to my brain—the ignoring me; the nearly always mumbled 'hi'; the name forgetting; the swinger scenarios; the European mafia crime ring; being tethered up out the back and kept as a sex slave; the football—they're all gone.

All I see is Frankie.

I step forward as the woman leaves. I'm so distracted, woozy and swoony that I have to lean against the counter to have any hope of maintaining an upright position. I am far more sixteen-year-old schoolgirl with a crush on her teacher than divine goddess. Every part of me is shaking. I feel like a human maraca.

I try to calm myself by wondering whether I should ask Frankie for star anise. Not that I need it but it's a spice that'd take some time to find. The thought only seems to make things worse after the dream. I've been careful not to buy shallots— thank Govinda that snake beans are out of season.

I manage to move my items forward for his convenience and, ever the helpful one, replace my basket behind me.

'Hi, Fiona,' he says and smiles as I turn back.

'Hi, Frankie.'

One of us should say something more surely, but we just stand there looking at each other. Even though I have no recollection of pulling a fifty-dollar note out of my pocket and handing it to him, he's getting my change, my items already bagged. We've been looking at each other the entire time.

Devo's 'Whip It' comes on, as though Spirit wants to expose me. I begin to overheat.

When Frankie touches the bottom of my right middle finger—yes, a single finger—the jolt of electricity that shoots up my arm and through my body is so forceful I jump as though I'm in an electric chair. The coins he's handed me fall from my hand. We both reach for them, but I'm so embarrassed that I race to scrape them up first.

'Ta!' I grab my shopping bag and scurry away like one of the rat family from my ceiling, not turning back.

By the time I'm home I've rewound back to Frankie's greeting as I entered. I do a little squeal of delight and dance around my apartment to Florence + the Machine's 'Spectrum (Say My Name)', Tove Styrke's 'Say My Name', Peking Duk's 'Say My Name', (No Destiny's Child's 'Say My Name'—I don't want to draw in that cheating-man energy), the Ting Ting's 'That's Not My Name' and then the 'Say My Name's again until YouTube has eaten up my remaining data. The tornado of happiness spinning around inside me sweeps away everything else, even the voice that had berated me for running off like that. I spin until I go to bed and finally get to sleep.

In the pre-dawn silence when I wake, my mind zig-zags all over the place. I replay Frankie's 'Hi, Fiona' so many times it starts to become flavourless, like over-chewed bubble gum.

Then I think about the coin dropping and the way I ran out, which furls at the edges of my happiness.

Surely Frankie sending Ms Middle-of-the-Road careening off course like that, blowing a tyre every time I see him, means he can't be good for me?

160

23

'Sorry about last night,' I say to Jack. In the moments that I hadn't been caught up thinking about Frankie, I'd felt bad about striding past him. 'I was just in a hurry.'

He looks at me like he isn't sure what I'm talking about and continues frothing milk.

I begin my usual routine of flicking through the paper, but I can't really focus—I'm feeling a little dizzy. Too much spinning last night. Jack still doesn't speak. He seems distant, as though he's pretending not to be upset.

'Do you want to come out, I mean to a party, on Saturday night?' he eventually blurts.

Saturday—that's this week. Am I being too available if I say yes without checking?

But I owe him a direct response after last night. 'Sure.'

'Great.' His face lights up and he's back to sweet, smiling Jack.

Before we can say anything more, someone else comes in, though Jack winks as he hands me my coffee.

Am I ready for this? It feels way too fast and has disaster written all over it. Beyond caffeine complications, it's sheer stupidity mixing men who work less than fifty metres from each other. But then, all Frankie did was say my name. And it's not like I'm marrying Jack. It's not even really a date, which is a good thing because I hate dates. My modus operandi with relationships has been to get to know someone until we've drifted into being a couple. But this is just going to a party together.

It'll be fine.

On Thursday night, Jane calls. My intuition was spot on. Mr Mural has been occupying her energetic field, not to mention other parts of her, which, Jane tells me, he does exquisitely.

'And what else has been happening? What of Operation Baby Jane?' I still can't quite imagine Jane with a child.

'Still exploring my options. There's only certain countries that are single-parent friendly—China, Colombia, India, Bulgaria. There are a few others but their wait time is so long I'd be more like an adoptive grandmother.'

When Jane asks me what progress I've made with Frankie I can't tell her about Monday night. That would involve having to explain the backstory and her doing something like cutting Frankie's tongue out with his own Stanley knife for forgetting my name let alone not apologising. And then she'd get to work on me.

'I'm going to a party with Jack on Saturday,' I tell her chirpily.

'Christ, you should have told me to sit down. How did that come about?'

'He asked and I said yes.'

'Simple as that?'

'Yep—simple as that.' If I disregard what was going on in my head.

'Good on you, Kizzo. I told you nothing was going to change until you took action.'

As we end the call with a promise to catch up next week, I'm amazed at how easy it was not to ask Jane her opinion about Jack. So sensibly autumn. And really, the way things turned out there was no need to tell her the date with Jack is Lionel homework.

The next day my homework is not so easy to avoid. I really don't want to have to broach our upcoming 'date' at all, let alone before coffee, but I can't stand not knowing what's happening.

'So, um, are you still going to that party tomorrow night, Jack?' I ask as nonchalantly as I can, folding a serviette into tiny squares as someone's taken the paper.

'Only if you're still coming with me.' Jack smiles a little too intensely.

'Sure. What time should I come down?'

'Down?'

'Yeah, I'll just come down and meet you here.'

'No, if you're coming to a party with me, I'll come and collect you. Write down your address.' Jack reaches for the order pad.

'Oh no, it's fine. I don't need collecting. I'm so close.' I hate giving people my address. I like to maintain my anonymity and once my door is closed on the world, that's where I like the world to stay—out there, unless I invite them otherwise. The drop-in visit should be considered illegal, like trespassing.

'No, I insist.'

'Ha, you're going to have to desist because I'm going to pop down here on Saturday and meet you. Just tell me what time.'

The metal milk jug clangs against the dark wood of the counter as Jack slams it down. Little drops of milk get caught in the hair of his forearm.

'Don't take it personally, Jack. It's just how I am.'

'It's not how you treat a lady, to have her hike down.'

Oh, Govinda. *'Treat a lady'*? An alarm bell starts to sound somewhere deep within my brain. I ignore it. We're going to a party. That's all.

'It's hardly a hike, Jack. Please just tell me what time. I'll come down.' I'd tell him not to be so dramatic if I didn't think I'd done enough damage already. I really don't want to hurt his feelings. He's just trying to do what he thinks is the right thing, what so many women like.

'Seven.'

I smile. 'Thank you, Jack. I'll see you tomorrow.'

The next morning on my way to Diego my hairdresser (even a not-a-date requires a cut and colour—I was overdue any-way), I go into a café around the corner, out of sight of Jack's. Substandard coffee but I need to build some anticipation.

At 6.55pm I leave home totally Ms Middle-of-the-Road right down to my outfit. One of my classic tunic tops, char-coal grey, diagonally cut so as not to sit like a tent across my hips, and jeans with underwear (not even my lucky under-wear). I've only curled my eyelashes twice.

Jack's is in darkness, apart from the flickering of a candle on one of the tables. There might be a power outage in this block—it happens, although the street lights are on and so are the lights in the shop next door. Deep hypno-breath. I knock.

I can smell Jack's aftershave before he's got the door fully open. It's got an 'I've tried too desperately hard for this date' whiff about it that I can't miss. If we're going to a party, why is Jack dressed in a tuxedo with his hair slicked back? He didn't mention it was formal.

'Shaken or stirred?' Jack gives the cocktail shaker he's holding a little jiggle as I step in.

'My dear man, there are some things that don't mix and alcohol and I are two of them.'

Jack looks at me blankly, entirely missing my attempt at a Bond quip.

'Um, neither thanks, Jack. I don't really drink. I brought some soda water for the party.' I try to sound calm, natural and not at all freaked out as I put the bag with the soda water down on one of the tables. One that doesn't have a white tablecloth, cutlery, a flickering candle and a vase with a single red rose on it. There's only one of those.

'Yes, the party. Before we go I thought we might have dinner.' He waves his arms around the café in the manner of a magician's assistant.

Dharma it—I had a snack before I left home. Who knows with parties whether there will be food and I'm really not good with low blood sugar. I'll just have to eat dinner though. I can't be rude.

On the upside, I know I'm entirely safe here with Jack because everyone who should happen to walk past can see us. Unfortunately the fact makes me uncomfortable rather than reassured, because what if Frankie sees me here on what is so obviously a *date*-date with Jack? I put the thought out of my mind immediately. If Frankie wanted to ask me out on a *date*-date he could have. I'm here with Jack and I am going to enjoy the evening. We're at a table at the rear of the café, my back is to the door and my hair is up as Diego's apprentice had blow-dried it too big, which always makes me self-conscious. Frankie probably couldn't tell it's me anyway.

Maybe I should go home and change. Not to dress for dinner but Jack's outfit and the way he's slicked back his hair is a far cry from the sort of party I imagined we'd be going to. Before I've got time to ask him, Jack is pouring the contents of the cocktail shaker into a couple of martini glasses, complete with olives. Regardless of my earlier comments, he hands me one, which I immediately put on the table. I hate martinis and after cocktails with Jane, my no-alcohol stance is even greater.

'I'm just going to—'

Oh my Buddha, if he says, 'Slip into something more comfortable,' and comes out wearing a James Bond–style dressing gown I will walk the 195 steps right on out of here back to the sanctuary and comfort of home immediately.

'—put on some music.'

Ed Sheeran fills the room and I have to hold in a snort. But I must act with grace and give Jack a chance. The fact that I hate this sort of music more than anything is beside the point. Again, I'm really to blame. If I hadn't been so focussed on John Farnham after the PGGG incident, I would've also thought to add 'Does not listen to Ed Sheeran' to my What I Want and Need in My Next Male Love Relationship list. I should have also added Sam Smith and now I'm thinking on those lines both the Justins (Beiber and Timberlake) should've been on there, along with James Blunt and Norah Jones, as well as with Barry White, Michael x 2 (Buble and Bolton) and Celine Dion to be sure I cover those in the upper age range! If I'd done that, Jack was bound to have picked up on it energetically. Frankie's music is pure gold compared to this.

Back at the table, Jack pulls a chair out for me to sit down. I fight my instinct to bat him away and tell him I can do it for myself. That sort of thing makes me uncomfortable but I remind myself of Lionel's advice to 'be kind to myself', which I understand means letting other people be kind to me too.

Jack sits opposite and takes a sip of his martini.

I feel the need to fill the awkward silence that pervades the room despite the music. 'You're looking very dressed up, Jack.

Are we off to an awards ceremony or taking a stroll on a red carpet after this?'

'No. I don't know anyone famous, do you?'

'Not really. I was …' I trail off and go to pour myself some water.

'Here, I'll do it.' Jack practically flings himself across the table and wrestles the jug from my hand. It's like he's read a 1950s etiquette manual on How to Woo a Lady and is following all the essential steps. I feel so bad. He's eager to please but there's none of our usual easy banter. It's as though by taking it beyond the coffee exchange we're all at sea.

'It's OK, Jack, thank you, that's very sweet, but I can do it.' If I don't tell him, how can I expect him to know?

'I might get our entrée.' Jack disappears out the back again, just long enough to pick up a couple of plates. He places six oysters au naturel, shells bedded in rock salt, in front of me.

Oysters—I can't actually swallow an oyster, they make me gag. There's so much I could read into his choice if I wasn't busy panicking.

Jack looks at me expectantly.

'Wow, you've gone to so much trouble, Jack. This is lovely.' I poke at an oyster with the special little fork. He really has thought of everything, apart from asking what I do and don't eat—I don't mean to sound unappreciative but I have very particular tastes.

He's still watching me. There's no way around it, I have to put the oyster in my mouth. I slide it between my teeth and my cheek and pretend to swallow. As Jack pops an oyster in his mouth I bend down so my head is sort of under the table (I hope I don't give him any ideas), take a tissue from my handbag and spit the oyster into it. It's gross but there's nothing to do with the tissue other than put it back in my bag.

'Sorry, I just had to check my phone, my ... my mother's not been that well.' I sense a bout of bad karma on its way.

'Is everything OK with her, Fiona?' His concerned thoughtfulness makes his already younger-than-his-years voice sound even younger and sweeter.

I'm definitely going to come back as a bug in my next life. 'Oh yes, fine really. Thanks.' I poke at my plate. 'Would you like the rest of my oysters, Jack? I want to save myself for the main course.' I'm super careful not to say dessert in case he thinks I mean him.

He takes them eagerly and then I wonder if it was such a good idea—I don't want to send mixed messages by passing him a plate of aphrodisiacs. But too late now.

'And what do we have for main?' I ask, for something to say.

'Pumpkin and ricotta ravioli with sage burnt butter sauce.'

'Sounds delicious.' It really does.

It's good we're not at a restaurant, I think, as dinner moves on. At least we're spared the humiliation of being the awkward couple of a date. Though Jack seems oblivious, continuing to be stiflingly attentive and bounding along with his unfunny jokes while I have to explain every one of my quips.

I'm way too tired and it's way too late for me to think about going to a party by the time dinner has finished. Jack takes it quite well but insists on walking me home.

'Thanks so much, Jack,' I say when we reach the main gate of the apartments. Ingenious Ms Middle-of-the-Road solution—Jack can feel at peace, having met his gentlemanly obligation of seeing me home, and I get to avoid fully disclosing my address.

Jack doesn't say anything but purses his lips into a little goldfish pucker as I turn to walk away. I do try to kiss him—I'm fully intending to—but at the last moment I turn my head so his lips land on my cheek.

Inside, I slip into something more comfortable myself and flop on my bed. My face is tight from smiling but I realise I didn't actually laugh all night. I'd phone Jane if it wasn't so late. She's going to snort herself senseless when I tell her about tonight, we both will. Not poking fun at Jack—I'd accrued enough bad karma for one night—just at the ridiculousness of the situation and how something so theoretically right can be so wrong.

The internet groans with the load of Saturday night streaming, and it's slim pickings on TV. At first when the *Love Me, Love My Doll* opening credits come up I think of changing stations, not in the mood for twee little girls and their toys, but it's not at all pink tutus and tiaras. Of course it's not, this is SBS. The opening shot is of a guy sitting beside a row of silicone dolls on his settee (he's English). 'I much prefer living with and having relationships with these girls to people,' he tells the camera.

After recent events I could relate. 'Much easier that way.'

Then the guy switches his favourite doll's tongue over to one designed specifically for the purposes of pashing. Wow, they really think of everything, how terribly convenient. I'm so enthralled that even though he has a bit of an Ugly Rabbit Person look, I can't take my eyes off the TV.

A bolt of lightning hits me, Mr Sheening my tarnished aura, and I feel the immediate change in the way my chakras are whirring. A doll could be everything I need. If it's worked for other people, why not me?

Pen and notepad always at the ready, I begin to make a list of Silicone Partner Pros:

1. No concern about unmet emotional needs with a partner with a substandard EIQ (emotional intelligence quotient), i.e. name forgetting.
2. Easy conversation when I'm in the mood to chat—admit
   virtually same as talking to myself but at least I would
   be looking at someone else's head, or a silicone someone
   else's head.
3. No need to bother pretending I'm interested in a conversation I'd rather not be having, just to act like I
   care—also admit I don't actually do this with men (may
   be one of my issues with them?).
4. No jealous rumblings or insecurities about the likes of
   younger/blonder/leggier/bustier/flirtier/can 'look men in
   the eye easily and talk whipper snippering' women.
5. No risk to personal welfare or virtue at the hands of
   European Mafia members and suburban swingers.
6. No conversations or phone calls about needing milk
   or deciding what's for dinner, or things like, 'Jeffie
   from work wants to know if we're free to have
   brunch with him and Jazzie at Café So New So Now
   on Sunday.' (Jeffie and Jazzie were *bound* to be mad
   for that sort of thing. The thought of it left me unable
   to breathe.)
7. The convenience of interchangeable tongues wasn't to
   be underestimated—and the adaptability was certain
   to extend to other appendages.

The list could go on but item seven creates a bit of a road
block. I'm not sure I could muster any real physical desire for a silicone doll. Maybe if I secretly record Frankie
(I hadn't considered the doll being anyone else)—not his
twanging, but one of his soft, sweet interactions or maybe
singing. I'd also need to steal one of his T-shirts—tricky,

given I only ever have access to them on his person. Maybe something else that has his pheromones on it. Still tricky … I'll have to think on that.

Of course I'll have to surreptitiously get a photo of him for them to model Silicone Frankie on. I'll also have to do some research to find out who 'them' are.

Put together, all of that might give a doll the human quality I'd need for a sexual encounter.

I listen to another guy tell how it used to be all 'sex, sex, sex' until he found fulfilment with his dolls.

'Well, that's just greedy,' I say to the next man featured. He's busy applying lipstick to one doll after another, lining up his 'five girls', as he lovingly refers to them, for a group photo. One Silicone Frankie is all I'd need. But then I realise I shouldn't be so quick to judge. A silicone backup wouldn't go astray—I just can't think of anyone else I'd want it modelled on right now.

I don't think twice about going into Jack's on Sunday—I know he won't be there. The thing that surprises me is that on Monday I don't really think much about going in either, or at least *overthink* it. I do feel a bit awkward but there's no sick feeling in my stomach, no butterflies, which really just tells me that I was right, there really isn't anything between us. I just hope Jack's OK.

'Hi, Fiona.'

His greeting sounds pretty much the same as usual, maybe a tiny bit flatter. Perhaps I'd got him wrong. He's definitely not a Scorpio taking it so lightly, even a Sagittarian would be a bit fiery about it. He must be an Aquarian, they're very detached. Jack appears fine through the whole interaction. He's so fine that it makes me totally fine too and then we're both so fine that we're back to our usual banter as though Saturday night never happened.

24

Frankie and BIG are so immersed in their conversation that I'm seemingly invisible when I slip in straight off the bus from work. I hope all my pre-departure primping and preening has withstood the trip. In my Ms Middle-of-the-Road way I note they are having a serious conversation about the merchant fees for different credit cards—well, Frankie is delivering a nasally lecture and telling BIG what to do. Strangely, I find this loud, bossy side of Frankie quite appealing. It's not normally my style but there's something about the way he does it that makes it slightly endearing—not quite enough for me to list it as an official item on my mental list of Endearing Things About Frankie. Not for now anyway. I'll keep it on standby though.

I scoot around the shop in record time and am soon placing four items on the counter. 'Hello, Frankie,' I say, looking towards the doorway, where he is still talking merchant fees with BIG.

'Hello, Fiona.'

I stand at the counter, money gathering sweat in my hand. For a moment I consider not saying anything more, just looking down and waiting—he seems very pre-occupied with bossing BIG around.

Nothing is going to happen unless you make it happen. Jane's in my head reminding me, not that she'd endorse this situation.

'What time do you guys close?' My voice comes out soft and fluttery, as though carried by a breeze.

'It depends who's working,' says Frankie flirtatiously. I watch his hands move to his chest. 'If it's me, I'll wait for you.'

There's something about the way he holds his hands, the way he moves them. Whatever it is, it affects me deep inside, making me feel like I'm going to stop breathing.

Oh Great Govinda, look at those pecs. I can see them through his shirt. After my week of not looking in—I'd banned myself leading up to so-a-*date*-date to give Jack a chance—I feel like someone who's just come off a diet and there is Frankie, a big bowl of acquired-taste eye candy. Best of all, he is entirely calorie free. You can't ever be sure when opportunity will knock again, so I let my eyes linger. Pretending to be looking at his hands is the perfect excuse to appreciate the physicality of his pecs without appearing obvious (I'm on a spiritual path, not becoming a Buddhist nun). The black T-shirt he's wearing has a white rabbit on it and stripes of red and green that stretch across those pecs. Behold, my relationship corner Feng Shui bunny candles! Now Foreigner's 'Hot Blooded' has come on the radio.

Even though everything from my head down feels as though it has begun to melt, I'm not going to pass out. 'Should I phone ahead so you know whether you need to bother?' I say and Frankie laughs.

'Doesn't need my quips explained' will definitely make my mental list of Endearing Things About Frankie.

'Seven fifteen is safe, seven thirty is pushing it. I work Monday and Tuesday evenings,' Frankie says, adding to my delight by catering to my penchant for detail.

'Mondays are later?' I say, thinking that I have seen them open until eight on a Monday. The fear of sounding like a stalker doesn't enter my brain.

'Yeah.'

In my drifty state, I know that we have had some sort of eye contact during this exchange. It must have been broken at some point, though, as he is now ringing up my items and putting them into my enviro bag.

Frankie hands me my bag and we look into each other's eyes. *Someone get me a snorkel—I think I might be drowning!*

'Thanks.' I float out with my items, putting my head down as I squeeze past BIG, who shuffles to his left to let me through. He's been watching the entire time. I have a thought but I push it immediately out of my mind. Falling victim to Frankie and BIG is not a yoghurt-tethered-torture scenario I can afford to entertain.

It's just one step, and one long glide home. I don't feel my feet touch the ground.

'Now you've asked Jack out, why don't you consider asking Frankie out?' Lionel's suggestion nearly makes me flip out of the apricot recliner.

'Don't be ridiculous. I would never do that.' I'm far too surprised to clarify that, technically, I didn't quite ask Jack out.

'That just goes to show there's more at risk with Frankie, but I already knew that. It's obvious, the way you light up when you talk about him. That doesn't ever happen with

Jack.' Lionel's back on Team Frankie since being updated on recent events.

'So why make me go through it?'

'I wanted you to experience it for yourself so you'd learn to trust your own instincts.'

Lionel does get me thinking, though not about asking Frankie out—I might be making progress but I haven't had a complete personality transplant. I could do something less extreme, like write him a note although even that would be the equivalent of a major organ transplant. What would I say in it anyway?

Besides—I don't want to push my luck—the positive energies in my life are manifesting in another, crucial, way: the Universe had delivered me another potentially perfect job—admin manager at the College of Sinology Studies.

Back at work after my lunchtime session with Lionel I'm busy-bored. I even spark up at Rosemary Hatchment limping towards my desk, then notice she's brandishing half a filing cabinet of papers.

'Oh, look at you, you poor thing,' she says on arrival. 'Are you alright?'

'I'm fine, thanks, Rosemary. Just a bit tired.' I take the papers from her. Why she needs notes typed up when she's taught the subject for a million years I've no idea.

'So long as you're sure.' She's already limping away.

The next morning I don't so much wake, as am torpedoed from sleep. At 4.30 I sit bolt upright in a panic attack. Sure, I'd had a few lately but it was as though Rosemary and her concerned look had made me see things I'd been trying to ignore.

I calm myself slightly with some hypno-breathing and reach for my water bottle. My fingers land on something soft and sludgy. It takes a moment in the darkness to work out what it is. A slug! A sense of queasiness overcomes me. Even worse, I'm out of Rescue Remedy—for the panic attack, not the slug.

When I get to work—after two coffees, thanks to Jack and Bing—Broomstick has amped up her bitchiness to Super Bitch status. Definitely time for a new job and the College of Sinology Studies really does seem perfect. I'm desperate to draw all the energy I need to create the perfect application for the Sinology studies job I have to submit by the deadline tonight so it's a totally appropriate Ms Middle-of-the-Road manoeuvre to go into PGGG again on my way home. It's not like I'm going to throw myself at Frankie or go grabbing a bunch of shallots and spank him with them. I just need some milk. I'm ignoring the fact that there are five other shops I can go to and that I went in yesterday.

Though there is one concern that I can't quite get around, not necessarily restricted to just Frankie. On Saturday, when I bought some new foundation, the sales assistant gave me some free testers. Of course I took them eagerly. Who doesn't love a free tester? They're almost as good as a gift with purchase. Fossicking through my free tester booty I'd discovered not just an eye cream but an Intense Reinforcing Anti-Wrinkle Eye Cream. The hide of her! How very dare she infer that I need it! Sure, I have a teensy trace of a line or two but not nearly as many as other 35-year-olds and they're hardly noticeable, certainly not in a triple-whammy Intense and Reinforcing and Anti-Wrinkle eye cream needing sort of way, or so I'd thought.

Now in PGGG, Frankie is looking at my face and I am spiralling off and two and two have become something like a hundred and twenty-four and I know without a doubt that he's noticing all my cronish wrinkles that are apparently obvious to everyone but me. I had thought the way he focusses on my left side weird and hadn't been able to figure it out but I now have an answer: obviously it is the most crinkly side of me and he's been busy counting the Intense Reinforcing Anti-Wrinkle Eye Cream–needing lines of my left eye, to guess my age, like counting the rings of a tree trunk.

Although maybe there's another explanation. Perhaps it's the yang male energy of my left side that appeals to him. Maybe Frankie and Ms Terse-at-the-Till are nothing at all. He and BIG do seem very close, he spends an awful lot of time with him. Maybe he is gay and a feeder!

Thankfully before the image of Frankie and BIG in bed together—naked apart from BIG's bib, Frankie feeding him chocolate-dipped strawberries laden with whipped cream—has a chance to fully form in my mind's eye, I realise I'm being ridiculous. Even if I disregard all the stereotypes and the nice comfortable excuse for Frankie not making a move on me, if he were gay I'd have no trouble looking him in the eye and we'd be best friends by now. And, hello, a gay guy would not *ever* forget my name and even if he did, he'd cover it up so perfectly with a suitably endearing generic term I wouldn't even realise he had.

No, I was pretty sure Frankie wasn't gay. Which left me with only the confusing reality of Situation Frankie.

At the counter, Frankie's eyes settle on my hands for a second. I already liberally apply hand cream to them—not anti-wrinkle, I admit—but I'm not overly paranoid about them. I watch his eyes move from my hand to my face. We look at each other. He has that look people get when they're about to say something more meaningful than 'Would you like me to bag that for you?' or 'Do you have forty cents?' (That had been a disaster, expecting me to manage change—I'd almost died with the effort of trying to get it out, my hands shaking as they were). I hold my breath. I can feel the words so close to the tip of his tongue that I want to reach across, squeeze his cheeks and force them out.

'Frankie!' bloody BIG calls, waddling up to the doorway.

Seriously! Motherfornicating Goddess hell, haven't you got buns to eat or something, man?

'Thank you, please come again,' Frankie playfully reads the top of my receipt as he hands it to me but not before rolling his eyes and smiling because BIG has started talking even though Frankie doesn't quite appear to be listening.

'Thank you, Frankie,' I say in that sing-song way that over-takes me around him these days. As I turn to walk away, I knock my elbow on the stack of baskets. This clumsiness is to-tally torturous, making a spectacle in front of him when all Ms Middle-of-the-Road wants to do is maintain a cool, calm and collected appearance. I'm not klutzy or clumsy anywhere else.

I can't let it upset my energies though, I've got the application for the College of Sinology Studies to submit.

25

That is the way my life goes for several weeks, victim of super bitch Broomstick and frequent visits to PGGG without any real advancements with Frankie. But then I discover I've secured an interview.

When the day comes, I wake more excited than nervous.

The squelch of a dead gecko between my toes isn't the best way to start the day for me or the gecko but particularly the gecko—it hadn't been dead until I trod on it. I don't let the incident dampen my positivity; it must have just been the gecko's time.

Being able to walk to the College of Sinology Studies is just another plus to this apparently perfect role. I'm sure I'll immediately become a nicer person not having to endure the nightmare of public transport every day. Although I definitely won't do the walk in one and a half inch heels in future. My feet are screaming already and I'm only halfway. Not that I'm going to let scrunched toes come between me and my shiny new future, even if they are lethal weapons where geckos are concerned. I'm powered up with the Act My Life technique

Amethyst emailed out in her monthly newsletter this week (such timing!). It's all about acting confident over and over until I become it and it becomes me. So I'm sure meditating on the traits I want to embody, visualising myself having them, telling myself that today I'm going to be confident and professional and bracing myself for action will pay off. Lionel and I had also done some more work on my anxiety.

I'm dressed the part: a dark professional suit with some angular quirks so I still feel like me. I had considered my black and gold cheongsam momentarily; perhaps they'd appreciate a little cultural authenticity. But then a little voice inside my head reminded me I was going for an interview as an admin manager not a yum cha waitress.

Prepared with my spiritual fake it till I make it technique I head confidently across the road into the uni grounds. Even though I'm surrounded by lush green grass, I feel myself being wrapped in a blanket of fog. It's nothing tangible but the energy is all wrong. Oppression oozes up from the ground, presses down from the sky, squeezes in on me from the regal sandstone buildings and their mismatched neighbours. The black windows and broken venetian blinds of the ugly seventies concrete slabs make them seem as though they're blinking sadly against the beauty of their stained-glass counterparts.

Which method of dull, grey, suffocation is worse? I wonder. *The environment here or with Broomstick?*

Maybe it's just unfamiliar. I try to convince myself that my gut reaction to run is nothing more than the fear of facing the interview coming through now I'm closer.

However, things go from bad to worse when I walk into the building. A morgue would look like a nightclub in comparison. *I would die in here.* It's not so much a thought as a knowing.

Scratchy writing on a post-it note stuck to the door with yellowing sticky tape tells me I've arrived at Room 107. The writer has used a fine point pen. I hate fine point pens—people who use them as a preference are pedantic and mean spirited.

The office, when I enter it, is even more morgue-like. Neither of the people look up—they're both staring blankly at their computer screens—although one does show signs of life, flicking at woodgrain veneer that's peeling from the edge of her desk. I stand for a moment and still neither of them acknowledge me. I ring the little bell on the counter.

My mind wanders as I wait. Perhaps Spirit has sent me here as a reminder to be grateful for what I have—still, I can't quite see Broomstick as a gift, not even a dodgy thrice re-gifted Kris Kringle.

Then I'm called into the interview. By the time I've nodded and smiled and said, 'Lovely to meet you,' to each of the panel members, all of whom appear to be cardboard cut-outs from the crowd at the compliance workshop I attended with Broomstick, I'm quite dizzy. Six really is excessive.

I don't quite glide over the questions with the ease and grace of an Olympic skater but it's certainly not the disaster the Consulate interview was. I'm not sure if it's the work I've done with Lionel or because there's so much less at stake. I wouldn't want this job now if they paid me, which of course they would, and quite well.

The question of how something that seems so right can be so wrong raises itself in my head again.

With rats, slugs and dead geckos popping up as my totem animals and my perfect jobs being flops, things aren't looking up for me on the enlightenment front. But all of that is about to change. Today is Enlightenment Day—Amethyst's one-day inner urban retreat. Sure, it's a bit pricey but it's an investment in my future. I'm all geared up to embrace my femininity, harness the power of my intuitive female knowing and wisdom, and out the Goddess within.

To begin the day, Amethyst guides her Goddesses-in-Training through the Moon Goddess meditation. We're all lying on the carpeted floor of the hired healing space, since Amethyst's clinic is far too small to fit us in. 'You are the divine, heaven and earth, pure love and energy flow through each and every one of you. The karmic forces connect us, we are all as one. In your mind's eye I want you to visualise the light that connects you to your neighbour and all living things.

'Lie back and bathe in the radiance of connection and cosmic knowing, soak up the Goddess wisdom, strength and love.' Amethyst pauses, no doubt tuning in to her guides. 'Share that wisdom through your light, see it shining from you, radiating from every cell of your body, the very essence of your being ...' Her delivery takes on a near evangelical fervour.

I'm not really a moon howler, I realise, lying on the carpet. I'm bored, and quite itchy; I'm finding it hard to stay still.

By the time the Moon Goddess meditation finally ends I've relived virtually every interaction I've had with Frankie. I can't possibly manage to recount all the signs, even though I'd tried. There've been thousands. I see them everywhere—part of me is always on the lookout. I do need to be careful with that, though. I'd literally almost been hit by a bus yesterday.

Up off the floor, I work hard to emulate an authentically enlightened Goddess expression, smiling beatifically at each of my neighbours, taking their hands for the Moon Goddess Unification chant. The Goddesses-in-Training form a circle around Amethyst, who flings herself around the Intention Stick. We'd made the stick earlier, each tying a ribbon around it to symbolise our special intentions. I don't mean to be disrespectful but I can't imagine some of the moves she's doing would really appeal to the Moon Goddess—there's gyrating and thrusting, among other things—she looks like pole dancer doing interpretive dance in a kaftan. The circle moves clockwise as Amethyst continues to writhe. The little cymbals strapped to her fingers are making quite a din and kicking her feet around the way she is ensures maximum impact from her brass Indian ankle bells.

The blur of her kaftan returns to the solid colours of High Priestess purple and Goddess gold (the colours had come to her in a dream, she told us in the same way most people would say, 'I picked it up at a stocktake sale') as she slows. When her jingling and jangling stop, so do we.

I take a huge Pranayama-style meditation breath to disguise what is really a sigh of relief. The clanging of metal on metal, the chanting, the sweetness of the Nag Champa incense, the clamminess of the hands of people I don't know, Amethyst's spinning, us circling around her and the swirling colours had started to make me feel a little unwell.

With a clang of the cymbals on Amethyst's right hand and an 'Om Shrim Som Somaya Namah' we're off again. Oh Goddess, have mercy. Anticlockwise this time, which she indicates with some dramatic circling and cymbal snapping of her left arm and hand above her head. I imagine it's to balance out the energy from all our clockwise work but right now I'd give anything just to lie down for another Moon Goddess meditation. Or a nap.

Once Amethyst has received the message from the Moon Goddess that we've hit the right energetic note and reached our karmic chanting quota, she proudly announces that it's time for 'the special ceremony for the Goddesses who are having their divine feminine moon time'.

I'm not, but I wouldn't admit to it even if I was. There is no way I'd be going into the red tent in the corner of the room: a red sheet that has been strung up to cordon off one small section. I cannot believe she's scheduled this in just before lunch. It's a period not a spiritual experience, for Govinda's sake. It's not the Goddess worshipping her womb, it's messy, it's painful, it's inconvenient, you pig out, you puff up and you're either so wet and weepy that you could be mistaken for a depressed goldfish or you're spitting and kicking like a llama with lethal intentions—sometimes both simultaneously.

I zip my lips into a tight smile, feeling the words, 'Oh for fuck's sake,' buzzing at the base of my throat chakra like an angry wasp wanting to fly out from my Vishuddha to sting everyone in its path. I take the symbolic chunk of garnet from my neighbour and hold it against my abdomen as every woman before me has done, drawing on the energy of the crystal to reclaim our collective power and bond in the unity of womanhood and Goddess energy. As I pass it on to the next woman, whose name tag tells me she's Megan, she looks me up and down with a slightly superior look. Megan's wearing mauve. And not just Megan, nearly every other Goddess-in-Training is in mauve too. There's so much mauve it's upsetting my aura and it's *such* a try-hard cliché to choose the colour of spiritual awakening.

After the garnet passing, we break for lunch.

'I knew it, I knew there was something impure about your energy when I got the garnet from you,' Megan says to me, eyeing my takeaway coffee cup.

'I normally use a KeepCup but I'm so tired I left it on my kitchen bench.'

'I can't *believe* you putrefy your system with that,' she takes a sip of whatever is in her enviro cup, an almond milk turmeric latte no doubt.

I'd thought part of why she'd looked me up and down at the garnet exchange was because I'm all in black. She wouldn't have been the first person today to ask me if it was a conscious choice I was making to impede my energetic connection, drowning my energy field in such a negative colour. Two other Goddesses-in-Training had done so before the Welcoming Prayer. 'Actually on the label it's called Obsidian,' I could have retorted but I knew I'd only sound like a pretentious, unenlightened, superficial bitch.

A twenty-something in a white and, yes, mauve Lululemon outfit with a 'daily yoga by the beach at sunrise' vibe bounds up to Megan and me. 'I'm Goddess Phoenix,' she tells us and throws herself around Megan in a hug. She lets Megan go and turns to me. It's too late for me to make a getaway, there's nothing to do but reciprocate. I count to three, then let go.

'Can you believe she's toxifying her system with caffeine?' Megan sounds more aghast than she did when she said it to me directly, as though she's inferring they need to organise a purity intervention.

At afternoon tea (herbal) I text Jane to see if she can meet this evening. I'm so desperate to laugh, I'll beg her to snort for me if I have to. I know I should chat to my fellow Goddesses-in-Training but I'm all feminine-energied out. Jane's much more yang than yin. And busying myself with my phone gives me the perfect excuse not to join in the 'What came to me in my afternoon meditation' discussion; the visions are getting extreme and I'd never be able to come up with anything as close to Nirvana as they claimed to have experienced—I'd actually fallen asleep, which practically is a spiritual experience for me these days. I'm still feeling a bit groggy but Amethyst's 'Lessons from Hindsight' talk—the final thing on today's agenda—will get me buzzing. She's in the workshop room seeking guidance from her guides about which experiences to share now. It's going to be amazing.

And it is—very reassuring.

Dusk is descending on Enlightenment Day and Jane and I huddle in the corner of a café. Much to my relief, our hug felt almost normal again. It's been a while since we caught up, mostly because we just haven't been able coordinate our schedules and a full debrief of the Jack so-a-*date*-date was still to be had. I've already filled Jane in on the mauve brigade and the red tent. I can't repeat what she said about that.

'So, you know when someone says, "Wait for it, this is the hysterical bit," you pretty much know it's going to be disap-pointing?'

'Oh god, the worst.'

'That and more. But he seems totally fine now. It's as though it never happened, he still flirts like a frisky little ferret and tries to touch my hand even though he's got to know it's pointless. I couldn't even kiss him, for Buddha's sake.'

'I told you he would. He probably doesn't get it. Men are pretty dumb really, Kizzo. He might just think—forget that, men really don't think.'

For all her ease with men, Jane isn't the male gender's biggest fan, beyond their obvious purpose.

'Is Mr Mural still around?'

Jane flicks her hand in the air and leans forward. 'I did, how-ever, have a bit of an interlude with this guy I met on Friday night.'

I spoon some non-crisis chocolate cake (Megan and Phoenix would have a fit) into my mouth as Jane embarks on the tale of Mr Friday Night. I watch her, trying to imagine her at the school gate with other mothers. I can't.

'Will you see him again?' I ask after we've snorted our way through some of her more risqué anecdotes.

'No, definitely a once-in-a-lifetime experience, that one.' Jane proclaims, then does her eye-narrowing thing again and brings up Frankie.

'Nothing really,' I say. 'I mean, nothing that's a big deal. I'm doing really well being Ms Middle-of-the-Road, just seeing what happens.' I shove another spoonful of chocolate cake in my mouth, hoping it will get me out of having to disclose anything more.

'Honestly, Kismet—'

'I went for a job interview. It was perfect, except when it wasn't.'

'How so?'

Credit to her for not pushing me on Frankie. I know how much she loves to voice her opinion.

I fill in the blanks of the what and where of the interview before I declare it, 'Dead boring, serious and stifling beyond even Broomstick.'

Jane looks shocked. 'That bad?'

'Unfortunately so.'

'What are you going to do?'

'You know—I really don't know. Keep looking, I guess.' I shrug. 'What about you. How's life in the land of art?'

'Pretty quiet, actually. I haven't been getting much work since the mural. Not even any hideous corporate commissions in the offing but something will come up. It always does.'

It will. Jane was born under a pretty lucky star. Even so, I have a scarily Catherine-esque thought: If Jane is going to be providing for two maybe she should find something more stable.

'Would you ever consider becoming an art teacher?' The words are out before I can stop them.

Jane shoots me a look that tells me Ms Middle-of-the-Road has ventured way too far onto the straight and narrow, and I have to agree.

'Just a thought, not saying it was a good one.'

'You're the one that's good with kids not me. I'll be fine with one of my own but a room full of them ...' Jane pulls a horrified face.

'How's your mum with it now, has she adjusted?' I ask, Spirit having provided the perfect segue.

'Freaking hell, Kiz, she's so adjusted that I've had to tell her to back off. I'm pretty sure I'm going to do it, but it's not one hundred per cent and she's already talking about plans for when we go overseas. I mean that'll be ages away yet, if it ever happens. There are so many forms and red tape. I'll have killed her if she keeps this up.'

I laugh, even though inside, a little coil of disappointment is unfurling. When I've thought about it, I'd imagined me going with Jane. We'd always done big events together. I'm not going to get upset about it now; like she said, even if it did happen, it would be ages away. Anything could happen between now and then.

Someone's chakras are out of balance this morning. Unusually for a Monday morning they're not mine, Buddha be blessed. A guy has trundled up to the bus stop screaming blue murder and wanting to fight people. Having one of those old lady shopping carts is ruining his tough guy image somewhat, as is being hunched over and about seventy-five.

The herd of commuters waiting for the bus, ready if not willing to be transported to their slaughter houses for the working week, focus even more intently than usual on their phones. All except me.

As I do every day, I've strategically positioned myself at the bus stop to be in Frankie's line of vision should he come out to do some very environmentally unfriendly disposal of cardboard into the bin (one day when I can speak to him like a normal person, I really must tell him to recycle). I admit, all this primping, preening and constantly being on anxious alert is exhausting, but on the upside, it's great for my posture. No matter how tired I feel, I've become so chronically aware of the way I stand that I won't allow myself even a glimmer of a slump. Everything has a positive. Of course I'm hoping to manifest something a little more positive than just good postural alignment with Frankie quite soon but it's important to practise gratitude: it fuels the positive energies.

There's a collective sigh of relief when the 509 arrives and the crowd merges forward in the bus-boarding hustle—all except Mr I-Don't-Like-Mondays, who pushes and shoves, ramming his way to the front. We wait as he struggles with his cart and attempts to board the bus.

'You fucking dog bastard, I bet you fucked your fucking mother last night, didn't you?' It is entirely understandable that no one has offered to help him. 'You motherfucking bastard! And then you would have sucked your father's dick.' He starts backing away, still at war with his trolley.

'Off—not on my route,' I imagine the driver has said to him.

Top marks to the old guy for expletive expression, though! Even with my former fondness for swearing I couldn't have come up with a tirade like that. Not that I would've ever hurled abuse at anyone directly but pre-Amethyst I had such a penchant for the foul mouth. 'Too much negative energy attached to cursing and cussing,' she told me. I secretly relish my occasional lapses.

The Universe delivers its gifts in unexpected ways—I notice Frankie has come out to watch the kerfuffle. I set my manifesting in motion, and visualise him tearing down the street like a knight in shining armour to protect his delicate flower (that would be me) from such outrageous behaviour—my life hanging in the balance, at risk of being mowed down and run over repeatedly by an insane, foul-mouthed old man with a granny cart until she is nothing but a mound of pulverised flesh in a designer outfit. I even close my eyes really hard because everyone knows the tighter you close your eyes, the more likely your wish is to come true but when I open them, not only is there no sign of Frankie transforming his sneakers into a white steed to rush to my rescue, he's laughing and chatting with another woman. And she's younger than me and not at all dowdy.

How dare he, *how very dare he*!

I have the tiniest flutter of a thought to get Beyoncé beyond my butt and storm down there to F that bitch up, while singing 'Hold Up' to Frankie—but I'd already waited so long for the bus—and I was on a higher plane than that. People who had an Enlightenment Day attendance certificate calling them a Moon Goddess didn't go bitch-slapping people in the street. Although Enlightenment Day hadn't quite brought what I'd hoped for in the way of miracles, insights or epiphanies. I'd be sticking to one-on-one sessions with Amethyst from now on. (I don't know what I was thinking—I'm really not a group person.) It had, however, provided me with the details of Marcus, Phoenix's shaman, and Charisma, Megan's past-life person. There were obviously just a few more stepping stones on the path to enlightenment than I'd initially imagined.

By the end of the day I've made appointments with both Marcus and Charisma. Charisma's first available is four weeks away. He must be fantastic. Some people may deem having a Spiritual Support Pit Crew of four practitioners excessive. But while Amethyst and Lionel are working on the mechanics of the lock, I still feel like I need to find the key that will slide perfectly into it and open up the chamber that holds all the answers. It's not like I'm going to be seeing them all every day, and having a back-up is always a good idea; who knows when a girl might have to pull in to the energetic healing pits for an emergency tune-up or quick spiritual grease and oil change. Even though I'm doing quite well as Ms Middle-of-the-Road there's always the risk that even a finely tuned machine can malfunction.

In my fully-in-control state, focussed on the white centre line, I decided not to go into PGGG after work. It's one thing to turn away from me in the street and forget my name but Frankie had flaunted his flirtation as I'd faced imminent death, for Buddha's sake. That sort of behaviour is totally unacceptable and unacceptable behaviour of that magnitude officially calls for a huff, so I'll flounce past with a flick of my hair this evening. Even if Frankie doesn't notice, which given how oblivious he'd been to my rampaging-hippo act in store weeks ago, I don't imagine he will—I'll know and that's all that matters.

Clearly I'm making progress with Lionel.

Which all (somehow) brings me to another point. Why, with his long legs and big Adidas feet, hasn't Frankie offered to carry my shopping for me? It would take him under five minutes on a round trip. I'd witnessed him make it back from the street to behind the counter in nearly a single bound on several occasions. True, the expectation may be a little premature given that he'd only just managed to remember my name but everyone else seemed more than fine with the idea of providing home delivery—at least of them doing it, not Frankie. Jack was still making moves to deliver my coffee after everything and even Derek from the little supermarket that doesn't even rate a mention in my world had almost begged me to let him do home delivery the other day. Frankie would be well advised to get in touch with his chivalry genes. Of course I'd decline but I'd like the right of refusal to a chivalrous offer by him.

Unfortunately that train of thought leads me into the very dark tunnel of wondering why Frankie didn't say, 'Sorry, you did tell me your name but I've forgotten it,' like any normal, civilised, reasonably caring person would do.

Deep hypno-breath—I can't afford to get dragged under by thoughts like that if I'm going to maintain my huff but I also can't afford to undo it by overriding the thought with items from my mental list of Endearing Things About Frankie. I'm not sure if it is appropriate to take a Ms Middle-of-the-Road approach to a huff but I do, so as not to topple too far either way. It works quite spectacularly. As I pass by PGGG on my way home I flounce like I've never flounced before.

26

It's the chocolate brown recliner with Positively for my Lionel session this week. My lack of sleep is making me fragile and the bear really is quite comforting. I look deeply into his glass button eyes for a little pre-cuddle permission, then hold him against me.

'You seem to be growing quite attached to Positively, Kismet. You might get one for your birthday—Oh, I see I'm a month or so too late,' Lionel says.

Am I the only one in this trio (I include Positively) still clinging to the hope that I might get a real-life, breathing, non-stuffed bedfellow?

As lovely as Lionel is and as much as I've relaxed into our now customary end-of-session hugs, I certainly wouldn't ever be able to sleep with a bear he gave me. And if I were to live out the remainder of my days—or nights—sleeping with an inanimate object, Silicone Frankie was going to win big, work-roughened hands down every time. I begin to wonder if I influenced Lionel's inability to imagine me with a real-life bedfellow with so many thoughts of Silicone Frankie. But again realise I need to get down to business.

I tell Lionel about the College of Sinology Studies job first. I swear if he says, 'Getting clarity on what you don't want helps you refine what you do want,' I'll scream. I know that's true but I'm tired and over trying to figure out what I should do.

Mercifully he doesn't.

'That must have been very disappointing. It really did sound perfect for you.'

'I know. I can't believe it. I can't figure out what I'm doing wrong.'

'Don't be so hard on yourself. You've only had two interviews. Getting to the interview is a success in itself. You're doing that every time, most people don't. So tell me, how did you go with the anxiety?'

'Better, not nearly as bad. Maybe that was because I didn't really want it.'

'Or maybe there's been some improvement. Give yourself that. It's just a matter of time. Now, Frankie?'

'There's not much to tell ...' I begin but somehow find myself talking about Frankie for ages. The bus stop incident with the old man is turned into an amusing anecdote by my OTT indignant outrage.

'I want you to tell me about your past relationships, Kismet.' Lionel rubs his beard.

'I really don't want to do this, Lionel.' When I say I really don't want to do it I mean, I really, really don't want to do it. I've promised myself I won't ever cry over a man again and if we do this, I will. When I say I've moved on from my relationships, it's more that I've locked those events and memories in a dark room and thrown away the key. Now here is Lionel with a bobby pin, trying to unpick the lock.

'Why?'

'They weren't great relationships and I'm a different person now. Some things are just best left in the past.'

'But you've brought that past with you—you're lugging it around, letting it get in the way. Do you know what I think? I think you're afraid of being hurt again. Don't kid yourself into believing I can't see that pain. All your imaginings, fantasising and dramatics, as endearing and amusing as they are, they're just a decoy.'

Seriously, if I'd known that Lionel was going to turn everything around on me I would've kept it to myself. I blink furiously to try to get rid of the tears already bubbling.

'No, I just get bored easily, Lionel. I need to entertain myself.'

'True in part, perhaps, but there are much healthier ways to exercise your imagination. The way you get all prickly and huffy is nothing more than an echidna using its quills to protect itself from pain. Even the rigidity and tension in the way you hold yourself works to keep people away.'

We're both quiet for a moment.

'Fine, Lionel. You win.' I reach for a tissue. Now we've started this I may as well get it over with. I clutch Positively a little more tightly. My voice has none of the smooth slowness it usually has when I'm under hypnosis. It quavers and quakes, dragging through the pieces of rubble that didn't get swept away when I rebuilt my heart.

What Lionel finds most interesting is not the fact that, yes, both my exes happened to marry someone else before they were exes, but that I've always chosen men who are not quite available. In my defence, it wasn't like Tommy Tung had really wanted to marry someone else—it was his obligation to his family. Then there was Wang Kang Qi—Wang Ka, as he became known after he'd been meant to come for dinner and just didn't show up—not a word. When I bumped into his brother and he told me Wang had got married, I'd wanted to kill him. I hadn't. He was much less of a loss than Tommy Tung had been. Of course I could have phoned Wang when he didn't turn up, even if to check he was OK, but deep down I knew he was—even then my intuition was strong. And to call and demand an explanation wasn't really me. I'd always had a bit of an issue with my pride.

'Is your freedom really that important to you, Kismet?' Lionel asks over the buzzer.

As I leave Lionel's office, I think back to family lunch on Sunday. Mum had insisted on driving me home, which meant Dad drove and she came along for the ride. Not that Mum can't drive, I've just never seen her do it when Dad's around.

A trip with Mum and Dad is always excruciating, their bickering intensified in the confines of the car, and there's always a detour: Dad seeking an out-of-the-way newsagency he'd heard stocked back copies of *Golfing Weekly*, and Mum just wanting to drop something off to Mrs So-and-So, seeing as we'd sort of be passing—if passing meant a ten- or twenty-minute diversion.

'Now, about our anniversary dinner, you haven't forgotten, have you?' Mum said as soon as our seatbelts were clicked.

I honestly can't remember ever hearing about it but, then again, things had been getting a bit hazy lately. There's a good reason sleep deprivation is used as torture.

'Bev, give the girl a break. Can't you see she's exhausted?'

Oh holy Govinda, I'd thought, *if Dad's noticed it's worse than I'd realised.*

'I'm just *mentioning* it, Reggie. You're not the law on what I can say.'

Those sort of nagging domestic differences and the way Catherine is with Brian, the claustrophobic nature of it all, were exactly the answer to Lionel's question I needed. Yes. If that was the alternative, my freedom really was that important.

The fact that I can't decide whether I need a jacket or not as I prepare to head down to PGGG after all my usual preparations on Monday night reminds me how quickly time is passing. *If I'm going to wear a jacket is this the best one to wear? I think I better curl my eyelashes one more time. Am I sure I really do need this jacket?* It was all critical, given Frankie had been laughing with that younger woman. Even though, as Lionel had pointed out, I may have been overreacting slightly.

It isn't until I'm at the till at PGGG that Frankie suddenly appears. He shuffles the young guy away from the counter and gestures towards the storeroom. 'You go pack up back there, I'll do this.'

Ms Middle-of-the-Road score ten out of ten—I don't even have to stop the thought that he's using a secret code to prepare my hostage quarters because it doesn't come.

'Hi, Fiona.'

'Hi, Frankie.'

He's nonchalant, I'm sing-song.

'You didn't come in last week.'

'No, I got caught at work.' I remain pokerfaced to stop the grinning fool inside of me from escaping.

'I see.' Frankie's smile seems to have a knowingness to it. Maybe he did see me flounce by.

We look at each other, silent—I don't think either of us is going to be taking up a spot on the public-speaking circuit anytime soon. I blame all my pent-up Goddess energy from Enlightenment Day for what I do next.

'Um, have you got any cinnamon, please?' I double-check there's no one who can see me, then indulge in physical appreciation of his torso as he stretches to the spices above the counter. If BIG comes waddling in I'll die.

'Sticks or ground?' Frankie's up on tiptoes, head out of sight.

Shiva. I am not good on the spot, especially as I'm quite preoccupied hyperventilating at the sight of him reaching up like that. Blind panic makes me squeak, 'Just one of each would be great, thanks.'

He starts singing along to Bonnie Tyler's 'I Need a Hero' and I keep watching, thanking Buddha, Govinda and every God and Goddess known to man, woman, dog and spirit that he is taking so long.

'Thanks.' I'm not quite able to meet his eye as he scans the spices.

When I do look up, Frankie is looking at me, smiling broadly. I can't help but look right into his eyes. It's like I'm standing on the edge of a volcano and I can feel myself tumbling into a place that I may not ever get out of alive.

'Fiona.' Frankie brings me back to reality.

'Oh. Sorry.'

'Twenty-five fifty, please.'

For this evening's in-store clumsiness, I trip over my own feet as I walk away. I grab the end of the counter to steady myself and turn back—Frankie is still smiling at me.

I somehow arrive home via a trip to Planet Swoon.

You have the power to say no or to walk away, the Lovers' Oracle card tells me. Of course I do—technically—but it's as though a furnace has been lit under the energetic powerhouse of my hara. From the fire it's creating in my belly I realise that no matter what I do or don't know about Frankie, any question of walking away has disappeared into the ether. Whatever crazy experiment the Universe has going on in the test tube of my life, as illogical as it seems, something's going to happen with Frankie and me—I know it.

27

The thing with exceptionally good moods, like the one I'm in after last night, is that they can be suddenly ripped away from you. Work will do it every time. Mine begins to waver when I see Rosemary Hatchment hobbling towards me.

We keep our greetings brief.

'Fiona, I just wanted to check up on those notes I left the other week.'

'Oh yes, of course, your notes.' I scramble around my desk, desperately trying to find the right pile of papers. 'Here they are.'

'They'll be ready for my class tomorrow afternoon, won't they?' Rosemary sounds doubtful.

'Absolutely, Rosemary.' I nod reassuringly as I leaf through her scratchy, hand-written fiscal policy notes. Though I'm not sure how—I haven't even looked at them.

'By the way, are you *sure* you're OK, Fiona? You really don't seem yourself lately and you don't look it either.'

'Fine, thanks, Rosemary. Best I get on with these.' Honestly, as if I didn't have enough issues and paranoia about my appearance without everyone telling me how crap I look, not to mention the insult of the Intense Reinforcing Anti-Wrinkle Eye Cream sample.

'Do take it easy. I see you have stuff everywhere. You can only do what you can do. As the saying goes: how do you eat an elephant?'

'One bite at a time,' I reply. Part of me knows she's right but there's a bigger part that wants a circus elephant to sit on her just so I can say, 'Now chew!' She might come closer to understanding that I feel like I have a whole herd of elephants to be eaten and I can't even manage to catch one to tie it down and start chomping.

She's right though, my desk is a shambles. The extreme clutter quotient is very bad Feng Shui for productivity. No wonder I'm not coping quite as well as I usually would.

An hour later, I'm close to having the piles on my desk sorted into 'Red Hot Super Urgent', 'Super Urgent', 'Quite Urgent', 'Average Urgent', 'Below Average Urgent', 'Important But Not Vital', 'Less Important', 'Might Get to It One Day' and 'Can't Even Remember—Hide it in Desmond's Office for Future Shredding'. I can feel my chakras whirring more harmoniously and a sense of control returning as I survey the neatly ordered piles. I would've loved to create a list of the piles and potentially a matrix of what was in them to tick off as I got through them but Ms Middle-of-the-Road had to rein my compulsive side in. *The Thirteenth Tale,* the book that Marianne from Customer Service gave me months ago, had appeared sandwiched between a working copy of *Prioritising Compliance Within the Organisational and Academic Structure* and a fact sheet on government funding requirements. (Kill me now.) I throw it in my handbag. Not that I'm planning on reading it—like I've got the time—but everything that

isn't essential has to go. And I don't want to offend Marianne
by giving it back unread.

On Saturday morning I head down to PGGG wearing an extra
layer of foundation. (Insomnia does nothing for a girl's complexion, not to mention the dark circles!) Unfortunately despite
multiple attempts, my eyelashes haven't curled well and I now
look like I've got a couple of squashed spiders on my eyelids.

'WDE, GI's announced his retirement. SSFC are done for—
RC must be devo. With SB already VC and performing the way
he is, he's bound to get the captaincy. Sutto will be so PO'd.'
Frankie comes down the aisle as though he's about to face a
firing squad.

I assume the acronyms he's hurling around are directed at
Ms Terse-at-the-Till because he's looking at her and doesn't
see me.

'What?' Ms Terse-at-the-Till drawls, barely looking up
from her phone. I'm with her, I haven't got a clue what he's
going on about, but from the desolation in Frankie's voice, it's
the worst thing to happen since Buddha was a boy in his last
incarnation.

Listening in on Frankie's translation to Ms Terse-at-the-
Till—in a totally appropriate, just curious way—I gather that
it's the 'Worst day ever, Greg Inglis has retired, South Sydney
Football Club are done for.' Frankie assumes Russell Crowe
must be devastated and Sam Burgess will be the new captain
and this might piss John Sutton off.

Ms Terse-at-the-Till doesn't say anything, just looks back
at her phone. *Tap, tap, tap,* she goes on her screen. I very
much doubt she's tweeting about it.

I feel a bit bad for Frankie, he looks so crestfallen. There's something sweetly appealing about the way he's so affected, even if it *is* about football!

He's so caught up in it all he doesn't register me, but he's never as friendly when Ms Terse-at-the-Till is around. There's something about her presence that interferes with our energies.

I can't refute that the whole football thing is a blow of mine-blasting proportions. But ever since I'd noticed the bunny logo on Frankie's shirt a while ago, I've been seeing them everywhere. Sammy had even had one on his hoodie on Sunday. Who would've thought the Universe would take it quite so literally when I put those two little red and green bunnies in my relationship corner?

But gratitude where gratitude is due. I have to count my blessings that I hadn't manifested an ugly rabbit person.

'Why didn't you mention those football players—try to connect to him? It's obviously something he's interested in,' Lionel says after I've filled him in on recent events.

I knew Spirit had provided me with a gift—the perfect time to have said, 'Hey, Frankie, guess what? John Sutton and two other Souths players asked me for directions the other week.' I only knew who they were because of Sammy, not that I'd ever be able to tell Sammy I'd seen them. He'd never forgive me for not getting their autographs, or maybe kids wanted selfies these days, but I hadn't done either. The guys had seemed so set on not letting their heart rates drop as they jogged on the spot while I pointed to where they needed to go and I was pretty sure that the reason they'd approached me was because in my black outfit I looked like the girl least likely to know who they were. The guilt at not asking for Sammy's sake was still eating away at me so I'd been trying to put it out of my mind.

'I don't really think I could sustain a conversation about football, Lionel, and why would I want to? I must've lost my mind. A football fanatic? Seriously!'

'You're overthinking it, life isn't always logical. Remember that session we did on just saying the first thing that comes into your mind with Frankie? Actually, you need to stop censoring yourself full stop, not just around Frankie. That's going to be your homework this week—well, forever, actually.'

Oh holy singing Hare Krishnas! Does Lionel have any idea what he would be unleashing on the world if I stopped censoring myself? Surely he knows how dangerous that could be!

I don't do anything other than look shocked, or maybe amused. I'm not even sure which I feel.

Lionel continues, 'No—it won't be that bad. Just do and say what you feel, whether it be in words or in action—just be, Kismet, *just be*.'

'I'm not sure ...' I stop, trying to find the right way to put it. I imagine Broomstick with a chopstick through her chest (or maybe a pile of unravelled paperclips fashioned into a weapon) and people hiding under chairs and tables in the office and on the street, cowering from all the things I currently keep inside. 'I don't know that it's really a safe idea.' My mind had moved on to the carnage I'd create on public transport.

'I know it's an unusual concept. You will have that negative voice inside you that tries to stop you but it's not *you*. It's your anxiety that puts you into this state of censorship. You assume you'll fuck up because you think that just being you is somehow fatally flawed. Just say to it: "Fuck off, like you're so perfect!"'

Lionel has me counting down into hypnosis before I've even come to terms with the fact he just used the word fuck. Twice.

Later, still with the same warm plasticine feeling that hypnosis leaves me with, I walk past the closed shopfront of PGGG. I slow down and look longingly at the store, thinking, *Oh my fated one, why do you forsake me, my Singing Fruiterer?* (Even Ms Middle-of-the-Road needs to get a little Jane Austen occasionally.)

Dharma it to destiny and back. BIG has taken time out from his buns and is on the street, observing my fascination with the PGGG doorway. Karmic curses to him and his cupcake- and cream horn–congested arteries. No doubt he has noted the look of longing on my face and will tell Frankie I looked like a bunny-boiling stalker!

'I can see you've already been doing quite a lot of work on yourself,' Marcus, the shaman that Phoenix recommended, observes as I enter his treatment room. My chakras are humming in their freshly re-harmonised state after my morning session with Amethyst. That's how it is with deep spiritual work: to the untrained eye, progress isn't necessarily obvious, but as a shaman, Marcus can spot it on sight. 'It's my unique combination of marrying the ancient energetic and spiritual-healing wisdom of shamanism and tribal insights with psychotherapy and working physically and neurologically that creates the vital potency of my healing techniques.'

I'm slightly distracted by the way his middle-aged man ponytail bobs and swishes as he speaks but his words hold great promise. The hair is probably just to compensate for his very-sensible-for-a-shaman attire of relaxed business wear.

'Oh no, no, no—this won't do. We can't commence yet,' Marcus says as I lie face up on the treatment table. I imagine he's just realised he's forgotten his feather, and what of his dream catcher?

'There's no way I can get to any other issues until I've reset your body clock. It's totally out of sync.'

I'm not surprised.

'No, there's still something else,' he says ponderously after resetting my body clock. He rests his hands on my head, then my shoulders and then my feet. 'Have you always felt different, like you don't quite belong?'

Phoenix was right, he is very intuitive.

'You landed in the wrong tribe, always on the outside. That's created a sorrow pattern. It's all around having no choice.'

I really had no idea I had so many layers of dysfunction until I started all my healing work—thank Buddha I came upon it.

'I want you to imagine yourself being in a flirty situation with a man you find attractive,' Marcus instructs, once my body clock is ticking in perfect harmony and I'm sorrow-pattern free and have had the chance to address some of the issues on my mind.

Naturally I begin to visualise myself opposite Frankie at the PGGG counter. Well aware that most women would go for something a little more sophisticated—at least a decent bar—I can't help but put myself in the most likely situation. It's only practical. And it's a good benchmark for me to see the progress I've made from when I'd imagined myself opposite him in my Alex the Anxiety session with Lionel.

I do, however, become a little distracted, trying to focus on what song Frankie might be singing. I'm going for gold with The Killers but I can't choose between 'Change Your Mind' and 'Glamorous Indie Rock Roll' and the clearing happens before I have time to conjure the image fully. No harm done.

Marcus assures me that the pattern he uncovered has been released.

I'm quite unsteady on my feet as I get up, so much so that I have to grip the bed.

'Put yourself in silver light for protection till you get home,' Marcus recommends as he sees me out to the reception area. I sit for ten minutes to return fully to my body before I feel ready to navigate public transport.

I'd intended to phone Stephanie when I got home. I hadn't heard from her since leaving some brownies with James the day Mum and Dad had dropped me back. It was the only thing I could think to do to make things a bit easier, Stephanie was so busy running her mum to chemo and other appointments. I'd sent her texts to let her know I was thinking of her but I didn't want to bombard her, or make her feel pressured to reply.

I'd thought about calling Jane too but as soon as I make it home I drop like a boulder onto my bed. I take painkillers for my throbbing head and close my eyes in the hope that it will ease the wooziness. It's probably all the energetic toxins shifting out of my system and my unearthed foundations settling into place, I think, as I slide off my bed to the floor. I crawl to the bathroom. I'm too ill and exhausted to stand up so I have to crouch over the toilet bowl, vomiting.

Back in bed, I can't sleep. Even though my skull feels like it's been pierced with a red hot poker, I pick up *The Thirteenth Tale*.

'Don't be ridiculous, Kismet,' I tell myself. 'You're not going to be getting messages from Spirit via the crinkly pages of a borrowed novel.' But before I get to the end of the page, the words I've just read are planting the seed of an idea that I can feel runs the risk of propagating into an out-of-control vine. I may not be big into whipper-snippering but I need to snip the thought right off at the roots and forget I ever had it. I don't even let myself think it fully for fear of it wrapping its sticky tendrils into my brain. Still, it hovers there as I manage to drift back to sleep.

28

Sunday morning, my chakras settled, clear of my migraine and nausea, I wake from a dream that feels like déjà vu, so real I could swear I'd astro travelled and was back there again. 'There' being Shanghai, in the area I'd visited for my birthday a few years ago.

In the dream I relived it all, walking down the same streets, smelling the same incense from the popular temple, street food being fried in sesame oil, large trees creating the cleanest air in the city, surrounded by the same sense of comfort and familiarity—chatting easily, giving Chinese tourists directions in Mandarin, chatting to stallholders on the street and shop-keepers, completely at ease, happier than I have ever been. It's probably just because I'm catching up with Bing and his family for yum cha today.

I've got just enough time to get to the second closest bedding supply store and back before I'm due to meet them in Chinatown. Going to the closest would obviously be more convenient, but it's in a shopping centre. Shopping centres must be avoided at all costs—they bring me out in hives, agitate my aura and play havoc with my energetic equilibrium.

I run down the street via Jack's.

'Woo hoo—look at you. I've definitely never seen you in that shirt before, Fiona.' To my surprise, Jack is there to greet me.

His comment heightens my self-conscious state because I'm standing out like a beacon in my red checked shirt. A bright colour and a pattern—normally I wouldn't be seen dead in either, let alone both simultaneously, but it's desperate times where my washing is concerned. I had planned on doing that last night too. I'd pulled the shirt off the hanger it's called home since I unwrapped it on my birthday two years ago and forced myself to button it up, as though I were taking medicine.

'I thought you weren't working Sundays?' I don't want to make any more of a big deal about my shirt than it's making of itself.

'What's it matter? I didn't have anyone to go out with me last night.' He sighs dramatically and waves his 'I couldn't ever fall in love with you' forearms around, his face all sad puppy-dog eyes.

'I'm sure you have a hundred girls to go out with, Jack. I've seen the way you chat to all your customers.' I take a stab at not censoring myself. I won't be guilted into feeling bad about not wanting to go out with him. It's not my fault fate hasn't set our paths to cross in a seriously romantic way.

Speaking of fate, I'm still in a bit of a state over looking like a human beacon when I see Frankie sitting out the front of PGGG.

'Hi, Frankie,' I say in a perky voice that doesn't seem to be mine.

'Hi, Fiona,' Frankie says, just before he pops a spoonful of yoghurt in his mouth.

I slow down. I've no doubt that both the yoghurt and being on my way to get new bed linen are a sign.

He gives me a restricted smile. A few words tumble out of my mouth, I've no idea what they are. I'm back on board the rocket to Planet Swoon.

'Have a good day, Fiona,' Frankie calls after me as I speed off.

'You too, Frankie,' I throw flirtatiously over my shoulder. Twisting back to look at him lowers my guard and my smile comes more naturally, bigger, brighter. I'm sure I feel his smile follow me down the street.

I wish I could be mad at him for not calling me Kismet but I'm just so dharmaed happy seeing him and hearing him say my name in any form. Although it's going to be tricky to ever correct him now. But like Bibby said—no one's perfect.

An hour later, laden with five large Bed Linen Wonderland bags, I hail a cab. If there's going to be someone new in my bed (which Marcus assured me there would be soon), energetically, it's only fitting to have new sheets ... and a new quilt, pillows, pillow cases, doona, doona cover. And throw cushions don't ever go to waste! This morning's Lovers' Oracle card—*Success—all will work out*—helped me rationalise the expense.

There's quick kisses and hugs with Bing, Jie and Lulu when I run up to them at the restaurant but today I'm more focussed on Bibby. I stand back from her and smile expectantly. Bibby turns the bundle containing Bau Bau—their cute, chubby-faced new addition—towards me. Bau Bau gurgles and burbles as I take him.

'Aiya!' Bing and Bibby say in playful shock, laughing at Bau Bau. He normally doesn't like going near people and cries if anyone comes close to him, they tell me.

I slip into Bing's family like it's a second skin, cradling Bau Bau, nattering to Bing, Bibby, Jie and Lulu as we wait for our yum cha number to be called.

One thing about most Chinese I've known is that they pride themselves on being the perfect hosts. 'Mei Mei, have you tried this?', 'You might like this', 'You should eat this, it's good for you', 'I remember once before you said you like this.' There's isn't a trolley that passes that Bing doesn't choose something from. There's barely time to chew before he's thrusting another dumpling or sticky rice triangle in my bowl.

I may like to leave yum cha full and groaning but this is a safety hazard—I'm sure the table is about to collapse, plus my stomach's started to press against my diaphragm and it's getting hard to breathe.

'Come on, girls, help out here before I explode,' I say to Jie and Lulu. They've been holding back—taking their cue from Bing and Bibby. As lovely as it all is, them treating me like a guest, and the distance the formality creates, brings a slight itch to my second skin.

29

Monday has become my regular early-mark day and by 'early' I mean 6pm. If I were blessed with the ability to form a forty-three-word sentence around Frankie what I'd say tonight is: 'Frankie, excuse me, it's not easy to concentrate and maintain my Ms Middle-of-the-Road composure when you launch into "I Wanna Be a Cowboy", full of chirpiness and swinging an imaginary lasso—particularly when the song isn't even on the radio!' But after a minute or two, he stops—as though he's remembered something he doesn't want to think about.

I don't understand his sudden change of mood but I do understand that this is about yesterday's bloody red shirt. I knew a pattern *and* a colour were trouble. In my state of confused fluster, I go to the beverage section.

I feel Frankie's eyes on me as he comes bouncing by, singing 10cc's 'I'm Not In Love'.

My Spiritual Support Pit Crew sessions are really paying off. Twice in a matter of weeks Spirit has sent me this sort of test. I don't imagine Frankie belting out the line about keeping the picture on the wall is a sign he has a shrine out in his dungeon, with chains and a yoghurt pot ready for the whole sex-slave scenario. I don't even flinch.

In fact it's me who has a shrine, of sorts. It's not like I'm collecting strands of Frankie's hair or anything (I would've felt compelled to return them to him given his slight deficit); when I got home the other night, I realised I'd thrown my change from our nicest interactions into the bowl of crystals I keep in my creativity corner for good Feng Shui. What can I say? I'm sentimental.

I try to muster a cool, calm and collected exterior but all my energy is going to trying to contain my laughter at his wildly out-of-tune singing. I feel like I've fallen into the centre of that volcano I'd been imagining.

By now I'm at the fridge. He's come to a stop next to me. I'm back to that item on my mental list of Endearing Things About Frankie of him having no sense of humiliation.

'Hi Frankie, great singing.' I smile. 'Are you practising for *The Voice*?'

'Do you like my chances?'

Oh great Goddess of Mercy, what does he mean by that?

'If you don't give it a shot you won't ever know.' I grip the fridge's handle, my smile widening.

'Maybe *Australia's Next Top Model*,' he says enthusiastically.

I have to look down to hold in a snort. 'Why not?' is all I manage when I look at him again. 'Beauty is in the eye of the beholder, I think you have a really beautiful energy,' is what Amethyst or one of the Goddesses-in-Training would be saying right now. I can virtually hear Amethyst screaming at me to say it but those aren't the sort of words that form in my mouth. It's just not me to actually come right out and say something like that to anyone, let alone try it with Frankie.

Almost composed but not quite, after Frankie has zipped off again and I've spent a moment or two leaning against the fridge to calm and cool myself down, I head to the counter.

Frankie does his bustle-in thing when I get to the till (it's definitely a thing now). He and the young guy working in tandem to serve me sends me all atwitter. Frankie is more than enough male energy for me to cope with.

'You don't normally buy avocadoes, Fiona,' Frankie observes.

I'm pulling items out of my basket as though they're rabbits out of a hat. Some of them, like the avocadoes, are a mystery even to me. Seriously, avocadoes? The mere thought of eating them makes me ill. But I can't be expected to maintain Ms Middle-of-the-Road *and* know what I'm buying with Frankie carrying on the way he had been. This revelation of him knowing what I buy is almost more than I can take.

'Thanks, Fiona.'

I get a full, unrestricted smile from Frankie as I pay. We hold our look for a millisecond. It's not a deep meaningful glance. Before I can set off on my journey to Planet Swoon, he pogos off, back to whatever he was doing before I got to the counter.

I'd like to say I float through the week, swooning over Frankie knowing what I buy but at 4am on Tuesday, I'm jolted from sleep with whiplash-inducing force. I've been acting like an ostrich, burying my head in the sand and thinking that my super organised piles meant I was on top of things at work when they're no more effective than a band-aid on a severed limb.

I try hypno-breathing in the darkness to calm myself down but tasks, deadlines, the fallout of not meeting them and feeling personally responsible for it all race through my mind as though I'm in a Hollywood car chase, guaranteed to end in a spectacularly explosive crash. Regardless of how much I work to get on top of it, I can't. Broomstick and the board keep changing things, adding new, more urgent, priorities and having me rewrite equally urgent reports to align with them. Broomstick has also got me covering the work of someone who's on extended leave. I'm living in deadline hell and the fallout if I don't meet them will be fatal—for the college at least. Everything feels out of control.

By the time I head out the door to work I am so pissed off that I'm positively ready to explode. All the better to stop censoring myself around Broomstick, I think, searching for a positive. The one time I'd tried to get her to take some responsibility in a polite and civilised manner hadn't worked so I don't have anything to lose.

I rush past PGGG clutching my coffee, fully focussed on what a bad mood I'm in so I can embody it and be authentic about it. I *feel* Frankie looking at me from not far inside the entrance. He's chatting to someone in his sweet Frankie voice. It's a cliché but my heart really does skip a beat, or maybe it's palpitations from the anxiety and the caffeine. Then I hear him laugh and there's no question. How dare he go ruining my bad mood and delighting my heart with his energetic zing, making me happy and bringing me joy just hearing his laughter? How am I meant to stay mad at Broomstick now?

Turns out it's pretty easy, especially when she's sending emails that bark super snappy demands like: *Strategic Plan!*

I'm tempted to email back and say: *I'm sorry I'm not sure what you meant by that? Did you mean: 'Fiona could you please send me a copy of the Strategic Plan when you have a moment, thanks!'*

It's because I'd suggested she should probably take some responsibility. Ever since then her behaviour has gotten worse, as though she has her sights set on me and is trying to break me—get me to leave.

I know I should probably work on my job anxiety and coming up with some strategies to deal with Broomstick in my session with Lionel on Thursday but it's so much nicer to talk about Frankie. He's an escape from all that crap. Besides, work is not going to get any better until I'm employed somewhere else but at the moment I haven't got the time or energy to apply for anything.

It must be full moon because even Lionel's quite Jekyll and Hydish this week. On one hand he's intuitively picking up on things, insightfully saying, 'We only stay in circumstances or repeat behaviours when they're not painful enough for us to change, no matter how uncomfortable we claim them to be. On some level we're getting something out of them, even if it's just staying in our safety zone, avoiding change or conflict.'

On the other: 'Have you thought any more about giving Frankie the Cuddle Card?'

'There is no way I'm doing that with or without censorship. And if I were giving him anything, it wouldn't be the Cuddle Card.' Oh my Buddha, I can't believe that's come out of my mouth. I wasn't intending to tell Lionel about the quote. I'd been trying so hard to forget I'd even had my initial thought about it. I have to tell him now, there's no way he'll let me back out of this. He's already leaning forward in anticipation, bushy eyebrow raised.

'And what's that, Kismet?'

'I read a line or three in a book that feel so perfectly suited to my Frankie situation. You know I'd normally hack myself to death rather than do anything remotely like this, but the thought just came to me and now it's there, it won't go away.'

'The thought?'

'Well, I've been thinking about writing it out and giving it to him. Not that I will.'

'Excellent idea! I can't tell you how happy I am to hear you even think of doing something like that.' Lionel beams at me as though I'm his star patient.

'I don't know that it is. But it's such a convoluted story, how I came to have the book, why I found it and even just the timing of me reading it. I almost feel I can't ignore it, it's as though it's meant to be.'

'It's obvious that you're starting to feel safer with Frankie. I'm not going to make you do it for homework but if you feel safe, why not do it, Kismet?'

I could give Lionel a thousand reasons—probably more—but the buzzer goes.

30

GJ! SOS—Hit with bad bout of the Bevs. All I want to do is stay at home and bake some brownies to take down to Frankie. Germaine would so disappointed in me! Kxxx

That's the text I'd be sending Jane the following Monday morning if I'd done anything more than skate around the edges of Frankie with her lately. We love Germaine Greer, Jane and I. The fact that she's gone extremely OTT and is erring on the best side of brilliantly crazy these days only makes us love her all the more. GJ would be none too pleased with the concept of me wanting to stay home and bake brownies for Frankie either. She's busy anyway, too busy to deal with me worrying I'm turning into my mother.

After her concern that she didn't have any work coming up, Jane had landed on her feet in that cat-like way she has with a commission from 'I can't divulge but a big name in music' or so she'd said on the voicemail she left the other night. I'd intended to phone her after my immediate temporary measure response of: *Yay for you. Congratulations GJ xxx*. I really had, I just hadn't quite got round to it with work and ... well, work. Intention is everything. Surely she will have picked up on my intent to call, even if I have been a little light on the action side of things?

Still in bed, I feel grotty and hung over, as though I've crawled out from a month under a pile of damp straw. I force myself up. I may not be brownie baking for Frankie but I do have the carrot of a trip to PGGG dangling before me at the end of the day.

Holy flapping prayer flags, I think I just accidentally winked at Frankie.

Hopefully he'll think it was a nervous tick from a hard day at work.

It began innocuously enough. 'Hi.' I'd walked into PGGG and turned to Frankie at the counter, simply intending to smile. For all the times I hadn't been able to find any, words chose that moment to possess me. 'Don't you ever do anything but work?' floated from my mouth on a flirtatious upwind. It didn't even make sense for Govinda's sake—he was always there at this time.

'Yes, sleep,' Frankie deadpanned without an ounce of innuendo as we looked each other in the eye.

I'd attempted a return to the safety of plan A— simply smiling—but even that was fraught with unforeseen risk. As if my words having taken on a life of their own wasn't bad enough, my right eye (with twice-curled lashes) followed suit and rather than just crinkling with my smile, it had winked at him.

Kismet, you idiot! Of all the times to go randomly winking, you do it when he's talking about sleeping!

But I wasn't going to let a little wink bother me, or at least I'd give it my best shot not to.

As if he'd rung Retro FM to request it, Carly Simon's 'You're So Vain' comes on and Frankie starts humming, giving me a look I can't quite read.

Last week things had been going so well. 'He's a very good teacher for you.' Amethyst once said to me. I'd gathered she wasn't talking elocution. I am learning resilience.

'I'm going for a break,' he calls to the young guy on the casual shift, gesturing for him to take over the till.

I'm quite relieved. He doesn't seem himself today and with my unwieldy words and randomly winking eyes, who knows what might happen if I end up in front of him at the counter?

However, when I get to the checkout queue and there's no sign of Frankie my relief evaporates. He hasn't returned to serve me. His absence leaves me strangely bereft.

At work on Wednesday I go through my to-do list. It could be mistaken for the Magna Carta but I have to say, if Frankie called up and said, 'Oh for God's sake, come home early, I want to shag you senseless on the new freezer,' I doubt that my response would be: 'Oh, I'm sorry, I have the *Prioritising Compliance Within the Organisational and Academic Structure* report to finish and documents to format. Far too much to do for that sort of caper.'

Pity he has no idea where I work or what my number is, but that doesn't stop me thinking about it.

When I'm so far into my fantasy that I've considered whether I'd even be bothered by the cold of the freezer and decided I wouldn't as I'm so gagging for him, I take the scenario a step further, concluding that the cold of the freezer could add to the experience—heightening the intensity of the sensations.

Maybe baking brownies for Frankie isn't what I need to be doing for him.

As dissatisfying as it is, particularly given the potential of the imagined alternative, I should really get back to the report.

'Come to Friday night drinks with us tonight, Fiona, you hardly ever come anymore.' Angela and Tiffany teeter up to my desk, clutching each other's arms for balance. They haven't been drinking already, it's just the height of their shoes.

Tiffany holds up her hand as I start offering excuses. 'No, Fiona, this time you're coming. No arguments.'

Angela giggles. 'Handbags at happy hour, no later than five-fifteen.'

Bless them. I watch them wobble back to the Creative Think Tank, as they refer to their Marketing Department desks. True, they have all the substance of two dandelion puffs in a gale-force wind but they're adorably sweet and well intentioned and they're always good for a laugh, even if they weren't likely to provide a full snort. I'm at serious risk of acquiring Snort Deprivation Syndrome, spending so little time with Jane.

'You have so much to offer, it would be such a pity if you wasted your life stuck in that place, running around after Broomstick,' Tiffany says to me on Friday once we're settled with drinks in the outside area of the bar.

Angela's too occupied with her first mouthful of chardonnay to speak but nods in agreement.

'You don't want to become a prune woman,' Tiffany continues. 'Prune women' was what we called those late-middle-aged women who worked long hours at soulless jobs, their work–life balance way out of whack, the life sucked out them, puckered up like prunes.

For a wisp of millisecond I consider telling Tiffany and Angela about Frankie, or at least about Jack, holding them up to say, 'See, there's life and surprises in me yet—no prune woman here!' But I smile and say, 'You're probably right.'

The whole so-a-*date*-date with Jack feels surreal now, like a bad dream. Jack behaving exactly the same as he did before only makes me more confused as to whether it really did happen. As for Frankie, destiny is not something Tiffany and Angela would be keen to hear about. They want something solid, tangible. They'd only pressure me to be moving forward. Harmless enough as they are, they'd be unrelenting if they thought there might be a chance of some girly gossip. Apart from not needing the pressure, I'm not into displaying my private life like laundry on a Hills hoist. I know Tiffany and Angela, they'd be cracking Situation Frankie open like a walnut, wanting to know every detail about it and picking him apart with their prescriptive how-men-should-be ways. Beyond the parameters of my Spiritual Support Pit Crew and, within limits, Jane, Frankie is something I want to keep to myself.

'Too right we're right,' Angela says, flushed with her post-chardonnay-coital glow.

'It's not that easy when you don't really drink, or hang out in the usual pick-up spots.' I sip from my soda water. 'It's like a sea of relationship short straws ended up here—just filling in time to retire.'

'Some people like older men.' Angela's constant perky positivity sometimes makes me want to slap her, but not tonight.

'Don't be ridiculous, Angela. Not like *this* sort of older man. Ones with money or who are at least a bit distinguished or something.' Tiffany is forever pulling the rug out from Angela's blitheness but in a way that doesn't ever seem the slightest bit nasty.

Angela looks at me. 'I don't mean to be rude, but I think you might need to lose that Chinese liniment of yours. I passed you in the street the other day and I knew it was you before I saw you. It's not that it stinks, but it certainly isn't Britney's Believe in terms of perfume.'

'I know,' I say, even though I haven't a clue as to what Believe actually smells like. 'It's my neck and my headaches. I'm killing myself with aspirin as well.' I'm always careful not to apply the liniment on PGGG days but I've needed to use so much of it lately it still probably oozes through my skin like grog on an alcoholic.

'The internet then!' Angela has a eureka moment.

'Yes, you have to get on e-hilarity or RSDD.'

Their 'cat that swallowed the cream' smiles twitch into giggles. I know they're bursting to tell me whatever it is that they've come up with in the Creative Think Tank.

'RSDD?'

'Yes, RSDD!' Angela says, giving way to laughter.

'Regrettably Shagless, Desperate and Dateless.' Tiffany follows Angela into laughter.

'We can look at all the profile photos with you, cull them.'

'Yes! Let's write you a profile now.'

'We're good at this sort of thing. Remember, we're professional marketers. We'll have you running off the shelf. Oh! I didn't mean you were "on the shelf"—you know what I mean.' Angela falls over herself to clarify.

'Thanks, but the whole online-dating thing isn't really me. What about the chemistry?' I'd rather die than be posted on an internet dating site, and when it comes to chemistry, you either have it or you don't, and I know exactly who turns the flame of my Bunsen burner up to full heat.

Tiffany and Angela both need a constant supply of men. Not that they have a string of them, they're just the sort of girls who always have a man. Not just a boyfriend either, they have to be living with him and if it doesn't work out, they're out of there faster than they'd have the guys calling Roses Direct if they'd forgotten their anniversary. As ditsy as they appear, a single look or word cracked like a whip from Tiffany or Angela can fell a man before he has time to blink.

'It's about training them,' they'd once counselled me. 'Start out as you mean to go on.' To be honest, I haven't ever quite understood the whole 'needing a man' thing let alone the 'having them live in fear of you' thing.

'I've just remembered. I've got a friend,' Angela blurts.

'Oh, you mean apart from us,' Tiffany and I say in unison.

'Ha, ha—funny. You're *so* amusing aren't you, biatches? No, this is entirely new and it's brilliant. My friend has set up a site: Meet My Friend.'

'What? Why don't I know about this?' Tiffany asks.

'Not like you need it. It's brilliant—you get a friend that sees the best in you to promote you and screen your respondents.'

'I don't mean to be rude, but that sounds a bit like a pimp to me.' I stab at the lemon at the bottom of my glass with my straw.

'Oh, let us, Fiona,' Tiffany pleads. 'It'll be fun.'

'Darling, you'd have more chance of Broomstick telling me I've done an excellent job and offering me a pay rise.'

In our session this week Lionel asks me if I've always worried so much about doing what Jane thought I should do.

'Well, maybe,' I reply, 'but it hasn't been an issue before.'

'Perhaps that's because you're finding your own voice. It sounds like there's been a history of codependence.'

'Strong female friendships aren't necessarily codependent, Lionel. If we were a couple everyone would think it was normal.' The way people had questioned our closeness over the years had made me defensive.

'My point exactly. You're friends, not a couple, and now you're both looking for something more—her potentially with a baby and you maybe with Frankie or a new relationship. It's only natural that things have to change.'

I sit quietly for a moment, cuddling Positively and not correcting Lionel. Technically I hadn't been 'looking for a new relationship', it was only because Amethyst had mentioned him being in my aura as my destiny that I'd ventured down that path again.

'Have you thought anymore about giving Frankie the quote?'

'I have it in my diary. I wrote it and rewrote it until my writing was as close as it could be to perfect.' The tell-tale talking-Frankie lightness returns to my voice.

'Sweet, but in your diary isn't going to help anyone. Are you actually going to give it to him?'

'One day, if it feels right, I might, but I doubt it.' I sigh and pull at my hair in frustration. 'It isn't something I'd ever do but then I have this weird feeling that I will. Not that I can imagine *actually* doing it. I feel sick just thinking about it.'

'Remember the work we did on your fears and that voice that tells you to keep everyone away so you don't get hurt?

Don't give into it. Isn't it worth taking the chance? You haven't told me what the quote says yet. I can be your independent judiciary.'

Beaten, I repeat the line from *The Thirteenth Tale* verbatim.

'That is the perfect note for you to give him,' Lionel says. 'Any man would be flattered to receive it from you.'

It's unusual for Catherine to call me to meet up when it's not a whole family thing but Mum and Dad have gone away for the weekend with Johnny and Vonnie—a golfing trip (don't think I hadn't had Mum on the phone about it)—and Brian is working, apparently.

About half an hour into our park outing, Catherine announces she needs to phone Brian and moves away. She's been prickly all day even for her—her texts about the time and place to meet were bordering on hostile. From where I'm playing with Sammy and Sonja I can see her pacing up and down the path that leads through the park. The latest model iPhone is firm against her ear. The tension in her face could be straining to hear or stress, I can't tell.

'For God's sake, Brian, you should have thought about that sooner!' she screams.

Definitely stress.

'Sammy, I hear GI's retired.' The thought comes miraculously to mind in my desperation to distract the children from their mother.

'I know, Aunty Fee, that was *weeks* ago.'

Of course he knew.

'Well, that's it then,' Catherine declares, marching over.

My throat constricts and I feel like I'm going to vomit. What is she doing? Is she just going to blurt out their crisis in front of the children?

'We're not going to be able to go skiing in New Zealand with the other families during the holidays.'

'Skiing in New Zealand! Seriously, Catherine, I thought something really *awful* was happening.'

'It is awful! All the other school families we're friends with are going. We'll be ostracised as paupers. Sammy and Sonja won't have any friends, no one will want to play with them. It's a *complete* disaster. Not to mention the humiliation.'

And they call me dramatic.

I slip immediately into solutions mode. 'Maybe Sammy and Sonja could each go with one of their friends? Then you'd only have to afford the stuff for them.'

'Oh yes, that's a great suggestion, Fiona. Looking like we have to put our children into care and they're off on some charity holiday.'

I think I liked her better when she was being Mother Teresa.

'What? Why are we going into care?' Sonja screams.

'Now look what you've done, Fiona.'

'Oh for Buddha's sake! It's Kismet! Call me Kismet! That's who I am, so get over it. And you created this situation, not me.' My anger kick starts an internal emergency generator and I discover energy I didn't think I had anymore. Lionel's non-censoring is really coming to the fore.

'Oh, get a real problem!' Catherine screams as though hers is.

Yep, definitely liked her better when she was being all Mother Teresa but I don't bite back. *Compassion—even for Catherine*, I remind myself.

I massage my temples. All this hostility has made my head hurt. Actually, it's been hurting for weeks but this has made it worse.

31

I'm like a rubber ball, bouncing from practitioner to practitioner, trying to find an answer to something I can't explain.

'It's so beautiful, they welcome you with a song,' Megan had said dreamily at Enlightenment Day when she told me about Charisma, her past-life therapist, and his wife, Crystal.

The three of us are sitting on the floor of their lounge room, Charisma and Crystal with their legs crossed perfectly in lotus position on saffron-coloured cushions, me more like an oversized kindergartener, trying my best to behave. Being badly serenaded by Frankie is one thing but being strummed at on an out-of-tune guitar by these two, in their matching rainbow tie-dyed cheesecloth with their home-penned lyrics is something else. I feel like I've landed in the middle of a church youth group camp—they'll probably sing 'Kumbaya' next.

Charisma stops strumming and puts the guitar down, a welcome relief, though short lived. He stands, raises his head, indicating for me to do the same, then takes both my hands in his.

He looks deeply into my eyes. 'I think you're ready.' He leads me into the meditation room. 'Can you feel the energy?'

He's still holding my hand as I lower myself onto another saffron cushion. I'm careful to choose the one closest to the door. There's something just slightly creepy about him. What if this is one of those free-love hippie scenarios?

Charisma explains how he'll take me through a meditation that will lead me into my past-life regression. I close my eyes and he begins.

'Allow yourself to relax into the comfortable embrace of this experience, knowing that in this lifetime you are safe, safe to journey through that which has come before this incarnation no matter—'

'Charisma! Charisssmmmaaaa! Come here. I need you for a minute.' Crystal's voice cuts through the beginning of my meditation like a chainsaw. Gone is all trace of her gentle, calming manner. She sounds possessed.

'Forgive me.' Charisma slips out the door.

From what I can understand from Crystal's screaming and Charisma's attempts to sooth her, something or someone has escaped. Oh Buddha above—I do need to be more careful with my thoughts. Maybe I've manifested a sex-slave scenario. I should have never come into a room alone with a man dressed in cheesecloth, let alone a room with Sacred Sexuality brochures lying on the floor next to the meditation cushions, which I've only just seen. Despite Frankie's amusingly out-of-tune rendition of The Police's 'Message in a Bottle' the other week, he wasn't Sting. I couldn't image myself let alone Frankie in a blissed-out crowd of tantra types—dancing the divine, learning what he can do to my jade pavilion with his heavenly dragon stem that will make our inner flutes sing.

'Here, kitty, kitty.' Charisma's calling alleviates my sex-slave scenario concerns. Still, I'm definitely going to add 'Does not think attending Sacred Sexuality Workshops is a good idea' to my What I Want and Need in My Next Male Love Relationship list when I get home.

There's scuffling outside—quite a lot of it—followed by a strangled meow.

Charisma returns, small scratches on the inside of his arms and cat hair covering his top. 'Apologies. We're minding our neighbour's prize Burmese. He escaped and was on the balcony ledge. I'm allergic but Crystal couldn't cope by herself.'

Charisma's sneezing, snuffling and scratching make it difficult for me to find the flow of my meditation but eventually I find my past-life path. I retrace until I am an advisor in a Chinese court, serving an emperor.

'Charisssmmmaaaa!' Crystal screeches again just as I am about to ask for an explanation of why I feel so connected to Frankie. Both Charisma and I can tell that the bloody Houdini of cats has escaped again.

'I'm sorry,' Charisma says. 'Maybe we should make a time when we're not cat-minding. I don't know why he's doing this; he's never done it before. It's like he's set on throwing himself from the balcony. I think I need to give him some reiki, draw in some universal love energy to calm him down.'

'I'll give you a call,' I lie. Suicidal Houdini cats and tantra definitely aren't good signs.

'No one was ever a housewife or an office worker or an accountant or council worker,' Stephanie says when I meet her on Saturday afternoon and tell her about my past life in the Chinese Emperor's court.

She has a point. When I think about it, I've never heard of anyone's past-life regression bringing up something boringly ordinary. And even if she didn't, I wouldn't be taking her to task on it now. I've only told her as an amusing distraction; I knew she wouldn't take it seriously and I'm happy to let her make fun of it.

When she'd taken a call from James, it was obvious just how badly she isn't coping. She was all mushy and deferring to him. She hadn't yelled at him once! Then I'd watched her gaze dance around the room, trying to run from the tears as she'd told me of her mum. 'They're saying she hasn't got very long. Three months maybe, max. I always thought she'd be around till I was oldish and grey and she was older and greyer,' Stephanie says, off past lives and back to those cut short.

I stir my coffee clockwise then anti-clockwise and watch the latte art swill into muddy milk, trying to think of something comforting to say. 'Miracles happen.' People say it all the time but it sounds so twee and you might as well be saying, 'Oh well, there's no hope then—best you get praying.' Besides, I'm sure Stephanie's reaction would be much the same if I suggested her mother consider crystal healing: she'd probably lean across the table and strangle me. I know there's nothing I can say that will make it better. I can't fix it, *words* can't fix it.

I lean over and take Stephanie's shaking hand. Her chin quivers.

'We think that life goes on forever, that tragedy only happens to other people, that other people's mothers die young or things happen to other people's families but not to your own. But you know what, Kismet? It does, it can happen to us.'

It's more than grief with Stephanie, I realise. This is the first thing that's ever happened to her that she didn't have planned behind the doors of the Advent calendar of her life and she has no control over it. For Stephanie, that must be nearly as terrifying as facing her mother's death.

We all had our challenges with family but Stephanie was right, you did just take it for granted that they'd always be there. I knew this wasn't about me, still I couldn't miss the message that it was another reminder not to keep hitting the snooze button on life.

32

I smell a rat—a dying rat. And so my week begins.

I tear around my kitchen with the fervour of a sniffer dog at a dance party, poking my nose into every nook, cranny and cupboard to rule out other possible explanations for the stench. Nothing. It could be the entire troupe of Riverdancing rats dead up there, from the power of the pong emanating from the thin layer between my place and the one above.

Someone must have Ratsaked them.

I'd really grown quite fond of them being there. Their middle-of-the-night scurrying had become comforting, because no matter what thoughts I had in the darkness, I didn't ever feel alone.

I reach for a Kleenex. I can't say if it's the rat homicide or still feeling nauseous, tired and headachy whenever I'm not distracted from my life that is sending tears trickling down my cheeks.

I wade through Monday and the days that follow as though they're wet concrete.

On Thursday night I catch up with Jane.

'Sorry I'm late.' I know Jane isn't happy from the texts we'd exchanged. I was already on the back foot as I'd had to ask her to change from Bar Monk. I'm too brittle for a full-on noisy environment and I really just needed to go somewhere quiet that was easy for us to get to.

'Fuck, Kiz, you look like shit,' Jane says.

'Not you too. Everyone's saying that.' More tears spike at my eyes as we hug. I don't know what's wrong with me. I can barely keep it together.

'With good reason. You really don't look good, like *unwell* not good, not simply a bad hair day.'

'I'm just tired and my life is one long bad hair day lately. Enough about me. Can you tell me who the big name in music you did the mural for was yet?'

'Not yet.'

'You know if it was John Farnham I'm not going to speak to you ever again.' My words come out flat. I've lost my spark and I'm also trying too hard to be how I used to be, when I know nothing ever stays the same—well, almost nothing.

'I can't believe it,' Jane says, changing the subject. 'We're here months later and the only thing that's changed is you're the one running late and you look like—well, I won't say it again.'

'I know, time just goes so fast.'

'I'm not even going to blame Frankie. I'm not saying he's not a fuckwit but one look at you and it's obvious your problems are well beyond a man. Even during the worst of times I've never seen you like this.'

'Can't we talk about something else? Something fun, like what's happening with you. How are things progressing with Baby Jane?'

'No, this is serious, Kiz. I want you to promise me you'll do something: go to the doctor and get yourself checked out.

You must have loads of holidays banked up. Take advantage and take a break, I say.'

I promise to see a doctor then and again as we say good-bye, which makes Jane happy. I just don't promise when.

The next day begins with what has to be the most painful meeting of my life. I struggle to stay awake as Broomstick babbles on, praising her compliance strategy as though it will save the world from war and starvation. Perhaps it's just an accumulation of all the meetings lately and I've hit a toxic level of Boring Meeting Syndrome. We're about to enter the third hour, so I wouldn't be surprised. Sitting here listening to her go on really is the last thing I want to be doing. I'm so over compliance that I don't care whether we're moving to-wards it, strategically prioritising it or fraudulently filling out paperwork and manufacturing documents to look like we're achieving it.

'Well, that shouldn't matter as most students wouldn't know if a lecturer is good or not.' Broomstick's jowls flap as she scoffs at 'Point 8: Monitoring Student Satisfaction'.

'We do need to ensure some level of student satisfaction.' I try to keep the murderous venom from my voice. Didn't she get that students pay her inflated salary? (Desmond wasn't backward in telling any of us what they paid her—sometimes I wonder if dealing with confidential information is really a job he should have.)

'Fiona, we're not running a party,' she snaps.

Oh for Buddha's sake! Like anyone would have invited her if we were.

I refuse to let Broomstick know she's getting to me, so I close my eyes and take a deep breath, drawing in all the strength and haughtiness I can muster. I roll my shoulders back, sit tall and, with all the outward calmness of Amethyst leading a meditation, say, 'I didn't say we were, Dr Raynard, but it is a private college, a business, so we rely on students—'

She cuts me off with a scowl and her bitter words come at me like bullets, 'And your qualifications to speak on that are, Fiona? If you look to the agenda you'll note that you are only here for administrative and procedural reference.'

Higher ground, I remind myself and take another deep breath.

As the meeting moves on, the pleasure she takes in any opportunity to humiliate or degrade me is obvious. She may as well be licking her finger and stroking a point in the air with each put-down.

This is an excellent opportunity to practise getting used to dealing with confrontation and not censoring myself. If I wasn't dragging the last of my strength up from the bottom of the barrel to keep it together and not humiliate myself by letting Broomstick know she's humiliating me, I might have been grateful for the opportunity and whatever lesson Spirit was trying to teach me here. But the reality is that I feel far more like walking out, especially when she pulls a face at me after I *agree* with a comment she makes.

It isn't a good day to be robbed of my workday sliver of sanity—my lunchtime trip to the gym—but with only fifteen minutes' respite until we're due back in the meeting, all I have time for is to run down and see Bing.

'You won't believe what that old bitch said to me,' I say and laugh. Turning it into an amusing anecdote will help—it always does.

'What?' Bing looks up as I pace by the counter. 'Oh Mei Mei, what's wrong?'

I touch my face and realise there are trails of tears down my cheeks so fine that I hadn't known they were there.

Bing puts down my cup, comes around the counter and forces me to stand still as he wraps his arms around me.

I dissolve, I knew I would, tears soaking the shoulder of his shirt as I take heaving sobs. Broomstick's abuse is really just the icing on the freaking untenable cake. I feel like I can no longer breathe, I've got no life anymore, I can no longer even hope to muster the energy to complete a job application and I can't quite get over the disappointment of how those 'perfect jobs' became so hopeless at the interviews. I feel trapped and I have no idea what I'm going to do or how I'm ever going to escape.

That's what I'd tell one of my Spiritual Support Pit Crew but it's Bing who's hugging me—I'd never say any of that to anyone I didn't pay.

'Kill me now! Broomstick's a fucking bitch,' I say instead, laughing to stop the tears.

'I kill *her* now! Anyone that upset my Mei Mei is a goner.' Bing turns his hand into a pistol, making shooting actions. Bing likes to think he knows people, but it's just a tough-guy fantasy he entertains. The truth is he's about as bad boy as Bau Bau having a tantrum in his bassinet.

By Sunday I've moved beyond Broomstick.

'Is it an all-female gym you go to, Fiona?' Frankie asks as I stand at the counter of PGGG.

I give an inner scoff. My world is filled with too many women as it is. It's a bit off the middle of the road but I'm hoping he might be writhing internally with jealousy at the thought of me on the gym floor with other men. 'No, it's called Definition.' I don't know how it is that Frankie and I even started talking about our exercise routines.

'That's a great name for a gym.'

Two more items for my mental list of Endearing Things About Frankie—'animated' and 'likes words'.

He fills me in on his preferred exercise routine. A wave of concern about whether I'd be able to keep up with him flies up my thighs at his mention of spin classes. The only time I tried one, I thought I was going to die in any of three ways: as a sweat spot on the uncomfortably pointy little bike seat or of a heart attack or heat stroke. Not that I'll mention that to Frankie. I'll deal with any stamina issues in my own way, should—Goddess willing—the chance ever arrive.

Despite my concerns, the intimacy level of this interaction is quite good, very good in fact: an overall 8 out of 10.

Mutual Smiling: 8.5—I really do like the way his smile crinkles his eyes.

Conversation: 8—Free-flowing and a good deal of personal information shared but not earth-shatteringly exciting or romantic, although a big leap beyond our previous efforts, so I gave an extra point for that.

Mutual Eye Contact: 7.5—The dip there was my fault.

With things going as well as they are there's no need to force the issue. Still, I'm acting like a drug mule at Customs whose heroin-filled condom has burst on the plane: edgy and fidgety and my eyes keep darting out to the street. I'd asked the Universe for a sign this morning to tell me without a doubt what to do.

Nodding and murmuring in the appropriate places as Frankie chats on, I search for sausage dogs or at least someone in one of those bunny-adorned Souths caps or shirts or *something*. When none of that appears my gaze zips around inside the shop for a sign. Nothing. I take another quick look outside.

Frankie has stopped talking and I know it's time for me to leave, but I'm standing there, signless, unable to move. Except for my hand, which reaches into my bag.

'I just have to give you this.' I pull the note from between the pages of my diary and thrust it at Frankie, with all the grace of a gymnast missing the bar, landing on their arse. It's my take on the quote from *The Thirteenth Tale: If you hypnotise a man with green eyes, he will never know there is a girl behind those eyes looking back at him.*

It is such a flustered and ungainly manoeuvre that I can only pray to Spirit, the Universe and every deity in existence that he will find something endearing in my clunkiness.

Once I've handed over the note it's as though I've accepted a baton in a relay race. I take off, running from the store. Holy motherfornicating Goddess hell, Ms Middle-of-the-Road is so out of control that I should be arrested for reckless driving. In my defence, Stephanie's 'We think life goes on forever' comment has played a part here. Her words had been hovering in my mind all week.

Oh, Kismet, what have you done? I scream silently, hurtling home as quickly as I can. Which, given I feel as though I'll die if my humiliation catches up with me, is faster than I've ever moved before. I barely even notice a red short-haired dachshund as I run past it.

Doing things like that at 2.15pm when you haven't eaten all day. Ridiculous! I should know better. Plus I'd promised myself I wasn't going to do anything extreme until I'd consulted with Amethyst. Yet I'd done it. And, oh my Buddha, I freaking did it in front of someone; there was someone behind me.

When I get home I google whether it's possible to die of humiliation.

'OK, Kismet, calm down. This may be confronting and a bit embarrassing and it may mean that right now you're feeling quite traumatised and you may have to go to the other bus stop tomorrow. But your life is not going to end, for Govinda's sake—Google just proved it.'

But what if Google is wrong. What if I'm the first?

Obviously if Frankie doesn't do anything, like come out and see me or mention it as I'm passing or pursue me in some way, I can't ever go back into PGGG. Simple. The name forgetting was one thing but this—well, this is something else entirely.

On the upside—which I do take quite a while to find—at least I'm not waiting for him to call as I didn't give him my number. That would be the drawn-out torture of peeling off a never-ending band-aid, minute by minute, hour by hour. I mean, someone 'normal' would have probably just given him their number and said, 'Give me a call sometime.' Or better still, just kept the conversation going with something like, 'Hey, I've noticed you're a Souths fan, would you believe John Sutton and some other players once asked me for directions?'

But not me, I had to go all Jane Austen again and pass over a handwritten quote from a freaking novel that may make me sense to me and to Lionel but probably not to Frankie. Now he's really going to think I'm some conceited bunny-boiling maniac!

The magnitude of my trauma is evidenced by the fact that in my Post Note Passing Trauma State I've even blanked out what songs were playing in PGGG. But if I were going with the theme of my behaviour, Retro FM would have been spinning Gnarls Barkley's 'Crazy' or maybe Prince's 'Let's Go Crazy'—it certainly appeared I had—or even Cheap Trick's 'I Want You to Want Me', seeing as I'd been pushed to such extremes … the possibilities are endless. Running through them provides a brief respite from my thoughts but as soon as I hope I might be on the verge of not so much calming down as slightly de-escalating my hysteria, they're back again.

I put on Aurora's 'I Went Too Far' and Sarah Blasko's 'No Turning Back' and sing and dance around for a few minutes to buy myself a little more time to escape my thoughts, but as soon as they're over my head is flooded again. Rescue Remedy proves fraudulently ineffectual—twenty drops under my tongue doesn't even take the edge off. Hypno-breathing is hopeless.

I think I'm going to vomit. I run to the bathroom but it's a false alarm. A good thing I hadn't eaten. I definitely won't be able to eat tonight.

I spin around, not sure what to do. I tidy things that don't need tidying, I wash up, I vacuum, I search for jobs, I do anything. Every time my body and brain stop simultaneously what I've done hits me and I feel ill again, paranoia snapping through my thoughts like a starved pelican at a fish market.

You're a fucking idiot, Fiona. Everything was going fine—you'd had quite a nice chat and everything was fine. That's the worst thing—it was all perfectly lovely and now you've gone and ruined everything!

My paranoia is set on calling me Fiona—I'm sure Amethyst and Lionel would have a field day with that.

Maybe I can pretend it was just a dream. Back on my bed, I throw my *Meditation for Monkey Minds* CD across the room— as effective as the bloody Rescue Remedy and hypno-breathing!

Dying mothers indeed. I should have known better than to act on someone else's karmic journey.

33

I'm not having a nervous breakdown, I'm putting my make-up on, I'm curling my eyelashes. I've set my intentions, I've picked my *Meditations for a Monkey Mind* CD up off the floor, and I am going to *om* myself into a state of elevated consciousness. Sure, I might have been googling natural rat repellents and throwing liniment and peppermint oil around my kitchen cupboards at 2am when I heard the rustling of rats, but I am perfectly in control now.

My previous distress was misguided. The rats, apart from the one I can still smell decaying in my ceiling, have decided that my kitchen cupboard, with its cosy little hot water system, can provide them comfort in their grief. I was pleased to discover it had only been one member of the rat troupe that had died in the ceiling—from the sound of the rustling the others were alive and very comfortable snuggled in with my hot water system. I didn't want to cast them out to the street, but they need to find new quarters and another rehearsal space for their Riverdancing ways.

And in terms of my not having a nervous breakdown, I may have only got four hours of broken sleep but I'm not crying, I'm not collapsed on my bed, surrounded by tissues, bunkered down and planning to watch daytime TV and eat triple chocolate mud cake for the rest of my life, or even just today. I'm going to walk out the door and face the world.

All those people you think are looking at you as you go by their shops, Kismet, they're not, you are just being paranoid. Ms Middle-of-the-Road's cogs grind as I try to get her into gear. I begin counting my steps in Chinese on a loop of eight. It's the most calming thing I can do and it keeps my feet moving, one in front of the other.

It's not too late to turn around and head back to the bus stop in the other direction. It would be so easy. But I have to be stronger than I think I am. If I don't do this today, I won't ever be able to go past PGGG again. My breath scratches at my throat. I have a coffee in my hand, though I'm not sure how it got there—Jack, obviously, but I'd blanked out the whole interaction.

Holy mother of Buddha, I'm going to die—there's someone walking out of PGGG as I approach. My glassy eyes can't focus enough to recognise who it is. I may not be having a nervous breakdown but I think I am definitely about to have a stroke.

Ms Paranoid-Nowhere-Near-the-Middle-of-the-Road has taken over the wheel and I wonder, *Have shopkeeper secret messages tumbled down the street like dominoes to tell Frankie I'm coming?*

Without looking again, I lower my head. I take furtive glances from under the veil of my hair. Relief or devastation—I don't know which emotion to choose when I recognise the socks as Raymond's.

The street is still a warzone with the road works that have been going on for weeks. Angels disguised as council workers in high-vis vests have barricaded the footpath so I don't have to walk directly past the doorway of the PGGG but I can feel Raymond's eyes on me.

No, I'm not having a nervous breakdown, I tell myself again. My breath might now just be skimming the opening of my nostrils, little droplets of coffee might be shaking through the lid of the cup, and someone might ask me if I need a hand as I try to navigate extracting my card from my bag to tap on as I board the bus. The bus Spirit sent immediately on my arrival at the bus stop to scoop me up from my humiliation. (Thank you, Spirit.) But I'm fine. The worst is over. I've done it.

I billow out a breath of relief and sink onto the bus seat. A strange sense of calm washes over me (a miracle really, given I'm on public transport) and I feel more free and less focussed on the outcome of my actions. Letting go and letting the Goddess.

It takes only till the bus stops at the next traffic light for this to change. In my not-moving state, my mind unoccupied by cycling from 'yi' to 'ba' to count my steps, the murky waters of fear come washing over me. What will my next interaction with Frankie be?

Of course I'm not going into PGGG, that would be insane—humiliating and insane. If Frankie doesn't pursue me, I shall forfeit my purchases from the Purveyor of Putney's Finest Fresh Produce since 1963 and seek my salad greens elsewhere.

Waves of nausea rise, their undertow pulling me further down with each turn of the bus's tyres. I fight against them, momentarily settling back in to *Everything will be fine—Spirit has it all under control,* before a fresh swell rises to submerge me.

I arrive at work and try to pretend everything is normal. 'Fine, thanks. Yes, a nice weekend, yours?' I say as people pass my desk on their way in, my voice as taut as a tightrope.

My movements match my robotic response. I shift files from the Quite Urgent pile on my left to the Super Urgent pile on my right, then move them to the Extremely Urgent pile in front of me. Steel girder straight and strong, I type furiously in my effort to block Frankie and what I've done from my mind.

But as the morning wears on the lulls become fewer and the swells become bigger, building to tsunamic waves of nausea. At lunchtime the day remains a sign desert. On the treadmill I'm so desperate that I beg Spirit for a sign. Two tiny sporty logos appear, but I think they're only half a straw I'm clutching at.

This is weird and fabulous, this is fabulously weird, I think, reaching some sort of high when I get back to my desk. It could be the endorphins from the gym.

Sitting opposite Broomstick, the *Prioritising Compliance within the Organisational and Academic Structure Report* on her desk between us, I smile at her. I watch her Adam's apple bob up and down as she prattles on, thinking, *No, I think I have actually gone insane. I can't believe I did that.* But in this instant I feel fabulous and free and like nothing at all matters anymore. Even the desire to beat Broomstick to death with the report, stapler, phone handset or hole punch as I'd visualised myself doing in some karmically unsound moments has disappeared.

Maybe I haven't gone insane, maybe I've reached enlightenment.

I'm not sure how to tell.

Thursday brings a freakishly hot day—global warming refusing to be ignored. Facing a furnace of thirty-five degrees, the city is set to become a pressure cooker. For four and a half days, the note and every other interaction, look, thought and feeling I've ever had with or about Frankie has been thrust under the microscope of my mind, magnified until there's no room for anything else. It's not just every waking hour; they take over my scraps of sleep as well, tormenting me through my dreams. I toss and turn, feeling as though I haven't slept at all.

I've cast Lovers' Oracle cards and 'Manifesting my Mojo' meditations aside for hypno-breathing and Amethyst's 'Acting My Life' meditations. I need them to get me out the door. Today I'm trying *I make the right choices every time and everything is perfect in my life as it is right now* on for size.

I'll miss the flirtation, the mystery, the build-up, the wonder and the fantasy of Frankie. I might even miss Frankie a bit too.

Lost in thought, outside Jack's I nearly run directly into someone wearing a T-shirt similar to the style Frankie wears. At least the signs have returned but sporty logos, Souths bunnies and even sausage dogs are cold comfort in the harsh light of Frankie's complete lack of response.

'You look cute, like a teenager.' Jack eyes me in my Chinese-influenced sleeveless top and black three-quarter pants.

'It's so hot, I can't stand it,' I say.

My breath catches on my way to the bus stop as a bald spot emerges from the entrance of PGGG. *Bloody Frankie!* I think. Now so much time has passed I was hoping I wouldn't have to deal with him until I'd sought guidance from Lionel.

Calm yourself, Kismet, false alarm. Closer to the PGGG, I realise it's Raymond again.

My angels of the high-vis vest wearing variety have inched their earthly pavement digging and cabling mission to almost directly outside PGGG. They part like a sea and down shovels as I walk through them. I keep my eyes on the ground, but I feel them watching me.

Thank you, great Goddess of salvaging some pride, I think, hoping Raymond is still watching. Working on the principle that people can catch your thoughts (Amethyst, of course) I put so much effort into giving power to my next thought that I fear I could burst a blood vessel in my brain. *See, Frankie? I'm not some desperate freak—I can still turn heads, so you should be gobsmacked, delighted and flattered that you've driven me so close to the point of insanity that I'm indulging in bizarre non-me behaviour like thrusting quotes at you.*

I admit it's asking a lot of someone to catch a thought that long but eventually Spirit was going to come up with the proof of the pudding; as everyone I encountered on the spiritual path kept reminding me: 'Spirit has an infinite capacity to deliver.'

On the bus, I stare out the window. As the adrenalin of the perving angels abates, I'm hit with an awful thought. Maybe Ms Terse-at-the-Till is Frankie's partner and she's found the note and killed him. Perhaps that's why Raymond keeps coming out, he's trying to work up the courage to tell me. It's alarming that I haven't even heard a sneaker squeak since the incident.

'Not that you care, Kismet, you're practising non-attachment, remember?' The echo of Amethyst on Enlightenment Day comes screeching through like a parrot on my shoulder. But I'm not failing at non-attachment; I simply hate unanswered questions.

The niggling feeling that I'll see Frankie tonight creeps up on me and stays all day. I'm sure it's intuitive knowing, although it could just be the hope that I'll solve the mystery of his imagined demise.

Even though I'm trying to be non-attached, I can't say I don't experience a slight surge of disappointment when I pass PGGG that evening and it's closed. Then I remind myself it's perfect, because I need to see Lionel before Frankie.

A few steps down the street, I look up and there's the bald spot I've been longing to see.

'Hi, Fiona, how are you?' Frankie turns from the quartet of shopkeepers when I reach him.

'Hi, Frankie.' Oh Great Govinda, I think I just arched an eyebrow. What has become of me? Why can't I control myself around him?

His eyes move towards me—towards my chest, to be precise. Seems the message in the note may have been entirely wasted on him, but good to know he has manly desires—a girl can't live on deep drowning glances alone.

Fuck, fuck, fuck! (Yes, fuck, sorry, Spirit!) I think and keep walking, wondering if he's watching. Ms Completely-off-the-Centre-of-the-Road is wishing/hoping that he will follow but Ms Middle-of-the-Road knows he won't.

There's a time and a place to practise non-attachment and I'm afraid this isn't it. I don't even seem to have the power to—the spell that overtakes me whenever I see Frankie has been cast again. I swoon down the street, legs weaving into each other like the strands of plaits.

34

Tonight I have the excitement of supervising an exam. Well, 'invigilating', as Broomstick insists we call it now. I'm sitting at the front of a large room full of students. With the electricity of exam nerves buzzing around, every hair follicle within a hundred-metre radius must be standing on end. I could do something like read the new Government Compliance Guidelines to kill the time, or I could slash myself to death with them. Death by papercuts would be preferable. Looking at the sea of anxious faces, I remind myself that I have a responsibility to provide conditions that are conducive to exam sitting, so I don't think the latter would be appropriate.

To make productive use of my time I try doing a little of the proofreading I've brought with me. I can't concentrate on it. Not that it requires great concentration, however, I can't really think of anything but the inexplicable way Frankie affects me.

I'm too protective of the kernel of him that's growing in the seed of my heart to Phone-a-Friend for answers.

Even though a few months ago I would have been madly poking my finger at the favourites on my phone to call Jane before Frankie's eyes were back in their sockets last night, I hadn't even thought to text her about it. I'm having a hard enough time as it is trying to cling to my friendships, just managing to hang onto most of them by a thread with one-line texts because I have nothing more to give. The last thing I need is to have to defend myself or listen to anyone tell me what I *should* do. I knew what people would say if I told them about Frankie and I didn't want to hear it. They wouldn't get it, whatever 'it' was exactly. More than ever before Frankie had become the terrain of trained professionals.

And beyond everything else it'd seem too weird to go calling Jane, saying, 'Oh, by the way, I know I've been skirting around the edges of Situation Frankie with you for months but I went insane and gave him a quote from a book and he hasn't acted on it.' She'd want to have a full-on bitchfest about Frankie's fuckwittedness. I can hear her now and I just don't have the stomach for an 'all men are bastards' session, or the fuel for the rage.

Goddess above, I must be in a bad way—I don't even have the strength to get angry at men anymore!

As the students work away at their papers, my mind drifts further. Too bad if someone pulls their text book out of their bag or gets on their digital device to look up the answers—I won't even notice, I'm too busy imagining myself pulling a new trick out of my bag every time I go in to PGGG.

It's a pity I threw out the Cuddle Card, telling myself, 'I'd never do anything like that', but there's a postcard I have at home that used to be on my desk pre-Broomstick with 'Shut Up and Kiss Me You Fool' on it. Maybe that could be my next move! Really make him squirm. Perhaps I should pop the postcard in my diary on the off chance that Sixpence None the Richer's song 'Kiss Me' is playing on Retro FM one day when I am in PGGG. Who could ignore a sign like that?

I could have all manner of fun coming up with things to hand over to Frankie until he either screams at me to stop, calls the police to have me escorted off the premises, calls the mental health crisis team for them to come and get me or takes me on the counter. Sometimes it isn't until someone is backed into a corner that they show their true colours.

I check the clock that ticks ominously on the wall. Buddha above, it's only half an hour into a three-hour exam. Without any distraction, the sensation of how badly I need to shag Frankie is getting worse. I wrap my right thigh over my left, then twist my right foot around my left calf, squeezing my legs together, and chew, but don't bite, my nails.

Three long hours later, I'm at the station. Tiredness has pruned all of my desire and turned it to mulch. I don't even give a second thought to the concept of Frankie whipper snippering some other woman's edges, or co-composting at my pruning analogy. With his environmentally unfriendly rubbish disposal ways, I'm sure he's not a composter anyway.

I listen to a voicemail from Stephanie: 'I need to get away from everything for an hour. Can you meet me near mine tomorrow?'

I can't say no. As much as I hate relatively impromptu catch-ups (I'm a week-in-advance girl) there is no question that I'll be there for her.

'What's happening with that guy?' Stephanie tries to be bright.

I know I've told her Frankie's name but she's got a lot on her mind; besides, forgiving your friends is much easier than say—no, I'm not going to think about it.

'Nothing really—slow progress. I haven't got much time for anything with work at the moment.' I take a smoke and mirrors approach then change the subject back to her.

We share a tear and a laugh over cake and coffee—Stephanie tells me about her mother, I stick to safe territory and make her feel lucky she no longer works full-time. I'm careful not to take on too much of her 'life doesn't go on forever energy' after what I'd done last time.

On the bus heading home I get chatting to the guy sitting next to me. Obviously he starts it, I definitely wouldn't.

'I'm Hawaiian,' he tells me.

'Oh, a friend of mine goes to Hawaii every year, she loves it.' Pleasant chit-chat with strangers is quite my forte—no demands, nothing at stake, so I can pleasantly bob along the surface.

We get off the bus at the same stop (as fate would have it) and he appears to have misinterpreted my enthusiastic banter—he's writing his details on a piece of paper for me. I glance at it and note his name is Kainoa Pukui.

'Oh, one more thing,' Kainoa calls after me once we've said our goodbyes and I've disinterestedly dropped his note into my handbag. I turn back. 'I'm thirty-seven, I know I look younger.'

'That's OK—I like older men,' I say, laughing, and fly off down the street, delighted he felt the need to clarify that. Who says I need Intense Reinforcing Anti-Wrinkle Eye Cream?

35

Hello, my name is Kismet Johnson and I'm a Frankie addict.

Surely there must be some kind of twelve-step program for this sort of behaviour? Possessed by a force far greater than good sense, my survival instincts seem to have gone into hiding. One week on from the note passing, prepped to the max—my eyelashes have been curled at least a thousand times, underwear packed in my bag to pop on later, I'm walking down the street to PGGG. I may as well just get facing Frankie out of the way. How much worse can it get? I'm so nervous every time I leave the house that surely whatever happens is going to be better than living with that constant sick feeling. And after his physical appreciation of my chest on Thursday night, I don't feel overly repellent to him. I'm not throwing myself at him by making a special trip—I'm just popping by on my way to lunch with my family (hence the underwear in my bag). Baking is still beyond me.

I give myself a last-minute talk. *It will be fine. Only what is best for my highest good can play out here. What doesn't kill me will make me stronger. I can handle this. In for five hundred grams of salad greens, in for a kilo!* But only Ms Terse-at-the-Till is there. Frankie is nowhere to be seen or heard.

Of course he didn't see you and has run out the back to hide—Ms Middle-of-the-Road wrestles her evil twin, Ms Paranoid-and-Chronically-Insecure, who is sure she saw the flash of a male figure risk life and limb as he leapt from the ladder to dash out the side.

I'm scouring safe dessert selections like nougat and biscuits—innocuous if dropped and reasonably easy to handle when shaking like a leaf —when the squeak of a sneaker startles me. I look up just as Frankie is passing.

'Hi,' he says in a 'fuck, I'd rather not talk to you at all' manner.

'Hi, Frankie,' I squawk, certain I sound like a chain-smoking cockatoo.

Ms Terse-at-the-Till comes out from behind the counter holding a broom. She moves closer, pretending she's sweeping to get a better view—or maybe she's going to fly into a jealous rage and beat me to death. Hard to know.

Focus on what's in front of you, I remind myself, one of Amethyst's tips to manage my anxiety. I turn back to the biscuits and nougat, all blurry now. I close my eyes, try to breathe and regain my emotional equilibrium, and clear my eyes. The only sound I hear is the shattering of all hope in my head. *Just grab something—anything—then all you have to do is walk to the till and pay, you can do that.*

Without looking, I reach forward and take the first packet my hand lands on.

Who was I kidding? I've got about as much of a karmic connection with Frankie as I do with one of the cucumbers my gaze has landed on. Bad choice, too phallic and they make me sick. I look at the cauliflowers instead.

You started it, Frankie, you with your seagull eyes looking at me like I was a hot chip!

Frankie moves away from the counter as I approach. He's been using Ms Terse-at-the-Till as a human shield. I put my head down and scuff at the floor as she rings up my purchase—Cardamom, Macadamia, Kumquat and Pineapple Nougat, that's going to go down a treat, not. But I'm in no position to care. I pay and get out of there as fast as possible.

Honestly, Frankie wouldn't have noticed if I'd been wearing a pair of nanna knickers as a beanie let alone had a hint of visible panty line.

I package my disappointment up in a tight bundle and return to Plan A: living in Shanghai with a Silicone Frankie. That'd have to be better than living with the real thing. I tell Lionel as much in our next session.

'If you *truly* didn't care and were over him, you wouldn't be sitting here talking about him.' Lionel sounds a little peeved.

Touché, Lionel.

I try to sit up tall in the apricot Jason recliner to give my Frankie declaration some dignity. Not easy considering my ankles are up around my ears.

'I want you to email the Hawaiian guy, see what happens.' He puts his hand up at my objection. 'As an exercise. Maybe you just need to freshen things up a bit. Frankie probably feels too safe now. Time to snap the rubber band.'

'What?'

'Snap the rubber band: pulling back a bit so Frankie can snap back to you. Be open to other opportunities. Better still—create them.'

'I do try to entertain the possibility of other men but, to be honest, no one else does it for me.' I push myself up as far as I can on the chair.

'The Hawaiian, Kismet, write an email and send it.'

After what happened last time I took Lionel's advice I'm not sure it's a good idea but I agree. Exploring other options can't hurt anything. I know any semi-decent bookie would put the odds of anything happening between Frankie and me lower than Hitler reaching enlightenment the next time he's incarnated, but bookies probably don't believe in signs and destiny.

'Sure, I'll do it when I get home from work tonight,' I promise as I rush out to get back to work.

36

Sorry, Spirit, but fuck, shit and hell, I think that's Frankie.

I squint down the street as I walk to the bus stop and have a louder than sneaking suspicion that the figure I can see surrounded by workmen is said fruitologist.

Kill me now a thousand times over, maybe more. A few steps closer I realise it's definitely him. I prepare to enter Humiliation Central and try not to drop dead from anxiety. Although why I'm trying not to die from anxiety when it'd be preferable to facing him with all these men around, I'm not sure. Could Spirit have thrown a more torturous situation in my path? Do I speak? Do I look in his direction? Do I not? He seems pretty immersed in the conversation. What if I speak to him or even just look at him and he blanks me in front of everyone?

I'm not good saying 'hi' to someone if they're engaged in conversation with another person, let alone a group. I can't even do it at work, never mind with Frankie and a gang of workmen first thing in the morning. I haven't even finished my coffee.

My mouth gets drier with each step. If my hands weren't shaking so much I'd take another sip of coffee to lubricate it a little. I look at the ground, trying to figure out what to do. I have so many butterflies that if I can manage to open my mouth I fear they'll come flying out like racing pigeons. My near constant state of queasiness amps up—if it's only butter-flies that come out when I open my mouth I'll be happy. If I vomit in front of them I will die, I'm sure of it.

I'm sure the rapid side-step I've just made to dodge a guy delivering pig carcasses to the butchers, then another to avoid a cable layer's legs sticking out of a ditch don't help the sit-uation. The actual pig's carcass itself is probably not helping either, nor is being precariously close to being hit in the head with a pig's trotter for all to see.

Oh no, I can't do it—I can't say 'hi' to him. But I make myself lift my head and half-look at him so if he ignores me it won't be obvious that I was expecting him to acknowl-edge me.

'Hi, Fiona, how are you?' Bless Frankie. He stops talking to the workmen and turns to me in full Mr Putney-Road-Alpha-Male mode.

I look at him fully and deliver another original, 'Hi, Frankie.'

Beyond not getting a gig on the public speaking circuit, I doubt either of us will be writing a *How to Make Your Mark Mingling and Maximising Small Talk* book anytime soon either.

Frankie looks into my eyes and I look back into his. I raise my eyebrow slightly, not intentionally—it's another one of those 'no control over my physical functions or actions' things that hit me around him. I hope it compensates for the lack of enthusiasm in my tired, timid voice.

As Frankie and I look at each other I can feel the workmen looking at us. There is so much sizzle going on that when a second guy comes by labouring under the weight of a pig carcass on each shoulder, I expect the meat to have crispy crackling by the time he gets it inside the butcher.

Why him? I can almost hear the cogs of the workmen's brains as they watch me turn to a steamy pile of mush, while Frankie puffs out his chest and broadens his shoulders.

'Have a good day, Frankie.' I give him a wave, fingers fluttering like snowflakes. I don't skip (even though if I weren't so tired I'd want to) but I do trot down to the bus stop, asking myself exactly the same question the workmen were thinking.

On Saturday the weather is spectacular. The sun glistens off the waters of the bay. It's so bright coming through the floor-to-ceiling windows of Amethyst's waiting room I have to put my sunglasses on.

'Can't you just fix it?' I say jokingly to Amethyst, head in my hands, when I get into my session. Of course I'm talking about Situation Frankie.

'I can fix it when you're ready for it to be fixed,' she says. 'But you can't bypass the process, Kismet. You need to live through your karmic lessons to evolve. You can't run screaming down your spiritual path. Our energetic and physical journeys are really very similar: you must crawl before you can walk.'

Oh my Buddha, I've been crawling so long my knees are bloody and my hands raw. I want to ask if there isn't some sort of spiritual bullet train that I can take to put an end to this ordeal but I don't imagine she'll find the humour in it.

'Trust more, Kismet ... the Universe, yourself, the signs— that's what my guides say you need to hear.' Forefingers and middle fingers rubbing her temples. 'But there's something more. I'm not getting it clearly right now. Let me get you on the table. I'm sure it'll come through when your energetic field is less congested.'

Once I'm on the table, Amethyst waves a chunk of turquoise around my aura, darting it this way and that. 'It's a potent healer, this one. It bridges the space between heaven and earth and will—Oh, hang on, I knew this would happen.' She lays the piece of turquoise on the table beside me and moves her fingers to her temples again. 'Yes, yes. I thought so. Vulnerability, Kismet. You need to show him your vulnerability, exposing that side of yourself to him will help, they tell me.'

'I'm pretty sure I might have already done that.'

'No, no. I knew there was a reason I chose turquoise for you today. It's not a crystal I'd normally think aligns with your energy but it was calling me so strongly and now I know why. Turquoise helps you speak your truth. You're still putting up a front around him.'

She picks up the turquoise again. 'Oh my, oh dear, what's going on there?' Amethyst's not expecting an answer—I know she's talking to my energy. 'Kismet, your root chakra is turning the crystal into a hot rock.'

Well, I did mention the sizzle, I think, but to tell her about the full level of my desire would only make me feel like I was exposing another of my spiritual failings.

As I leave she reminds me, 'Be grateful to Frankie, he's an excellent spiritual teacher for you. He's really pushing your energetic evolution to heights you wouldn't have reached so quickly if you'd stayed in your comfort zone.'

Spiritual teacher, my karmic asana, some people would say. But I really do need to have faith and trust. I haven't spent this long on the spiritual path for nothing.

I'm not madly excited when I finally get an email back from the Hawaiian guy on Tuesday. I'd contacted him as per Lionel's homework, though I'd nearly stalled at his email address. Supa_bambang_like2partay@gmail.com so isn't me.

I open the email, not really caring what he says, but I am curious, that's just my nature.

It's totally BLANK! Not a keystroke in there.

I close it and re-open it to check.

Nope, definitely blank.

The third time I look at it, I see that the sender's name is different from the one he gave me. Kainoa Pukui is really Suparman Bambang Prakoso!

Not that being Indonesian, as his name indicates, is a problem. It was the dishonesty about being Hawaiian. At least it proved my intuition was correct—I'd known something didn't feel right. There had to be some reason I wasn't attracted to him—I'd always fancied dating a Hawaiian.

The following day another email comes through from him with *CALL ME* and his number in the subject line. Nothing in the body of the email again!

What am I, some sort of dog? I don't think so, sweetheart. What good is a man who doesn't use words?

Unlike Frankie, I bandy Suparman Bambang Prakoso around the office for entertainment. I feel a new lease of life, having a little fun again. According to everyone there, I should 'Stop being a princess about how you were approached. Just go out with him as practice for when someone you really like comes along.'

Everyone apart from Bing that is—he is outraged at Suparman lying to me.

I don't intend to even email Suparman back, let alone call him. Apart from the fact that I have less than no desire to, I'm totally irritated by the email.

Maybe I should direct my rubber banding energies back to Jack? What did it matter if he didn't have the same sense of humour as me; I could always snort with Jane. As for chemistry, maybe it would develop. I mean, you hear about people being just friends at the outset all the time. They probably even learnt to overlook things like unattractive forearms.

37

There are three reasons I once again decide to bite the bullet and return to PGGG on Monday night:

1. My obvious Frankie addiction—am yet to locate a Frankie Fetishes Anonymous (not that I've tried).
2. The dismal failure of the email exchange with Suparman in Mission Moving On/Rubber Banding.
3. Amethyst's words of wisdom—I'm committing to my spiritual path, being bigger than my ego, having faith and trusting.

After Pig Carcass Friday, I'm feeling hopeful for another positive interaction. I've been trying to block the actual pig carcasses out, since I'm not sure they're such a good sign. I mean, it's all well and good for Google to tell me about pigs and their spiritual significance in agriculture and being symbols of fertility but what about their carcasses?

'Hi, Fiona,' Frankie says in the midst of a phone call.

'Hi, Frankie.' I look at the floor and don't slow my step. He resumes his phone call.

At least we're back to our scintillating style of conversation and the choppy waters of his mood from the last visit definitely seem to have calmed.

I start to gather the items on my list. *Oh fuck!* Between the salad greens and red cabbages, my first two items, I realise there's only Frankie here. I try to gather my senses and not spin around in circles.

I move on with my shopping but struggle to locate things I buy every week. I'm feeling—and, I fear, looking—slightly bewildered. I know I'm meant to be having faith but panic seems to have taken over. There's only one way out and unless I choose to drop my basket and make a run for it, I must face Frankie at the counter.

I look around. There's no one else in the shop and no queue so I can't even tailgate someone for protection and not face Frankie alone. I could take A Flock of Seagulls' 'I Ran' being on the radio as a sign, I think, as I hide in the deli area to try to gather some courage. Frankie is only semi-singing along—there's none of his usual gusto.

What's the point if you're going to give up now, Kismet? I remind myself that no one ever died of embarrassment or humiliation—according to Google at least.

I steel plate my aura and gird my chakras.

One steps, two steps ... then I'm at the counter, unloading my produce opposite Frankie.

Clunk! Crash!

Fantastic! First I hit the wall with my basket as I turn to put it away, *then* I have trouble getting it to sit in the other baskets. Blame my shaking hands—well, my shaking everything.

I turn back to see Frankie about to put my things in a plastic bag.

'Oh, don't worry about a bag, thanks,' I say, hopefully sweetly. I point to my bag.

It's more smog than sizzle between us right now, all awkward and stilted. The air has a monsoonish heaviness to it. Frankie seems nervous and unable to even look at me, but regardless of what's going on inside, I'm obviously looking warm, open and friendly as he finds it in himself to say, 'I'll talk to you later, I've been really busy and …'

Oh Great Guru, have mercy! The way things are going whatever he says next is only going to result in more humiliation. I'm about to be totally rejected and become the first person ever to die of humiliation.

Frankie does not specifically mention the note, though I can feel his discomfort at having to say what he *is* saying and I'm sure he's wishing I hadn't put him in this situation.

Fuck, fuck, fuck. Now I feel awful for making Frankie feel bad.

I dance my hand around my face dismissively, which is what I do when I'm very uncomfortable. 'Oh, that's OK, don't worry about it. Sorry, I still can't believe that I did it.' I'm not quite able to keep a tremor from my voice.

My left hand moves into my hair at my forehead and—I can't help myself—I gather strands between my fingers and pull them down over my face. Oh Goddess, I can't believe I'm doing this in front of Frankie. It's as though all my 'this is what I do when I want the ground to open up and swallow me' traits and tricks have come out in one fell swoop.

At least the shock of my obvious discomfort seems to put Frankie at ease. Not my usual approach to making people feel more comfortable but what would I expect? Nothing I do around Frankie is usual.

'You don't need to apologise.' There's no twang in his voice.

'I don't do things like that.' I feel myself cycle from dusky pink through magenta to puce, a rainbow of humiliation.

'Why not?'

Seriously, Frankie, 'why not' should be obvious—look at where it has led.

'I can't believe I did that, I don't know why I even did it. I didn't even *plan* to do it,' I babble. Then we look into each other's eyes and I disappear into Frankie and want to stay in the moment forever. (Maybe not exactly *this* moment, as it is quite excruciating.)

Even though I'm looking into his eyes, I've gone into my super chronic anxiety mode. My hand has moved from my hair and my little finger is in my mouth and I'm biting on it with my incisor. It's a state that shocks people, particularly as I look like I'm going to cry.

Frankie appears a bit traumatised. 'I'll talk to you later,' he says again.

Kill me now a trillion times over—the rejection must be so bad he can't bring himself to do it now.

I step away. We're still looking into each other's eyes. There are words floating between us but now I've got one foot on Planet Swoon and one on Planet Kill Me Now if I Don't Die of Humiliation Immediately, I don't register what they actually are.

I have to force myself to turn away from him and walk out of the store and when I do, I fucking well go in the wrong direction! (Get over the swearing, Spirit—I have bigger fish to fry right now.)

At first I think, *Oh, I'll just run with it, head up the street and go home the back way so it'll look completely intentional.* But after one step I decide I'm just going to run straight home, so now I look like I've totally lost the plot.

I realise I still haven't told Frankie the note was a quote from a book and that I'm not so up myself that I wrote it about me. Although, there'll be time to clear that up 'later', I think, in an effort to deescalate my internal situation.

I dump my stuff home. Even though it's 8.15pm, I'll implode or explode or something if I don't keep moving. I take myself for a walk around the park to try to expend some of my energy and emotion and clear my head (insofar as that is going to be possible).

When I get home, I reflect on things in place of sleep.

It's interesting timing, there being no coincidences and all, that just last week Lionel and I worked specifically on me feeling that I can't look people in the eye if I like them or am uncomfortable with them or intimidated by them, or I'm upset with someone, or afraid of them, as I don't want them to see my softness. If they see it, they will hurt me.

And Lionel also just happened to feel the need to tell me that if a man likes someone he'll find shyness and clumsiness endearing, if not then he won't. So simple with men really sometimes.

Amethyst has been priming me along those lines too: 'Don't ever lose that shyness—lose its power to debilitate you, but don't lose the sweetness of it.'

And I can't overlook the message from Amethyst's guides about appealing to Frankie by showing him my vulnerability. I think that box has been ticked. And I did succeed at looking at him in the eye.

Even Katy my old kinesiologist said I would always be sweet and self-conscious when guys fancied me—not that we have any evidence that Frankie really does.

38

For fourteen days I've been stuck in an Adidas-adorned-feet desert. My life is a nasal-twang-free zone, devoid of bald spots, apart from Desmond's, which is definitely not the one I want to be seeing. At work Tiffany and Angela—and everyone really—have been unbearable, nagging me to 'Just go on a date with Suparman, for God's sake, Fiona, what's it going to hurt?'

I've kept them at bay by claiming I'm too busy, which I am. Of course being busy isn't the *only* reason. Even though the post-note visit to PGGG was torturous, there was still something sweet and comforting in his response when I went all haywire that means I just can't shake that Frankie feeling.

I'm sitting at my desk on a short trip to Planet Swoon when my office phone rings.

'Centre for Strategic and Financial Excellence, this is Fiona,' I answer, distracted.

'Fiona, Fiona Johnson?' a timid-sounding male voice asks.

'Speaking.'

'I believe from my friend Mitchell that I should meet you.'

'I'm sorry?'

'My friend Mitchell said I should meet you.'

'I'm sorry, I don't understand.' But then the penny drops. I know exactly what's going on here and I know exactly who is responsible! He's talking about Meet My Friend. 'I'm awfully sorry, there seems to have been some mistake,' I say and get him off the phone as quickly as possible.

'Angela! Tiffany!' I scream across the office. Heads pop up over petitions like meerkats and follow me as I march to their desks.

They're doubled over, laughing.

'I will not be prostituted for your amusement and entertainment, ladies.' I try to keep a straight face but their laughter is contagious. 'Take it down now, please.'

Tiffany smirks. 'Only if you agree to go on a date with Suparman.'

'No. You can't hijack my love life. I can't believe you've done this. It's an invasion of my civil liberties.' I'm still laughing so it does detract from the force of my demand but, honestly, as if Mum and Catherine hadn't been bad enough with Grant (who, as it turns out, wasn't Tindering at all; he'd just got back with his wife).

'Please.' I turn pleadingly to Angela, always a softer touch.

She opens up my profile immediately. Oh Great Govinda, I really must get some sleep. The photo Tiffany had snuck of me was hideous. I wouldn't have ever found anyone decent with that. And they called themselves marketers!

'Angela, we agreed,' Tiffany barks. 'Fiona, this is officially an intervention.'

Angela's hands fly off her keyboard just as she was about to hit delete.

'OK.' I glare at Tiffany. 'I'm not promising anything but I'll call Suparman tonight and just see what happens.'

But first there's something I need to do.

'Hi, Fiona,' Frankie says when I walk into PGGG that evening.

It's not like I'm giving Frankie one last chance but if nothing tangible happens tonight I will go on a date with Suparman, if he asks.

'Hi, Frankie.' My nerves steal a little of the sing-song from my voice. I can't quite look at him. Neither of us seem to know what to say. 'Have you got any ground ginger?' I blurt, mortifyingly forgetting a 'please'. I'm not asking for the ginger just for the chance to appreciate his physicality, although I won't be complaining when he reaches up to get it; I'm throwing it in all my food these days because it's supposed to help with queasiness.

I focus on trying to turn this encounter into something, anything, other than the 'later' Frankie mentioned last time. I'd prefer to forget the note ever happened and not have it, or any fallout from it, ever mentioned again.

'Have you been busy?' I ask, eyes on his torso as his head disappears behind the spices.

'Yes,' he says, 'always two thousand things to do.'

I love it that he doesn't say an ordinary hundred or even a thousand or million. Another item for my mental list of Endearing Things About Frankie that I resurrected after post-note-fiasco night.

'Oh, not two thousand and ten?' I tease.

I see his body relax. He gives a little laugh but maybe he's just putting on a front. I immediately worry that he's thinking I'm having a go at him. But if we're worrying about sensitivity, Frankie choosing to sing along to The Human League's 'Don't You Want Me' when it comes on doesn't get a top score.

I'm the one suffering here, Frankie. If allowances are to be made for anyone's behaviour right now it is mine, so don't go sulking about my dysfunctional synapses and what they make me say when I'm around you, I think, hoping to transmit it mentally.

It'd help if I could figure out his star sign but I can't. He's too much of a chameleon for me to pin him down.

With visibly shaking hands I pass over my cash and we look into each other's eyes—a medium length but still delicious gaze.

My right shoulder moves of its own accord, giving him a coy shrug as I leave.

'See ya, Frankie.' I flick my hair, look back and smile at him.

Arrgghh. I can't believe I get so dharmaed girly around him, not to mention my body taking on a mind of its own.

I don't want anything or anyone to break the Frankie bubble I'm in, but still a promise is a promise and surely one date with Suparman has to be better than random callers from Meet My Friend.

And so it is that on Friday, Tiffany, Angela and I are gathered at my desk, preparing for my lunch date with Suparman. Tiffany is coaching me in suitable topics of conversation and what to order in front of a man (she insisted), while Angela is doing my hair in a half-up/half-down style (which will make the most of my 'to die for cheekbones' apparently), when Rosemary Hatchment limps up.

'No Dr Cybil again today, I gather?'

There's no hostility in Rosemary's voice but I start making excuses—I don't want her telling Broomstick we've taken to holding virtual slumber parties in her absence.

'We're priming Fiona, she's going on a date,' Tiffany says over me.

Rosemary smiles. 'Good for you, Fiona, you deserve some fun. My advice: if your toes don't curl when he kisses you, he's not for you.'

Rosemary winks and lurches off, leaving Tiffany, Angela and I gaping at each other.

At 12.30 I meet Suparman outside a café a few blocks from work. I didn't want him to be able to find me again.

'Hi. Are you hungry? I'm starving.' I hurry him inside, not feeling anything, but then I am a bit distracted; Angela and Tiffany are only about five metres behind me. I appreciate that a lunchtime date isn't high risk but it feels like more fun to have them on the case with me.

'That table would be great,' I say to the sweet-looking waitress, pointing at a corner table towards the back of the café. I almost throw myself into a seat that puts my back to the room.

Angela and Tiffany are coming through the door, I can hear them. As planned, they'll choose a table where they can see Suparman and me. I've got hand signals for 'intervene immediately' and 'five minutes till take-off' to give them the cue to leave.

Suparman pulls his mobile out and sits it, screen up, on the table as soon as we're seated. Call me old-fashioned, but if you're having a conversation with someone or—hello—a lunch date, you show the good manners of actually focussing on them. Still, we're all different, live and let live, we all make mistakes (random winking and note passing, for example).

'Wow, you must be popular—two mobiles,' I say as he pulls out a second and places it next to the first. I knew this was a bad idea. Suparman the fibbing non-Hawaiian wasn't ideal but a man with two mobiles cannot be trusted.

'One work and one personal,' he says.

Likely story. 'What do you do for work?'

'A broker.'

'Oh really, that sounds—' *boring as Broomstick* '—interesting.'

'Yes, I'm an estate broker.'

'Is that the same thing as a real estate agent?'

'Are you ready to order?' The waitress's return saves him from having to answer and me from having to endure an explanation.

'The risotto and a side salad for me, please,' I say, passing my menu to her with a smile. I'll probably hear it from Tiffany about the risotto. It's a bit carb-heavy for date food according to her guidelines but I'm starving and pasta is definitely out—way too messy.

'I'll have the zucchini fritters.' Suparman doesn't look at the waitress as he orders, then puts his menu down on the table, ignoring her outstretched hand.

She scoops it up and sails off. She's probably used to that sort of thing but, really, how hard is it to say please and hand her the menu?

'What do you do for work, Fiona?'

Yes, I've told him my name's Fiona. I mean, Kismet just took more explaining than I could be bothered with for a one-off, which I was sure this was going to be.

'Oh, admin stuff, boring.' Normally I'd wave my hands around as emphasis but I don't want to mistakenly make the panic button signal and have Tiffany and Angela rush over. Actually, it's sort of distracting having them here. I can hear them laughing. It's making me feel like I'm missing out on something.

'Was it easy for you to get here?' I ask, keeping things in neutral, Tiffany-endorsed territory, then stifle a yawn as he gives a detailed explanation of his transport connections.

'Don't you need a car as a real estate agent?'

'It's estate *broker* and we have company cars for work. I'm not working today.'

'Oh, I see,' I say because I really can't think of anything else.

Suparman takes the opportunity of the lull in our conversation to play a game of One Hundred Personal Questions You Probably Shouldn't Ask Someone You've Just Met. Not that I'm too fazed by them. Still, being quizzed is exhausting.

Somewhere around question fifty the waitress arrives with our food. I'm pleased for something to occupy him other than questions, but I notice he doesn't thank her or even look up as she delivers our meals.

'This is delicious, how's yours?' I say after a couple of mouthfuls.

'Too salty,' Suparman says. As though to prove his point, he refills his water glass and glugs down half, which would be no big deal if my glass weren't also empty. I don't mean to go on about it but, hello, manners! I know I can refill my own glass and I know Jack being overly attentive put me off but when the other person's is also empty it's purely a matter of consideration.

He clangs his cutlery down then sits there watching me eat. The scrutiny doesn't bode well for a girl enjoying her lunch, not to mention good digestion.

'Have you been married?' he asks. He really did seem so much nicer on the bus but then again, I wasn't that invested in the conversation.

'No. You?'

'No. So you don't have children?'

'No, I've got a niece and nephew, they're adorable.' I stop short of showing him some photos.

'Do you want children?' he asks before I have a chance to ask him if he has children.

'No, it's just not my thing. I love kids but being an aunty is enough for me.'

'Isn't that selfish? Women should want to be mothers, it's what they're made to do. You'll change your mind. Women always do. They say they don't want children but then they wake up one day and their biological clock's alarm has gone off and all they can see in a man is someone to father their children.'

Thank Buddha Germaine is still alive, because if she weren't she'd be spinning in her grave that, after all her work, men were still making such comments. Maybe he'd been burnt—we all carried some baggage. I could forgive him that. But if there's one thing I cannot stand it's being told I don't know my own mind.

'It sounds like maybe you've had a bad experience,' I say, reaching over to fill his glass before mine. It's both a hint and a move to try to remain composed.

'This was a bad experience.' He points at his plate so I gather he doesn't mean me.

'Oh, look, is that the time? I really should be getting back to work.' I've totally lost my appetite. I need to get away from his toxic negativity before it eats any further into my aura. I don't even care about the five-minute signal for Angela and Tiffany.

I almost die when Suparman snaps his fingers to get the waitress's attention for the bill. Who does that?

I'm sure I do die for just a moment when he shoves his chair in, loudly announcing to the waitress and everyone else in the café, 'That was crap.'

Govinda, how I hate a scene.

I've always said I would walk out on a date if they were rude to wait staff, or rude full stop, and here I am, walking out, even if the date has technically ended.

I put my head down to be sure not to look at Angela and Tiffany as I pass.

'Split bill. She had more than me,' Suparman says as we pay.

Buddha above, someone give this guy a gold medal for being an obnoxious prick. I wasn't expecting him to pay for me but quibbling over a couple of bucks and not simply halving it just shows a meanness of spirit. And that was a definite deal breaker, as if everything else wasn't enough.

I'm careful not to get too close to him as we make our way outside. I don't want anyone to think I really know him.

'I'd like to see you again sometime,' he says, as we stand and wait for the lights to change.

Is he insane? Now would be the perfect time to call him out on his lie but why waste my energy? I poke at the button again and it seems to work miraculously. The green man flashes immediately. 'I'm very busy at the moment, actually, I'm busy till next year,' I say, running across the street.

Frankie wouldn't ever be rude to a waitress, I think, but then Frankie hasn't done anything and for all intents and purposes it looks like he never will.

So much for Mission Moving On.

39

When Sunday comes, I'm strung out like a trapeze artist on speed—restless, fidgety, edgy and distracted. I lie on my bed and try to become a flowing stream, drifting around the rocks of life, without force, without aggression, moving fluidly, with grace and beauty in my own perfect rhythm.

But it's hopeless. Lying there only makes me feel worse. I start to think, start trying to figure things out. Fate, the signs, the list, Frankie.

So much for Lao Tzu and his single step. If I wore a Fitbit it would be well over a thousand miles by now and I felt like I'd got nowhere, or worse.

I needed a definitive sign.

True, a sausage dog probably isn't likely to come sniffing at my door but I'd asked to see one in the flesh (or hair) during my intention setting this morning so I'll know what to do. The only way to get an answer is to head out.

At the end of my block I get tangled in the confusion of pedestrians and cars turning in and out of the narrow T-intersection—everyone and everything going in different directions.

Karmic crumpets! A sausage dog is tied up outside a shop on the side street. I only see it because of the confusion. My fate is sealed for today at least.

I'm reaching in to get my yoghurt when I hear Frankie's voice from the deli section.

'Hi, Fiona,' he calls, breaking his sing along to The Pretenders' 'Don't Get Me Wrong'.

I'm not sure if I flinch or what—there's really no explanation—but two little pots of yoghurt leap from the refrigerator shelf. I can't do anything but watch as they hit the floor with a devastating splat. Fucking fantastic! Just fabulous!

I rescue the slightly battered and bent one and pop it back, then pick up the spewing offender and step away, careful not to tread in the soft pink blobs and splatters of yoghurt around my feet. Rather than head to the front, I go in search of Frankie, who has disappeared.

A voice from beyond (Frankie's not God's) starts singing the Little River Band's 'Help is on its Way'. I have no idea how he knows what's happened. Maybe they have a Clumsy Girl Yoghurt Alarm that whoever is at the counter has activated.

'You've got to be unlucky.' Frankie appears, mop and bucket in hand.

He joins me for the journey back to the scene of the yoghurt disaster.

'Oh my god, I am so sorry. How embarrassing. Sorry.' My cheeks on fire, I cycle through my humiliation rainbow.

'I've just finished cleaning up another mess.' Frankie points to the large wet patch on the floor nearby. That explains the 'unlucky' comment so I can forego worrying that it was anything untoward being directed at me. 'A dropped dip,' he explains and shakes his head. 'It was a nightmare, such a mess, took me forever to clean up. Yours is nothing compared to that.'

Still I can't look at him properly. I'm beyond my humiliation rainbow now and bordering on post-note-fiasco-reaction—I've just started the hair-pulling thing.

This is where things go a little hazy.

We're standing at the fridge together, and I must pass him the ruined yoghurt that I still have in my hand. 'I should pay for that,' I say.

'Don't worry about it,' he says in his soothing way.

Obviously I open the fridge to get out the yoghurt I need because I'm standing in front of it. Frankie is behind me, one large hand propping the fridge door open, and—oh my fucking God—his other one is on my waist, resting on the upper curve of my hip!

It is so intimate and comforting. If I thought I'd felt like a melting ice cap before, that was nothing to what I'm feeling now. I have no desire to say, 'Unhand me young (or middle-aged) man,' or even, 'Get your fucking hands off me,' like I would do with anyone else.

But of all the things I could say, 'Oh God, now I can't remember what I wanted,' is what comes out, as Frankie removes his hand from my waist.

Seriously, what is wrong with me? It's perfectly obvious that what I want is right behind me. Why didn't I turn around and just freaking well kiss him?

'That's OK,' Frankie says, standing so close behind me that I can feel him—his warmth, his breath in my hair. It is absolutely the most reassuring thing for me to hear.

Then, as I put a pot of yoghurt into my basket, he says, 'That's not the sort you normally get.'

'Oh, yeah, thanks.' Good thing someone has managed to keep their wits about them here. I force every cell in my body to concentrate on not creating any other disasters as I put the wrong one back and retrieve my usual brand.

Frankie starts to mop up my mess. I move away, offering more apologies with each mop stroke. One hand clutches my basket so tightly my knuckles are white, while the other flutters around my face in embarrassment. But Frankie just reminds me of the dropped dip, as though trying to make me feel that everything's alright.

I rally myself to toss a couple of humorous lines at him as I step away. I'm not really aware of what I'm saying or doing but I gather they're amusing, because Frankie and Thuga, who I now see has been watching from the till, both give a small laugh. Ms Totally-Middle-of-the-Road doesn't even entertain the paranoid notion that they might be laughing at me. A breakthrough of sorts.

'Don't stop now, Fiona, go for a trifecta,' Frankie says as he passes me in the deli section.

'I'm just looking for what will make the most mess.' I gathered he was talking about the mopping up rather than the fantastically humiliating moments I'd created with the note and the spillage.

Frankie runs around the shop in his hurricane-like way, singing along to Toni Basil's 'Mickey'. I only lift my head to watch him when I know he and Thuga can't see me.

'Man, I'm so problematic today,' I say to Thuga at the counter, as Frankie has to run off to check a price on something I've bought.

Thuga looks at me and smiles when I pass him my fifty dollars, once Frankie has yelled out, 'Three twenty-five!'

'Thanks,' I say, smiling. I walk home feeling like I've had the spiritual equivalent of electric shock therapy—I even forgot to say goodbye to Frankie.

When I get there I'm off in every direction—mentally and physically. By the end of the evening I have cooked, I have cleaned and I have reflected on Situation Frankie from every angle. The conclusion: I am officially more confused than I have ever been.

I sit on the bus, I drink coffee, I work, I run on the treadmill, I go to meetings, I lie in bed, I sit at my desk, I use my computer, I watch TV, I walk along the street, I chat … I do all the things I do and every so often a little smirk appears on my face and if anyone is around and aware enough to catch it they ask, 'What are you thinking about?'

'Oh, nothing,' I reply every time, not once sharing that it's Frankie who curls the corners of my mouth with affection, girlish skittishness and a longing for our next interaction. And we have them. My life becomes a movie trailer of Frankie highlights. Everything else exists in the shadows.

The Monday after Yoghurtgate, Desmond needs counselling as he's having trouble with his fiancée, Valeria. We all knew there was trouble in paradise when he stopped referring to her as 'my beautiful bride-to-be'. I feel terrible when he walks away dissatisfied—I'm really off my life-advice game. I just can't concentrate.

A week after, at one of our family lunches, I keep drifting off, thinking about Frankie and slipping into how I felt with his hand on my waist. I'm so awash with desire that waves of heat spring up like spot fires, taking over my body. In every conversation I'm in two minds: one on the words, the other on Frankie.

'Fiona, what's wrong with you? You keep blushing or flushing or something. It can't be the menopause, you're too young for that. It's not in our genes to get it early,' Catherine says in her way, thankfully not in front of anyone else.

Of course I tell her nothing.

I don't even tell Jane. It's not that I'm avoiding her, technically. I knew she'd probably be pleased to hear that desire had rapidly overtaken destiny, but I still haven't been to the doctor like I promised and work has been so busy and she's busy and that's just the way life is sometimes, I guess. She seems fine in our texts and my Suparman disaster date had been fantastic for defrosting any autumn chill left in the air. We just both seem to have a lot going on.

And Stephanie, things aren't good with her mum, so I only text her to see how she is and let her know I'm here if she needs me.

Before I know it, it's over a month since Yoghurtgate. Even as time moves on, the thought of Frankie with his arm around my waist can give me goosebumps and make me swoony. Sometimes when I run to the bathroom or rush to the gym—the only times I have a moment to breathe, think or feel at work these days—I want to call just so I can hear him.

The couple of near-death experiences I have at the gym—so distracted that I nearly fly off the treadmill—are reminders that I should probably come back down to earth.

It's not just Yoghurtgate. Over the next few weeks as we chat and become more familiar, he gets past my safety mode of deflection and humour. I lower the drawbridge that I don't open for anyone, and he doesn't even know it.

It's not like I don't still have a mini meltdown, lose the plot and also my ability to function around Frankie each and every time. Yet I find a strange comfort in being around him, more comfort than I've ever found in anything. It's the way he says something so simple but so perfectly soothing or calming whenever I need to hear it. Like recently when I was feeling timid about going in because I thought they were about to close. He was there, doing his unforgivably sexy lean against the door, and he came out with, 'You're right, Fiona,' with a softness that caught at my heart.

Sometimes the way he appears in front of me on the street like an apparition, the rest of the world swept away, makes me wonder if he's even real.

This Frankie feeling is so many tiny things, from the conversations we have where my words tumble out as I tell him about the simple things of my life. It's the considered questions he asks that are so inconsequential and ordinary that they conceal how much they truly matter.

It's the way he laughs at my stupid asides, the way I'm all crazy nervous around him and the way the clumsiness this causes has become a joke between us. It's also the fact that not even my clothes behave themselves in his proximity now and do crazy things like slipping off my shoulders. My feet turn into lead weights whenever I'm close to him, making it hard to leave. The world washes away when I look in his eyes. He doesn't demand anything from me; I can come and go as I please.

I'm still one hundred per cent Urthboy's 'Crushing Hard'. Well, I would be if Retro FM would play it for me to serenade Frankie and that's never going to happen. Not that I'd be likely to go singing to Frankie, least of all a song that would give the game away.

I've managed to clock up so many things on my mental list of Endearing Things About Frankie that I can no longer tally what they all are. Even the way he pretends not to look at my arse or down my shirt is appealing.

But some days I want to scream, 'Frankie, you're a fuck-wit!', thinking Jane's original assessment is right. Like when I push the conversation too far or my words come out wrong, explaining rather than just letting it be, or Frankie's tired and cranky days. There's also a distance between us still and if I step too close, he recoils like a cobra preparing to strike.

Signs swirl around me in the manner of incense smoke at a temple on a windy day, even to the point of a sausage dog appearing at my feet when I walk down to PGGG.

There is all of this yet there is nothing!

Nothing happens!

'Later' doesn't ever come to talk about the note and Yo-ghurtgate isn't mentioned.

There's an energetic elephant in the eggplants that neither of us want to name, and I don't mean one in Lycra and leg-warmers working out to Jane Fonda like Bev used to do. This elephant has 'not free to be fully with me' written all over it. Item ten gazillion and twenty on my What I Want and Need in my Next Male Love Relationship list requires exactly the opposite.

40

The first person I see when I walk into the nursing home is an old lady in the corner, tears washing her eye make-up into bruises that streak her face.

'Don't mind her, love,' one of the other residents says, 'she just sits there every day, waiting. Sometimes she cries, sometimes she doesn't. She's not having a good day today.'

I ignore the man and walk over to her. You can tell she was attractive once, with high cheekbones and cut-glass green eyes that have become clouded and dull. She's mumbling something to herself. When I get close enough her fingers become claws that wrap around my forearm.

'Where's Frankie? Is he with you? I've been waiting for him so long.'

I kneel beside her and brush the wisps of grey hair that the carers haven't managed to catch in her bun away from the crepe paper of her face. Wet with tears, the hair sticks to my fingers, as though every part of her is trying to find something to cling to.

'Not today,' I tell her. 'Maybe tomorrow.'

She whimpers like a wounded dog.

'Definitely tomorrow. I remember now, he said definitely, one hundred per cent tomorrow, he'll be here,' I say because I can't stand to see her like this.

Her eyes light up and her face loses twenty years.

I wake from the dream in a cold sweat. No dream analyst required to understand what *that* was about. Great Govinda, I couldn't let it be my future.

'What would you do if you didn't consider anything or anyone else, Kismet?' Lionel asks me when I tell him about the dream.

'Oh, that's easy. I'd study Mandarin in China.'

'You seem very sure of that.'

'I am. I've wanted to ever since I started learning it. I just haven't got around to it.'

'Sorry, I don't quite understand. You've studied for years but never got yourself there?'

'I've been but not to study. You know me, more tortoise than hare.'

Lionel nods in the way I've come to recognise as his way of saying, 'It's OK, that's just you. You can't un-be who you are. I'm here to help you know what's you and what's other people—to know yourself well enough to spot the difference, believe in yourself and find the courage to overcome what stops you.'

'I've probably been all or nothing with that too, thinking that unless I do a full three-year degree, or even a year, it isn't worth it. I know there are shorter intensives.'

'That's what I want you do to for your homework this week: research some courses you could do,' Lionel says before he hugs me goodbye. I'm even more comfortable with Lionel hugging me now, he's got a quirky, kind-grandpa way about him that I've grown quite fond of, even though he sometimes challenges me.

Over the next few days, the idea of studying in China starts to take root properly. Once again Lionel has really hit the nail on the head. I just had to be pushed. Obviously I need to be in Shanghai to land my perfect job. I can't believe I hadn't realised that for myself.

Despite the fact that it's after midnight when I do it, I find a couple of places to email. I have loads of leave. I'm not sure how I'll wrangle it with Broomstick and everything that's going on but, once again, I had to find faith. An answer would come.

The medical centre is busy for a Friday. Each time one of the consulting doors opens I look up from the vintage copy of *The Australian Women's Weekly* I've taken from the stack. Perhaps there's a universal waiting room law against having anything too current and interesting in case it causes someone to miss their name being called. Four people who aren't me are called for their appointments, which leaves me with more time to think about why I'm here, and I really don't want to be doing that.

It isn't that my insomnia and anxiety have, in medical terms, become chronic and I spend most of my time feeling that I can't breathe. And even though waking up each morning to the room spinning and having to steady myself to get out of bed would be just cause to be here, it's not that either. Nor is it the constant queasiness and weakness—unless I know Frankie is around, then I summon all my postural poise for him. It's also not the constant headaches and migraines, or that all the painkillers are eating away my stomach lining. Despite the fact I'd been trying to pretend it wasn't there, the tingling from my neck down my right arm, the pain in my wrist, elbow and forearm that mean I sometimes can't use my right hand and that the pain of this RSI fights with the anxiety to see which one will propel me from sleep first is a valid reason too. I know that will take care of itself when I have a more reasonable workload, so it's not that either.

It's one hundred percent pure vanity. When the guy sitting on the seats outside the station near work spoke to me this morning I'd had trouble making sense of his slurring, indecipherable drawl.

'What, sorry?' I'd asked.

He tried again. 'You jus bin dussip la?'

'Sorry, still didn't get it.'

We went through it a few more times, and by the fifth go we got there. Turns out 'You just been dosed up, love?' was what he was saying.

Motherfornicating bastards of Buddha hell! He thinks I've just come from the methadone clinic! *How shit do I look?*

Not really the image I was going for. No wonder Frankie hasn't taken the note or Yoghurtgate any further. It's not that he's not available, he probably thinks I'm a junky whore with a novel approach to turning tricks.

'Fiona Johnson?' Finally! One of the conveyor belt doctors calls me in.

'How can I help you today?'

'I feel nauseous all the time.'

'Hmm. You're not likely to be pregnant are you?'

'No,' I snap. I don't mean to be rude but I really don't need the reminder of how long it is since I've had sex or that it doesn't seem to be likely in the foreseeable future. Bugger

Frankie throwing a Molotov cocktail of desire at my loins then running off like I was the cops about to charge him with arson.

'Anything else unusual happening?' the doctor asks as though he's ticking off his list.

'I'm a bit stressed but I manage that naturally.'

'How long has that been going on?'

'A while.' Seriously, why is he asking me probing questions? I specifically chose a medical centre so I could duck in and out. Just grab something for my nausea because I was sure if I could get rid of that, everything else would be easier.

'How long exactly?'

'Oh, I don't know, a few months, maybe longer.' I really couldn't remember.

'How's your sleep?'

'Not great.'

'How many hours a night do you get?'

'A few, I mean four, maybe.'

'You seem quite agitated.'

I realise I've got my hands shoved under my thighs, my legs jiggling. I feel like a cornered animal. Honestly what did he think he was playing at? Should I remind him that he works in a medical centre? 'Look, I don't want to take up too much of your time. I just came in to get something for my nausea.'

'Any other symptoms?'

'I'm getting a lot of headaches.'

Big mistake. After taking my blood pressure, which is fine, he picks up his little torchy thing. Quite a bit of *hmm*ing ensues as he examines each eye, then makes me follow his finger with my eyes and finally touch my nose with my finger.

'Well, I can tell you I'm pretty sure it's not a brain tumour.'

I hadn't thought I was dying, not in a serious way. I mean Amethyst would have picked it up in my energy field, surely?

'What's happening in your life? Do you a supportive partner? Do you enjoy your work? How long since you've taken
a break from work?'

Those little questions cause treacherous tears to spring
from my eyes.

'Sorry, it's just that I'm not feeling well.' I wipe the tears
away. 'I'm fine, my life is fine. You know how things are with
insomnia. You get all brittle.'

Just because I'm crying at the drop of a hat every five minutes these days it doesn't mean anything. I'm not cracking up.
Not that there is anything wrong with cracking up. It's fine
for other people to do it, just not me. I cope, that's what I do,
I'd always coped and now wasn't going to be any different.

I'm in a state of complete mental, physical and emotional
exhaustion—burnout. That's the official medical opinion. It
sounds so much better than a breakdown, even if a breakdown is the next step if I don't do something, or so the doctor
says.

Walking into work with a medical certificate stating that I
need to take some serious leave and soon is one of the hardest
things I've ever had to do. Admitting I can't keep going is even
harder than any of the times I've made myself go into PGGG.
I'd been thinking about it all weekend, trying to find a way
around it. Maybe if I just made sure I worked shorter hours
and gave myself a break. I didn't want to have a big bang–type
breakdown, but I did feel that my catalyst to 'do something'
was a bit dull. I mean, most people have life-changing epiphanies after their world comes crashing down in a major event
or when they faced death, but my non-breakdown was more

like simmering a pot until it went dry—I'd been given the opportunity to grab it off the heat before it totally cracked. There I'd been, wanting an answer about what to do about my life and though it hadn't come in the form I would have chosen, it was all working out perfectly, in an imperfect sort of way. I'd even had emails back from two of the colleges I'd contacted about courses. The one that I had the best feeling about had a six-week intensive running in a month's time.

'You're just going to have to get a temp to cover me,' I say to Broomstick when she starts turkey gobbling. 'It's not like I'm going on leave tomorrow, I can do some handover.'

As soon as I'm back at my desk Angela and Tiffany come teetering up. Honestly, it's like they were born with supersonic gossip sensors.

'Fiona, have you done it, have you resigned?' they ask.

'No, I'm going to China!' I practically squeal with excitement.

'Oh, you're leaving us.' Their faces fall, which is pretty touching really.

'Only for six weeks. I'm doing a language course.'

They look at me blankly. I know it's not really their thing. It wouldn't be most people's thing. Most people ordered to take R&R would go sip cocktails on a tropical island but I'm not most people and I'm starting to feel more and more comfortable with that.

'Ohh, maybe you'll meet someone in China,' Angela says excitedly.

Tiffany and I shoot her a look. After Suparman, they'd agreed that maybe it was best they didn't force me back onto Meet My Friend and stayed out of my romantic affairs.

Of course I don't tell them exactly why and how I've been able to get leave so quickly. They don't even ask—they're so accustomed to asking for what they want and getting it that the question simply wouldn't occur to them. Broomstick's agreed not to mention the whole burnout thing to anyone. Not out of kindness and consideration, more out of the fear that I could launch some sort of worker's compensation claim, I'm sure.

Of course I've made a People to Call and Share My News With list. That night, I send my application to the college and there's no doubt in my mind that it's going to be accepted. I'm so certain that I book my flights too. It feels good to be doing something like this for myself again. I haven't planned a trip for years. Not that it's a trip, exactly. It's a research mission. I'll be intelligence gathering—looking for a job, scoping out my new life and laying foundations. Of course I won't tell anyone this.

Jane is the first person I tell. I am so excited that I can't hold it in.

'Jesus Christ, Kizzo, about fucking time,' she says when I call her after I've booked everything. I know she's not just referring to the study trip, but to putting my foot down with Broomstick and saying what I need and, yes, taking her advice to go to the doctor. I let her think it was her advice; it makes her happy.

Of course, she's also not protesting because it means I'm not mooning around, waiting for Frankie. I still haven't told her about the note or Yoghurtgate.

Lionel says people's immediate reaction always gives away who they are at their core. Actually maybe that was one of Mum's Dr Phil-isms, but whatever, it turns out to be pretty much true. Over the next few days there's:

Mum—'But you'll miss two family lunches.'

Dad—mute on all fronts; Mum speaks for him.

Catherine—'Do you get a qualification of some sort?'

Bing—'Mei Mei, I wish you'd wait and come with me and the family.'

Stephanie—'Good on you, you need to take your chances when they come and live your precious life.'

OK, so Stephanie's was a bit surprising, she's always so factual and efficient, but she's not herself lately. Who would be, in her shoes?

I don't really mention my burnout to any of them. It isn't that I'm embarrassed, I just wanted to focus on the positive.

Lionel, who of course I've told everything, is so happy that the hug he gives me actually brings a tear to my eye and not in an 'I can't control my emotions anymore' way.

41

The four weeks fly by. It's a bit of a blur really. There's so much to do between work and trying to pack up my life here so I can make a hasty permanent exit from it on my return. I'm still tired but my aura feels so alive and sparkly that I cancel my session with Amethyst. She could sense I was on the cusp of a major shift, she tells me. This must be it.

On the Monday of the week I'm due to leave, I'm waiting for Jack to make my coffee, staring at the doorway, when Frankie bounds in. Of all the things I fear in life, it isn't exactly *the* biggest, but still … timing, gentlemen. I give a little prayer for Jack not to say anything flirty or grab my fingers in front of Frankie.

'Hi, Frankie.' My words come dancing out loudly, and I fear a tad too enthusiastically given my surrounds. I may be heading to China to scope out my new life as Ms Middle-of-the-Road-Driving-Her-Own-Destiny-and-Moving-On but I'm immediately flushed with excitement at the sight of him.

Behind the coffee machine, Jack raises his eyebrows. 'Do you know Frankie?'

Jack's reaction makes me look at my pedicured toes peeking out of my sandals. They're almost touching Frankie's sneakers. It feels so perfectly natural and comfortable for me to be there, cocooned in Frankie's aura, that I hadn't realised how close we are. That zing—it's not my imagination.

'Yes, I *do* know Frankie,' I say, which may be a little over-familiar as I don't really *know* him or any of the details of his life.

'He's terrible,' Jack says, with what I assume is territorial jealousy.

I feel bad that I'm not able to contain my Frankie excitement even for the sake of Jack. He really is so much sweeter and more into me, in an overt way at least, not to mention technically more attractive (if I overlook his forearms). Still, here I am, every cell of my body tingling with life at being so close to Frankie.

As though we've been caught out, Frankie and I take a small step away from each other.

'Are you enjoying the cooler weather, Fiona?' Frankie asks me in a move towards one of our world-record-breaking scintillating conversations.

'Yes. The weekend was lovely. Did you have a nice one, Frankie?'

It's ridiculous, the way we're both looking at each other, trying not to smile, keeping our conversation so proper.

'Yes, I did have a nice weekend, thank you, Fiona. I had one of the best sleeps I've had in ages: nine pm to five am.'

'Oh my god, that's fantastic!'

'What time do you start work? You seem late,' Frankie says.

I am Ms Middle-of-the-Road-Driving-Her-Own-Destiny-and-Moving-On, I am not going to swoon or give an internal squeal of excitement that he notices what time I go by ... until I do.

'Fiona's work is busy, sometimes she has to go in really early, before you're even there, other days she goes in later because she's worked late!' Jack virtually spits in an attempt to put Frankie back in his place.

I can't help imagining them having a little tussle over me. I hold my breath for a dramatic moment when Frankie moves away from me and steps up to Jack at the counter, thinking it might happen.

I hadn't been expecting a duel but as Jack passes me my coffee, Frankie occupies himself looking at the paper. Before his fingers are barely off my cup, Jack is looking at the highlight that Frankie's making comment on, holding it up to show him. Had I wanted to force my hand, I could have chosen that moment to announce my trip to Shanghai—or try to. Announcements aren't really my style, not to even just one person, let alone two, and when one of those people is Frankie—forget it.

Not that I'm into game playing or playing one man off against another, but it would've been interesting to see how they responded, which one threw himself at my feet and whether the forearms that wrapped themselves around my ankles and begged me not to go were attractive to me or not. But here I am, veering off the white lines of the centre of the road again.

'Bye!' I turn to wave at them as I walk to the door. Of course I run into the coffee beans as I do it. All the times I've been in here, I've not once run into them before. Bloody Frankie!

At 7.55 Sunday morning I step outside my gate. Bing, who has insisted on taking me to the airport (much to Mum's distress) is parking his little black car.

Fuck it! (I'm not even going to apologise to Spirit for expletives today, I need the release—everything feels so intense.) I rush up before he has time to get out and give his cheek a quick peck through his half-open window.

'Da Ge, I'm just going to run down and grab a coffee. Want one?'

'Plenty of time, Mei Mei, I'm early.'

I freaking well know!

'Why don't I come with you and we can sit and have breakfast?' Bing starts to get out of the car. I lean my weight against the door to stop him opening it.

'Oh no, Da Ge, I'm a bit anxious to get to the airport. I'll only be a minute.' A volatile cocktail of sleep deprivation (four hours), amped-up excitement (if I could I'd be doing backflips and cartwheels), anticipation and urgency with a dash of desperation see me in no mood for fussing around and giving in to what other people want me to do. Before Bing has time to argue, I'm running down the street. My heart is beating so hard it's making my brain rattle.

I'm all Amy Shark in 'Adore'. She captures everything I feel in this moment so perfectly. Seeing Frankie before I go feels like the most important thing I've had to do in my life.

Putney Bridge Road is deserted, everything feels different. Maybe I've willed the street out of the suburb just so I can adore Frankie, or at least say goodbye. Or perhaps it's always this quiet at this hour on a Sunday, I just haven't witnessed it before.

What if BIG is there to cramp my style?

'Back off and get back to your buns, BIG.' I imagine giving him the same 'now is not the time to mess with me' treatment I just gave Bing.

Fuck it twice! No Jack. I'd hoped he might be there despite it being Sunday. I'm disappointed but not devastated. I'll see him when I get back.

I make it down to PGGG in about five desperately determined strides.

I gasp and think I am going to cry.

Fuck it thrice! Not open—devastation beyond devastation. Then I realise they are, it's just my bloody appalling eyesight again.

'Hi Frankie, I bet you didn't ever expect you'd see me here this early on a Sunday,' I sing-song as I swan in, blessing Spirit, the Universe and every single atom of the cosmos for having him there.

'It's nice to see you so early,' Frankie replies so sweetly it risks turning me into an instant diabetic.

If I was being suave and true to our Retro FM relationship I'd break out into Juice Newton's 'Angel of the Morning', but it doesn't cross my mind.

'Oh no, it isn't ever good to see me early really—I'm not a morning person.'

Frankie approaches me. I approach him. Soon we're facing each other with less than a foot between us.

'I wanted to come and say goodbye. I'm going to China for a while. I have to go because if I don't I'm just going to drop dead at my desk,' I blurt in one big whale spout of words as I look forlornly into his eyes. This isn't at all how I wanted it to happen—I'd spent half the night imagining a normal exchange: 'I'm going to China.' 'How long for?' 'Oh well, I'm not sure ...' 'What are you going to do there?' 'A language intensive course and I'll look for work while I do that.'

I feel like I'm going to cry or vomit or pass out or maybe all three. And if that happens, some bloody cosmic ombudsman will have hell to pay.

Frankie takes another step towards me. I assume we're going to hug, but—oh my fucking god! Frankie's mouth is on mine and he's kissing me on the lips! Don't ever let it be said I was easy—we do hug briefly as well.

I step back for a moment. Then all of a sudden we're pashing. I haven't a clue how this happens, it's as comfortable as slipping on my favourite coat. Lips, teeth, tongues—no Tantra happening here. His hand is on my breast then shifts to running up and down my side and then returns to my breast again and then—oh Buddha—I'm losing track.

I still have my coffee in my hand. (Hello, like I'd let go of my first coffee of the day for anything or anyone!) I throw my free arm around him and, in my clumsy state, I send snack packs of dried fruit flying from the stand next to us.

'Oh God, sorry,' I mumble, leaning into his neck, hugging him.

After pashing again, we release each other—I have no idea who lets go first. How am I ever meant to figure out what's going on if I don't catch the details?

As Frankie crouches down to pick up our debris I flee to the deli section to get a packet of coffee. 'Sorry, I knew I'd knock something off and I don't mean you.' *Mother freaking hell, where did that come from? What would possess me to actually say that? I am insane!*

I stand and look at the coffee. Even though I drink the same kind all the time I'm paralysed. Oh fuck, our moment at the counter would have been visible to anyone walking by.

When I see Frankie approaching, I notice he's wearing his South Sydney Rabbitohs T-shirt. Something must be wrong with me—I don't so much as register an internal groan about it. What if the doctor is wrong and I *am* dying of a brain tumour? Surely a brain tumour is the only possible explanation for my behaviour?

'Oh God, I don't know what I'm doing,' I say.

'That's OK,' Frankie says in his comforting way.

I turn to walk back to the counter but we end up in each other's arms once more. My body is against his, we're pashing, his hands explore me, running down my waist and inside my jeans at my hip.

We're all over each other during Grouplove's 'Ways to Go', and when we part, our conversation runs along the lines of:

'When are you going?'

'Now—my lift is waiting for me.'

'Oh dear,' he says, making me wonder if he's all hot and bothered and is expecting to take me out the back and have his way with me.

Goddess, that would be just my luck. After waiting so many years to study Mandarin in China I manifest that tethering-out-the-back scenario just when I am about to get on the plane.

Hang on, Grouplove's 'Ways to Go'? Someone must have either banned Frankie from Retro FM or one of the younger employees has been at the radio, but the song is perfect.

'I have to go,' I murmur, hugging him one last time.

We stand looking into each other's eyes. Then I tear myself away like we're two strips of Velcro.

'Take care of yourself.'

Fucking, Jesus, Hell! Of all the things I've wanted to say to him that's what I say as I walk out, not looking back even though I want to and even though I can feel his eyes on my back and his emotions in my aura. I can't. If I turn back and look at him now, I won't ever leave.

I straighten my shirt, try to regain my composure and walk sedately back up the street—straight past Bing's car.

'Mei Mei!' he calls.

'Oh my God, my eyes!' I laugh, hoping that'll explain.

'You didn't get your bag of coffee?'

'Oh no, I, um, I sort of got distracted.' Once we're inside my place the shockwaves I've been so busy containing take over and my composure evaporates. My mind spins, not achieving anything, and I'm hardly able to string two words together.

I can't believe I just pashed Frankie! I can't believe I just pashed someone who wears a football shirt! I can't believe I pashed Frankie when he was wearing his football shirt!

Not that I'm attached to my What I Want and Need In My Next Male Love Relationship list anymore. I'd ceremoniously shredded all twenty-five pages of it at work last week. I didn't bother thinking long and hard before I'd shredded it, I'd already spent way too much time overthinking things. I'd simply looked at the two hundred and thirty-six items and thought, *If the clipboard was in the other hand, would I want someone ticking off my traits like I was a second-hand car?* The technique had about as much spiritual essence as a shopping list—or less, in my case! When it was done I'd totally given up on men again, convinced relationships weren't meant for me.

There's another list I'd created that would be quite handy to have right now, but for the life of me I have no idea where I've put it. Without my Checklist for Shanghai Departure to focus on, I'm turning in actual circles, not a clue what I'm meant to be doing. I'm so obviously dysfunctional and unable to get it together that Bing takes over to get my stuff and me out the door.

'Oh look! My Mei Mei is so excited about going to Shanghai,' he says more than once.

'Oh yes, *very* excited to be going to Shanghai, Da Ge!' I fib.

He succeeds in his mission and we're off! I look into PGGG as we drive past and my heart stalls. Frankie is leaning on the counter, looking like he's having a D&M with Thuga. Just as well I got out safely when I did. That was so a sex-slave moment waiting to happen.

My phone becomes a hyperactive cricket, chirping constantly with texts flying between Jane and I, and Stephanie and I, interrupting my conversation with Bing. There's no way I could keep this from Jane, I'd burst if I even tried. And I had to come clean with Stephanie too. When we'd caught up recently, she'd asked me about him. 'I'm so tired of thinking about Mum's ... not living. Just tell me something entertaining to distract me from chemo talk and illness,' she'd said. At the time I'd disappointed her by providing another, 'Oh, nothing really, not much progress there.'

At the airport, checked in and baggage free, Bing and I head off for breakfast.

'What would you like, Da Ge? My treat.'

'No, no, no, Mei Mei. You not pay for my breakfast.'

'Da Ge, seriously, don't be so stubborn. It's tiny. You've managed to get me here and after all the coffees you've given me and everything you've done—'

'No, Mei Mei, stop. Sit down. I will get for both of us.'

I know better than to try to argue with Bing. I sit down but he doesn't get up.

'You know, if I met you long time ago I would be married to you,' he says.

Oh my motherfornicating Goddess, Jesus, Buddha, Hell! Seriously! What is going on with the Universe today? A good thing Jack wasn't there, who knows what he might have done?

'You know I'll always love you, Da Ge.' I lay heavy emphasis on the term of endearment to remind him he's my big brother.

'Who is it you are going to miss so much?' Bing says huffily as my phone goes off again, his Scorpio jealousy boiling over.

I know I wasn't being very Ms Middle-of-the-Road about the fact I'd just pashed Frankie, but this was not time for her, this was a time for squealing with girlfriends. Still, I put my phone down to give Bing some quality sole-focus time.

We both get a little nostalgic as we chat about life and how things work out. At least until he embarks on one of his super rants, knocking the nostalgia right out of me.

I need a moment away from Bing so I excuse myself to go to the bathroom, where I send Jane an informative text that will fill in the blanks.

When I get back, Bing is standing up. It's time.

He sighs. 'I wish you not going.' He tells me he will 'xian ni de yoa si le' (miss you to death) as he kisses and hugs me a thousand times (no pashing or even an attempt at a pash, thank Buddha). He confesses again how he wishes he'd met me years ago.

I finally get to set off on my dream trip. It's no one's fault but my own that it'd taken me so long to get here, 'fast mover' certainly isn't a term likely to be bandied around in my eulogy.

I'm not surprised when I get stopped and scanned as I pass through the security check, given the methadone comment of a few weeks ago and the fact that I'm not only sleep deprived but fidgety and hyped up as well. Mr National Security is full of questions about what I'm going to get up to over there. Like a blonde girl travelling alone to China is so dodgy. Though maybe they saw me with Bing and assume I'm up to something with some crime syndicate, as though Bing and I can't be family or even friends.

I get patted down for the second time that day. Unfortunately the woman is not nearly as friendly or welcome as Frankie. But after so many years without any action, a girl can only think to herself, *It's true, it never rains but it pours.*

I'm so perky and friendly in the face of their surliness that they seem quite taken aback. 'Fine, absolutely understand, better to be safe than sorry,' I say as we go through more scanning and bag screening.

At the Customs area we're herded like cattle. My text-a-thon with Jane continues. *I know I'm a bombshell but this is ridiculous!* she suggests as a response to the bomb scanners.

'Turn that off *now*! See the sign?' a truck driver–esque woman in a Customs uniform barks at me, pointing to a sign that has a picture of mobile under a big red circle with a line through it.

'Just give me a second, this is an emergency!' I surprise myself by yelling at her. And it was. I mean. holding this level of excitement in could have caused me to have a stroke or something.

Once we're seated on the plane, I look around. I'm the only blonde on the flight. Surrounded by a sea of Mandarin, I am happier than I imagine Frankie was when South Sydney won their first grand final in forty-three years back in 2014. Even though Sammy isn't old enough to remember it, he's inherited his father's love of statistics—our entire family knows that fact.

42

Shanghai! Bright lights, big city.

Delayed flights and customs queues don't do anything for anyone's mood and after the last twenty-four hours my coping mechanisms are significantly compromised. It's chaos at the taxi stand outside Pudong International Airport. The situation isn't helped by the aversion that the Chinese have to orderly queues and patiently waiting their turn. Understandable traits, having to live your life constantly trying to secure limited resources in a city with as much demand as Shanghai. Still, I'm in no fit state to deal with it or exercise love, light, compassion and understanding. I need a bed and I need to be asleep in it *now*.

When I finally get a cab, I lug my bags into the boot and flop into the back seat like a puppet whose strings have been cut. I draw on all my reserves and summon the energy to lean forward, passing the driver the address the uni have sent me. I lay back against the seat, close my eyes and wait to be whisked through the city to my accommodation. After a minute or two of no whisking—in fact we're still stationary—I open them again. The cab driver is looking quizzically at his sat nav, then clears it and enters the address again with the same result. He's been doing this *the entire time*?

I have a strong feeling I should get out of this cab and wait for another one. I'd like to claim the reason I don't is altruistic. However, I'm too tired to imagine myself swanning around in a kaftan at a meditation retreat telling people: 'I couldn't possibly get out, I knew from his regional accent that fate had put me in his cab for a reason and his entire village would starve if he didn't get the fare.' Which is along the lines of what I'd like people to believe. In truth, it's just exhaustion. The thought of doing battle for another cab is more than I can face.

'Don't think I don't know you're ripping me off. I'm just too tired to care!' I scream once we finally arrive. I always scream better in Chinese than in English. I needed him to know that I knew what he was up to, even if I was going to cough up the cash. Love, light and his karmic welfare had really deserted me now.

I get out, thinking, *Fuck, I hope this is the right place*, as he speeds off, my hand barely off the boot. It's the middle of nowhere, or it feels like it. If this isn't the place I'm just going to have to lie on my bags for what's left of the night and deal with it in daylight.

I look around, then, craning my head back, at the very top of the building in front of me I see a sign. I mean a physical one, floodlit, with writing on it, that tells me this is it. I breathe a sigh of relief, brush off my bad mood and head up the stairs.

Checking in is delightful and for all my tiredness, I'm blessed with a new lease of life. The concierge and I chat all the way to the room that will be my home for the next six weeks.

The hot water doesn't work and the toilet runs all night but I sleep, at least until the car horns start up. They accompany the sound of traffic—the sound of Shanghai waking up. After a cold shower and a challenging and frustrating exchange with reception about the hot water (what happened to the nice nightshift staff?), I head onto the streets, prepared to be infused with the feeling of being 'home'.

I'm surprised at how big and clumsy I feel, nothing like I felt like when I ran here to hide for the week of my thirtieth birthday. I'm so out of place on the footpath in this part of town. I walk for blocks, looking for something I might be able to stomach in the morning—nothing. Coffee is non-existent too. I go back to the student accommodation to forage at the shop downstairs. I search between instant noodles and packets of preservatives parading as food until I find something I can eat. I lie on my bed, eat my sweet Chinese bread, drink weak jasmine tea and think about everything, but mostly about Frankie.

The best part of the day is still in front of me and there's no point lying here complaining about bad food or thinking about Frankie, even if my toes still haven't uncurled from pashing him. I need to get out and find my place in the city again.

Heading through the uni grounds on my way to a destination I know guarantees coffee, a young Chinese couple cycle past so close I have to sidestep the girl's pedals. Then another couple laugh as I pass them. I hear the girl say, 'She couldn't be an international student, she's too old for that.'

'Bugger off,' I could tell her in Mandarin, or at least say, 'I understood that and by the way, it's totally obvious your designer handbag is fake.' Instead I ignore them, keep my head straight up and pretend I haven't understood.

Ten Australian dollars for an only semi-decent coffee when I get into the city. At that rate, I'll have to sell a kidney before my language intensive is over to feed my addiction. A forty-five-minute trip to get to my caffeine fix each day isn't going to work either, especially when classes start at 8am!

Caffeinated, I hop on the Metro out to where I stayed last time. I go in search of the traditional old hotel just off a big leafy street in the French Concession. I love the vibe there—it's like it captures the best of both worlds. I walk past a construction site three times before I'm certain that I'm standing in front of all that is left of the hotel.

Tiredness creeping up on me, I head back to the city, or I make the move to. It takes five Metro trains coming and going before I can force myself onto one through the crowd. Squeezed in sardine-tight, I can't help but think that all the people looking at me are thinking I shouldn't be here. Westerners don't have the economy of space that Chinese do; even when we're not physically bigger, we seem to take up more room. Maybe it's urban evolution and we've adapted to fill the space available.

From the city I walk along Nanjing Road until it becomes Nanjing Road West. I walk quite a long way until I reach 1168, the building I would have worked in if I'd got the job at the Australian Consulate. I stare at the black mirrored tower of un-me-ness whose height disappears into the haze of the sky.

Amethyst was right; in this case hindsight definitely held the answer.

As the day stretches into early afternoon the greyness that sits above the city hangs so low it's almost as though I could reach up, poke it and make it burst. Heat and humidity fester. I'm coated in dampness, a putrid combination of the moisture in the air and my own sweat. The grime of the city, the black fumes from the cars and my clothes cling to me. By the time I'm walking back from the Metro stop to the uni, I'm dripping. It's not even summer. My nose curls. What is that disgusting smell? It's way worse than a decomposing rat. It smells like sewage. At first I'm worried it might be me, with all this sweat and grime, and give myself a quick sniff. It's not. But it doesn't go, it's still there when I get back to the accommodation. I only stop smelling it once I'm well into the foyer.

I try to rest, watching saccharine-sweet Chinese MTV, but then I'm bored. I go out again in search of the supermarket I'd seen people walking back from. The stench of sewage is still in the air.

I just need time to get used to things, find my way around, get a routine happening and find my bearings, I tell myself as I walk through the grey buildings of the uni grounds, when all that I can think is that I want to go home. All this noise, so many people, dealing with the energy of the crowds, feeling out of place and out of sync, having to concentrate so much with every step—it's too exhausting.

In the supermarket, when I eventually find it, I am jostled and shoved and looked up and down as I browse the aisles. Even a woman out shopping in her flannelette pyjamas—in this heat—gives me a caustic once-over. There are definitely not any PGGG-worthy deli items either. And dharma it— instant coffee only.

Well, you're no Frankie, in fact Ms Terse-at-the-Till would get a customer service award before you, I think when the woman on the till barks at me to 'Hurry up', because I'm tak- ing too long to pass her my money.

It'll be better once I start class, I tell myself on the way back to my room. That's what I wanted, that's what I'm here for.

Day two of class, the teacher asks me, 'Why are you here?'

I can't help but wonder the same thing. I'm in a class lower than my comprehension and speaking level because my written characters are so weak. They're my least favourite aspect of the language and I've never really been the type to spend the endless hours of practice required to master them. I'm far more about connecting with people through the language. But here, my weakness makes me feel remedial.

By the end of week one, no matter how Ms Middle-of-the-Road I try to be about it, I'm struggling to convince myself that the situation is going to get better. The constant smell of sewage definitely hasn't. The heat makes the odour snake its way up from the city's drains and ooze out the open grates. Summer would be unbearable. For so many reasons, this is not the Shanghai I remember and I'm not the me I was before in Shanghai.

And I'm still so tired. I'm not sure if it's being woken at 5am every day by the traffic, the focus class and navigating the streets requires, trying to operate well below my full caffeine quota, or everything catching up with me. I wake from a nap on a Sunday afternoon and decide I'm going to phone Frankie. I feel a bit bad about the way I left everything up in the air. I'm so totally Ms Middle-of-the-Road I don't coin toss or anything, I just do it. I dial PGGG's number from memory. Even though I don't know if Frankie will be there, little bubbles of anticipation pop and fizz around my body.

A young guy answers.

'Hi, can I speak with Frankie if he's there, please?'

'I'll just get him.' He doesn't ask who's calling.

Bless you on two counts, Buddha—one that he's there and two that I get to surprise him.

'Frankie, speaking.'

'Hi, Frankie, it's Fiona.'

'Fiona, are you home?' His words rush out soft, gentle and breathy, without any nasal twang. His comforting voice.

'No, I'm still here. Sorry, I know you're probably busy, but I just wanted to ring and say hi.'

'I'm always busy, but I think I can manage time for you.' Frankie gets the balance of sweetness and playful flirtation perfect.

'Thanks.' I can hear the smile in my voice.

'How's it going over there? When are you coming home?'

'Good, you know—fine. How are you?'

'Fine. You didn't tell me when you're coming home.'

'Four weeks.'

'Oh, that's ... that's still quite a while. What date?'

'The twelfth.'

'The twelfth,' Frankie repeats as the warning beeps of low credit sound.

'I've got to go, we're about to get cut off. I'll see you when I get back, Frankie,' I say at the same time as he says, 'I'm looking forward to seeing you when you get back.'

Then the line goes dead.

I lie on my bed, the little bubbles of nervous anticipation I had just five minutes ago maturing into happiness. I think about all the things I know about Frankie. As far as my lists go, it's a pretty short one but I'm so awash with joy that, right now, it doesn't matter. I'm just going to appreciate the moment for what it is.

I have to admit that even though I'm here and even though I'm enjoying the moment, a part of me is looking forward, hoping that one day I'll get to discover more about who Frankie is in a completely non-obsessive, non-stalkerish way.

One afternoon a few weeks later, the phone wakes me from another afternoon nap.

'Wei?' I offer the standard Chinese phone greeting, my voice croaky with sleep.

'Would you like to attend one of the regional primary schools with me next week?' the voice asks.

It takes me a moment to figure out it's the college's English coordinator. 'Definitely,' I say. Most of the foreign English-speaking students get an invitation to a school in one of the villages outside Shanghai to do a guest appearance in an English lesson and I'd been waiting for my chance.

The morning of the English class I arrive at the appointed collection spot early, uncaffeinated but buoyed with excitement. Once I'm aboard the minibus with some local English-teaching students, we head east. After we've passed through the water town of Tongli—picture-postcard China with its ancient white buildings and black-tiled rooves—we drive another half-hour to arrive at a tiny village with an even tinier school.

I can tell all the kids' parents have made an effort to dress them in their very best, which in China means brightest, clothes. 'Nice to meet you, I like your skirt/top/pants,' I say as child after child introduces themselves, pointing at the relevant item to help their learning.

I can tell they're trying really hard to be on their best behaviour but there's a ripple of nervous excitement in the way they giggle at having to speak English to a Westerner.

They're so far out of the way here, this is probably the only chance they get.

My performance of 'Head and Shoulders, Knees and Toes' is a stroke of genius. The teacher-training students say as much, even if it does get a little out of hand for a moment when the children forget their best behaviour and let their excitement reign. I think it's hysterical, kids being kids, their teacher, not so much.

Back on the minibus a couple of hours later, I'm exhausted but I can't stop smiling. It was one of the best days I've had in ages (Frankie pashing departure day excluded). There's just one tiny thing tugging at my heart strings, unravelling the happiness a teensy bit. It'd been there all day.

I miss Sammy and Sonja.

I stare out the window and watch the scenery whip by. Tree after tree is coated with plastic bags, ugly tinsel come to rest on the spindly, leafless skeletons: Chinese Plastic Bag Forests. The blinkers I've been wearing for so long about a future in China seem to loosen at the passing of each tree.

The trainee teacher sitting across the aisle taps my shoulder to get my attention.

'Do you have a family, Fiona?'

There are so many things I could say to that: *Oh my Buddha do I, and don't they drive me crazy! No, I'm not married and I don't want kids. Absolutely not, it's always been my number-one priority to maintain my freedom.*

'Yes, quite a big one,' is what I actually say. Sure, not everyone I was counting was a blood relative but they were all my clan, pieces of the jigsaw puzzle and without them things just weren't complete. So what if my biological family were pieces you had to jam in a bit to make fit and my life wasn't made up of the neat shapes that other people's seemed to have?

Back in Shanghai, I dump my stuff in my room. I really didn't want to be cooped up, waiting for night to come. I could go to the computer room but it's almost impossible to navigate the Chinese software and even though I'd sent emails to a few places about work when I'd first arrived, my heart just isn't in it. I set out on a walk, with no real purpose or direction, just going where my feet take me.

I'm standing at a crossroads. I don't mean metaphorically—I'm physically positioned at a crossroads in the back streets of an outer suburb of Shanghai, wondering which way to go, and there it is, a miniature red short-haired dachshund trotting across the bitumen.

Oh my Buddha—just when I'd been having a little inner tingle, thinking about where Frankie will fit into the puzzle. Not that I needed a sign anymore, although it was a nice reinforcement.

43

I'm all up in the air, quite literally. The weeks have passed and I'm an hour into the flight home. Leaving China this time there was only the tiniest tug on my heart. That kicking and screaming toddler inside of me, whining to be allowed to stay, seemed to have grown up. There are things I'll miss but I would have missed what's waiting for me at home more. I don't just mean Frankie, I mean all the pieces of the puzzle. Of course Frankie is the first piece to be dealt with.

I admit I'm also a bit up in the air about him. I mean, I've really got no idea what his intentions—or his circumstances, for that matter—are. Ms Middle-of-the-Road is totally fine with that. Actually I'm madly excited about finding out, but who wouldn't be?

Putney Bridge Road is in darkness but as soon as the cab turns into it, I can feel my soul settle into place with the unmistakable sense of being home. I mean *really* home, as though everything has aligned perfectly and I can feel safe to let my roots grow into the earth again in a way I haven't for a very long time.

A pity my head and stomach won't follow suit in terms of settling. It's a migraine. I get one every time I fly home, which is why I always just get a cab from the airport. Once I'm inside, I throw my bags on the couch and take a shower—a long, hot one—even after repairs the hot water didn't get beyond lukewarm in Shanghai. I lie down and relish my bed, enjoying the cosiness, the softness of my sheets, the fluffiness of my doona. I curl up, shut my eyes and sleep.

The next morning, when I've given up all hope of my migraine leaving me completely, I rally myself as much as I can and go down to PGGG. Perhaps the migraine is a blessing in disguise—it's a stretch to ever think of a migraine as such, but I've got so many emotions I don't know how I'd manage them if I was well enough to feel them completely. Having to focus to stay upright and not vomit does reduce the intensity a bit.

As soon as I walk in, my heart sinks. I don't hear music. My heart plummets even further seeing Ms Terse-at-the-Till. I'm not well enough to get away in a hurry if she launches an attack with the broom today. Luckily she doesn't seem to be anywhere near it. I instinctively know Frankie isn't here.

I cannot believe we're back to this again. Seriously, why ask me when I'd be back and then not freaking well be here?

On Monday I'm feeling so much better. I've taken the day off work to settle into my life again and by that I mean getting myself organised with shopping and cooking. But not PGGG. Seriously, if Frankie can't be bothered to be there on my return I'm not going to act desperate and go searching for him.

'Fiona, you're back!' I'm so touched when I go into Jack's and not just from the warm hug he gives me but the fact that he has the postcard I sent him pinned next to the coffee machine. He beams. 'I've got some exciting news.'

'Oh great, what?' I'm a bit taken aback, I'd been expecting him to ask how China was.

'I met someone, a girl, while you were away.'

'That's fantastic, Jack.' I hug him again. 'I'm really happy for you.' I do a quick internal scan—no, there's not even the tiniest hint of jealousy. Although if *someone else* in the neighbourhood has moved on so quickly, it will be another story.

I scoot past PGGG, head held up, eyes straight ahead, stiff with pride. I mean, if Frankie sees me and wants me, he can come get me.

It's such a relief to be able to walk around the street and shop without 26 million other people and to drink Jack's coffee as I do so. I don't know what I was thinking, imagining myself living somewhere that just didn't ever get it quite right, caffeine wise.

On my way home I allow myself a little glance at PGGG. Frankie, Raymond and Thuga are chatting. Frankie looks at me, Raymond and Thuga look from Frankie to me then back to Frankie. I raise an eyebrow, take a breath in, making myself taller, then go back to looking straight ahead. So many people would want to shake me, but I'd already swallowed my pride so many times for Frankie.

It's fine; I'm fine. So it was just a pash-and-dash scenario, even if it hadn't seemed that way. He probably just said those things on the phone because that's what you're meant to say.

I've got one more stop to make before I go home and call everyone—I'll be so happy to reconnect with them that it'll be like Frankie never existed. I'm not sure what I'll say to Jane and Stephanie about him because they're going to be gagging to know.

I step backwards, away from the counter at the pharmacy, shoving the painkillers into my bag and thanking the pharmacist. It isn't until I'm about to tumble off the step that I turn. And there's Frankie, waiting for me right outside at the doorway.

'Hi, Fiona.'

'Hi, Frankie,' I say, my voice a little higher than usual. Actually it sounds a bit prissy and tight.

'You didn't come in.'

No shit, Sherlock. Hell hath no fury like a woman scorned.

'I came in yesterday,' I say pointedly.

'But you said you'd be back on the eleventh. I was here on the eleventh.'

'No, I said the twelfth.' By this time my hands are on my hips and because I'm on the step I'm half a head taller than him.

'I'm sure you said the eleventh, I waited all day.'

'I said the twelfth.' We stand there looking into each other's eyes, both a little fiery. Frankie's eyes crinkle as he smiles. I cock my eyebrow because that's what I need to do to maintain my huff and stop myself smiling. What Frankie does next will be crucial. I love a little huff and I love someone who can incite me to flounce. Part of the problem with my previous partners was that neither of the serious ones had been able to cope with a huff; they'd either sulked or got angry, both resulting in the silent treatment, which made me teary, insecure and pathetic. I hated that side of me.

'You must have missed your yoghurt.' A little glint of mischief flashes in Frankie's crinkly eyes.

'Yes, I did miss my yoghurt.'

'Why don't you come in and get some later, when it's quieter.'

'Maybe I will.' I'm grinning like a dharmaed fool and I can feel my face burning up but I flick my hair, step off the step and prepare to flounce. My elbow brushes him just slightly as I pass. I'm immediately awash with goosebumps.

'See you later, Fiona.'

'Possibly,' I toss over my shoulder.

I'm so cool I don't even run into anything.

It's amazing how little has happened in everyone else's lives while I've been away. That's the thing when you leave for an extended period, you come back expecting everyone's lives to have changed. But time had moved in its ordinary way.

Stephanie's happy that 'nothing major has changed', as she tells me when I call. Which of course means her mother is still alive. We'll talk about it in more detail, or whatever she wants to talk about, when we catch up on Saturday.

My mum is *exactly* the same: 'Dad's playing too much golf', 'Brian is the perfect husband', 'Catherine is lucky but then again Catherine deserves it. She's given me the greatest happiness any mother could want,' (she means Sammy and Sonja) and 'We're having lunch on Sunday. Make sure you're not late.' Too bad if I had other plans. I'm sure that somewhere in there she asked how my trip was.

Jane's the last person I phone, purely because I don't want to have to worry about getting off the phone to call anyone else. Unlike Mum and Stephanie, Jane being Jane is frustrated with everything being so much the same: 'I've made a big decision, now I just want things to be happening.'

We spend ages on the phone, squealing, laughing, snorting. Even though the autumn of our relationship is really entirely

over, Jane won't confirm that the 'big decision' is what I assume it is—she wants to tell me in person—and I don't ask
her whether she thinks I should go down to PGGG tonight.
I've already decided what I'm going to do.

44

'Hi, Frankie,' I say as I stride right up to him.

'Hi, Fiona, you made it.' He grimaces and looks down.

'Oops, sorry!' I step off his foot. So much for Ms Super-cool. I can barely breathe, not from anxiety but from the overwhelming mix of everything I feel being so close to him, breathing him in, his scent, feeling the warmth of him so close to me—happiness.

'Excuse me, can you help me find the water crackers?' A male customer chooses that moment to sidle up to us.

Seriously! Couldn't he sense this isn't a moment for interruptions? I'd purposefully timed my visit late so that it would be quiet—and to keep Frankie on his toes (although I think the Universe took my 'on his toes' thoughts too literally).

Franke rolls his eyes.

'There they are.' I lean across to the shelf, grab a box and pass it to the man.

'My wife told me to get cracked pepper ones,' the man says, studying the box.

This time, I roll my eyes.

'We haven't got any. Just go with those, plain goes with anything,' Frankie says. He looks as though he's trying not to laugh.

The man walks away, still looking uncertainly at the box in his hand.

Frankie turns towards the counter where the water cracker guy is. 'I better get that.'

'I better get my yoghurt. Seeing as that's what I came for.' I give him a fully intentional wink.

My heart is doing backflips. Then Frankie breaks into an impromptu rendition of David Bowie's 'China Girl' and it begins a whole gymnastic routine.

When I get to the counter, the young guy is back on the till next to Frankie.

Great Govinda, what does a girl need to do to cop a break in this town?

'Hey, Aaron, can you just pop out to the cool room and tidy up the boxes?' Frankie has tuned into my thoughts or he's having similar thoughts of his own.

'Whoa, be careful with my yoghurt,' I say, as he performs some fancy moves taking my items out of my basket.

'So, how's the weather? It seemed a little stormy earlier,' Frankie says, placing the pot into my bag with great care.

It only takes one of my big, booming heartbeats to understand that he's talking about my mood this afternoon. 'Much better, the storm clouds have passed, sun is shining.'

'Um ...' Frankie sounds nervous.

I'm still smiling, totally fine. Whatever it is he's going to say next will be the best thing for whatever is meant to happen, in whatever crazy way the Universe has decided things will play out.

Please, Universe, don't let it be 'I'm sorry, I made a huge slip-up, nothing like that can ever happen again.'

I stand there waiting, not looking at the ground or the counter. I'm looking at Frankie, my eyes wide, but I do seem to be blinking quite a lot.

'Are you free Friday night?' Frankie's words rush out in a nervously uncool way. (Definitely one for my mental list of Endearing Things About Frankie.)

'No, sorry—not that I don't want to be free. I would be free if I wasn't busy, if you know what I mean.'

'Saturday?' he says, seeming to totally understand.

'This weekend isn't good. I've got lots of catching up with everyone. Friends, family, you know.' He looks a little dejected. I can't stand to see Frankie looking sad. 'Next week?' I quickly offer.

'Next week for sure. What day works best for you?'

Ms Plan-a-Week-in-Advance loves that he's onto the details already. His keenness doesn't go unnoticed either.

'Let's do Friday, if that's good for you,' I say. The sooner, the better. From the smile that breaks across Frankie's face, I get the feeling he's thinking the same thing.

But having to wait that long feels like torture.

It's hardly like I'm going to forget it but once I've floated home and landed back on earth from Planet Swoon, I add it in my diary. I snort out loud—amazing! Friday is the twenty-fourth. That Friday, Saturday and Sunday are the twenty-fourth, twenty-fifth and twenty-sixth. I have to keep mentally pinching myself to check that my dream is really coming true. After so long, this stuff with Frankie feels monumental but at the same time so natural.

It's also pretty weird to be going to work in a good mood. I can't say I'm exactly happy to be back but I'm excited to be seeing *some* of my workmates. And there's Bing.

He wraps me in a hug when I walk into his café. I hold him tight, not squirming away from the oiliness of his cooking clothes. 'My Mei Mei is home.'

'My Da Ge.' I squeeze him even tighter. 'I missed you to death,' I tell him in Chinese.

'I told you that you should've waited and come with me and my family. Your Da Ge is always right,' Bing says when I tell him about it all. Some things won't ever change—Bing is one of them and I really wouldn't want him to.

'Fiona!' There's a flurry of excitement as people rush over to me when I walk into the office.

'Did you meet anyone over there?' Angela asks.

'No. Sorry to disappoint.'

I don't say: '*I'm going on a date with a guy that it's taken me months to get this far with, but according to all energetic influences and accounts, he's my destiny, I've never felt so much chemistry with someone in my life, I've never enjoyed pashing someone as much in my life, when I'm near him my hands itch to reach out and touch him because being close is not close enough.* Angela would absolutely self-combust, although I don't withhold it because I feel like I need to be protective of the Frankie kernel anymore. It's two-fold: it's nice to just have my own little secret and it's early days; Ms Middle-of-the-Road can't be getting ahead of herself.

When it comes to Jane, on the other hand ...

'Well, just look at you,' she says outside the restaurant that Friday night. It's pretty easy for us to fall into second hug immediately, given that neither of us have fully let each other go from the first one. We'd squeezed each other so tight we'd wheezed for breath.

'I missed you,' we say in unison. The way we look at each other, we both know we're talking about more than just the six weeks I was gone. Autumn is a season of the past. Here we were at spring, with new and, yes, slightly healthier growth.

'Oh my fucking God, guess what?' I've given up not swearing. Surely Spirit has much more to worry about than that, or even the occasional little white lie? Of course I don't leave a gap for Jane to even try. 'I'm going on a date with Frankie next Friday night.'

'Jesus H Christ, about fucking time!'

People on the street turn to look as Jane and I jump, whoop and squeal.

'You're going to have to ask him what all that hot, cold, fuckwit shit was about and what took him so long.'

After Frankie, after more on China, after work, Jane has an announcement of her own—the 'big decision'.

'I'm going to do it, Kiz, the adoption. I'm going to formally apply and see what happens.'

'Well, look who went and got all grown up while my back was turned,' I joke as I stand and lean across the table to kiss Jane's cheek and pinch it affectionately. I still can't imagine Jane as a mother, but she has every right to want what she wants. I knew Jane and, no matter what, that child would know it was loved. 'Have you narrowed down countries?'

'Colombia. It has relatively short waiting times. I mean, I don't want the poor little thing to be having to push me around in a wheelchair as soon as she can walk.'

South America is *so* Jane.

We might be speeding through stop signs, given there's the whole approval process yet, but the more Jane tells me, the more excited we get.

'I can't wait to be the number one aunty.'

'Super Aunty. Of course you'll be Godmother as well. The moral guardian, no less.' Jane laughs.

'Like I would've let anyone else!' Suddenly we're snorting and from there the night just rolls on.

Sadly, things aren't so positive with Stephanie when I see her the next day. We meet at the movies at her request. It's her way of saying, *I want to see you but I can't pretend to be OK.* Not that I expect her to be, but Stephanie expects herself to be.

'How are things?' I ask tentatively. Despite her protests I wrap her in a hug in the middle of the movie foyer. The skin around her eyes is drawn tight and dark blue with lack of sleep and there are tiny grooves splaying out from her lips.

'It's only a matter of weeks, a week—who knows?'

A feeling of guilt lands on me. I shouldn't be taking any of the precious time Stephanie has left with her mum, but she'd insisted. I also feel pretty crappy because I've got an inner glow that radiates from me—everyone's been saying it. I can't dim it even for Stephanie. I don't care that I won't get to tell her about China or Frankie. Although we should have timed things better, the only session for hours is a high-octane Hollywood blockbuster, the sort of movie that normally we'd do anything to avoid. As tyres screech and gun shots ring out, I look at Stephanie. She's focussed on her phone, waiting for a text or a call. An explosion on the screen lights up her face, and I see tears flowing down her cheeks.

I squint down at her phone to double-check there isn't anything there that might have caused the tears—all clear. I rest my upper arm against hers and turn back to the drama and carnage. Stephanie knows I'd do anything for her—I just can't do what she needs the most.

45

Even though I'm longing to bound into PGGG, I glide by each morning, looking properly in, sipping on my new platonic friendship–infused coffee from Jack. I give Frankie a wave and a full smile if I see him. My heart may flutter when I catch sight of him but I don't want to go setting any false expectations by encouraging conversation at that hour. Mornings are never going to be my thing.

Sunday is family lunch.

'Can you let us go, Aunty Fee? I can't breathe,' Sammy gasps when I wrap myself around him and his sister.

I'd easily won the battle with Mum to get to them first. She was a bit off her game after her meltdown when she saw me: 'Fiona! I thought I'd lost you, that you'd never come home, that you'd stay there forever.'

I didn't have the heart to correct her to Kismet, it didn't feel like it really mattered. And naturally I don't tell her that staying was what I'd originally planned. It's best not to pour fuel on her drama fires.

'Just one second longer, then you get your presents,' I promise Sammy as he squirms. I know how to buy my time with kids.

They love their presents, everyone does. Well, almost everyone.

'An abacus. Thanks, that's different.' Brian is impassive.

Of course it's different, Brian, that's exactly the point! Anyone could have brought you back a T-shirt. He was normally so appreciative but he really doesn't seem himself at all. He's distracted, stressed, having to go outside and 'make an important call' three times. I even overhear him snap at Catherine after she follows him outside when he's making one of the calls. He's really taking his life into his own hands there.

Speaking of Catherine, she actually *loved* the silk scarf I'd bought her.

The Chinese moon cakes I'd brought back for dessert weren't the biggest hit. I guess lotus seed paste is an acquired taste, but everyone agreed they were an improvement on nougat.

Everything had improved since the nougat lunch. Not that I told them I was going on a date with Frankie. I didn't mention him at all. There was so much to catch up on and, well, I was still trying to come to terms with the fact that I was going on a date with someone my family might actually be able to relate to.

It's Monday. That means that on Friday night, I'm going on a date with Frankie. Which means I shouldn't go into PGGG tonight. I should hold out, let the anticipation build. But of course I'm going into PGGG and I'm not even going home to recurl my eyelashes! Really, there's been months of anticipation and as for the eyelashes, on departure day they were pretty flat and it hadn't made a scrap of difference. Perhaps Frankie has a thing for girls with flat eyelashes or maybe he didn't really notice them that much. Men!

There's no path of rose petals laid along the floor to the fridge where my yoghurt is in anticipation of my visit—not that I was expecting it. A good thing, as it turns out, because my body temperature would have wilted them immediately. My temperature always seems to rise a few degrees around Frankie and now, after the taste test of departure day and with date night ahead, I feel like a bush fire is running wild in my body.

Rose petals are clichéd anyway. Frankie's snort-inducing version of Michael Jackson's 'Rock With You' is not. As he hands over my bag he says, 'You know Friday is only four sleeps away. If you have a number you would be so kind as to give me for preparation purposes, that would be pretty handy.'

'Who can sleep?' I say, which is really just one of my dramatic-effect fibs. I *am* sleeping, and so relieved about it.

We're grinning at each other like Cheshire Cats as I take an exaggerated step backwards. It's the only way I can stop myself reaching out to grab him. I don't know how I'm going to make it through a whole evening without throwing him on the table at the restaurant and having my way with him. I know I'm meant to want him to woo me and all of that but, really, it feels a bit like trying to put a runaway train in reverse.

When I get home I find Frankie has snuck a chocolate bonbon into my bag. I spin around and squeal.

But then I put thoughts of the date with Frankie on a low simmer. Something else requires my attention before Friday.

Being at the Centre for Strategic and Financial Excellence just really isn't where I want to be. The excitement of seeing everyone at work waned very quickly and I've realised that even if I did find a role that involved speaking Mandarin, doing admin and/or compliance isn't what I want to be doing. Surprise, surprise!

Kids are the answer. It isn't so much an epiphany as a crystallisation of an idea that had begun to percolate after the visit to the tiny school in China. Not having kids or adopting them, but working with them. So I've rejigged my job alerts and put positive vibes out to the Universe.

It doesn't waste any time. A solution that seems too good to be true floats seamlessly into my inbox—no desperate searches required. The job is as a teacher's assistant at an intensive English centre, working with newly arrived, primary-aged students. They want someone who can assist with their bilingual Chinese classes. I know just the girl for the job. And I can walk there. Slight negative: the pay is less but I've done the maths (I cannot believe I'm saying that) and I can manage it with some cutbacks. I won't be flush, but it's the perfect way to dip my toe in the water to see if I might find a future in teaching. Some of the units I'd done previously in my false starts of degrees could feasibly go towards a qualification and, looking at the school's website, I'd discovered they offer an annual bursary for staff training. Not that I'm putting the cart before the horse, I'm just going to do the application and see what happens.

The points for this application are particularly easy and, as I start typing, the answers just roll out of my fingers. Deep down, I know it's the right thing—if not this job, then one similar. I haven't even had to ask Lionel or Amethyst about it. There'll be savings there too. I'll definitely see Amethyst again in the future but my chakras are humming along pretty happily of their own accord at the moment. When I do see her it'll be more for a tune-up than answers, and I know exactly what she'll say: 'Didn't I tell you everything would be clear in hindsight? Now can you relax, trust and have faith. Wasn't it looking Frankie in the eyes and your vulnerability that got you to where you are? Are you prepared to admit that the Universe and Spirit have it under control and everything really is as it's meant to be?'

And Lionel, he's going to have a fit—in a good way—when I tell him about Frankie and everything else, like my China realisations, and the whole working-with-kids thing. I can just hear him on that too: 'Great idea, Kismet, use your imagination and that creative side of you for good, rather than self-paralysing evil.'

It feels way more important for me to see Lionel than Amethyst. In his own funny way, Lionel has been the most invested in my welfare and understands who I am. If I were to be honest, while Amethyst has taught me to trust the Universe, Lionel has perhaps given me the greatest gift in helping me trust myself.

Now that Ms Middle-of-the-Road feels OK staying reasonably close to the centre line without the need for training wheels, I won't be tearing up to have sessions every week, but I like Lionel. I've learnt to enjoy talking to him and opening up. I even miss his hugs—a bit. It's good to know he's there whenever I feel the need for a completely unbiased ear. There's no shame in needing someone removed from everything to talk to occasionally.

46

I'm meeting Frankie at PGGG tonight. Yes—oh my Buddha—
it's Friday! In approximately eight hours, at 7pm (they close
early on Fridays) I will be rat-a-tat-tatting on their door using
the code Frankie and I have arranged so he knows it's me.
He'd offered to come and collect me, but I'd declined. I'm not
concerned about Frankie knowing where I live—it's just more
exciting this way.

With our secret knock and getting in after hours, I've begun imagining myself as a cross between a spy and the Queen;
I think it's the Queen that Harrods opens up for after hours.
Not that I'll be shopping and not that Frankie and I will be
having a picnic of fresh produce on the floor, reminiscent of
the so-a-*date*-date, I'm sure.

I don't actually know where we're going or what we're doing. I hope it's quiet, but not too quiet—not the sort of quiet
where everyone can hear everything you say, or with that awful
empty-restaurant feeling where every word seems magnified
and the waiters loom, listening and being over-attentive, interrupting every five seconds just to pass the time.

I'm just back from the beautician when my mobile rings. My stomach doesn't lurch in a 'if that is Frankie calling to postpone, my life is over' way, but it does do a little hiccup.

I look at my phone and breathe a sigh of relief. It's Mum. I'd changed her to a normal ringtone, as the alarm tone had started to feel mean.

Mum's sobs are audible before I've got the phone to my ear. A hundred things run through my mind, the most obvious being that someone has died. My head races trying to figure out who. Dad—surely Catherine or Brian would have called? Catherine—Dad would have called. If something has happened to the kids that would be Dad too—Mum and Catherine and Brian would be too distressed. It must be ...

'It's Brian.' Mum's voice quakes in response when I ask her what's wrong.

At first I imagine he's killed himself—he was so stressed. Oh my God, Sammy and Sonja are going to be devastated. I've no time to google 'suicide rates of accountants' before my next thought comes galloping in: I hope I didn't manifest Catherine killing him with my 'taking his life is his own hands' thoughts—I understand that's inappropriate to think right now but I can't be held responsible, I'm in shock. Even if he's only left them for someone less, well, Catherine-ish, they're going to be shattered.

'He's been stood down from work,' Mum says before I get any words out.

'Oh my God, Mum, seriously? I thought he'd died or something.' I fossick in my bag for my Rescue Remedy.

'No, Fiona, you don't understand, he's been stood down—suspended, pending an investigation by a forensic accountant.'

'Oh. Holy shit,' I say before I squirt Rescue Remedy under my tongue. If it weren't so serious I'd be making a joke about a slightly balding, bland man in thick glasses and a white coat with a fingerprint kit and a scientific-style calculator or something. But this is officially a family crisis.

'Your sister is a complete mess,' Mum whispers into the phone. Obviously Catherine and Brian are with them. 'We need you to collect the kids from school, take them home to their place. Keep it all normal.'

'Sure. What time?' Saying, 'No, I can't, I have a date with that fruit guy' doesn't enter my head; this is Sammy and Sonja. But honestly, fucking hell, I really cannot believe it. How hard can it be to kick one relationship off?

I email Broomstick. I've got heaps of time before school is out but there's a sense of urgency about getting there. I don't wait for her permission to leave.

Catherine or Frankie—who to call first, I wonder as I run to the station.

'Frankie, it's Fiona,' I say when he answers.

'Fiona, are you OK?'

I must sound breathless from my run to the station. 'Yes, sort of. I'm really sorry, but I'm going to have to take a raincheck on tonight.'

'OK, then. What's up?' His voice carries a slight edge of something ... defensive disappointment?

'I'm fine, it's my—it's a bit of a family crisis. My family doesn't usually really have crises, I mean *I* am the family crisis.' Jesus Christ, as always with Frankie, my words take on a life of their own, tumbling out without any regard to how I want them to sound. It really is as though they'd felt trapped, holed up inside of me during all the months of not being able to speak to him and now they're like rebellious kids racing out of school on the last day of the year: un-wieldy, excited and free. 'I'm sorry, Frankie. I can't believe it, today of all days.'

'That's OK, Fiona. I can wait. We'll do it soon. I hope everything's OK,' Frankie says in his soothing way, adding just the right amount of a chuckle at my crisis comment. I'd even appreciated that edge to his voice. Being sweet *all* the time would make me want to kill someone. Or go off them very quickly at least.

Frankie may be able to wait, but I'm not sure I can. How-ever, there's no choice.

Next, I call Catherine. There's so much revenge to be had if I wanted it. So many jabs, so many accusations, so many things Catherine would probably say to me if the situation were reversed.

Her phone rings so long that I've nearly given up on her answering when a snuffly voice says, 'Hello.'

'Catherine, are you OK? Cancel that, I know you're not. I just wanted to ring and let you know I'm here, I'm on my way to the school. What do you need me to do?'

'How about pizza for dinner?' I ask Sammy and Sonja after surveying the neatly stacked delivery menus that Catherine keeps underneath the phone.

'Why don't we have Chinese instead?' Sammy suggests.

He and Sonja are leaping around the lounge room, still on the high of the excitement of catching a taxi home from school. They'd bought my excuse about their parents having forgotten about a party they were going to and Gran and Oompa being out with the Smithsons so easily, I feel quite guilty. Now is not the time to worry about the bad karma of a lie—as if I'd have done anything else.

'Great idea,' I say, high fiving him even though I hate the thought of Chinese takeaway food. It's hardly going to kill me to suffer it for them. 'But before dinner, who's going to help me with Operation Hoover?' Popcorn had been flying around the room while we watched *Cloudy with a Chance of Meatballs*. Catherine will be far less reactive about a stray piece of popcorn than last time but it's important to act normal, which means cleaning up to conceal the evidence to some degree.

After dinner, we sing and dance to Carly Rae Jepsen's 'Call Me Maybe'. Sonja's choice, not really my style, but again, anything for them. Actually, Sammy's not really dancing, he's standing on the spot moving his limbs slightly, eyeing the Souths football card collection that he's lined up on the coffee table. He's waiting for his turn to call the shots. I'm not sure what we're going to do; I mean, once you've looked at football cards, haven't you seen them? But like I've said, whatever they want.

I barely hear my phone over the music. It occurs to me that I probably should've been more responsible about that, in case Mum or Catherine had called, but I'm sure they'd ring the landline.

It's Frankie.

'Sorry, did you have to run for the phone?' he asks.

This is the second time today I've sort of been heavy-breathing down the phone to Frankie and I'm not the slightest bit concerned. It's like Ms Middle-of-the-Road is on cruise control.

'Oh no, I'm just having a sing and dance off with my niece and nephew.'

'Oh.' Frankie sounds confused, which I guess makes sense—
it probably isn't what you expect of a family crisis.

'It's a distraction,' I explain in a whisper.

'Sounds like a fun sort of distraction.'

'It is. We love them. Maybe one day you—' I stop short.
These words of mine just won't behave.

'Maybe, that might be nice ... one day,' he says.

'Come on, Aunty Fee, you're missing my best moves!'
Sonja calls.

'Sorry, I better go.'

'I just wanted to see if you—if everything was OK?'

'Thank you. I am. Everything else I'll have to explain later.'

I don't get home until late Saturday, way too late to catch
PGGG open. Sunday, going there is the first thing I do—OK,
second. I hadn't had a decent coffee yesterday either. Jack isn't
there. I imagine he's off with his new girlfriend. He's smitten
with her.

There are two reasons I haven't phoned ahead to see if
Frankie is at work today:

1) I like the sense of anticipation; and

2) I want to surprise him.

'It's me,' I say to Frankie who, as timing would have it (thank
you, Spirit), is singing along to Men At Work's 'Who Can It Be
Now?'.

'Fiona.' He spins around, a smile spreading across his face.
'Is everything sorted out?'

'In a way.'

Catherine and Brian had eventually got it together enough
to return home. The plan is that Sammy and Sonja will stay

with Mum and Dad and everyone will pretend that Catherine and Brian are off on another little holiday while the investigation is carried out. Why the kids can't just be told that Daddy is taking some time off work, I have no idea, but things have a way of getting unnecessarily complicated once everyone gets involved. I find that a lot in life.

'So,' Frankie says.

'So.'

'That Friday night thing. You know it needs to be rearranged.' Frankie looks around, perhaps to double check that no one can hear, or maybe to check no one's about to interrupt us.

'Yep.' I feel myself heating up as I look at him, trying not to smile too broadly but failing. Playing it cool is overrated anyway.

Frankie raises an eyebrow. 'Are you free tonight? We could go for dinner.'

'I'd prefer home delivery. I see on your sign out there that you offer it.'

I don't know who is more shocked, me or Frankie. I can't believe I said that—well, in a roundabout way, I sort of can. I really am quite tired after the last couple of days and would prefer home delivery. Not that I want to appear like a sure thing but given that the Universe created such extreme circumstances to get out of going a date, I have to take my chances. Playing hard to get at this point in time seems unnecessary, and since when had things gone the normal route where Frankie and I were concerned anyway?

47

At 7.05pm there's a knock at my door. It's exactly the knock I was meant to give on the PGGG door on Friday night, so there's no mystery who it is.

I'm already smiling when I open it and see Frankie standing there, holding a pot of my yoghurt. It's got a stick-on bow on top of it.

'Thanks,' I say through my laughter as he holds it out to me. 'Have you ever tried it?'

'No, not that one.'

'You really should, it's delicious. I only ever eat it for break-fast.' I cannot believe I maintain a straight face as I say that but I do and I look at him in the eye.

'So.' Frankie seems a little nervous as I close the door and we go into the lounge room.

'What happened ... did you break up with your boyfriend?' I nod in the direction of BIG's bakery. Someone else may think me a sarcastic bitch but I sense it's exactly the sort of thing Frankie needs to help ease his nervousness.

Frankie gives a huge guffaw. 'Something like that.' He leans towards me and kisses me and, oh great Ganesha have mercy, it's back to Departure Day and more.

'We should talk,' Frankie says, pulling away.

Fucking pent-up-frustrations hell—he wants to talk? *Talk?* Seriously, can't we talk later? But then I hear Angela's voice in my head, reminding me that we set the way things are going to play out from the start. I should encourage conversation.

'Great place,' Frankie calls as I run my yoghurt out to the fridge (priorities). I'd noticed him looking around at my rather eclectic Chinese-themed decor.

'Thanks. Would you like a drink? I can offer you water or water or water. Sorry, I'm not very organised at the moment.'

I can't believe I didn't go and get stuff in but I got caught up on the phone with Mum about Situation Family Crisis after I got back from PGGG.

Actually it's a bit of a Ms Middle-of-the-Road coup for me to keep it basic. Normally I would have got about fifty different beverages and at least a hundred snacks. I do have tea but Frankie doesn't seem the tea type. If I'm being entirely honest, I had maybe taken more than the absolute essential amount of time to get ready. I tried on multiple outfits, even if they were all jeans, and different hair styles, and adjusted my make-up and then there was the critical element of the playlist. Flight Facilities' 'Crave You' wasn't getting as many plays these days, Mallrat's 'Groceries' certainly was, still it felt a bit too obvious—so I started off with Kira Puru's 'Tension', followed by Major Lazer's 'Powerful' and took it from there. But all of that was part of the process of getting into the mood.

'Maybe water.' I hear the smile in Frankie's voice.

'Here, have some water.' I return from the kitchen and pass him his glass. I set mine on the coffee table beside the couch and take my spot, not quite as close to him as I'd like to. I have to sit on one hand to stop myself reaching out and touching him again. It's all I can do not to say, 'So you wanted to talk, talk—and hurry up about it.'

'You certainly aren't listening to Love Song Dedications here, Fiona.' Frankie chuckles as the Middle Kids' 'On My Knees' comes on.

If I hadn't happened to say, 'You forgot my name,' at exactly the same time, I might have made a joke about bringing his musical taste into this decade, but I've grown rather fond of his Retro FM ways. As for forgetting my name, I can't believe I said that, it was just another one of those things that fought its way out.

'I just said your name.' Frankie seems totally confused. Actually, beyond confused, he looks a little wounded and the way his hair is tufting out at the sides after our 'greeting', he looks quite vulnerable. Gah! It's impossible to really feel mad at him.

'No, when I originally told you, you forgot it.' I try to act a little huffy at least.

'Oh. Oh, yeah.' There's a dawning across his face and he looks at the floor. 'That wasn't good. I had a lot on my mind. I guess I should explain.'

'If you want.' *Hell yes, spit it out and make it snappy. I've been dying to know what's going on here since, like, forever.*

'I've sort of got a wife.'

How does one 'sort of' have a wife? Why is he on a date with me if he's married? I think I'm really going to have a stroke—blood has begun to pound in my head.

'It's OK, Fiona, we're separated,' he continues, which is just as well as I'd lost the ability to speak there again for a second.

'Oh.'

He tells me everything as though he wants to get it all out of the way at once so we don't ever have to go back and talk about the past again. Which suits me just fine, though I feel a bit like I'm in a confessional.

'We're separated *now* but it was playing out over the last ten months,' is where Frankie begins. 'It's a long story but, basically, there were some problems that meant things went downhill.'

I nod and look at him. I really don't know what to say. Of course I'm more than dying to ask the obvious questions that any woman would want to ask and also whether it's Ms Terse-at-the-Till—this one is essential information for my personal safety but beyond the inappropriateness of an interrogation, I need to let him explain without interruption—that's what he seems to want to do.

'It was kids,' Frankie continues. 'We couldn't have them. We tried the whole IVF thing for years and it just didn't work.'

OK, I'm not going to cry. I'm not going to say, 'Well, sorry, I better not waste your time.' Honestly, how cruel could fate be? But Frankie's not finished.

'It wasn't so important to me. I mean, I love kids but my—well, she really wanted them.' He scuffs at the floor with his sneaker. 'It was so much pressure in every sense. And in the end, it was me: I shoot blanks.'

I've heard and seen what IVF does to a lot of the couples who go through it. There's the financial pressure, the emotional pressure, the physical toll, tests, poking, prodding, prescriptions, the clinical nature of the process, the hope, the disappointment, the dreaded question asked time and time again by everyone who knows they're trying, the complete overtaking of the couple's life.

'My ex, she's a midwife, so it's particularly hard for her.'

At least now I know his ex isn't Ms Terse-at-the-Till.

'In the end, everything just seemed like a disappointment for her, especially me. I couldn't do anything right. I was just an irritating reminder, right down to the way I breathed. All we did was fight.'

Frankie doesn't go on to call his ex a bitch or say anything nasty about her, which is yet another thing for my mental list of Endearing Things About Frankie.

I know it's a dangerous thought to have about a guy, considering Angela and Tiffany's approach to men, but I really don't want Frankie ever to feel like just being him is wrong again. I know what that's like.

'It was over, it *is* over, but you came along in the middle of it ending and I thought maybe there was a chance to salvage it somehow, so it was tricky. I know I was ...'

A fuckwit, Jane would say here but I leave Frankie to continue.

'It wasn't an easy time and I was ... confused, I guess is the word. Not that I was weighing up my options. I wasn't going to do anything till it was over, and I really didn't think I'd stand a chance with someone like you. But then you were so ... you weren't the way you looked or seemed, with all your running into things and stuff.'

I snort as though to prove his point. Which breaks the atmosphere as well, thankfully. As appreciative as I am of Frankie being honest and opening up, it was heavy-going. Naturally, I would quite like him to list *all* the things he thought I was but there'll be time for that later. There's only one thing I need to ask immediately.

As though I'm a kid in class, I put up my hand and say, 'Excuse me, Mr Frankie, can I ask a question?'

In hindsight the whole kid thing may not be ideal but Frankie laughs and nods.

'Can I kiss you again now?'

I'm already clambering onto his lap when he nods again, enthusiastically. I press myself against him and lean in to kiss him but before I do, I take a chance and whisper, 'I'll tell you a secret: I don't want kids.'

To say it was the best sex I've ever had would be a big call, but, oh sweet Goddess above, it was *so* beyond the best sex I've ever had that I can't believe it. By Monday morning, I am one very satisfied customer indeed.

MY LIST OF 20 THINGS
I WILL KNOW
TWELVE MONTHS FROM NOW

(In no particular order)

1. Confucius was right: 'Choose a job you love and you will never have to work a day in your life.' I love my new job working as a teacher's assistant.
2. Ms Middle-of-the-Road can be a state of automatic transmission—sure I'll always have a dramatic imagination but Lionel was right, working with kids will help balance that.
3. Happiness is the greatest chakra aligner there is.
4. Frankie will always sing his feelings, and we'll have a secret language that no one else understands, even as we understand each other perfectly.
5. GI—these two letters can say more than I ever thought possible when Frankie and I look into each other's eyes and say them to each other: 'I want you', 'Sorry' (Frankie won't ever say it in its five-letter form), 'Love', 'Don't be mad at me', 'You're crazy but I love you for it', 'You're hopeless but I love you for it', 'All is forgiven', and so much more.

6. Jane won't quite get what I see in Frankie but we'll be fine with that—and when she sees us together, she'll get that there's *something*.
7. Everything with Brian will have been a false alarm. Well, there won't be enough evidence to prove otherwise, however, he will move onto a job with a less prestigious firm because in people's minds, where there's smoke, there's fire.
8. Not everyone learns from their experiences—Catherine won't change. It's just the way she is.
9. Jane can stay Jane and still be a fantastic mother. So long as Baby Jane can cope with having a lot of special uncles, everything will be great.
10. When I look into Frankie's eyes, I will always feel a bit like Alice falling through the looking glass.
11. Take your happiness where you can get it, and don't spend too much time analysing it—just enjoy things for what they are. There is very little point to overthinking things.
12. Frankie doesn't snort, he's more of a guffawer.
13. Frankie will always have a terrible memory and run late—these things will drive me insane but in an endearing way and I won't ever be able to stay really mad with him.
14. Frankie will never be able to say the name I give the dachshund puppy he buys me—Xin Xin (Faith)—properly. I won't care because it's more than enough that he gave it to me.
15. The Universe did Jack and I a favour by letting him find the woman he's going to marry.
16. I won't believe it of myself, but each week during the NRL season I'll know whether South Sydney win or

lose. It's not pretending to be someone I'm not—it's about embracing someone else's passion, being scooped up in the dragnet of their excitement and enthusiasm, and wanting to share their happiness. Still, I won't ever go to a game with Frankie—Sammy will.

17. Frankie and I will sing and dance together even when there are no kids around.

18. I love lists and while, yes, 236 items of What I Want and Need in my Next Male Love Relationship list was ridiculous, there's no need to give them up entirely.

19. Grief transforms people—this I will learn from Stephanie when she is knocked sideways by it. One day, when your parents are gone, it won't matter in the slightest that they couldn't remember to call you Kismet, all that will matter is that they're no longer here. Enjoy them while they are—they do the best they can.

20. Mick Jagger got it right—'You Can't Always Get What You Want' but sometimes you get what you need.

About the Author

PJ Mayhem is a Sydney based writer and dachshund wrangler, who swore she'd never write a romance—yet here we are! In her time as a copywriter for a natural therapies college, she didn't once hear anyone utter the words 'Oh my Buddha', but there was much talk of signs. Her favourite thing to do is laugh out loud, and that's what she hopes her writing will make people do. For more on PJ visit www.pjmayhem.com